Prize Stories 1956: The O. Henry Awards

PRIZE STORIES 1956:

The O. Henry Awards

Society of Arts and Sciences

Selected and Edited by

PAUL ENGLE and HANSFORD MARTIN

Doubleday & Company, Inc., Garden City, New York, 1956

Library of Congress Catalog Card Number: 21-9372

Copyright © 1956, By Doubleday & Company, Inc.
All Rights Reserved
Printed in the United States
at The Country Life Press, Garden City, N. Y.
First Edition

PUBLISHER'S NOTE

The present volume is the thirty-sixth in the O. Henry Memorial Award series, and the third to be edited by Paul Engle and Hansford Martin. No collections appeared in 1952 and 1953, when the continuity of the series was interrupted by the death of Herschel Brickell, who had been the editor for ten years.

In 1918 the Society of Arts and Sciences met to vote upon a monument to the American master of the short story, O. Henry. They decided that this memorial should be in the form of two prizes for the best short stories published by American authors in American magazines during the year 1919. Originally thought of as just these two prizes for a single year, the memorial promptly became an annual anthology of the best American short stories. With the exception of the two years mentioned above, it has been published by Doubleday & Company continuously ever since. Blanche Colton Williams, one of the founders of the awards, was editor from 1919 to 1932; Harry Hansen took over from 1933 to 1940; and Herschel Brickell edited the collection from 1941 to 1951.

The stories chosen for this volume were published in the period from August 1954 to July 1955 and subsequent volumes will also cover the period from August through July. A list of the magazines consulted appears at the back of the book. The choice of stories and the selection of prize winners is exclusively the responsibility of the editors.

CONTENTS

After the three prize stories the order is alphabetical by author

INTRODUCTION

The Awards for 1956

First prize: To John Cheever, for "The Country Husband," published in *The New Yorker*.

Second prize: To James Buechler, for "Pepicelli," published in *The Harvard Advocate*.

Third prize: To R. V. Cassill, for "The Prize," published in *Perspective*.

The prize winners have this in common: while being all stories of vision, they work close to a daily texture of reality.

For a steady number of years John Cheever has written some of the most attractive and solidly shaped short stories to be found in American magazines. Behind his perfectly achieved sophistication are the warmly alive men and women of suburbia. The fact that his insights about them are often achieved by a wicked wit should not conceal their accuracy and human perceptiveness.

James Buechler's story is a touching account of another modern man's search for the apocalyptic moment. When, after years of sober employment, having a house, daily repetition of meal, of leaving for work, of return, he at last acquires a motorcycle, Pepicelli roars off on it like a furious angel ascending to heaven on a fiery chariot. The machine age has provided its own supreme image.

Verlin Cassill has for some years written his stories of insight into the haunted and moving lives of ordinary people. In "The

Prize" he has taken a plain, definite, modern fact, the prize contest. He has used it to heighten the relationships of son to mother and father and brothers, and the great American dream of winning the big dough. The scene of the boy miserable at the thought of walking over his father, whom he knows to be hidden in a culvert beneath him, is not merely a meaningful act, but a perfectly dramatic incident in a story.

The 1956 stories present a variety which proves the vitality of the short tale in the United States. They divide roughly into two groups, one the work of skilled hands from whom we expect, and certainly in these examples get, solid and attractive writing. From William Faulkner there is a story of his recent sort, wonderfully full of details of hunting and weather and animals, pushed at the end into his sense of mankind at large beyond the old and certain associations of individual white and colored men in Mississippi. And as usual, there are only excellence and power from Saul Bellow, Jean Stafford, John Steinbeck.

The other group of stories includes work by little known and little published writers. Here is the first American publication (the original having appeared in Botteghe Oscure, Rome) by Alfred Chester, who deserves attention from American magazines. James Buechler has had only three published pieces—all in *The Harvard Advocate*—and all stories of a rich and supple prose culminating in a realized and direct vision. (It should be mentioned that the fiction published in *The Harvard Advocate* in the past year was astonishingly fine.) It is also heartening to note that "Able Baker" by Joseph Whitehill was an Atlantic First, by a talent who can really be said to resemble no one else.

Fiction is sometimes praised by being said to "sound true." But it is equal praise of a record of reality to say that it has the imaginative quality of the best fiction. Archie Carr's "The Black Beach" is proof of this. For art does not achieve its impact merely by imitating the experienced fact, but by shaping and heightening it. The lyrical encounter with the old woman at the sea's edge has the living presence of that concentrated human scene which is the substance of the modern short story.

The editors were pleased to add *New World Writing, Discovery* and *Botteghe Oscure* to the list of publications appearing at regular intervals which they read in search of excellence in the short story. They pray for the continuance of these useful outlets for the writer, especially the young one who needs places that will take a chance on him. We trust that the rumored discontinuance of fiction in *Charm,* and the total extinction of *Discovery,* will turn out, happily, to have been wrong.

Prize Stories 1956: The O. Henry Awards

JOHN CHEEVER was born in Quincy, Massachusetts, in 1912 and attended Thayer Academy in Braintree. He first appeared in the O. Henry Prize Stories in 1941 with "I'm Going to Asia" and again in 1950 with "Vega." His stories have appeared in The New Yorker, Harper's Bazaar, Mademoiselle, Collier's, The Atlantic Monthly, New Republic *and others. His story, "The Five-Forty-Eight" was included in the 1955 edition of the O. Henry Prize Stories. He is the father of two children and has spent most of his time since leaving college in New York and Washington.*

THE COUNTRY HUSBAND

From THE NEW YORKER

To begin at the beginning, the airplane from Minneapolis in which Francis Weed was travelling East ran into heavy weather. The sky had been a hazy blue, with the clouds below the plane lying so close together that nothing could be seen of the earth. Then mist began to form outside the windows, and they flew into a white cloud of such density that it reflected the exhaust fires. The color of the cloud darkened to grey, and the plane began to rock. Francis had been in heavy weather before, but he had never been shaken up so much. The man in the seat beside him pulled a flask out of his pocket and took a drink. Francis smiled at his neighbor, but the man looked away; he wasn't sharing his painkiller with anyone. The plane had begun to drop and flounder wildly. A child was crying. The air in the cabin was overheated and stale, and Francis' left foot went to sleep. He read a little from a paper book that he had bought at the airport, but the violence of the storm divided his attention. It was black outside the ports. The exhaust fires blazed and shed sparks in the dark, and, inside, the shaded lights, the stuffiness, and the window curtains gave the cabin an atmosphere of intense and misplaced domesticity. Then the lights flickered and went out. "You know what I've always wanted to do?" the man beside Francis said suddenly. "I've always wanted to buy a farm in New Hampshire and raise cattle beef." The stewardess announced that they were going to make an emergency landing. All but the child saw in their minds the spreading wings of the Angel of Death. The pilot could be heard singing faintly, "I've got sixpence, jolly, jolly sixpence. I've got sixpence to last me all my life . . ." There was no other sound.

The loud groaning of the hydraulic valves swallowed up the pilot's song, and there was a shrieking high in the air, like automobile brakes, and the plane hit flat on its belly in a cornfield and shook them so violently that an old man up forward howled, "Me kidneys! Me kidneys!" The stewardess flung open the doors, and someone opened an emergency door at the back, letting in the sweet noise of their continuing mortality—the idle splash and smell of a heavy rain. Anxious for their lives, they filed out of the doors and scattered over the cornfield in all directions, praying that the thread would hold. It did. Nothing happened. When it was clear that the plane would not burn or explode, the crew and the stewardess gathered the passengers together and led them to the shelter of a barn. They were not far from Philadelphia, and in a little while a string of taxis took them into the city. "It's just like the Marne," someone said, but there was surprisingly little relaxation of that suspiciousness with which many Americans regard their fellow-travellers.

In Philadelphia, Francis Weed got a train to New York. At the end of that journey, he crossed the city and caught, just as it was about to pull out, the commuting train that he took five nights a week to his home in Shady Hill.

He sat with Trace Bearden. "You know, I was in that plane that just crashed outside Philadelphia," he said. "We came down in a field . . ." He had travelled faster than the newspapers or the rain, and the weather in New York was sunny and mild. It was a day in late September, as fragrant and shapely as an apple. Trace listened to the story, but how could he get excited? Francis had no powers that would let him re-create a brush with death—particularly in the atmosphere of a commuting train, journeying through a sunny countryside where already, in the slum gardens, there were signs of harvest. Trace picked up his newspaper, and Francis was left alone with his thoughts. He said good night to Trace on the platform at Shady Hill and drove in his second-hand Volkswagen up to the Blenhollow neighborhood, where he lived.

The Weed's Dutch Colonial house was larger than it appeared to be from the driveway. The living room was spacious and divided like Gaul into three parts. Around an ell to the left as one entered from the vestibule was the long table, laid for six, with candles and a bowl of fruit in the centre. The sounds and smells that came from the open kitchen door were appetizing, for Julia Weed was a good cook. The largest part of the living room centered around a fireplace. On the right were some bookshelves and a piano. The room was polished and tranquil, and from the windows that opened to the west there was some late-summer sunlight, brilliant and as clear as water. Nothing here was neglected; nothing had not been burnished. It was not the kind of household where, after prying open a stuck cigarette box, you would find an old shirt button and a tarnished nickel. The hearth was swept, the roses on the piano were reflected in the polish of the broad top, and there was an album of Schubert waltzes on the rack. Louisa Weed, a pretty girl of nine, was looking out the western windows. Her younger brother Henry was standing beside her. Her still younger brother, Toby, was studying the figures of some tonsured monks drinking beer on the polished brass of the wood box. Francis, taking off his hat and putting down his paper, was not consciously pleased with the scene; he was not that reflective. It was his element, his creation, and he returned to it with that sense of lightness and strength with which any creature returns to its home. "Hi, everybody," he said. "The plane from Minneapolis . . ."

Nine times out of ten, Francis would be greeted with affection, but tonight the children are absorbed in their own antagonisms. Francis has not finished his sentence about the plane crash before Henry plants a kick in Louisa's behind. Louisa swings around

saying *"Damn* you!" Francis makes the mistake of scolding Louisa
for bad language before he punishes Henry. Now Louisa turns on
her father and accuses him of favoritism. Henry is always right;
she is persecuted and lonely; her lot is hopeless. Francis turns to
his son, but the boy has justification for the kick—she hit him first;
she hit him on the ear, which is dangerous. Louisa agrees with this
passionately. She hit him on the ear, and she *meant* to hit him on
the ear, because he messed up her china collection. Henry says
that this is a lie. Little Toby turns away from the wood box to
throw in some evidence for Louisa. Henry claps his hands over
little Toby's mouth. Francis separates the two boys but acci-
dentally pushes Toby into the wood box. Toby begins to cry.
Louisa is already crying. Just then, Julia Weed comes into that
part of the room where the table is laid. She is a pretty, intelligent
woman, and the white in her hair is premature. She does not seem
to notice the fracas. "Hello, darling," she says serenely to Francis.
"Wash your hands, everyone. Dinner is ready." She strikes a
match and lights the six candles in this vale of tears.

This simple announcement, like the war cries of the Scottish
chieftains, only refreshes the ferocity of the combatants. Louisa
gives Henry a blow on the shoulder. Henry, although he seldom
cries, has pitched nine innings and is tired. He bursts into tears.
Little Toby discovers a splinter in his hand and begins to howl.
Francis says loudly that he had been in a plane crash and that he
is tired. Julia appears again, from the kitchen, and, still ignoring
the chaos, asks Francis to go upstairs and tell Helen that everything is ready. Francis is happy to go; it is like getting back to
headquarters company. He is planning to tell his oldest daughter
about the airplane crash, but Helen is lying on her bed reading
a *True Romance* magazine, and the first thing Francis does is to
take the magazine from her hand and remind Helen that he has
forbidden her to buy it. She did not buy it, Helen replies. It was
given to her by her best friend, Bessie Black. Everybody reads
True Romance. Bessie Black's father reads *True Romance.* There
isn't a girl in Helen's class who doesn't read *True Romance.*
Francis expresses his detestation of the magazine and then tells
her that dinner is ready—although from the sounds downstairs it
doesn't seem so. Helen follows him down the stairs. Julia has

seated herself in the candlelight and spread a napkin over her lap. Neither Louisa nor Henry has come to the table. Little Toby is still howling, lying face down on the floor. Francis speaks to him gently: "Daddy was in a plane crash this afternoon, Toby, don't you want to hear about it?" Toby goes on crying. "If you don't come to the table now, Toby," Francis says, "I'll have to send you to bed without any supper." The little boy rises, gives him a cutting look, flies up the stairs to his bedroom, and slams the door. "Oh dear," Julia says, and starts to go after him. Francis says that she will spoil him. Julia says that Toby is ten pounds underweight and has to be encouraged to eat. Winter is coming, and he will spend the cold months in bed unless he has his dinner. Julia goes upstairs. Francis sits down at the table with Helen. Helen is suffering from the dismal feeling of having read too intently on a fine day, and she gives her father and the room a jaded look. She doesn't understand about the plane crash, because there wasn't a drop of rain in Shady Hill.

Julia returns with Toby, and they all sit down and are served. "Do I have to look at that big, fat slob?" Henry says of Louisa. Everybody but Toby enters into this skirmish, and it rages up and down the table for five minutes. Toward the end, Henry puts his napkin over his head and tries to eat that way, spills spinach all over his shirt. Francis asks Julia if the children couldn't have their dinner earlier. Julia's guns are loaded for this. She can't cook two dinners and lay two tables. She paints with lightning strokes that panorama of drudgery in which her youth, her beauty, and her wit have been lost. Francis says that he must be understood; he was nearly killed in an airplane crash, and he doesn't like to come home every night to a battlefield. Now Julia is deeply committed. Her voice trembles. He doesn't come home every night to a battlefield. The accusation is stupid and mean. Everything was tranquil until he arrived. She stops speaking, puts down her knife and fork, and looks into her plate as if it is a gulf. She begins to cry. "Poor Mummy!" Toby says, and when Julia gets up from the table, Toby goes to her side. "Poor Mummy," he says. "Poor Mummy!" And they climb the stairs together. The other children drift away from the battlefield, and Francis goes into the back garden for a cigarette and some air

It was a pleasant garden, with walks and flower beds and places to sit. The sunset had nearly burned out, but there was still plenty of light. Put into a thoughtful mood by the crash and the battle, Francis listened to the evening sounds of Shady Hill. "Varmits! Rascals!" old Mr. Nixon shouted to the squirrels in his bird-feeding station. "Avaunt and quit my sight!" A door slammed. Someone was playing tennis on the Babcock's court; someone was cutting grass. Then Donald Goslin, who lived at the corner, began to play the "Moonlight Sonata." He did this nearly every night. He threw the tempo out the window and played it *rubato* from beginning to end, like an outpouring of tearful petulance, lonesomeness, and self-pity—of everything it was Beethoven's greatness not to know. The music rang up and down the street beneath the trees like an appeal for love, for tenderness, aimed at some lonely housemaid—some fresh-faced, homesick girl from Galway, looking at old snapshots in her third-floor room. "Here, Jupiter, here, Jupiter," Francis called to the Mercers' retriever. Jupiter crashed through the tomato vines with the remains of a felt hat in his mouth.

Jupiter was an anomaly. His retrieving instincts and his high spirits were out of place in Shady Hill. He was as black as coal, with a long, alert, intelligent, rakehell face. His eyes gleamed with mischief, and he held his head high. It was the fierce, heavily collared dog's head that appeared in heraldry, in tapestry, and that used to appear on umbrella handles and walking sticks. Jupiter went where he pleased, ransacking wastebaskets, clotheslines, garbage pails, and shoe bags. He broke up garden parties and tennis matches, and got mixed up in the processional at Christ's Church on Sunday, barking at the men in red dresses. He crashed through old Mr. Nixon's rose garden two or three times a day, cutting a wide swath through the Condesa de Sastagos, and as soon as Donald Goslin lighted his barbecue fire on Thursday nights, Jupiter would get the scent. Nothing the Goslins did could drive him away. Sticks and stones and rude commands only moved him to the edge of the terrace, where he remained, with his gallant and heraldic muzzle, waiting for Donald Goslin to turn his back and reach for the salt. Then he would spring onto the terrace, lift the steak lightly off the fire, and run away with the

Goslin's dinner. Jupiter's days were numbered. The Wrightsons' German gardener or the Farquarsons' cook would soon poison him. Even old Mr. Nixon might put some arsenic in the garbage that Jupiter loved. "Here, Jupiter, Jupiter!" Francis called, but the dog pranced off, shaking the hat in his white teeth. Looking in at the windows of his house, Francis saw Julia had come down and was blowing out the candles.

Julia and Francis Weed went out a great deal. Julia was well liked and gregarious, and her love of parties sprang from a most natural dread of chaos and loneliness. She went through her morning mail with real anxiety, looking for invitations, and she usually found some, but she was insatiable, and if she had gone out seven nights a week, it would not have cured her of a reflective look—the look of someone who hears distant music—for she would always suppose that there was a more brilliant party somewhere else. Francis limited her to two week-night parties, putting a flexible interpretation on Friday, and rode through the weekend like a dory in a gale. The day after the airplane crash, the Weeds were to have dinner with the Farquarsons.

Francis got home late from town, and Julia got the sitter while he dressed, and then hurried him out of the house. The party was small and pleasant, and Francis settled down to enjoy himself. A new maid passed the drinks. Her hair was dark, and her face was round and pale and seemed familiar to Francis. He had not developed his memory as a sentimental faculty. Wood smoke, lilac, and other such perfumes did not stir him, a᷑ ' his memory was something like his appendix—a vestigial repository. It was not his limitation at all to be unable to escape the past; it was perhaps his limitation that he had escaped it so successfully. He might have seen the maid at other parties, he might have seen her taking a walk on Sunday afternoons, but in either case he would not be searching his memory now. Her face was, in a wonderful way, a moon face—Norman or Irish—but it was not beautiful enough to account for his feeling that he had seen her before, in circumstances that he ought to be able to remember. He asked Nellie Farquarson who she was. Nellie said that the maid had come through an agency, and that her home was Trénon, in Normandy

—a small place with a church and a restaurant that Nellie had once visited. While Nellie talked on about her travels abroad, Francis realized where he had seen the woman before. It had been at the end of the war. He had left a replacement depot with some other men and taken a three-day pass in Trénon. On their second day, they had walked out to a crossroads to see the public chastisement of a young woman who had lived with the German commandant during the Occupation.

It was a cool morning in the fall. The sky was overcast, and poured down onto the dirt crossroads a very discouraging light. They were on high land and could see how like one another the shapes of the clouds and the hills were as they stretched off toward the sea. The prisoner arrived sitting on a three-legged stool in a farm cart while the mayor read the accusation and the sentence. Her head was bent and her face was set in that empty half smile behind which the whipped soul is suspended. When the mayor was finished, she undid her hair and let it fall across her back. A little man with a grey mustache cut off her hair with shears and dropped it on the ground. Then, with a bowl of soapy water and a straight razor, he shaved her skull clean. A woman approached and began to undo the fastenings of her clothes, but the prisoner pushed her aside and undressed herself. When she pulled the chemise over her head and threw it on the ground, she was naked. The women jeered; the men were still. There was no change in the falseness or the plaintiveness of the prisoner's smile. The cold wind made her white skin rough and hardened the nipples of her breasts. The jeering ended gradually, put down by the recognition of their common humanity. One woman spat on her, but some inviolable grandeur in her nakedness lasted through the ordeal. When the crowd was quiet, she turned—she had begun to cry—and with nothing on but a pair of worn black shoes and stockings, walked down the dirt road alone, away from the village. The round white face had aged a little, but there was no question but that the maid who passed his cocktails and later served Francis his dinner was the woman who had been punished at the crossroads.

The war now seemed so distant and that world where the cost of partisanship had been death or torture so long ago. Francis had lost track of the men who had been with him in Vésey. He could not count on Julia's discretion. He could not tell anyone. And if he had told the story now, at the dinner table, it would have been a social as well as a human error. The people in the Farquarsons' living room seemed united in their tacit claim that there had been no past, no war—that there was no danger or trouble in the world. In the recorded history of human arrangements, this extraordinary meeting would have fallen into place, but the atmosphere of Shady Hill made the memory unseemly and impolite. The prisoner withdrew after passing the coffee, but the encounter left Francis feeling languid; it had opened his memory and his senses, and left them dilated. He and Julia drove home when the party ended, and Julia went into the house. Francis stayed in the car to take the sitter home.

Expecting to see Mrs. Henlein, the old lady who usually stayed with the children, he was surprised when a young girl opened the door and came out onto the lighted stoop. She stayed in the light to count her textbooks. She was frowning and beautiful. Now, the world is full of beautiful young girls, but Francis saw here the difference between beauty and perfection. All those endearing flaws, moles, birthmarks, and healed wounds were missing, and he experienced in his consciousness that moment when music breaks glass, and felt a pang of recognition as strange, deep, and wonderful as anything in his life. It hung from her frown, from an impalpable darkness in her face—a look that impressed him as a direct appeal for love. When she had counted her books, she came down the steps and opened the car door. In the light, he saw that her cheeks were wet. She got in and shut the door.

"You're new," Francis said.

"Yes. Mrs. Henlein is sick. I'm Anne Murchison."

"Did the children give you any trouble?"

"Oh, no, no." She turned and smiled at him unhappily in the dim dashboard light. Her light hair caught on the collar of her jacket, and she shook her head to set it loose.

"You've been crying."

"Yes."

"I hope it was nothing that happened in our house."

"No, no, it was nothing that happened in your house." Her voice was bleak. "It's no secret. Everybody in the village knows. Daddy's an alcoholic, and he just called me from some saloon and gave me a piece of his mind. He thinks I'm immoral. He called just before Mrs. Weed came back."

"I'm sorry."

"Oh, *Lord!*" she gasped and began to cry. She turned toward Francis, and he took her in his arms and let her cry on his shoulder. She shook in his embrace, and this movement accentuated his sense of the fineness of her flesh and bone. The layers of their clothing felt thin, and when her shuddering began to diminish, it was so much like a paroxysm of love that Francis lost his head and pulled her roughly against him. She drew away. "I live on Belleview Avenue," she said. "You go down Lansing Street to the railroad bridge."

"All right." He started the car.

"You turn left at that traffic light. . . . Now you turn right here and go straight on toward the tracks."

The road Francis took brought him right out of his own neighborhood, across the tracks, and toward the river, to a street where the near-poor lived, in houses whose peaked gables and trimmings of wooden lace conveyed the purest feelings of pride and romance, although the houses themselves could not have offered much privacy or comfort, they were all so small. The street was dark, and, stirred by the grace and beauty of the troubled girl, he seemed, in turning into it, to have come to the deepest part of some submerged memory. In the distance, he saw a porch light burning. It was the only one, and she said that the house with the light was where she lived. When he stopped the car, he could see beyond the porch light into a dimly lighted hallway with an old-fashioned clothes tree. "Well, here we are," he said, conscious that a young man would have said something different.

She did not move her hands from the books, where they were folded, and she turned and faced him. There were tears of lust in his eyes. Determinedly—not sadly—he opened the door on his side and walked around to open hers. He took her free hand, letting his fingers in between hers, climbed at her side the two concrete steps, and went up a narrow walk through a front garden where dahlias, marigolds, and roses—things that had withstood the light frosts—still bloomed, and made a bittersweet smell in the night air. At the steps, she freed her hand and then turned and kissed him swiftly. Then she crossed the porch and shut the door. The porch light went out, then the light in the hall. A second later, a light went on upstairs at the side of the house, shining into a tree that was still covered with leaves. It took her only a few minutes to undress and get into bed, and then the house was dark.

Julia was asleep when Francis got home. He opened a second window and got into bed to shut his eyes on that night, but as soon as they were shut—as soon as he had dropped off to sleep— the girl entered his mind, moving with perfect freedom through its shut doors and filling chamber after chamber with her light, her perfume, and the music of her voice. He was crossing the Atlantic with her on the old Mauretania and, later, living with her in Paris. When he woke from this dream, he got up and smoked a cigarette at the open window. Getting back into bed, he cast around in his mind for something he desired to do that would injure no one, and he thought of skiing. Up through the dimness in his mind rose the image of a mountain deep in snow. It was late in the day. Wherever his eyes looked, he saw broad and heartening things. Over his shoulder, there was a snow-filled valley, rising into wooded hills where the trees dimmed the white- ness like a sparse coat of hair. The cold deadened all sound but the loud, iron clanking of the lift machinery. The light on the trails was blue, and it was harder than it had been a minute or two earlier to pick the turns, harder to judge—now that the snow was all deep blue—the crust, the ice, the bare spots, and the deep piles of dry powder. Down the mountain he swung, matching his speed against the contours of a slope that had been formed in the first ice age, seeking with ardor some simplicity of feeling and circumstance. Night fell then, and he drank a Martini with some old friend in a dirty country bar.

In the morning, Francis's snow-covered mountain was gone, and he was left with vivid memories of Paris and the Mauretania. He had been bitten gravely. He washed his body, shaved his jaws, drank his coffee, and missed the seven-thirty-one. The train pulled out just as he brought his car to the station, and the longing he felt for the coaches as they drew stubbornly away from him reminded him of the humors of love. He waited for the eight-two, on what was now an empty platform. It was a clear morning; the morning seemed thrown like a gleaming bridge of light over his mixed affairs. His spirits were feverish and high. The image of the girl seemed to put him into a relationship to the world that was mysterious and enthralling. Cars were beginning to fill up the parking lot, and he noticed that those that had driven down from the high land above Shady Hill were white with hoarfrost. This first clear sign of autumn thrilled him. An express train—a night train from Buffalo or Albany—came down the tracks between the platforms, and he saw that the roofs of the foremost cars were covered with a skin of ice. Struck by the miraculous physicalness of everything, he smiled at the passengers in the dining car, who could be seen eating eggs and wiping their mouths with napkins as they travelled. The sleeping-car compartments, with their soiled bed linen, trailed through the fresh morning like a string of rooming-house windows. Then he saw an extraordinary thing; at one of the bedroom windows sat an unclothed woman of exceptional beauty, combing her golden hair, and Francis followed her with his eyes until she was out of sight. Then old Mrs. Wrightson joined him on the platform and began to talk.

"Well, I guess you must be surprised to see me here the third morning in a row," she said, "but because of my window curtains I'm becoming a regular commuter. The curtains I bought on Monday I returned on Tuesday, and the curtains I bought Tuesday I'm returning today. On Monday, I got exactly what I wanted—it's a wool tapestry with roses and birds—but when I got them home, I found they were the wrong length. Well, I exchanged them yesterday, and when I got them home, I found they were still the wrong length. Now I'm praying to high Heaven that the decorator will have them in the right length, because you know my house, you *know* my living-room windows, and you can imagine what a problem they present. I don't know what to do with them."

"I know what to do with them," Francis said.

"What?"

"Paint them black on the inside, and shut up."

There was a gasp from Mrs. Wrightson, and Francis looked down at her to be sure that she knew he meant to be rude. She turned and walked away from him, so damaged in spirit that she limped. A wonderful feeling enveloped him, as if light were being shaken about him, and he thought again of Venus combing and combing her hair as she drifted through the Bronx. The realization of how many years had passed since he had enjoyed being deliberately impolite sobered him. Among his friends and neighbors, there were brilliant and gifted people—he saw that—but many of them, also, were bores and fools, and he had made the mistake of listening to them all with equal attention. He had confused a lack of discrimination with Christian love, and the confusion seemed general and destructive. He was grateful to the girl for this bracing sensation of independence. Birds were singing—cardinals and the last of the robins. The sky shone like enamel. Even the smell of ink from his morning paper honed his appetite for life, and the world that was spread out around him was plainly a paradise.

If Francis believed in some hierarchy of love—in spirits armed with hunting bows, in the capriciousness of Venus or Eros—or even in magical potions, philtres, and stews, in scapulae and quarters of the moon, it might have explained his susceptibility and his feverish high spirits. The autumnal loves of middle age are well publicized, and he guessed he was face to face with one of these, but there was not a trace of autumn in what he felt. He wanted to sport in the green woods, scratch where he itched, and drink from the same cup.

His secretary, Miss Rainey, was late that morning—she went to a psychiatrist three mornings a week—and when she came in, Francis wondered what advice a psychiatrist would have for him. But the girl promised to bring back into his life something like the sound of music. The realization that this music might lead him straight to a trial at the county courthouse collapsed his happiness. The photograph of his four children laughing into the camera on the beach at Gay Head reproached him. On the letterhead of his firm there was a drawing of the Laocoön, and the figure of the priest and his sons in the coils of the snake appeared to him to have the deepest meaning.

He had lunch with Pinky Trabert, who told him a couple of dirty stories. At a conversational level, the mores of his friends were robust and elastic, but he knew that the moral card house would come down on them all—on Julia and the children as well—if he got caught taking advantage of a baby sitter. Looking back over the recent history of Shady Hill for some precedent, he found there was none. There was no turpitude; there had not been a divorce since he lived there; there had not even been a breath of scandal. Things seemed arranged with more propriety even than in the Kingdom of Heaven. After leaving Pinky, Francis went to a jeweller's and bought the girl a bracelet. How happy this clandestine purchase made him, how stuffy and comical the jeweller's clerks seemed, how sweet the women who passed at his back smelled! On Fifth Avenue, passing Atlas with his shoulders bent under the weight of the world, Francis thought of the strenuousness of containing his physicalness within the patterns he had chosen.

He did not know when he would see the girl next. He had the bracelet in his inside pocket when he got home. Opening the door of his house, he found her in the hall. Her back was to him, and she turned when she heard the door close. Her smile was open and loving. Her perfection stunned him like a fine day—a day after a thunderstorm. He seized her and covered her lips with his, and she struggled but she did not have to struggle for long, because just then little Gertrude Flannery appeared from somewhere and said, "Oh, Mr. Weed . . ."

Gertrude was a stray. She had been born with a taste for exploration, and she did not have it in her to centre her life with her affectionate parents. People who did not know the Flannerys concluded from Gertrude's behavior that she was the child of a bitterly divided family, where drunken quarrels were the rule. This was not true. The fact that little Gertrude's clothing was ragged and thin was her own triumph over her mother's struggle to dress her warmly and neatly. Garrulous, skinny, and unwashed, she drifted from house to house around the Blenhollow neighborhood, forming and breaking alliances based on an attachment to babies, animals, children her own age, adolescents, and sometimes adults. Opening your front door in the morning, you would find

Gertrude sitting on your stoop. Going into the bathroom to shave, you would find Gertrude using the toilet. Looking into your son's crib, you would find it empty, and, looking further, you would find that Gertrude had pushed him in his baby carriage into the next village. She was helpful, pervasive, honest, hungry and loyal. She never went home of her own choice. When the time to go arrived she was indifferent to all its signs. "Go home, Gertrude" people could be heard saying in one house or another, night after night. "Go home, Gertrude." "It's time for you to go home now, Gertrude." "You had better go home and get your supper, Gertrude." "I told you to go home twenty minutes ago, Gertrude." "Your mother will be worrying about you, Gertrude." "Go home, Gertrude, go home."

There are times when the lines around the human eye seem like shelves of eroded stone and when the staring eye itself strikes us with such a wilderness of animal feeling that we are at a loss. The look Francis gave the little girl was ugly and queer, and it frightened her. He reached into his pocket—his hands were shaking—and took out a quarter. "Go home, Gertrude, go home, and don't tell anyone, Gertrude. "Don't—" He choked and ran into the living room as Julia called down to him from upstairs to hurry up and dress.

The thought that he would drive Anne Murchison home later that night ran like a golden thread through the events of the party that Francis and Julia went to, and he laughed uproariously at dull jokes, dried a tear when Mabel Mercer told him about the death of her kitten, and stretched, yawned, sighed, and grunted like any other man with a rendezvous at the back of his mind. The bracelet was in his pocket. As he sat talking, the smell of grass was in his nose, and he was wondering where he would park the car. Nobody lived in the old Parker mansion, and the driveway was used as a lover's lane. Townsend Street was a dead end, and he could park there, beyond the last house. The old lane that used to connect Elm Street to the riverbanks was overgrown, but he had walked there with his children, and he could drive his car deep enough into the brushwoods to be concealed.

The Weeds were the last to leave the party, and their host and hostess spoke of their own married happiness while they all four stood in the hallway saying good night. "She's my girl," their host said, squeezing his wife. "She's my blue sky. After sixteen years, I still bite her shoulders. She makes me feel like Hannibal crossing the Alps."

The Weeds drove home in silence. Francis brought his car up to the driveway and sat still, with the motor running. "You can put the car in the garage," Julia said as she got out. "I told the Murchison girl she could leave at eleven. Someone drove her home." She shut the door, and Francis sat in the dark. He would be spared nothing then, it seemed, that a fool was not spared: ravening, lewdness, jealousy, this hurt to his feelings that put tears in his eyes, even scorn—for he could see clearly the image he now presented, his arms spread over the steering wheel and his head buried in them for love.

Francis had been a dedicated Boy Scout when he was young, and, remembering the precepts of his youth, he left his office early the next afternoon and played some round-robin squash, but, with his body toned up by exercise and a shower, he realized that he might better have stayed at his desk. It was a frosty night when he got home. The air smelled sharply of change. When he stepped into the house, he sensed an unusual stir. The children were in their best clothes, and when Julia came down she was wearing a lavender dress and her diamond sunburst. She explained the stir: Mr. Hubber was coming at seven to take their photograph for the Christmas card. She had put out Francis' blue suit and a tie with some color in it, because the picture was going to be in color this year. Julia was light-hearted at the thought of being photographed for Christmas. It was the kind of ceremony she enjoyed.

Francis went upstairs to change his clothes. He was tired from the day's work and tired with longing, and sitting on the edge of the bed had the effect of deepening his weariness. He thought of Anne Murchison, and the physical need to express himself, instead of being restrained by the pink lamps on Julia's dressing table, engulfed him. He went to Julia's desk, took a piece of writing paper, and began to write on it. "Dear Anne, I love you, I love you, I love you . . ." No one would see the letter, and he used no restraint. He used phrases like "Heavenly bliss," and "love nest." He salivated, sighed, and trembled. When Julia called him to come down, the abyss between his fantasy and the practical world opened so wide that he felt it affect the muscles of his heart.

Julia and the children were on the stoop, and the photographer and his assistant had set up a double battery of floodlights to show the family and architectural beauty of the entrance to their house. People who had come home on a late train slowed their cars to see the Weeds being photographed for their Christmas card. A few waved and called to the family. It took half an hour of smiling and wetting their lips before Mr. Hubber was satisfied. The heat of the lights made an unfresh smell in the frosty air, and when they were turned off, they lingered on the retina of Francis' eyes.

Later that night, while Francis and Julia were drinking their coffee in the living room, the doorbell rang. Julia answered the door and let in Clayton Thomas. He had come to pay her for some theatre tickets that she had given his mother some time ago, and that Helen Thomas had scrupulously insisted on paying for, though Julia had asked her not to. Julia invited him in to have a cup of coffee. "I won't have any coffee," Clayton said, "but I will come in for a minute." He followed her into the living room, said good evening to Francis, and sat down awkwardly in a chair.

Clayton's father had been killed in the war, and the young man's fatherlessness surrounded him like an element. This may have been conspicuous in Shady Hill because the Thomases were the only family that lacked a piece; all the other marriages were intact and productive. Clayton was in his second or third year of college, and he and his mother lived alone in a large house which she hoped to sell. Clayton had once made some trouble. Years ago, he had stolen some money and run away; he had got to California before they caught up with him. He was tall and homely, wore horn-rimmed glasses, and spoke in a deep voice.

"When do you go back to college, Clayton?" Francis asked.

"I'm not going back," Clayton said. "Mother doesn't have the money, and there's no sense in all this pretense. I'm going to get a job, and if we sell the house, we'll take an apartment in New York."

"Won't you miss Shady Hill?" Julia asked.

"No," Clayton said. "I don't like it."

"Why not?" Francis asked.

"Well, there's a lot here I don't approve of," Clayton said gravely. "Things like the club dances. Last Saturday night, I looked in toward the end and saw Mr. Granner trying to put Mrs. Minot into the trophy case. They were both drunk. I disapprove of so much drinking."

"It was Saturday night," Francis said.

"And all the dovecotes are phony," Clayton said. "And the way people clutter up their lives. I've thought about it a lot, and what seems to me to be really wrong with Shady Hill is that it doesn't have any future. So much energy is spent in perpetuating the place—in keeping out undesirables, and so forth—that the only idea of the future anyone has is just more and more commuting trains and more parties. I don't think that's healthy. I think people ought to be able to dream big dreams about the future. I think people ought to be able to dream great dreams."

"It's too bad you couldn't continue with college," Julia said.

"I wanted to go to divinity school," Clayton said.

"What's your church?" Francis asked.

"Unitarian, Theosophist, Transcendentalist, Humanist," Clayton said.

"Wasn't Emerson a transcendentalist?" Julia asked.

"I mean the English transcendentalists." Clayton said. "All the American transcendentalists were goops."

"What kind of job do you expect to get?" Francis asked.

"Well, I'd like to work for a publisher," Clayton said. "But everyone tells me there's nothing doing. But it's the kind of thing I'm interested in. I'm writing a long verse play about good and evil. Uncle Charlie might get me into a bank, and that would be good for me. I need the discipline. I have a long way to go in forming my character. I have some terrible habits. I talk too much. I think I ought to take vows of silence. I ought to try not to speak for a week, and discipline myself. I've thought of making a retreat at one of the Episcopalian monasteries, but I don't like Trinitarianism."

"Do you have any girl friends?" Francis asked.

"I'm engaged to be married," Clayton said. "Of course, I'm not old enough or rich enough to have my engagement observed or respected or anything, but I bought a simulated emerald for Anne Murchison with the money I made cutting lawns this summer. We're going to be married as soon as she finishes school."

Francis recoiled at the mention of the girl's name. Then a dingy light seemed to emanate from his spirit, showing everything —Julia, the boy, the chairs—in their true colorlessness. It was like a bitter turn of the weather.

"We're going to have a large family," Clayton said. "Her father's a terrible rummy, and I've had my hard times, and we want to have lots of children. Oh, she's wonderful, Mr. and Mrs. Weed, and we have so much in common. We like all the same things. We sent out the same Christmas card last year without planning it, and we both have an allergy to tomatoes, and our eyebrows grow together in the middle. Well, good night."

Julia went to the door with him. When she returned, Francis said that Clayton was lazy, irresponsible, affected, and smelly. Julia said that Francis seemed to be getting intolerant; the Thomas boy was young and should be given a chance. Julia had noticed other cases where Francis had been short-tempered. "Mrs. Wrightson has asked everyone in Shady Hill to her anniversary party but us," she said.

"I'm sorry, Julia."

"Do you know why they didn't ask us?"

"Why?"

"Because you insulted Mrs. Wrightson."

"Then you know about it?"

"June Masterson told me. She was standing behind you."

Julia walked in front of the sofa with a small step that expressed, Francis knew, a feeling of anger.

"I did insult Mrs. Wrightson, Julia, and I meant to. I've never liked her parties, and I'm glad she's dropped us."

"What about Helen?"

"How does Helen come into this?"

"Mrs. Wrightson's the one who decides who goes to assemblies."

"You mean she can keep Helen from going to the dances?"

"Yes."

"I hadn't thought of that."

"Oh, I knew you hadn't thought of it," Julia cried thrusting hilt-deep into this chink of his armor. "And it makes me furious to see this kind of stupid thoughtlessness wreck everyone's happiness."

"I don't think I've wrecked anyone's happiness."

"Mrs. Wrightson runs Shady Hill and has run it for the last forty years. I don't know what makes you think that in a community like this you can indulge every impulse you have to be insulting, vulgar, and offensive."

"I have very good manners," Francis said, trying to give the evening a turn toward the light.

"Damn you, Francis Weed!" Julia cried, and the spit of her words struck him in the face. "I've worked hard for the social position we enjoy in this place, and I won't stand by and see you wreck it. You must have understood when you settled here that you couldn't expect to live like a bear in a cave."

"I've got to express my likes and dislikes."

"You can conceal your dislikes. You don't have to meet everything head-on, like a child. Unless you're anxious to be a social leper. It's no accident that we get asked out a great deal. It's no accident that Helen has so many friends. How would you like to spend your Saturday nights at the movies? How would you like to spend your Sundays raking up dead leaves? How would you like it if your daughter spent the assembly nights sitting at her window, listening to the music from the club? How would you like it—" He did something then that was, after all, not so unaccountable, since her words seemed to raise up between them a wall so deadening that he gagged: he struck her full in the face. She staggered and then, a moment later, seemed composed. She went up the stairs to their room. She didn't slam the door. When Francis followed, a few minutes later, he found her packing a suitcase.

"Julia, I'm very sorry."

"It doesn't matter," she said. She was crying.

"Where do you think you're going?"

"I don't know. I just looked at the timetable. There's an eleven-sixteen into New York. I'll take that."

"You can't go, Julia."

"I can't stay. I know that."

"I'm sorry about Mrs. Wrightson, Julia, and I'm—"

"It doesn't matter about Mrs. Wrightson. That isn't the trouble."

"What is the trouble?"

"You don't love me."

"I do love you, Julia."

"No, you don't."

"Julia, I do love you, and I would like to be as we were—sweet and bawdy and dark—but now there are so many people."

"You hate me."

"I don't hate you, Julia."

"You have no idea of how much you hate me. I think it's subconscious. You don't realize the cruel things you've done."

"What cruel things, Julia?"

"The cruel acts your subconscious drives you to in order to express your hatred of me."

"What, Julia?"

"I've never complained."

"Tell me."

"Your clothes."

"What do you mean?"

"I mean the way you leave your dirty clothes around in order to express your subconscious hatred of me."

"I don't understand."

"I mean your dirty socks and your dirty pajamas and your dirty underwear and your dirty shirts!" She rose from kneeling by the suitcase and faced him, her eyes blazing and her voice ringing with emotion. "I'm talking about the fact that you've never learned to hang up anything. You just leave your clothes all over the floor where they drop, in order to humiliate me. You do it on purpose!" She fell on the bed, sobbing.

"Julia, darling!" he said, but when she felt his hand on her shoulder she got up.

"Leave me alone," she said. "I have to go." She brushed past him to the closet and came back with a dress. "I'm not taking any of the things you've given me," she said. "I'm leaving my pearls and the fur jacket."

"Oh, Julia!" Her figure, so helpless in its self-deceptions, bent over the suitcase made him nearly sick with pity. She did not understand how desolate her life would be without him. She didn't understand the hours that working women have to keep. She didn't understand that most of her friendships existed within the framework of their marriage, and that without this she would find herself alone. She didn't understand about travel, about hotels, about money. "Julia, I can't let you go! What you don't understand, Julia, is that you've come to be dependent on me."

She tossed her head back and covered her face with her hands. "Did you say I was dependent on *you?*" she asked. "Is that what you said? And who is it that tells you what time to get up in the morning and when to go to bed at night? Who is it that prepares your meals and picks up your dirty closet and invites your friends to dinner? If it weren't for me your neckties would be greasy and your clothing would be full of moth holes. You were alone when I met you, Francis Weed, and you'll be alone when I leave. When mother asked you for a list to send out invitations to our wedding, how many names did you have to give her? Fourteen!"

"Cleveland wasn't my home, Julia."

"And how many of your friends came to the church? Two!"

"Since I'm not taking the fur jacket," she said quietly, "you'd better put it back into storage. There's an insurance policy on the pearls that comes due in January. The name of the laundry and the maid's telephone number—all those things are in my desk. I hope you won't drink too much, Francis. I hope that nothing bad will happen to you. If you do get into serious trouble, you can call me."

"Oh my darling, I can't let you go!" Francis said. "I can't let you go, Julia!" He took her in his arms.

"I guess I'd better stay and take care of you for a little while longer," she said.

Riding to work in the morning, Francis saw the girl walk down the aisle of the coach. He was surprised; he hadn't realized that the school she went to was in the city, but she was carrying books, she seemed to be going to school. His surprise delayed his reaction, but then he got up clumsily and stepped into the aisle. Several people had come between them, but he could see her ahead of him, waiting for someone to open the car door, and then, as the train swerved, putting out her hand to support herself as she crossed the platform into the next car. He followed her through that car and halfway through another before calling her name— "Anne! Anne!"—but she didn't turn. He followed her into still another car, and she sat down in an aisle seat. Coming up to her, all his feelings warm and bent in her direction, he put his hand on the back of her seat—even this touch warmed him—and leaning down to speak to her, he saw that it was not Anne. It was an older woman wearing glasses. He went on deliberately into another car, his face red with embarrassment and the much deeper feeling of having his good sense challenged; for if he couldn't tell one person from another, what evidence was there that his life with Julia and the children had as much reality as his dreams of iniquity in Paris or the litter, the grass smell, and the cave-shaped trees in Lover's Lane.

Late that afternoon, Julia called to remind Francis that they were going out for dinner. A few minutes later Trace Bearden called. "Look fellar," Trace said. "I'm calling for Mrs. Thomas. You know, Clayton, that boy of hers doesn't seem to be able to get a job and I wondered if you could help. If you'd call Charlie Bell —I know he's indebted to you—and say a good word for the kid, I think Charlie would—"

"Trace, I hate to say this," Francis said, "but I don't feel that I can do anything for that boy. The kid's worthless. I know it's a harsh thing to say, but it's a fact. Any kindness done for him would backfire in everybody's face. He's just a worthless kid, Trace, and there's nothing to be done about it. Even if we got him a job, he wouldn't be able to keep it for a week. I know that to be a fact. It's an awful thing, Trace, and I know it is, but instead of recommending that kid, I'd feel obliged to warn people against him—people who knew his father and would naturally want to step in and do something. I'd feel obliged to warn them. He's a thief . . ."

The moment this conversation was finished, Miss Rainey came in and stood by his desk. "I'm not going to be able to work for you any more, Mr. Weed," she said. "I can stay until the seventeenth if you need me, but I've been offered a whirlwind of a job, and I'd like to leave as soon as possible."

She went out, leaving him to face alone the wickedness of what he had done to the Thomas boy. His children in their photograph laughed and laughed, glazed with all the bright colors of summer, and he remembered that they had met a bagpiper on the beach that day and he had paid the piper a dollar to play them a battle song of the Black Watch. The girl would be at the house when he got home. He would spend another evening among his kind neighbors, picking and choosing dead-end streets, cart tracks, and the driveways of abandoned houses. There was nothing to mitigate his feeling—nothing that laughter or a game of softball with his children would change—and, thinking back over the plane crash, the Farquarsons' new maid, and Anne Murchison's difficulties with her drunken father, he wondred how he could have avoided arriving at just where he was. He was in trouble. He had been lost once in his life, coming back from a trout stream in the north woods, and he had now the same bleak realization that no amount of cheerfulness or hopefulness or valor or perseverance could help him find, in the gathering dark, the path that he had lost. He smelled the forest. The feeling of bleakness was intolerable, and he saw clearly that he had reached the point where he would have to make a choice.

He could go to a psychiatrist, like Miss Rainey; he could go to church and confess his lusts; he could go to a Danish massage parlor in the West Seventies that had been recommended by a salesman; he could rape the girl or trust that he would somehow be prevented from doing this; or he could get drunk. It was his life, his boat, and, like every other man, he was made to be the father of thousands, and what harm could there be in a tryst that would make them both feel more kindly toward the world? This was the wrong train of thought, and he came back to the first, the psychiatrist. He had the telephone number of Miss Rainey's doctor, and he called and asked for an immediate appointment. He was insistent with the doctor's secretary—it was his manner in business—and when she said that the doctor's schedule was full for the next few weeks, Francis demanded an appointment that day and was told to come at five.

The psychiatrist's office was in a building that was used mostly by doctors and dentists and the hallways were filled with the candy smell of mouth-wash and the memories of pain. Francis' character had been formed upon a series of private resolves—resolves about cleanliness, about going off the high diving board or repeating any other feat that challenged his courage, about punctuality, honesty, and virtue. To abdicate the perfect loneliness in which he had made his most vital decisions shattered his concept of character and left him now in a condition that felt like shock. He was stupefied. The scene for his *miserere mei Deus* was, like the waiting room of so many doctors' offices, a crude token gesture toward the sweets of domestic bliss: a place arranged with antiques, coffee tables, potted plants, and etchings of snow-covered bridges and geese in flight, although there were no children, no marriage bed, no stove, even, in this travesty of a house, where no one had ever spent the night and where the curtained windows looked straight onto a dark air shaft. Francis gave his name and address to a secretary and then saw, at the side of the room, a policeman moving toward him. "Hold it, hold it," the policeman said. "Don't move. Keep your hands where they are."

"I think it's all right, Officer," the secretary began. "I think it will be—"

"Let's make sure," the policeman said, and he began to slap Francis' clothes, looking for what—pistols, knives, an icepick? Finding nothing, he went off, and the secretary began a nervous apology: "When you called on the telephone, Mr. Weed, you seemed very excited, and one of the doctor's patients has been threatening his life, and we have to be careful. If you want to go in now?" Francis pushed open a door connected to an electrical chime, and in the doctor's lair sat down heavily, blew his nose into a handkerchief, searched in his pockets for cigarettes, for matches, for something, and said hoarsely, with tears in his eyes, "I'm in love, Dr. Herzog."

It is a week or ten days later in Shady Hill. The seven-fourteen has come and gone, and here and there dinner is finished and the dishes are in the dish washing machine. The village hangs, morally and economically, by its thread in the evening light. Donald Goslin has begun to worry the "Moonlight Sonata" again. *Marcatoma sempre pianissimo!* He seems to be wringing out a

wet bath towel, but the housemaid does not heed him. She is
writing a letter to Arthur Godfrey. In the cellar of his house,
Francis Weed is building a coffee table. Dr. Herzog recommended
woodwork as a therapy, and Francis finds some true consolation
in the simple arithmetic involved and in the holy smell of new
wood. Francis is happy. Upstairs, little Toby is crying, because
he is tired. He puts off his cowboy hat, gloves and fringed jacket,
unbuckles the belt studded with gold and rubies, the silver bullets
and holsters, slips off his suspenders, his checked shirt, and Levis,
and sits on the edge of his bed to pull off his high boots. Leaving
this equipment in a heap, he goes to the closet and takes his space
suit off a nail. It is a struggle for him to get into the long tights,
but he succeeds. He loops the magic cape over his shoulders and,
climbing onto the footboard of his bed, he spreads his arms and
flies the short distance to the floor, landing with a thump that is
audible to everyone in the house but himself.

"Go home, Gertrude, go home," Mrs. Masterson says. "I told
you to go home an hour ago, Gertrude. It's way past your suppertime and your mother will be worried. Go home!" A door on the
Babcock's terrace flies open, and out comes Mrs. Babcock without
any clothes on, pursued by her naked husband. (Their children
are away at boarding school, and their terrace is screened by a
hedge.) Over the terrace they go and in at the kitchen door, as
passionate and handsome a nymph and satyr as you will find on
any wall in Venice. Cutting the last of her roses in her garden,
Julia hears old Mr. Nixon shouting at the squirrels in his bird-
feeding station. "Rapscallions! Varmits! Avaunt and quit my
sight!" A miserable cat wanders into the garden, sunk in spiritual
and physical discomfort. Tied to its head is a small straw hat—a
doll's hat—and it is securely buttoned into a doll's dress, from the
skirts of which protrudes its long, hairy tail. As it walks, it shakes
its feet, as if it had fallen into water.

"Here, pussy, pussy, pussy!" Julia calls.

"Here, pussy, here, poor pussy!" But the cat gives her a skeptical
look and stumbles away in its skirts. The last to come is Jupiter.
He prances through the tomato vines, holding in his generous
mouth the remains of an evening slipper. Then it is dark; it is a
night where kings in golden suits ride elephants over the
mountains.

JAMES BUECHLER was born in Albany, New York, but has lived most of his life in Sche-nectady. He attended local public schools until going to Harvard on a scholarship. He graduated from Harvard, summa cum laude, in June, 1955. While there, he studied in the classes of Archibald MacLeish and Albert Guerard, Jr. He was married shortly after graduation and is spending his honey-moon on a travelling fellowship in Europe.

PEPICELLI

From THE HARVARD ADVOCATE

Pepicelli: he came half-running home one night around seven-thirty, pushing the thing in front of him. It was a motorcycle of all things, which was pretty much what Kate said to herself when she saw it coming up the street from the front window of the flat. It was something to look at, anyway, you didn't really see that many motorcyles on Third Street, and then it was mostly young kids in big leather belts that squeezed their fannies out behind them and hats like state troopers or something; big shots, a lot littler than the thing they were riding though, just sitting up there on their behinds until it ran away on them one time and killed them. You didn't see the squirts like that pushing the things either, they might get their big gloves or something else dirty. But here came somebody pushing this one, hopping along, puffing, in the almost-dark; a little man, but thick enough, who might be anywhere from thirty-eight-or-nine to fifty years old. He was as a matter of fact forty-six. His name was Pepicelli and he was Kate's husband—something she didn't realize or anyway believe until the thing, that is the cycle, turned its head, its wheel, like a big black dog, took a bite of the curb, then jumped it and went trotting out the alleyway that led to the Pepicellis' and the new people living upstairs' backyard. Pretty soon you could call it just the Pepicellis' yard as Pepicelli was meaning to buy the house. Seeing they were there going on thirty years it was about time now.

Motorcycles or not Kate had been waiting for him; and now he had shown up she went out to the kitchen to warm supper. It wasn't any wonder he was late—he was probably afraid somebody might see him pushing a thing like that up the street in daylight.

Just at dark Nick, the man next door, liked to hose down his grass. He saw the big cycle come rolling out from the alley, and Pepicelli running with it but sort of hanging on behind, like a boy exercising a big black horse. Pepicelli, moving, shuffling, breathing heavily, trotted it in an arc across his grass, around and into an open space between his house siding and Nick's fence. There it stood up by itself. Pepicelli had never had a garage.

He let go the grips, and came out from between the machine and the fence, and there was Nick come up on his side.

"Now holy smoke," said Nick, "what kind of a thing do you call that, there?" Although like Kate he saw very well what it was. Pepicelli, still breathing hard, told him as much:

"You care now, Nick? You see it."

Nick edged down along the fence to see it better. The thing was big, long, black, the handlebars wide black antlers, wheels as big as a car's, silver-rimmed, the saddle a size for two or three men.

That was a good-size machine, Nick said; and he asked, what it was for. But Pepicelli, back a little from the fence, squatted down, running his hot fingers through the grass. It was a heavy thing. It put a track in his lawn. When he rose up he could feel his legs. Nick was agreeing, that the sons of bitches weighed, and what was she, a Harley-Davison?—They used to make the good ones when Nick was a kid. When Pepicelli was a kid. "You should of rode her home," said Nick.

"Let me see that hose," said Pepicelli, "I need a little drink." So Nick did, and watched this little Pepicelli as he drank, who looked so hot and jumpy, and kind of worked up. "You're as old as I am," said Nick. "Hell." And he asked again, what make Pepicelli said she was.

"I don't know nothing about it," said Pepicelli, "I just bought it. Off a kid. Don't ask me so much unless you want to buy it."

Nick said sure, he could just see himself; he could just see himself buying it. But he didn't buy it anyway, Pepicelli did. He said so. "You're the one has bought her," he said.

Pepicelli stood there for a moment in the dark. Now he was no longer puffing, the sweat was beginning to cool on him, he had drunk some water, and he could give some attention to this Nick. And that made him see all at once that Nick was saying the truth, and he, Pepicelli, was the one who had her, the cycle. So he began to think all about this idea of him having the motorcycle; and right away he thought it was like having his own house, the same kind of thing, and he would have to take care of her. He didn't have a garage, but his brother-in-law did; but just a canvas to throw over would be better, as that would keep her home where he could keep his eye on her. She was a big machine, and worth something, and had to be taken care of. That was what he thought about it, just then.

Nick had a tarp; Pepicelli said he wanted it. Nick said, to wait a minute, he had to shut off the hose, and he'd find it; and he went out around the bulk of his house. Pretty soon he was back with a piece of stiff paraffined canvas that he and Pepicelli on either side of the fence tucked around the big motorcycle. Nick had to say again, by God, whatever she was, that was a machine! —and wanted to know how long Pepicelli was going to want his tarp.

But Pepicelli, still fidgeting with his edge of the canvas, couldn't say. He was strung-up, he felt reckless, he said things. He said maybe he'd buy his own and if he did Nick would get his back. He said, tell Nick what, he'd just hang on to this canvas and Nick could take it out in rides. Him and Nick, they'd ride to work every day; save Nick's gas. Nick wasn't worrying about his gas, Pepicelli paid him for it anyway. "You think that's what you bought it for, is it?" said Nick.

Pepicelli said, sure, Nick, and thought this was pretty good, the way you could kid Nick. You could say anything. Nick on his side was thinking, why, Pepicelli, he'd kill himself, he'd wrap around a pole, he'd break his neck, he was crazy, he wasn't very sensible. Pepicelli and him, Nick, *they'd* ride to work—sure, Nick!

But Pepicelli just said again, Sure, Nick, because you could say anything; and grinned, and said, "I got to go inside," and started toward his porch; while Nick muttering, sure, got busy, as he had a hose that wanted coiling.

Kate was waiting in the kitchen, where things were now as warmed and ready as they had been at quarter to six and nobody had shown up to eat them. She had made up her mind she was going to make a little noise about it, but for the most part she didn't care. Pepicelli never gave her much trouble like that, and even when he did it was never more than a few hours; and she could think of times years ago when they wouldn't see her father for days. But that was years ago, and now even he didn't do it anymore, if only because he hadn't anyplace to go, no place not to come back from, Kate thought.

Kate's maiden name was Brennan. This father of hers had worked for most of his life in the Municipal Department of Parks and Recreation. His wife was dead some few years now; he himself still lived with one son, who wasn't married, and was getting old, in the house where, when he wasn't working, or nobody knew where he was, he had brought up six other sons and his wife had brought up Kate. When Kate was something over eighteen the father brought home one night a young man, named Pepicelli, who said he was twenty-two, who also worked for the City, and who as the father said, was a "steady boy." Maybe the mother believed at first or maybe she didn't, but she must have come round to it sometime before the year was out. At all events she was glad enough then to see Kate married to Pepicelli and Kate seemed glad enough of it too. Old Brennan hadn't paid much attention to the whole thing until the wedding but he spent most of the reception telling his wife, one way and another, how pleased he was, as Kate was his only daughter and for that reason the last woman he'd have to worry about taking care of, as she, his wife, could understand.

And then right after the wedding the two of them, Kate and Pepicelli, had moved into this house on Third Street, that he had already brought her to look at weeks ahead. They had lived in the upstairs flat for the first five years. All that time there was plenty to do. The house was not so old then but it was not in such good shape either. It needed everything done to it, inside and outside too; painting and papering and roofing and rebuilding, and building some new additions as well, new plumbing, even a part of the foundation repoured, and a sidewalk poured and then the yard cleared and graded and seeded and fenced-off, finally, with a place left for a garden. They had worked very hard and steadily at all this, mostly because after all, as Pepicelli would say, they were the ones going to live in the place; but partly, too, because the landlord, who was living downstairs then, kept the rent low and was always talking about selling to Pepicelli. He never did, but after he moved out Pepicelli became pretty much the man of the house, even collecting rent for him from the new people; and by then, with a lot of the early work done, and all the people they had got to know, they were pretty well settled in Third Street.

They liked it there. Pepicelli was working in the parks with Old Brennan, who it turned out at the wedding, was the one to get him the job. After awhile Pepicelli found himself having less and less to do with the older man, what with his wife and the work on his house and all. And after the five years they never went over to the old house any more, except when Kate wanted to see her mother; and by and by Pepicelli let her go by herself even to do that, until finally the old woman herself had to come over to Third Street when she wanted to see them. The father never came with her but once he showed up by himself. Pepicelli said, well! to come into the house, and after, did he want to drink? He did; and so they did. Later they got up, and Pepicelli did the leading, and all the talking, and away they went, all over the house, out front, round back, so the old man could see it all; he had to see everything. He had a fine time, too, just wouldn't stop laughing all night, and every time Pepicelli stopped, and pointed, and started talking away, the old man took him under his arm and listened, and grinned, and leaned so hard Pepicelli could hardly stand up. And so around they went. Brennan laughed, listened, took his shoulder, leaned; thought it was all "pretty good." "Well now Peppy that's pretty good," he kept saying. "Isn't that pretty good, now!" Pepicelli said *he* guessed so, and it went on like that till pretty late. Then the old man left, and come back, said Pepicelli, come see us again; but he never did, and they didn't expect him to, as they didn't expect him a first time either. But Pepicelli used to see him in the parks, till when he got a better job that was more permanent than just a laborer, a little city park to take care of alone, with a tool shed on it. Then later the mother died, and there was a funeral, and then there wasn't even that between the old house and Third Street. Once in awhile they saw one of the brothers, who was married, and owned the garage Pepicelli was thinking of.

Things went on easily enough, Pepicelli and his wife got older. They didn't think much about it. The only thing that changed so far as they could see was the rent, that had got considerably higher of later years. This bothered them very much. Pepicelli still had a sort of stewardship, but after awhile he lost contact with the old owner and began to discharge even this to a downtown real estate agent. Just lately he had learned from the agent that the owner had died in New York City somewhere, and he started to deal with the agent about buying the house, to settle it once and for all. And this one night, when he had not come home, that is where Kate had expected he would be. He may have been there; but he must have been someplace else too, because here he came with something she didn't even want to think about, he just disgusted her so—that great big machine. Not that she worried at all, if you thought about thirty years without worrying, but it decided her she was going to say something.

She heard him mounting the back steps. She hurried and pulled open the back door. In walked Pepicelli, into the kitchen, right by her where she stood at the door. Pepicelli didn't so much as look at her. He saw her well enough—was there any reason for expecting not to see her? He just didn't look or wasn't thinking about her. She watched him. He went straight to the sink; turned on the tap; passed his hands and wrists under water. He lowered his head, he began slapping. He slapped his face, he slapped his neck, he slapped his entire head, with the water. He made noises, he snorted, his shirt and all got wet, she could see. She watched him snap down a dishtowel, and scrub and dry awhile, and she didn't like it at all. He belonged in the bathroom, he knew it.

But she shrugged, and with her eyebrows up and her eyelids down, closed the door.

Then Pepicelli looked up at her; but now it was she who was busy, you know, she could be preoccupied too, with pots and the putting of things upon the table. She told him, sit down; he did. She told him shortly, to go ahead, start, and don't wait for *her;* and after a little sat down herself across from him. Pepicelli ate. His wife sat and watched him. He didn't say anything, nothing at all, and this worked on his wife the longer it went on, till finally she started in:

—Well! And wasn't it pretty nice the way some people could run around all night and still have supper and things ready for them the minute they thought to come home! And didn't have to worry about anything; and just took care of their little selves! And what was the matter, didn't think he had to *bother* about a person that might be expecting him did he? And no telephones he could call a person up on?

On she went like this, scolding, but it didn't sound right, she wasn't used to it, and pretty soon it died down. But she couldn't stop there, and what about it, she wanted to know, did he see about the house, or what?

Pepicelli for his part went right on eating. He felt better from the water, but he was all tightened up, he felt light-headed, he was tired in his legs. He was still thinking about that motorcycle, and how he, Pepicelli, was the one who had her, how he should take care of her, all the things he might do with her, and then about Nick, that crazy Nick. Nick had everything so figured-out all the time, you could say anything to him. All this was jumping and running around in his mind without his so much as touching it, so to speak, but all of a sudden it stopped, still. Pepicelli listened. He heard his wife talking. She was talking at him; it was loud, he discovered she was scolding. Pepicelli considered; he decided he didn't like it, he was ready to shout back. But he realized he didn't have it all together, he wasn't really mad—it wouldn't be sensible; he felt he wanted to be sensible. So he answered, no, that he didn't have time to get downtown.

—He didn't have time! No, she guessed she saw what the time was for, it was for kid's tricks. It was time for that great big thing he brought home but it wasn't time for the house. What was he doing, bringing one of those things around here? Pepicelli, he must think he was one of those squirt kids!—One of those squirt kids! repeated Kate, who except for her mother was the biggest person in both the houses she'd ever lived in.

Pepicelli listened to all this, and although it was thirty years, and he meant to be sensible, things were pulling inside him. He could feel them; all the way home he had felt them as he ran along, shuffled, the big cycle moving heavily but easily beside him. Then there was Nick, and now here was his wife, and everything else was getting thrown into it besides. But this Pepicelli was a small man, thickly set, sturdy-looking, and in him this kind of density or weightiness went further than just being what he looked like: it almost told you just to look at him, that here was a man in whom things were made so well, or so badly, as never to snap. Now he felt he had been touched, things had to be put right. He set about it directly, for all the running and jumping in his mind, and said more suddenly and sternly than his wife had ever heard him, to close up her mouth; or he'd slap it for her. It was a man's business.

It struck Kate very hard, his saying that, and he looked at her so serious. She couldn't stand it, she got up and bustled for the stove. She didn't know what to do there; she couldn't think what to say; she hadn't expected that, or anything; thought the last word was already said, by her. She was flustered, she wouldn't say frightened. From behind her turned back there came something about business, it was some business, it was nice business.

To which Pepicelli did not answer, seemed to pay no attention, as if in fact he did not have to and so proved it. Kate remained at the stove, back turned, and did nothing at all. When Pepicelli was through he got up, making no more noise about it than ever —it just sounded that way—and went off into the living room.

But now Pepicelli found himself a lot more serious and deliberate about his new motorcycle. He went directly to one corner of the living room, where they kept a sort of tall cabinet, with shelves for things like books or knick-knacks in the top of it, and lower a door that could be pulled down, like the door of a stove-oven, and used as a desk to write at, with some small drawers and desk compartments behind it, in which were all the bills, bank-books, receipts, rent-books, tax forms, official letters, pens, ink, blotters, paper clips, stamps, and any other pieces of official-dom to do with the Pepicellis, including birth certificates. Pepicelli unlocked this board, lowered it, brought over the proper chair, and sat himself up to it. He spread out in front of him all the things he was going to need, dipped his pen, wrote out a check for a hundred dollars, payable to the kid, blotted it, filled in the stub, blotted that too, entered the thing in a separate little notebook, slipped the check into an envelope that he sealed and stamped and addressed to the kid's mother and finally, again, blotted; then he put things back, dried the pen, closed up, and set the envelope out on one of the upper shelves, to go. Then he sat down in an armchair because, as he told himself, he was tired.

He supposed he had a right to be tired. That morning he had been up early. Right after breakfast he had gone out, around to the front, where he had strolled in the early sunlight up and down his sidewalk, while it grew lighter and warmer, until finally Nick, tired and without much to say, had backed his car out into the street. Nick had dropped him at his park. And then he had walked in his steady way across the grass, under the trees, while the squirrels ran about like crazy and jibber-jabbered, chased one another up and down trees; he had watched them, and liked it, and said to himself they were funny little buggers; but he didn't stop or even take his time, he just went right on, out to the little brick tool house. Once there he had thought he would wait a bit for the kid to show up, but then he remembered, that was right, this was the day, the kid wasn't showing at all. So he had set a couple of bushel-baskets and a rake in the wheelbarrow; then walked the barrow in front of him back out onto the lawn, that he had gone over the day before behind a power mower; and he had begun to rake up the grass.

For awhile he worked. The squirrels tired out; it was very quiet. The sun rose higher, the loose grass dried in it. He became hot with the raking, he pulled off his jacket and hung it over the handle of the wheelbarrow. There were no cars on the street run-ning by the park; few people ever showed themselves there or made much of a movement. And then about nine had come from off behind the houses, sound; muttering, humming, roaring and thundering; metallic, and more; staccato, yet undulating even in this; bursts of expression shortly and sharply strung together in a sound, power, an announcement; all making itself heard now from off behind the houses. Pepicelli at his raking listened; he recognized it was a motorcycle, or something very like it, and he wondered, whether it might be the kid. Then in a sudden moment he had found out; the sound had swollen, sharpened, and there had come running up the street the cycle, big, black, the kid up on her easy and jaunty and then quickly crouched up forward as she roared in a burst of the engine, took the driveway, came down running, bounding on the cinderpath, then wheeled not breaking stride, speed at all and tore off now across the grass at Pepicelli with a rush that was more than sound, the kid now back and high on the big machine, knee-gripping her, calling in a high kid's voice that came with the rush, at Pepicelli who stepped back grasping his rake as the kid tore by between his grass-filled baskets: "Pep . . . i . . . cellleeeee!": which was part of the rush, the sound of the thing, and went off streaming after it, over the cinderpath, across the ball diamond, up into the wooded hills behind, where Pepicelli could hear it, and see it now and then, plunging, wheeling, shaking the brush, rattling the leaves on the trees. And then the kid had brought her back, raging down from the hills like some raiding barbarian, over the diamond, the lawn, again to Pepicelli still clutching his rake; where the kid stopped her, pulled her back but kept one knee dug into her, while she roared and roared under the hand throttle and dug and pawed at the ground as he played with the clutch, bouncing a little, cocky in the saddle, a thin young kid who grinned and yelled with the roar and snort of the machine: "Pepicellee! Buy her?—Hunnerd dollars!" Off again in a spurt of torn out grass and dirt to the edge of the course, the grass, skidding, wheeling, pivoting around the kid's grounded leg, then up, straightaway at Pepicelli and his bushel-baskets in a rush and high-voiced shout—"Hunnerd dollars!"—and past, while Pepicelli just stood there, grinned a little and thought, what a bastard kid, but watched closely, more and more so as the big machine lunged, pawed, raced past him in another—"Hunnerd dollars"—rush, to be kicked about again by the kid for another pass—"Hunnerd dollars!"—and so again until, the next time, Pepicelli had grinned and nodded and when the kid had called out the—"Hunnerd dollars!"—he had said it with him: which the kid had seen if he could not hear it, and so after the pivot had throttled her to a rolling trot and then a walk over the grass and she had come rolling bouncing slightly on her shocks to where Pepicelli stood with his rake.

They had talked about it then, the terms and the agreement, which Pepicelli felt he ought to be more or less grave about; but he couldn't help it, he kept grinning and laughing with the kid. The kid explained everything, "Look here, old Pepicelli, see this thing here, watch this now," and Pepicelli looked, and the kid said, you watching, old Pepicelli? and Pepicelli said shut up, he was, and then something would happen with the machine. Finally the kid drove out behind the tool house and came walking back. He said more things to old Pepicelli and then went off; he was going to the army, he had to be there by noon. Late in the after-noon Pepicelli had rolled the wheelbarrow slowly out back to the tool house and shut up his bushel baskets and rake. Then he had wheeled the big motorcycle along the cinderpath out to the street. He had rolled her all the way home, roundabout to the other side of the city, and it had taken him three hours.

And now he was very tired. He judged it would be a good thing to go to bed early, right away would be very good. He didn't want to do anything right now. So he pulled himself from his chair and standing, felt himself so very very heavy and tired, much too tired to be able to think even; and he went off to bed without saying anything more to his wife.

Next morning things seemed much better in the Pepicelli house. Pepicelli himself was awake very early. His wife was already out of bed but he could not yet hear the crackle of the frying pan from the kitchen. Out the window he could see the gray boards of Nick's house. When he stood up his thighs ached, and the bunches of flesh behind his knees, but he said to himself, it showed the muscles were there all right. He went round the bed to a chair by the window, which sat there dressed in his clothes. One by one he pulled them off the chair and onto him-self; and when the chair was pretty well bared he sat down on it to pull on his shoes and lace them up over his ankles. He stood up then, close to the window. The sun was upon the topmost bricks of Nick's chimney. Pepicelli raised the window all the way, to air out the room; and then, feeling really good this morning, as he told himself, he went on out for breakfast.

When he came walking into the kitchen, there was Kate, standing again at the stove, her back turned, as if, almost, she had stood there all night, had never closed the scene but waited there to get her answer, or a vindication, or something; as if in fact she had stood there perpetually, all their life together; and Pepicelli, though he never thought about it quite that way, was really most used to seeing her just like that. When he was off at the park and he thought of his wife for a moment, that is what he would see— the full back of a large woman in a clean cotton dress, whose dry black hair was braided thickly and rolled up closely and neatly at the back of her head; and who stood at a white and clean stove, doing something.

Right now she was cracking his eggs into the pan and as they fell they began to sputter, lowly; which pleased him, as the morning and all pleased him, and after he had sat and drunk off two glasses of milk he went so far as to say, "Ah!" It was only after this that there came from the stove his wife's asking, how he had slept, then? How he had slept? Why he had slept good, good. And then, but not right away, she observed, that he felt good this morning . . . that was good; it was a good morning. A good morning— Pepicelli thought so too and he was happy enough to say so, again; which led Kate, serving him now, to go on and say, what a good summer it had been all along; and then, why didn't he look at the paper, there, that she had set there for him, she could see it later; so he did, and they talked, about what the paper said, and once she mentioned that she had those screens she wished he would paint, and he answered he would do it; and Kate talked more and more, feeling how things were all good this morning, until when time came for him to go she gave him his jacket, that he slipped into, and she said, she would see him then, for supper, here was his lunchbox, and Pepicelli said, sure, took the box, and stepped out through the door into the morning.

He was down the steps on the back walk when he looked toward the motorcycle. It was partly concealed behind the shoulder of the house. Its body was hooded by the canvas.

Pepicelli thought to himself, so, his new property, his machine, it was still there. He would go over and see what the night had done to it. He crumpled back the half-stiff canvas. There was the cycle, supporting herself between the fence and the side of the house, her metal cold to the hands, her sable paint job dulled in the morning damp. She had a large chromium-plated headlight, dull-silvered now, shaped like the half of a great pearl, mounted upon her forehead above her handlebars; when he stroked it to wipe away the mist the morning flashed out suddenly brightly from it, and startled him a little, and he saw his hand reflected in it, grotesquely swollen and tapering down to be part of a tiny squat Pepicelli. For a minute then he looked at her, just looked, and then he told himself, she was all right, she would be all right where she was; and he retucked the canvas around her.

A door slammed in the next house. Pepicelli strode out onto his grass. Nick came shuffling down his own steps, going out toward the garage. Pepicelli said, "Hey!" Nick without stopping looked over and yelled, "Hey!" You ready? Get out there!"

"Sure, Nick," said Pepicelli. He went round front and both of them drove off to work.

Pepicelli was a man who had always liked to work; he liked working especially in a cool summer. But that day he had trouble; it bothered him for some reason, just having to stay there, filling his bushel-baskets; and before the sun was up to noon, even, he had already considered with himself, that it might not be a bad thing today, to get a bus home early, and take some time to inspect that thing—look her over good—that he had picked up the day before.

So that is what he did. He caught his early bus and by mid-afternoon he was back at his house, around in the yard, had slid his lunchbox tinnily across the porch and seen through the screen into the kitchen that his wife was out, shopping, or somewhere. He went over to the cycle then. He drew off her canvas tarp and folded it over the fence. Then he took her handlegrips and she rolled with him as he stepped her backwards, out onto the grass. He stood her up there, placing a wooden chock between her kickstand and the soft ground.

She stood on the grass in the sunlight, her front wheel nodded slightly with the lean of her to one side, the sunlight glinting in her finish, flashing circular from her silvered rims and from her headlight too; and to Pepicelli, standing back, it seemed a little queer, incredible, the way she showed herself so well, standing clear; how long she was, her body thick-made, heavy, but rounded and containing herself, which showed you something of her strength, right there; how her tank, shining black, bulged out above her engine on both sides before the saddle, like strong hunched-up shoulders, and she thinned back behind to just the rounded fender, rounded with the gleaming rim. But her motor, that was the heart of her, really, her power, just as it was with any car; and how she carried it, a drab piece of cast-iron, a little rusted, acid-stained, cylinder-abutted, infested with innumerable wires, bound around with gauges, carburetor, generator, battery: how she carried it, beneath her body, yet part of her, rounding her lines about it, unapologetic so to speak, proving that it was not ugly, no more than the rest of her, if you could see it there massed in its power while its sparkplug caps glittered like metallic stones in the sunlight.

Pepicelli was going to inspect her, look her over. He went to get a cloth and then he went all over her, rubbing and cleaning, wiping away what grease and bits of dirt he could find. With his hands he felt each of the tires for their hardness. Pepicelli liked motors as much as anybody else, what little he knew about them from talking cars with Nick; he checked what he could, traced a few wires, but for the most part touched the motor very gingerly. He looked at the rocker foot clutch too, and standing by the handlebars he worked the accelerator a little and squeezed the hand brakes a few times. They needed strong hands. The shift looked all right. He tried the saddle-springs once, twice, with his hand, and told himself, that they seemed good too. Then he walked around the machine, again and again, feeling that there was something more to be done, and trying to find it, eventually re-doing all of the things he had done already, until, later, his wife appeared upon the porch, and looking him straight in the face so as almost not to see what he was about, called:

"It's ready! You going to come?"

"Sure," said Pepicelli. "Right now." And he wheeled the big cycle back across the grass, installed her between the fence and the house-siding, and wrapped her again in her canvas.

The next day, and the one after, went very much the same. Pepicelli would be up early, and coming out of the house would walk over to the motorcycle to see how she had weathered the night. And then by the middle of the afternoon he would be home again and the cycle would be out on the grass, braced upon the wooden chock in the sunlight. The third day Pepicelli was again late for supper. But it was not a matter for Kate's worrying, as he had gone to see the agent about the house. When he came home Pepicelli didn't say anything and Kate wanted to know, what about it? He had seen him, Pepicelli said. Well, and what? He would have to go back, Pepicelli said.

After supper the two of them sat for awhile in the living room. Pepicelli read a newspaper, that he fidgeted with, and kept changing from one page to another. But Kate did not notice, because tonight it was she who was tired, and after a little she put away what she was doing and went off to bed. She fell asleep before she knew that Pepicelli had not come in too.

By that time Pepicelli was no longer in the house even, but was standing in the dark in the backyard. For a moment he stood there, until he could see better; then he went over to the side of the house. His two hands grasped the canvas covering the motor-cycle and carefully drew it from her. There she was, standing large and dark beside him, so that he could scarcely make her out, but against his leg he could feel the rough abutments of the motor, and higher, the smoothness of the tank. The metal of the tank was cool. With a sudden groping, reaching then he found the handlegrips, took hold of them and swinging a thick leg across her fender was suddenly up in the saddle. Pepicelli, how he felt the size and power of her swelling under him then; his legs wide-straddling the great motor, fitting tightly into her frame as they should, his feet finding naturally where they belonged, close-ready on the brake and clutch, while he seemed to hold all her power, everything, tight in control in his strong clasp upon her handlebars. He moved up forward on her, pressed his knees against the tank as if for a jump, settled back, raised himself easily in the saddle, then came down upon it, bouncing, but none too lightly, in his seat. The springs made a noise. Pepicelli heard it, and then for some reason it struck him; everything he had been feeling began to pass out of him; he almost thought he felt ashamed. There was no other sound; the cycle was quiet and immobile under him. Without saying so to himself Pepicelli knew it was nothing at all like it had been in the park. And after sitting there quietly for a short time he drew the canvas back over the machine and went into the house.

But he did not sleep, although he went straight to bed. And the next day, although he remained for the full time at the park because, as he told himself, he had been going home early too many times that week, he did not work much either—hardly at all.

When at supper he took nothing but a cup of strong coffee his wife said, to eat, what was the matter? Pepicelli answered, to never mind about it, he wasn't hungry. Yes—the heat, his wife said then; the days were hotter now, the heat was coming. "Who said, heat!" burst out Pepicelli. He wasn't hungry, that's what he'd said. "I've had mine!" And he shoved his cup toward the middle of the table, shoved himself up, then pushed, half-kicked his way out through the screen door.

Once outside there was no pause, or hesitation. Pepicelli began to move with all his own steadiness. He pulled off the tarpaulin, laid it over the fence unfolded, backed out the big motorcycle to where she could turn around; and then the two of them, Pepicelli walking deliberately, conducting the cycle by her saddle and one handlegrip, passed over the concrete walk, out the Pepicelli alleyway into the road: while across the street three little girls were playing jump-rope, two of them twirling, the rope splat-splatting, the other girl, who lived across there somewhere, hopping, breathless, counting; when there appeared coming out the driveway opposite her a man, pushing something, a machine, how big it was! and she missed: which stopped the rope and the game too, because she ran across the road then to see the thing, and watch the man, who was bending over it, looking, touching it, like he was getting ready to do something; and he wouldn't look at her or the other two girls who came over, didn't he see them? But she knew who he was then and she asked,

"Whose is that, Mr. Pepicelli? Where'd you get that?"

But Pepicelli whether he heard or not said nothing; just straightened up, sat himself very carefully in the saddle, balanced the big machine the best he could with one foot against the curb; his eyes were all the while intently downward on the cycle herself, on her ignition, gauges, pedals, where his feet should place themselves, until, finally, they fixed upon the kick starter, close up behind on the right; he cocked his leg and brought the heel of his work shoe up to it. All this the little girls watched, and had no attention paid them, even though, now, there were more than little girls to watch, bicycles racing up, one, then more, skid-whistling, stopping in a cluster about the motorcycle, kids' voices talking to Pepicelli, to one another, one of them yelling—"Art— hey Art! Here! Come on!"—with more and more people coming up now, looking on, no longer only children: men with lunchboxes, newspapers, a woman from a nearby house, all standing round on the sidewalk watching the thick little black-haired man, Mr. Pepicelli, who was sitting upon a motorcycle and—there!—he kicked at something now: which Pepicelli in the saddle felt kick back at him, hard, redoubling up his leg, almost so hard as to throw him, and he had to get off, back onto the road for fear to fall, and to have a look at that starter; while the people wondered, and more crowded up, men in neckties now, draftsmen or clerks or something, a woman or two with a shopping bag; and then a young girl and with her a young fellow—just a kid, red-headed, very freckled, extremely tall, who could see above the necessary heads without much trouble; he saw the motorcycle, and what was going on, was in a moment standing in the road above the squat Pepicelli, whom he got back a little from the machine, threw a gangling leg of his own over her, and was in the saddle. And then, everybody watching, he rose above them all, incredibly high, in the air; his red head came down flashing, and with it a clap of thunder, deafening, more than a clap, perpetual thunder, rolling along the street, bounding against the house-faces, filling the valley of houses that was Third Street.

The roar shoved back the bystanders, cleared away the bicycles, and the young man sat the machine in a little space rolling her sound with a thin wrist that was freckled and jeweled with a silver wrist-watch. He grinned at the people watching and at Pepicelli too, who had hardly moved from right beside the cycle, and to whom he tried to say something now; but nobody could make it out above the noise, which overwhelmed everything, until Pepicelli could be heard shouting harshly, "All right! All right! Get offa her!" So the young man did, and came back to stand by the girl, who smiled at him just a very little, while Pepicelli remounted his motorcycle.

Pepicelli: how he felt it all then, the real power of her, pounding and harsh, but fluctuating into infinite nuance within her where her pistons moved unseen and strong; how he felt her throbbing unbelievably between his knees, vibrating the very air, filling his ears, and hammering there; shocking her strength into him through his arms, responding to his heavy throttle hand with a force that was almost fearful to him! What might she do? He must know, she must run; urge her to it even, to her utmost swiftness, as hard as she would ride; conquer everything, roads, hills, wherever she might carry him; he had known horses, but she was so much bigger for a man, and more beautiful, and he had seen her run; and now he was on her, she roaring under him, ready, and everybody giving her room like a rearing animal!

By that time the roar in the street had opened front doors, called up faces in windows, brought people out on front porches. What, what was it, what was all the noise? There was something there, look, all those people; what was it, the police? What were they doing up here? That was what it sounded like, a motorcycle, like the police have. Sure, there; see. No, that man lived around here somewhere didn't he; what was his name, that little Italian fella, works for the City—Pepicelli. Lives right across the way. What was he doing on that thing, a man going on fifty years old? Although he looked pretty good on her didn't he, like a kid. But where was his wife; she was the one ought to see him.

Kate saw everything well enough. She stood in the living room, looking out through her summer curtains. The sound of the thing filled the room. She was disgusted, she told herself; she was thinking about them all, the kind of men who would go and buy a motorcycle. Most of her brothers had been like that. The roar became louder for a moment and outside she saw Pepicelli sitting sturdy and straight upon the machine move out from the curb in jerks and bucks, to go on slowly down the street. He came back more smoothly, but not too fast, and the bicycles got out of the way to let him pass. But then the third time she could hear the sound, still far away, raising pitch, expanding as it came, until the sound, the rush, Pepicelli unbentover in the wind, swept at once through the street and away, out of sight, then hearing, altogether. When he did not make another pass right away the people began to go home.

Kate waited. She waited until midnight, and then it was late, and she went to bed. She waited for a long time the next day, but then she began to call people. On the days following she called everybody she could think of. Somebody told old Brennan about it and he laughed, and said, maybe he would have her come and keep his house. But within a few weeks Kate had moved in with her married brother, and her sister-in-law, and none of them ever heard of Pepicelli again.

R. V. CASSILL *grew up in Iowa and taught at the State University there after service in the United States Army in the South Pacific. He received his M.A. from the University of Iowa in 1947, and later taught in the Writers' Workshop there. Following a year in Paris on a Fulbright scholarship, he now lives in New York City. He has published a novel,* The Eagle on the Coin, *and many short stories, one of which, "The Inland Years," appeared in the 1955 edition of the O. Henry Prize Stories.*

THE PRIZE

From PERSPECTIVE

The first prize in the contest sponsored by the Goodyear Tire Company early in the Depression was, I remember, an overwhelmingly large one. It was a sum on that scale, one large enough to inspire a variety of religious experience among contestants, and the scattering of lesser prizes had been conceived with similar grandeur. Looking back from a removal of two decades and from some comprehension of the economic and political turns of those years I am impelled to visualize the Goodyear Co., struggling with titanic anxiety to shake free of the chaos that threatened organizations as well as individuals, and willy-nilly I have to admire the scale of their effort. They knew how big a battle we were in.

And I remember with a twinge that at the time of the contest I didn't even know there was a Depression. I knew we had moved out of the city to live near Chesterfield—where my father was to work in his cousin's grain elevator—for reasons that were not very happy or decent. But it seemed to me when I weighed everything that we had been expelled because of some thing shameful or ugly that my family had done or because of some shameful inadequacy in us into which it was best not to inquire too far. When I learned, from eavesdropping on adult conversation, that my father had lost $380 in a bank failure, I was ashamed of him for not having had more on deposit. We lost our car then, too, and I was pretty sure that this need not have happened if he had had more of the installments paid on it.

There was very little talk between my parents which named the name of Depression. Since they were both faithful Republicans who supported Hoover to the end, it might well have seemed traitorous to them to use such a term—I figured then it was like not holding your breath when something very important depended on your holding it.

A big green van took our furniture to the house near Chesterfield, and the family followed in the car borrowed from my father's cousin. We arrived on a rainy evening just before dark, and there was the van backed up to the house with the moving men carrying our familiar things into its dark interior. Our rocking chairs, the fernery, and the radio were going in where they didn't belong. The thought struck me that we were moving into a house that no one lived in. That was so strange. And whatever mystery was being enacted, I didn't want it to happen. I wanted to hold my breath long enough to keep it from happening.

Through the rainy fall of our first year in Chesterfield, while I was trying to get used to the tiny school, to the overpowering skills of the farm boys who were my new classmates, and to the big old house we now lived in, I concentrated fiercely and stupidly on the problem of our expulsion from the city and began to see it as an omen of a world committed totally to sorrow. I learned to read the most trivial disappointments as signs that the race itself was doomed.

Walking home after school between the cornfields that bordered the road I would hear the brittle noise of rain on the cornleaves and the surliness inside me would cry back to it, "Yes, that's the way things are, all right." In the dripping of the rain from the porch roof outside my window I saw a melting of even my memories of the time when things had been fun, and whatever I found disheartening or miserable I cherished.

Separating myself more than formerly from my brothers, who were two and three years older than I, I cultivated an almost erotic pursuit of tokens of decay. In this I was aided by one of the rooms on the second floor that had served all the former tenants in lieu of an attic.

Books, old magazines, a sewing machine, dress forms, and trunks of many funny sorts were piled in this room. Probably there was some sort of stipulation in the rental agreement that we were to have only "the rest" of the house, for my brothers and I had been forbidden to play in there. But if I was quiet I could slip into it from my own room without my mother's hearing me where she worked in the downstairs kitchen.

In the room a smell of paper decomposing welcomed me and alerted my senses to a kind of dream that was detailed by the thousand articles of use and the souvenirs I stirred out of the trunks. I found an old cane with a metal bust of Lincoln for its head, the metal bearing an inscription linking it to the Republican convention of 1884. One of the trunks was half full of arrowheads and stone knives, some of them bearing paper tags that indicated they had been found in the river bluffs east of town. There was a stack of tintypes in another trunk which included pictures of the depot and the dedication of the Methodist Church. (If I wanted to I could look up and see this church through the window, sitting shabbily at the edge of a cornfield, now arched over with the elms that appeared in the tintype as twigs stuck in the loam around it. As far as one could see in such views the half-luminous white of ripe corn floored the river valley. I'd heard my father say in one of his moments of optimism that this was the richst soil on earth except for the Nile valley, and I worked on this idea too, converting it so I could gloat on these riches strung senselessly under the rains and consoling my bitterness by noting how universal the waste of things was.)

A green trunk in that room yielded a box of nickled instruments which I now realize were the old-fashioned paraphernalia of a woman's douche, and which had for me then, ignorant as I was of their function, some quality of terminated ferocity, like the arrowheads piled in the trunk bottom—no longer an arsenal, but something oddly more than a mass of junk.

When my mother found out that I had been playing in the forbidden room and asked what right I had to be there, I told her

I had been reading the old magazines and books—which was not entirely untrue. I didn't tell her that I had jimmied the locks on most of the trunks or that I had read batches of old letters I found in them. Anyway, she discoverd more trespasses by finding some of the arrowheads in my treasure box that I kept in one of my drawers and by noting small bits of vandalism. I had broken the head of Lincoln from the cane and for no good reason (except to mock at earthly vanity) had rubbed its nose off on the sharp edge of a lock.

She came after me with some determination then. She really insisted on an explanation of why I liked that room well enough to play there so much. "With that dirty old stuff," she said.

"Like with the arrowheads," I told her solemnly, "it would help me remember there used to be Indians right around here in the olden times."

"Ah," she said, mildly impressed and placated. "I see. With them you could sort of pretend that the Indians were still alive and more real. I see. Then I suppose you could understand your history better and the way things are by using that Republican cane."

She looked at me sharply. "Why did you break the cane then?"

"I don't know."

"You shouldn't have done that to Lincoln. He was such a great man," she said with a faraway look that seemed to suggest he should have been my father. "It was awfully wrong to break him up like that, but I'm glad if otherwise you learned anything."

My pretended agreement with her was a great fraud because her optimistic interpretation was so exactly wrong in its tendency. It had not been any sense of life in these trinkets that excited me. As they went through my hands I had exulted in them because they were evidence that so many who had been alive were dead and gone.

II

Far as she was from appreciating the content of my play in the closed room, my mother must have worried about it and found it inadequate.

She had a bundle of grievances, and I think sometimes that what carried us through that winter and marked all of us forever with a special stamp was her refusal to admit the slipping downward that obviously accompanied our move to the little town. She had to take it but she wouldn't have it. She was going to lure me out of the old storeroom into some healthy activity whatever the cost, and for a while there was talk of getting me a subscription to the YOUTH'S COMPANION even if that meant showing favoritism to me, since nothing comparable could be afforded "just then" for the older boys.

With the same frustrated force she approached the problem of utilities. There was no electricity in Chesterfield then and no bathroom in our house. From our arrival on she set the resources of her anguish to work on getting us a Delco light plant and plumbing, though with all her emotional heave in this direction and her heckling of my father she never worked out a practical plan by which we might expect to have them. She merely made us all hate fetching water from the pump more than we might have otherwise and made us feel we would go stone blind from reading by a kerosene lamp.

What she couldn't hold onto with a full grasp she meant to cling to, as long as necessary, with her fingernails, and the obvious pity of this was that she could get her nails into nothing solid except us.

It was her passion's refusal to admit that things had changed which swept us into the Goodyear contest with such velocity and finally made it intolerable not to win.

Winter had come by the time the contest was announced. The evening we heard of it my brother George and I were in the kitchen helping my mother with the dishes while my father and older brother listened to the radio in the dining room.

"Hear that?" my mother cried out all at once. I thought she'd at least heard a car stopping at our front gate. But she motioned us to be still and we got most of the announcement, not quite all. She marched into the dining room and demanded that my father explain the details she had missed.

"I wasn't entirely listening," he said guiltily, sleepily. "Just enjoying what they had to say."

"Enjoying? I don't see what there is to enjoy when he's talking about a contest. You ought to be listening attentively, or I don't know what's the point of listening at all."

"I know," he agreed. "I'll tell you what. It sounded like someone was going to get a patch of money, all right. I did hear them say there was a first prize of twenty-five thousand dollars. Moreover there's a whole kaboodle of little prizes."

"Little?" my mother wailed indignantly. "Why . . . why . . . Little! I heard myself that there were thousand dollar prizes."

"I meant even smaller ones. Little dee-rigibles and things."

"A thousand dollars," my mother mourned his unconcern for this.

"That's not so much it would wear our brains out figuring what to do with it. I wish you'd listen at the end of the program and be sure to get the details down on a piece of paper. No. You call me in if there's any more going to be said about it."

He took off his glasses and polished them slowly. "You sit down here and listen, Mother. The boys and I can finish the dishes. You're quicker at these things than I am."

"All I asked was for you to call me. Can't you even do that?" my mother demanded. "I know you're tired from your work and I wouldn't ask any more of you today."

Since he was in our big rocker and sitting as relaxed as a man can get and since it obviously wouldn't be much trouble for him to listen to the announcement, he naturally took her comment as sarcasm. So, when she'd gone back to her work, he tuned in another program.

"You hear that Mama?" George said, wiping away like a good fellow at the dishes. "He's turned it off."

"Well," she said, "he's tired and cranky. He worked awfully hard today. You know it's always hard work at the elevator."

Then my father appeared at the kitchen door. In those days he was still wearing some of his old business suits to work and they always had grain dust in their fibers no matter how well he brushed them when he came home. The whitish dust in his clothes gave him an air of being faded like a picture from which some of the ink has been rubbed. He made a curious gesture, half in anger, half in appeasement, like a doubter crossing himself.

"You know what these darn contests are, Sally," he pleaded. "They don't mean anyone any good. They're only done to advertise the product."

"We'll talk about it later," my mother said. This was recognized by all as a threat.

"Did you personally ever know anyone who had won his postage back in a contest like that?"

"We'll not discuss it until the boys are asleep," she warned him. I think he began making up his mind to submit right then. I saw him swallow and then nod reassurance to himself that it might not be all as bad as he feared it could be.

From that first evening on, for weeks, our family had the contest like a vocation or a disease. Of course it was easy enough for my mother to find out the details of competition once she had made up our minds, and by the end of the week she and each of us boys were working on our individual lists of words that could be made from the letters comprised in the name GOODYEAR TIRE AND RUBBER COMPANY. That was the task of the contest.

You can see that the first words come easily: dog, god, ray, rite, and so on. It is when these are all put down that the game becomes tantalizing and demoralizing. Then the tongue tries nonsense syllables and combinations in the hope that some lightly hidden word will fall out to be added to the list. And that makes quite a noise in the house.

Once at supper I began mumbling to myself and my father, driven beyond exasperation, slammed down his waterglass and howled, "Groggy wayorv, boogly, boogly, woogly, arf." Then he glared around the table with the tears of the rejected squeezing angrily out of the corners of his eyes.

"Not at the table," my mother cautioned me. She turned to my father. "I don't know why you're so set against what the boys are ambitious enough to try to do. I should think you might better want to help them."

"I won't. Great Jesus, I won't," he said helplessly. "What in His name would I be helping them to do? Lose their minds and jabber like apes?"

"They've been working with our dictionary, and I don't know

that that's bad for their education," my mother said. "The contest gives them something to look forward to." She satisfied herself with such explanations, and for my part I was thinking self-righteously that my father, in his outburst, had used f's and v's which, of course, were not permissible under the laws of the game.

According to my mother's first, rather easy-going plan, each of us was to work exclusively on his own list and even keep it partly secret from the others so there would be a sort of intra-family contest as well as the larger one. We worked from the dictionary by turns. It seemed to me sometimes when I was blundering unsystematically through it, dreaming by lamplight, that each of us might win a prize that suited his own intelligence and desserts. My mother would probably get one of the thousand dollar prizes. Dave and George might or might not get something. Maybe one of them would get a fifty dollar prize, since they were older than I. For myself, I thought and felt that I should win one of the chrome-plated models of the dirigible Akron, the lowest prize offered. I think probably a hundred of these models were being given away. I remember telling my mother that I didn't think I was good enough to win more than a model, but that this suited me because I would rather have it than money anyhow. Altogether I managed to make this model into an image of what I was worth and of what the world would pay me for being what I was.

"You have to work hard if that's the prize you want," my mother warned. "Don't forget there'll be people from all over the country trying to win, just like you are."

When the deadline for submitting entries was approaching, my mother decided that we needed a larger dictionary to work from and that we should borrow one from the school. The question of who should borrow it became major. One of us boys should ask our teacher, she thought, but we all balked at this as being too embarrassing. The other boys got away with this argument, but I was caught—perhaps because I had done more excited talking about the contest than they.

"There's nothing wicked about borrowing a dictionary," my mother bullied me. "We're not doing something dishonest. We're working as hard as we know how to earn something, and if more people would do that I expect our country would be better off. Just explain to your teacher. . ."

This is odd, but maybe if I had believed that we were in the contest for the sake of competition I wouldn't have minded explaining to my teacher why I wanted the dictionary. Caught as I was in the dream of certainly winning a thousand dollars and a dirigible, I couldn't face it. It seemed to me like putting on airs to go to my teacher and admit the glory my family was headed for.

So my mother finally borrowed it. I remember her coming in through the snowy yard, a little after I had come home from school, with the big dictionary wrapped in a shawl to protect it from the mist in the air. Her face before she saw me was set with a harsh intensity, as of someone who has refused humiliation by sheer refusal to recognize it. Seeing me, she smiled and said, "Look. I borrowed it from your teacher after you'd left. She was good about lending it. Now you see that she would have lent it to you if you'd only asked her. Don't you see?"

"But what's she going to think of us?" After all, it was I who had to go to school the next day and possibly face my teacher's amusement, envy, or scorn.

"I didn't tell her what we were using it for," my mother said with a sly grimace that meant to be comforting. "I fibbed to her, so don't you worry."

When I thought this over I announced that I didn't want to do the contest any more. My mother flung her arms around me and pressed my face very hard against her side. "Of course you do," she said. "We've worked so doggone hard this far that I'm convinced we're going to win. Maybe not the grand prize, but something. There's no reason why you can't win that dirigible if you want it. Don't you see that yet?" She frightened me with her determination, and even that was a lesser thing than the sheer giant onrush of the contest, beginning to reveal its true scope.

In the last week before the deadline—and this must have been in late January, at about the time of the thaws when the three of us boys would have liked to be playing outside—my mother bore down on us all. Some one of us had to be at the dictionary all the time. There wasn't any more talk of the contest's being educational or fun. It was work and we had to work hard enough to win. We combined our lists now, at least to the extent that our inefficient systems permitted. We had begun without much system at all and, except for my mother's, our penmanship was terrible. So, whether a word discovered in the dictionary at this late date or on someone else's list could legitimately be added to ours was a matter none of us could be quite sure of. Certainly each of us had duplications in his list, and none of us ever had quite the same total as any of the others though we tried to balance them for a while. Very late my mother tried to get us to alphabetize our lists, but this only got us in more tangles.

On the last afternoon Dave went to the post office immediately after school with his list and George's—that was a nervous precaution, since they had to be postmarked that day and some act of God might demolish the post office or block the road to it if we waited until too late.

On the other two lists at my mother's insistence we were adding all kinds of the nonsense combinations which earlier had been only a means of helping us find pure words. Some of these, she said, we might have missed in the dictionary, and it was the responsibility of the judges to decide if they were eligible or not. "Reay," she said. "That could be a girl's name. Put it down, anyway. Burrec. That sounds like a kind of donkey, I guess. Yarg. I don't see why that shouldn't be a word if there's a word yard. One doesn't sound like it meant any more than the other one does it?"

She had the clock sitting on the table where we worked—the post office closed at six—and I knew that now nothing but time running out would stop her. My father came into this intensity and stood behind us, watching us without saying anything. Pretty soon my mother spoke over her shoulder to him. "If you're not going to help, go somewhere else. Go start the fire in the kitchen. I'll get supper as soon as we're finished."

"I won't," he said; and then after a long deliberation, "God damn the Goodyear Tire and Rubber Corporation."

"Company," I said.

"I suppose you mean God damn me," my mother said.

"I don't," he said. "I mean. . ."

"Shoo. Go on. I can't think while you're staring at me."

He went into the bedroom and after some banging of dresser drawers returned to throw an envelope and two ten dollar bills on the list of words she was working on. "There," he said in a tone that was dignified only by its slightness. "There's some money and my insurance policy. I'm leaving."

"Ha," my mother said.

"You've turned the boys against me and driven them half crazy with this contest. I warned you not to do it."

"Then leave," my mother said. "Dooger."

After he was gone she kept muttering more and more absurd combinations of syllables. Her face flamed, and I could see a vein in her temple bulge with her effort, but she was not writing down any more of her inventions.

She looked up at George long enough to say, "Follow him and see where he goes." Then she glanced hard at the clock and told me to get my coat and rubbers and be ready to run for the post office. "We can't be late," she said. "You can run part of the way or go Scout's pace. You know how to do that."

With an attempt to cheer me, she said, "You and I have more words than the others now."

But, giving a last look at the physical ugliness of my list I said I wished there were time to copy at least this afternoon's work.

"Maybe if they can't quite make out some of them that will be a good thing," she said craftily. Her imagination apparently had strained to cover every accident of incompetence, weakness, taste, or unfairness on the part of the unknown judges, and it seemed to me that she had intended that each of our lists be somehow corrupt to fit the imagined corruptness of the major human types.

As I was going out with the big manila envelopes containing our two lists, George arrived back to report that my father had started west across the cornfield, had cut back within about a quarter of a mile, climbed the fence into the road, and was right now hiding inside a culvert about two hundred yards from the house.

"Ha," my mother said. Her voice crackled with unhappy triumph. "I supposed he wouldn't go far. He'll go hungry after a little while and come in. Now run," she commanded me. "Be sure you make it to the post office."

The culvert where my father was hiding was an obstacle in the road now. I could hardly bring myself to walk over him like that, but I knew I had to hurry. The road was wet. Now at sundown it was beginning to freeze and I could feel the delicate ice crunch under every step with a beautiful sound and sensation of touch. The rosy light over the cornfield, reflected in a thousand puddles islanded in the loam seemed to me too strongly and unhappily beautiful for me to stand, and it occurred to me that I might die right then, being so divided by feelings I had never encountered before, wakening to my first realization that living was something that one must choose against hardship to do.

At the culvert I left the road, knelt in the water of the ditch bottom and looked in at my father. He was sitting right in the middle of the concrete tube. In the dim light I could see his silhouette and the glitter of reflected light in his eyes. I am sure he saw me, but neither of us spoke.

Then I ran for the post office. I think I ran all the way, because I got there in plenty of time to put the envelopes in the letter box. Walking home afterward I felt how my knees were wet from where I knelt in the ditch.

III

Of course none of us won anything from the Goodyear Co. In about a month the winners of prizes over a thousand dollars were announced. First prize went to someone who had over three times as many words in his list as there had been in the largest of ours.

"Three times," my mother said. "That's a lie. That can't be. They must have used foreign words like French and German, Spanish and all. And they said that was against the rules."

My father commented, "Maybe one of you will win a littler prize. They're going to announce more next week." After the bad day of the mailing of the lists he had relaxed, had been permitted to relax, and by this time was even displaying a mild hope that something might come from all that bother.

But then the last of the cash prizes was announced and there was nothing left to wait for except the names of the winners of the model dirigibles.

"If the others didn't get any money I'm not going to win the dirigible," I said to my father, answering one of his soft optimisms aggressively.

"You don't know," he said. "I wouldn't wonder that your list would be just right for a smaller prize. You know, it might be like having the right tool," my mother said. "We should have had a typewriter. I can understand that now that it's too late. Even if they didn't specify that you had to use a typewriter."

"You told me that my words they couldn't read might be a good thing," I said.

"Well, on that. . . . ." Her lips worked carefully while she made up her mind how to answer me. "Yes, that may be so. Don't give up hope."

From this last posture she established against defeat and from my own premonitory sense of loss I began to develop the notion that they were all demanding that I win, and I added the strain of what I considered their expectations to my own. Partly for them, partly for myself I strained all the tricks of emotional force— on the order of holding my breath, crossing my fingers, figuratively—to affect what the announcer was going to say when he came to read the last list of winners. I accepted in a subterranean agreement, that I owed it to the family to win, for if I won that would help make up for my father's hiding in the culvert, my mother's fibbing to the teacher, and our general humiliation in prostrating ourselves before a big company that had so far ignored us.

Each name on that list of winners should have been mine and none was. I wanted to howl when the reading was over, and yet I felt that, having lost, I didn't even have the right to do that. For the first time it came to me with undeniable force that beyond our mere failure to win we had lost something that had been put at stake.

After the trial of listening my father sighed tranquilly and said it appeared to him that these last prizes had been awarded on a geographical basis. "Did you notice how there was hardly ever more than two from any state except New York? You heard how this gentleman up in Red Oak got one. Well sir, that's enough for this part of the world, they likely figured. You can't tell me these contests aren't rigged some way. Naturally you didn't have much of a chance when they did things like that," he told me.

He put out his hand to rumple my hair or pat my cheek, but I flung myself beyond his reach, behaving spitefully to cover my sense of worthlessness.

"There, there feller," he said. "There, there now."

"I worked hard," I screeched. "I had as good a list as anybody's."

"Sure you did. I'd lay money you had a better one than some of those as got the money."

I said, "I'm going to kill someone for this."

His head jerked as though I had burned him. Then his eyes searched beyond me for my mother and he seemed to be crawling humbly and with awkward slowness to some complicity with her. I saw this happen, but I chose then not to understand it. I thought I understood how every man's hand was against me. From then on.

"Everything comes to he who waits," my father said. "You'll see that, because that's the way things are. You remember when we came here we had such a hard job getting along without electricity and didn't think we'd ever have any?"

He paused for me to answer and I wouldn't.

"Now they're putting a line in," he said in a hearty tone, as though I might care about that. "They're going to bring the wire down from Parsons to Chesterfield and we'll have it out here, too. Then we can get us an electric radio and a lot of things, maybe. They were unloading poles on the other side of Chesterfield today."

"Somebody else got my dirigible," I whined.

"It would only be a little tin thing. You couldn't have any play out of it. Your mother and I thought that when the roads dry up we'd get you boys a bicycle. Wouldn't you rather have that?"

I set up an awful racket, protesting that I didn't want a bicycle

or anything else but the dirigible. To which my father replied
that I only wanted what I couldn't have and if that was the way
of it he couldn't help me. I believed this dictum, if nothing else
he said. I heard it wailing through my dreams that night like a
sentence of wrath to come. Maybe on purpose I dreamed toward
morning that all my family was dead. My father was dead in the
culvert where he had hidden, and I was kicking up wet grass
from the ditch to cover him in.

At school time I pretended to be sick so I could stay home.
As a matter of fact I sulked with such ugliness that my mother
suggested on her own part that I should go play in the store room,
where I had not been for some months. I considered her recom-
mendation and even walked upstairs to glance in at my former
retreat. The dead room would not receive me, and the chilly smell
of it really nauseated me. Losing the contest had even cut me off
from that.

Everything was so senseless I might as well go do it like the
rest until I was dead. I would just be too smart to hope for anything again, that was all.

But they tricked me back from that state too. I came from school
one evening about a month later to find my model of the dirigible
Akron on the dining room table. There was a mass of wrapping
paper broken back from around it and some excelsior that smelled
like newly sawed lumber.

It was a very shiny model, though somewhat smaller and
harsher looking than I had imagined it would be. It said GOOD-
YEAR TIRE AND RUBBER CO. on the side.

"What's it for?" I yelled to my mother as she came in from the
kitchen to see how I was going to receive it. "Did one of us win
after all?"

She smiled her best. "Sure," she said. "Isn't it a pretty thing,
now? I guess this proves that if you do your level best and really
want something you'll get it, doesn't it?"

I might have accepted the moral of her comment without
argument, for moral significances seemed to me at that point
lighter than air, but the practical accounting worried me. "How
come they didn't read our name on the radio if we won?"

"We didn't exactly win," my mother said. "Your father and I

thought that you'd worked so hard that you were a winner and deserved a prize. We wrote to that man in Red Oak and bought it from him."

"Oh," I said. Why did they do that to me on top of all the rest. I couldn't stand it and I said, "Thanks a lot."

Just before suppertime my brother Dave caught me outside in the yard and said, "All right you big jackass, you got your dee-ridge-able. Aren't you proud of it?"

"You leave me alone."

"I'm not going to leave you alone. They had to pay fifteen bucks for it and now maybe we can't have a bicycle this summer."

"I never asked them to do it."

"Oh no," he said. "Oh no, you didn't. Just whining like a pup that you didn't get anything in this contest. Did any of the rest of us get anything?"

"I didn't want them to buy it. I didn't know they'd be such big fools."

"I don't know," he said despairingly. "I guess they .. _re because you're such a big fool. Listen, if you don't make them think that you're real glad to get it I'll kill you."

It was not—or not exactly—his threat that weighed on me. When he left me I had nothing to face except—as on the evening of my father's flight—the width of sundown and spring air, empty but nonetheless resonant with things learned and half-learned, again multiplying by its beauty and silence the real threat of death if I turned away from my family and their organized ways of sting-ing me. I could see then that I would have to keep pretending the dirigible was fine, and I have never learned what else I could have said.

SAUL BELLOW writes "'A short autobiographical note' is like trying to write the Iliad with a grease-gun. I was born a Canadian (in 1915); I became, and have remained, a Chicagoan. I began, at an early age, to read and to write and have never stopped. I was educated in the literary conventions of naturalism but I do not like them. Something written should be something extraordinary. There is nothing ordinary about so-called ordinary events. This has always been clear to the best of the realistic writers. I have always thought of myself as a writer of comedies. Very few people have found my books funny. I am not willing to admit that the fault lies entirely with me. Who is!"

THE GONZAGA MANUSCRIPTS

From DISCOVERY NO. 4

Buttoned to the throat in a long, soft overcoat, dark green, Clarence Feiler got off the Hendaye Express in the Madrid Station. It was late afternoon and it was raining, and the station with its throng and its dim orange lights seemed sunken under darkness and noise. The gaunt horselike Spanish locomotives screamed off their steam and the hurrying passengers struggled in the narrow gates. Porters and touts approached Clarence, obviously a foreigner, by his small blond beard, blue eyes, almost brimless hat, long coat and crepe-soled shoes. But he carried his own bag and had no need of them. This was not his first visit to Madrid. An old limousine took him to the Pension La Granja where he had a room reserved. This limousine probably had run on the boulevards of Madrid before Clarence was born but it was mechanically still beautiful. In the spacious darkness of the back seat the windows were like the glass of an old cabinet, and he listened happily to the voice of the wonderful old motor. Where could you get another ride like this, on such an evening, through such a place? Clarence loved Spanish cities, even the poorest and barrenest, and the capitals stirred his heart as no other places did. He had first come as an undergraduate, a mere kid, studying Spanish literature at the University of Minnesota; and then he had come again and seen the ruins of the Civil War. This time he came not as a tourist but on a quest. He had heard from a Spanish Republican refugee in California, where he now lived, that there were more than a hundred poems by Manuel Gonzaga somewhere in Madrid. Not a single Spanish publishing house could print them because they were so critical of the Army and the State. It was hard to believe that poems by one of the greatest of modern Spanish geniuses could be suppressed, but the refugee gave Clarence reliable proof that it was so. He showed him letters to one of Gonzaga's nephews from a man named Gúzman del Nido, Gonzaga's friend and literary executor, with whom he had served in North Africa, admitting that he had once had the poems but had given them up to a certain Countess del Camino since most of them were love poems addressed to her. The Countess had died during the war, her home had been looted, and he didn't know what had become of the poems.

"Perhaps he doesn't care, either," said the refugee. "He's one of these people who think everything has come to an end anyway, and they might as well live comfortably. Gúzman del Nido lives very comfortably. He's rich. He is a member of the Córtes."

"Money doesn't have to do that to you," said Clarence, who had a little money himself. He was not exactly a rich man, but he didn't have to work for a living. "He must have a bad character not to care about his friend's work. And such work! You know, I was just killing time in Graduate School till I came across Gonzaga. The year I spent doing my thesis on *Los Huesos Secos* was the first good year I had had since I was a boy. There hasn't been anything like it since. I'm not much on modern poetry in English. Some of it is very fine, of course, but it doesn't express much wish to live. To live as a creature, that is. As if it were not good enough. But the first time I opened Gonzaga I read:

These few bits of calcium my teeth are,
And these few ohms my brain is,
May make you think I am nothing but puny.
Let me tell you, sir,
I am like any creature—
A creature.

I felt right away and in spite of this ironical turn that I was in touch with a poet who could show me how to go on, and what attitude to take toward life. The great, passionate poems carried me away, like *The Poem of Night* which I still know from beginning to end and which often seems like the only thing I really have got—" Clarence was sometimes given to exaggerating. "Or take the poem called *Confession,* the one that goes:

I used to welcome all
And now I fear all.
If it rained it was comforting
And if it shone, comforting,
But now my very weight is dreadful . . .

when I read that, Gonzaga made me understand how we lose everything by trying to become everything. This was the most valuable lesson of my life, I think. Gosh! There should be someone trying to find those posthumous poems. They ought not to be given up. They must be marvelous."

He felt, suddenly, as if he had been thrown into a race, terribly excited, full of effort, feverish—and profoundly grateful. For Clarence had not found his occupation and had nothing to do. He did not think it right to marry until he had found something and could offer a wife leadership. His beard was grown not to hide weaknesses but as a project, to give his life shape. He was becoming an eccentric; it was all he could do with his good impulses. As yet he did not realize that these impulses were religious. He was too timid to say he believed in God, and he couldn't think that it would matter to anyone what he believed. Since he was weak, it would be said, he must have some such belief. However, he was really enthusiastic about Gonzaga, and to recover this inspired Spaniard's poems was something that mattered. And "Does it really matter?" was always the test question. It filled Clarence with secret pleasure to know that he was not indifferent, at bottom pretending. It *did* matter, and what mattered might save him. He was in Madrid not to perform an act of cultural piety but to do a decent and necessary thing, namely, bring the testimony of a great man before the world. Which certainly could use it.

As soon as he arrived at the Pension La Granja and the lamps were lit in his room, a comfortable large room with balconies facing the trees of the Retiro, Madrid's biggest park, Clarence called for the porter and sent off two letters. One was addressed to Gúzman del Nido, Gonzaga's comrade-in-arms of the Moroccan War and literary executor, and the other to a Miss Faith Ungar on García de Paredes Street. This Miss Ungar was an art student, or rather student of art history; her fiancé was an airline pilot who brought in cheaper pesetas from Tangiers. Clarence disliked black-marketing, but the legal rate of exchange was ridiculous; he was prepared to pay a lot of money for those manuscripts and at eighteen-to-one he might spend a small fortune.

His landlady came to welcome him to the pension—a pale, big woman with a sort of turban of hair wound to a point. She came also to collect his passport and other travel papers for police inspection and to give him a briefing on her guests. A retired general was the oldest. She had also some people from British Shell and a widow of a Minister and six members of a Brazilian trade delegation, so the dining room was full. "And are you a tourist?" she said, glancing at the *triptico,* the elaborate police document all travelers have to carry in Spain.

"In a way," said Clarence, guardedly. He didn't like to be thought of as a tourist, and yet secrecy was necessary. Gonzaga's poems, though unpublished, would probably come under the head of national treasures.

"Or have you come to study something?"

"Yes, that's it."

"There's a great deal here to interest people from a country as new as yours."

"There certainly is," he said, his rosy beard-lengthened face turned to her, seeming perfectly sincere. The color of his mouth was especially vivid in the lamplight. It was not yet full evening and the rain was stopping. Beyond the trees of the Retiro the sky was making itself clear of clouds, and a last yellow daylight pierced the water-gray. Trolley sparks scratched green within the locust trees.

A bell rang, an old hand-bell, announcing dinner. A maid passed ringing it proudly, her shoulders thrown back.

The guests were eating soup in the dining room, an interior room, not very airy, with dark red, cloth covered walls. The Brazilians were having a lively conversation. The old general, feeble-headed, eyes nearly extinct, was bothering the soup with his spoon but not eating. Doña Elvia seated Clarence with a hefty British lady; he knew he must expect to have trouble with her. She was in a bad way. Her face was heavily made up; she thought she was a person of charm, and she did have a certain charm, but her eyes were burning. Tresses of dark-reddish hair fought strongly for position on her head.

"If you came here with the intention of having fun, you won't have it in Madrid. I've been here twenty years and never had any," she said. "By now I'm so tired out I don't even look for any. I don't read any books, I don't go to the cinema and I can just barely stand to read *Coyote* and look at the funnies. I can't understand why so many Americans want to come here. They're all over the place. One of your Bishops was arrested at Santander for bathing without the top of his costume."

"Really?"

"They're very strict in Spain about dress. I suppose if they had known he was a bishop they would have let him alone. However, in the water . . ."

"It's strange," said Clarence. "Well, anyway, he's not one of *my* bishops. I have no bishops."

"You do have Congressmen, though. Two of those had their pants stolen while taking a nap on the Barcelona Express. The thieves reached into the compartment from the roof. It happened in broad daylight. They carried about two thousand dollars each. Don't they have pocketbooks? Why do they carry so much money in their pockets?"

Clarence frowned. "Yes, I read about that," he said. "I can't tell you why they carry so much money in their trouser-pockets.

Maybe that's the custom down south. It's none of my business, though."

"I'm afraid I'm annoying you," she said. She was not afraid at all; a bold look of enjoyment had entered her eyes. She was trying to bait him. Why? he wondered; he found no ready answer.

"You're not annoying me."

"If I am," she said, "it's not absolutely my fault. You know Stendhal once wrote there was a secret principle of unhappiness in the English."

"Is that so?" he said. He looked at her with deep interest. What a busted-up face; full of unhappy energy and directionless intelligence. Yes, she was astonishing. He felt sorry for her and yet lucky to have met her.

"He may have been right. You see, I used to read widely once. I was a cultivated person. But the reason for it was sex, and that went."

"Oh, come, I wouldn't say . . ."

"I shouldn't be talking like this. It's partly the weather. It's been raining so hard. It isn't supposed to rain like this in the summer. I've never seen so much damned rain. You people may be to blame for that."

"*Who* people? Which people?"

"It could be because of the atom bomb," she said. "The weather has never been normal since the atom thing started. Nobody can tell what this radioactive stuff is doing. Perhaps it's the beginning of the end."

"You make me feel very strange," said Clarence. "But why are the American bombs the dangerous ones? There are other kinds."

"Because one always reads of the Americans exploding them. They do it under water. Holes are torn in the ocean bottom. The cold water rushes in and cools the core of the earth. Then the surface shrinks. No one can tell what will happen. It's affected the weather already."

Clarence's color grew very high and he looked dazed. He paid no attention to his broiled meat and French-fried potatoes. "I don't keep up much with science," he said. "I remember I did read somewhere that industry gives off six billion tons of carbon dioxide every year and so the earth is growing warmer because the carbon dioxide in the air is opaque to heat radiation. All that means that the glaciers won't be coming back."

"Yes, but what about Carbon 14? You Americans are filling the air with Carbon 14, which is very dangerous."

"I don't know about it. I am not all Americans. You are not all the English. You didn't lick the Armada, I didn't open the West. You are not Winston Churchill, I am not the Pentagon."

"I believe you are some sort of fanatic," she announced.

"And I believe you're a nasty old bag," he said, enraged. He left the table and went to his room.

Half an hour later she knocked at his door. "I'm terribly sorry," she said. "I suppose I did go too far. But it's all right, we're friends now, aren't we? It does you so much good to be angry. It really is good." She did, now, look very friendly and happy.

"It's all right. I'm sorry too," he said.

After all, how would feuding with this Englishwoman help him with his quest? And then there were wrong ways and right ways of going about it. Gonzaga's poems should be recovered in the spirit of Gonzaga himself. Otherwise, what was the use?

Considering it all next morning he saw that this Miss Walsh, the Englishwoman, had done him a service by baiting him. Unwittingly, she offered a test of his motive. He could not come to Spain and act badly, blindly. So he was deepened in his thought and his purpose, and felt how much already he owed to Gonzaga and to those poems.

He was in a hurry next morning to get to a bookstore and see what Gonzaga items there were in print. Impatiently he turned himself out of the comfortable bed, pulled on his underpants, dealt nervously with his cuff-buttons, washed at his little sink with the glass shelves and pointed faucets, and combed his hair and whiskers with his palms. Odors of soil and flowers came from the Retiro across the freshly watered street. The morning was clear, still and blue. He took one bite of the brick bits of toast the maid brought, sipped from the immense cup of bitter café-au-lait and then rushed out to find a bookstore.

At Bucholz's he found only a single volume he had not seen before, a collection of letters from Gonzaga to his father. The frontispiece showed Gonzaga in his lieutenant's uniform—a small man, by Clarence's standard—sitting up straight at the keyboard of an old-fashioned piano, his large eyes opened directly into the camera. Underneath he had noted, "Whenever I am lucky enough to come upon a piano in one of these Moroccan towns, I can, after playing for ten or fifteen minutes, discover how I really feel. Otherwise I am ignorant." Clarence's face colored with satisfaction as he stooped and looked. What a man this Gonzaga was—what a personality! On the very first page was an early version of a poem he had always admired, the one that began:

> Let me hear a sound
> Truly not my own;
> The voice of another,
> Truly other. . . .

The book engrossed him entirely until eleven o'clock. With a sort of hungry emotion, he sat at a café table and read it from cover to cover. It was beautiful. He thanked God for sending him the Republican refugee who had given him the idea of coming to Spain.

Reluctantly he left the café and took a cab to García de Paredes Street where Miss Ungar lived. He hated to do it, but he needed the pesetas, and it was unavoidable.

Again he was lucky. She was not at all the kind of person you would have expected a black-marketing art student to be; she was young and unusually attractive with a long, intelligent face of a white complexion, like the color of a snow-apple. Her hair was drawn tightly back over her enlongated head and tied off in an arched, sparkling tail. Her eyes were extremely clear. Clarence was greatly taken with her. Even the fact that her teeth, because of the contrast with her fair skin, were not too bright, impressed him. It proved to him that she was genuine. On a ribbon round her neck she wore a large silver medal.

"Is that a religious thing you're wearing?"

"No. Do you want to look at it?" She bent forward so that it swung free. He picked up the warm piece of silver and read: *Helena Waite Award for Historical Studies.*

"You won it?"

"Yes."

"Then why are you in this kind of business?"

"And what did you come here for?" she said.

"I need pesetas."

"And we need dollars. My fiancé and I want to buy a house."

"I see."

"Besides, it's a way of meeting a lot of people. You'd be surprised how few interesting people an American woman in Madrid can meet. I can't spend all my time in the Prado or at the Library. The embassy people are about as interesting as a plate of cold-cuts. My fiancé only gets here twice a month. Are you on a holiday?"

"Sort of."

She didn't believe him. She knew he had come with a definite purpose. He could not say why, but this pleased him.

"How do you like the Granja?"

"It's all right. An Englishwoman there lammed into me last night, first about the atom bomb and then saying that I must be a fanatic. She thought I was peculiar."

"Everybody has to make it as he can," she said.

"That's exactly the way I feel about it."

He had thought that the kind of woman who became engaged to an airplane pilot might look down on him. She didn't, not in the least. Soon he was wondering how that sort of man could interest her.

"If you have no other plans, why don't you come to lunch with me," he said, "and save me from that Miss Walsh?"

They went out to eat. Though the day had grown hot, she stopped in the courtyard to put on a pair of net gloves; barehanded women were considered common in Madrid. For his part Clarence thought the momentary grasp of her fingers as she worked them into the gloves was wonderful; what a lot of life she had! Her face gave off a pleasant heat. As they walked, she told him she couldn't give him many pesetas just yet; she'd pay whatever rate was quoted in the *Tribune* on the day the money arrived. That day, Clarence reflected, would also be the day on which her pilot arrived; he had no business to be disturbed by that, yet he was disturbed.

Near the Naval Ministry they were stopped by a procession. Priests with banners led, and next came a statue of the Virgin carried by four men. A group of barefooted widows followed them in their mourning and black mantillas. Old women passed carrying tapers. Most of these appeared to be old maids, and the flames made a clear additional light near each face. A band played Beethoven's Funeral March. Above the walls of the Ministry trees shot their leaves; there was the same odor of flowers and soil that Clarence had smelled that morning, of graves, of summer pines. Across the square, on the car tracks, a welding arc hummed and scalded. The dazzling mouths of the horns were carried past and the fires in the daylight moved away, but it was the bare white feet of the widows treading on the dusty asphalt paving that Clarence watched, and when they were gone he said to Miss Ungar, "Wasn't that splendid? I'm glad I'm here."

His brows had risen; his face was so lively that Miss Ungar laughed and said, "You take it big. I like the way you take it. You ought to be sure to visit Toledo. Have you ever been there?"

"No."

"I go often. I'm doing a study. Come with me next time I go. I can show you lots of things there."

"There's nothing I'd like better. When do you go next?"

"Tomorrow."

He was disappointed. "Oh, I'm sorry, I can't make it tomorrow," he said. "I arrived yesterday and I'm going to be very busy for a while. Just give me a rain-check, will you? I'll hold you to this. But there is something special I came to do—you guessed it, I suppose—and I can't take the time to go anywhere now. I'm all keyed up."

"Is this mission of yours a secret?"

"In a way. There's an illegal side to it, probably. But I don't think you'd tell on me, and I'm so full of it I'm willing to talk. Have you ever heard of a poet named Gonzaga?"

"Gonzaga? I must have. But I don't think I ever read his poems."

"You must read them. He was very great, one of the most original of modern Spanish poets, and in the class of Juan Ramón Jiménez, Lorca and Machado. I studied him at school and he means a lot to me. To understand what he did, you have to think first of modern literature as a sort of grand council considering what mankind should do next, how they should fill their mortal time, what they should feel, what they should see, where they should get their courage, how they should love, how they should be pure or great, and all the rest. This advice of Literature has never done much good. But you see God doesn't rule over men as he used to, and for a long time people haven't been able to feel that life was firmly attached at both ends so that they could stand confidently in the middle and trust the place where they were. That kind of faith is missing, and for many years poets have tried to supply a substitute. Like 'the unacknowledged legislators' or 'the best is yet to be,' or Walt Whitman saying that whoever touched him could be sure he was touching a man. Some have stood up for Beauty, and some have stood up for perfect proportion, and the very best have soon gotten tired of Art for its own sake. Some took it as their duty to behave like brave performers who try to hold down panic during a theater fire. Very great ones have quit, like Tolstoi who became a reformer, or like Rimbaud who went to Abyssinia, and at the end of his life was begging of a priest '*Montrez-moi Montrez* . . . Show me something.' Frightening, the lives some of these geniuses led. Maybe they assumed too much responsibility. They knew that if by their poems and novels *they* were fixing values, there must be something wrong with the values. One man can't furnish them. Oh, he may if his inspiration is for values, but not if his inspiration is for Literature. If you throw the full responsibility for meaning and for the establishment of good and evil on poets, they are doomed to go down. However, the poets reflected what was happening to everyone. As soon as people become free they feel that they are responsible for *everything*, and they feel it's up to them to be in charge. *Everything* is in their minds, their eyes and their bellies. Gonzaga is free from this form of despair, and that's why he absorbs me. Here. See what he says in some of these letters. I found this marvelous collection this morning."

His long hands shaking, he pressed flat the little book on the table of the restaurant. Miss Ungar's quiet face expressed more than intellectual interest. "Listen. He writes to his father: 'Many feel they must say it all, whereas all has been said, unsaid, resaid so many times that we are bound to feel futile unless we understand that we are merely adding our voices. Adding them when moved by the spirit. Then and then only.' Or this: 'A poem may outlive its subject—say, my poem about the girl who sang songs on the train—but the poet has no right to expect this. The poem has no greater privilege than the girl.' You see what kind of man he was?"

"Impressive—really!" she said. "I see that."

"I've come to Spain to find some of his unpublished poems. I have some money, and I've never really been able to find the thing that I wanted to do. I'm not original myself, except in some minor way. Anyhow, that's why I'm here. Lots of people call themselves leaders, healers, priests and spokesmen for God, prophets or witnesses but Gonzaga was a human being who spoke only as a human being; there was nothing spurious about him. He tried never to misrepresent; he wanted to see. To move you he didn't have to do anything, he merely had to be. We've made the most natural things the hardest of all. Unfortunately for us all, he was killed while still young. But he left some poems to a certain Countess del Camino, and I'm here to locate them."

"It's a grand thing. I wish you luck. I hope people will help you."

"Why shouldn't they?"

"I don't know, but don't you expect to run into trouble?"

"Do you think I ought to expect to?"

"If you want my honest opinion, yes."

"I may get the poems . . . why, just like that," he said. "You never can tell."

"Started, by God!" he said when he received an answer from Gúzman del Nido. The member of the Córtes invited him to dinner. All that day he was in a state, and the weather was peculiarly thick, first glaring sunshine, then explosive rains. "See what I told you," said Miss Walsh. But when Clarence went out late in the afternoon, the sky was clear and pale again and the Palm Sunday leaves braided in the ironwork of balconies were withering in the sunlight. He walked to the Puerta del Sol with its crowd of pleasure-seekers, beggars, curb-haunters, wealthy women, soldiers, cops, lottery-ticket and fountain-pen peddlers and priests, humble door-openers, chair-menders and musicians. At seven-thirty he boarded a street-car, following directions; it seemed to take him to every other point of the city first. Finally, with the wisp of trolley paper still in his hand, he got off and mounted a bare stony alley at the top of which was the del Nido villa. Suddenly there was another cloudburst—*una tormenta* was what the Madrilenos called it. No doorway offered cover and he was drenched. At the gate he had to wait a long while for the porter to answer his ring, perhaps five minutes in the hurtling rain. This would probably give comfort to the Englishwoman with her Atomic theories. His nervous long eyes seemed to catch some of the slaty blue of the pouring rain-cloud; his blond beard darkened, and he pulled in his shoulders. The tall gate opened. The porter held out an umbrella in his brown fist. Clarence walked past him to the door of the house. The rain stopped when he was halfway up the path.

So he was at a disadvantage when Gúzman del Nido came forward to meet him. He walked clumsily in his sodden wool suit. It had a shameful smell, like wet dog.

"How do you do, Señor Feiler. What a shame about the rain. It has ruined your suit but it gives your face a fine color."

They shook hands, and it came over Clarence with a thrill as he looked at the high-bridged nose and dark, fine-textured skin of del Nido that he was in touch with Gonzaga himself—this round-shouldered man in his linen suit, bowing his sloping head, smiling with sharp teeth, with his hairless hand and big-boned wrist and his awkward fanny, he had been Gonzaga's friend and belonged within the legend. Clarence at once sensed that he would make him look foolish if he could, through the irony of his very complete manners. He also realized that del Nido was the sort of person who cut everyone down to size, Gonzaga included; precisely the sort to whom Gonzaga had written: *"Go away! You have no holy ones."*

"The letter I sent you. . ." Clarence managed to begin. They were hurrying toward the dining room; other guests were waiting.

"We can discuss it later."

"I understand you gave certain poems to the Countess del Camino," he said.

But del Nido was speaking with another guest. The candles were lit and the company sat down.

Clarence had no appetite.

He was sitting between an Italian Monsignore and an Egyptian lady who had lived in New York and spoke a very slangy English. There was a German Gentleman, too, who headed some insurance company; he sat between Señora del Nido and her daughter. From his end of the table, del Nido with his narrow sleek head and forward-curved teeth and valuable crowns, dominated the conversation. About his eyes the skin was twisted in curious laugh-wrinkles. Impressed, appalled, too, Clarence asked himself again and again how Gonzaga could have trusted such a person. A maker of witticisms, as Pascal had said, a bad character. When these words of Pascal came into his head, Clarence turned to the Monsignore as to a man to whom this might make sense. But the Monsignore was interested mostly in stamp collecting. Clarence was not, so the Monsignore had nothing further to say to him. He was a gloomy, fleshy man whose hair grew strongly and low over the single deep wrinkle of his forehead.

Gúzman del Nido kept on talking. He talked about modern painting, about mystery stories, about old Russia, about the movies, about Nietzsche. Dreamy-looking, the daughter didn't seem to listen; his wife expanded some of his remarks. The daughter stared with close-set eyes into the candle flames. The Egyptian lady was amused by the strong smell of Clarence's rain-shrinking clothes. She made a remark about wet wool. He was grateful for the absence of electric lights.

"An American was arrested in Córdoba," said Gúzman del Nido. "He stole the hat of a *Guardia Civil* for a souvenir."

"Isn't that unusual!"

"He'll find the jail smaller than the jails at home. I hope you won't mind if I tell a story about Americans and the size of things in Spain."

"Why should I mind?" said Clarence.

"Splendid. Well, there was an American whose Spanish host could not impress him. Everything was larger in America. The skyscrapers were bigger than the palaces. The cars were bigger. The cats were bigger. At last his host placed a lobster between his sheets and when the horrified American saw it his host said, 'This is one of our bedbugs. I don't think you can beat that.'"

For some reason this fetched Clarence more than it did the others. He uttered a bark of laughter that made the candle-lights bend and flutter.

"Perhaps you'll tell us an American story," said del Nido.

Clarence thought. "Well, here's one," he said. "Two dogs meet in the street. Old friends. One says 'Hello.' The other answers, 'Cock-a-doodle-do!' 'What does that mean? What's that cock-a-doodle-do stuff?' 'Oh,' says he, 'I've been studying foreign languages.'"

Dead silence. No one laughed. The Egyptian lady said, "I'm afraid you laid an egg." Clarence was angry.

"Is this story told in English or in American?" del Nido asked.

That started a discussion. Was American really a sort of English? Was it a language? No one seemed sure, and Clarence at last said, "I don't know whether or not it is a language, but there is *something* spoken. I've seen people cry in it and so forth, just as elsewhere."

"We deserved that," said del Nido. "It's true, we're not fair to Americans. In reality the only true Europeans left are Americans."

"How so?"

"The Europeans themselves do not have the peace of mind to appreciate what's best. Life is too hard for us, society too unstable."

Clarence realized that he was being shafted; del Nido was satirizing his quest; he undoubtedly meant that Clarence could not comprehend Gonzaga's poems. An ugly hatred for del Nido grew knotted in his breast. He wanted to hit him, to strangle him, to trample him, to pick him up and hurl him at the wall. Luckily del Nido was called to the phone, and Clarence stared out his rage at the empty place, the napkin, the silver, the crest of the chair. Only Señorita del Nido seemed aware that he was offended.

Once more Clarence told himself that there was a wrong way to go about obtaining the poems, contrary to their spirit. That did much to calm him. He managed to get down a few spoonfuls of ice cream and mastered himself.

"Why are you so interested in Gonzaga?" said del Nido to him later in the garden, under the date palms with their sash-like leaves.

"I studied Spanish literature in college and became a Gonzagian."

"Wasn't that rather strange, though? You must forgive me, but I see my poor old friend Gonzaga, who was Spanish of the Spanish, in that terrible uniform we used to wear, and our hands and faces bruised and baked and chapped by the desert sun, and I ask myself why he should have had an effect. . ."

"I don't know why. I'd like to understand it myself; but the fact that he did is what you start with."

"I have made some interesting observations about poets and their lives. Some are better in real life than in their work. You read bitter poems and then you find the poet is personally very happy and good-tempered. Some are worse in their personality than you would guess from their work. They are luckier, in a way, because they have a chance to correct their faults and improve themselves. Best of all are the ones who are exactly the same inside and out, in the spoken word and the written. To be what you seem to be is the objective of true culture. Gonzaga was of the second type."

"Was he?" It occurred to Clarence that del Nido was trying to make himself more interesting to him than Gonzaga could be, to push Gonzaga out.

"I think I can tell you one reason why Gonzaga appeals to me," said Clarence. "He got away from solving *his own* problem. I often feel this way about it: A poem is great because it is absolutely necessary. Before it came silence. After it comes more silence. It begins when it must and ends when it must, and therefore it's not personal. It's 'the sound truly not my own'." Now he was proving to del Nido that he *could* comprehend; at the same time he knew that he was throwing away his effort. Gúzman del Nido was fundamentally indifferent. Indifferent, indifferent, indifferent! He fundamentally did not care. What can you do with people who don't fundamentally care! "But you know why I came to you. I want to know what became of Gonzaga's last poems. What were they like?"

"They were superb love poems. But I don't know where they

are now. They were dedicated to the Countess del Camino and I was supposed to hand them to her. Which I did."

"There aren't any copies?" said Clarence, trembling as del Nido spoke of the poems.

"No. They were for the Countess."

"Of course. But they were also for everyone else."

"There's plenty of poetry already, for everyone. Homer, Dante, Calderón, Shakespeare. Have you noticed how much difference it makes?"

"It should make a difference. Besides, Calderón wasn't your friend. But Gonzaga was. Where's the Countess now? The poor woman is dead, isn't she? And what happened to those poems? Where do you think the poems can be?"

"I don't know. She had a secretary named Polvo, a fine old man. A few years ago he died, too. The old man's nephews live in Alcalá de Henares. Where Cervantes was born, you know. They're in the Civil Service, and they're very decent people, I hear."

"You never even asked them what happened to your friend's poems?" cried Clarence, astonished. "Didn't you want to find them?"

"I thought eventually I'd try to trace them. I'm sure the Countess would have taken good care of her poems."

This was where the discussion stopped, and Clarence was just as glad that it couldn't continue; he sensed that Gúzman would have liked to give him the dirt on Gonzaga—revelations involving women, drunkenness and dope-taking, bribery, sickness or even murder. Gonzaga had escaped into the army; that was notorious. But Clarence didn't want to hear del Nido's reminiscences.

It's natural to suppose, that because a man is great, that the people around him must have known how to respond to his greatness, but when those people turn out to be no better than Gúzman del Nido you wonder what response greatness really needs.

This was what Clarence was saying to Miss Ungar several days later.

"He's glad he doesn't have the poems," said Miss Ungar. "If he had them he'd feel obliged to do something about them, and he's afraid of that because of his official position."

"That's right. Exactly," said Clarence. "But he did me one favor anyway. He put me on to the Countess's secretary's nephews. I've written to them and they've invited me to Alcalá de Henares. They didn't mention the poems but maybe they were just being discreet. I'd better start being more discreet myself. There's something unpleasant going on lately."

"What is it?"

"I think the police have an eye on me."

"Oh come!"

"I do. I'm serious. My room was searched yesterday. I know it was. My landlady didn't answer one way or another when I asked her. She didn't even bother."

"It's too peculiar for anything," Miss Ungar said, laughing in amazement. "But why should they search. . . ? What for?"

"I suppose I just inspire suspicion. And then I made a mistake with my landlady the day after my visit to del Nido. She's a very patriotic character. She has a retired general in the pension, too. Well, she was talking to me the other morning and among other things she told me how healthy she was, strong as a rock—*una roca* —a sort of Gibraltar. And like a dumbbell I said, without even thinking, '*Gibraltar Español!*' That was an awful boner."

"Why?"

"During the war, you see, when the British were taking such a pounding there was a great agitation for the return of Gibraltar to Spain. The slogan was Gibraltar Español! Of course they don't like to be reminded that they were dying for the British to get it good and hot from Germany. Well, she probably thinks I'm a political secret somebody. And she was just plain offended."

"But what difference does it make, as long as you don't do anything illegal?"

"When you're watched closely you're bound to do *something*," he said.

He went out to Alcalá on a Sunday afternoon and met the two nephews of Don Francisco Polvo and their wives and daughters.

They proved to be a family of laughers. They laughed when they spoke and when you answered. You saw nothing in the town but sleepy walls, and parched trees and stones. The brothers were squat, sandy, broad-bellied men.

"We're having tea in the garden," said Don Luis Polvo. He was called "the Englishman" by the others because he had lived in London for several months twenty years ago; they addressed him as "My Lord" and he obliged them by acting like an *Inglés*. He even owned a Scotch terrier named *Duglas*. The family cried to him, "Now's your chance to speak English, Luis. Speak English to him!"

"Jolly country, eh?" Luis said. That was about all he could manage.

"Very."

"More, more!"

"Charing Cross."

"Go on, Luis, say more."

"Piccadilly. And that's all I can remember."

The tea was served. Clarence drank and sweltered. Lizards raced in the knotty grapevines and by the well. . . . The wives were embroidering. The daughters were conversing in French, obviously about Clarence, and were laughing. Nobody appeared to believe what he said. Lanky and pained he sat in what looked to be a suit made of burlap, with his tea. Instead of a saucer, he felt as though he were holding on to the rim of Saturn.

After tea they showed him through the house. It was huge, old, bare, thick-walled and chill, and it was filled with the portraits and the clothing of ancestors—weapons, breastplates, helmets, daggers, guns. In one room where the picture of a general in the Napoleonic Wars was hung, a fun-making mood seized the brothers. They tried on plumed hats, then sabers, and finally full uniforms. Wearing spurs, medals, musty gloves, they went running back to the terrace where the women sat. Don Luis dragged a sword, his seat hung down and the cocked hat sagged broken, opening in the middle on his sandy baldness. With a Napoleonic musket, full of self-mockery, he performed the manual-at-arms to uproarious laughter. Clarence laughed, too, his cheeks creased; he couldn't explain however why his heart was growing heavier by the minute.

Don Luis aimed the musket and shouted, *"La bomba atómica! Poum!"*

The hit he scored with this was enormous. The women shrieked, swiveling their fans, and his brother fell on his behind in the sanded path, weeping with laughter. The terrier *Duglas* leaped into Don Luis's face, fiercely excited.

Don Luis threw a stick and cried, "Fetch, fetch, *Duglas! La bomba* atómica! La bomba atómica!"

The blood stormed Clarence's head so furiously he heard the uproar of it. This was another assault on him. Oh! he thought frantically, the things he had to bear! The punishment he had to take trying to salvage those poems!

As if in the distance, the voice of Don Luis cried, "*Hiroshima! Nagasaki! Bikini! Good show!*" He flung the stick and the dog bounded on taut legs, little *Duglas,* from the diminished figure of his master and back—the tiny white and brown animal, while laughter incessantly pierced the dry air of the garden.

It was not a decent joke, even though Don Luis in that split hat and the withered coat was mocking the dead military grandeur of his own country. That didn't even the score. The hideous stun of the bomb and its unbearable, death-brilliant mushroom cloud filled Clarence's brain. This was not right.

He managed to stop Don Luis. He approached him, laid a hand on the musket and asked to speak with him privately. It made the others laugh. The ladies started to murmur about him. An older woman said, "*Es gracioso*"; the girls seemed to disagree. He heard one of them answer, "*Non, il n'est pas gentil.*" Proudly polite, Clarence faced it out. "Damn their damn tea!" he said to himself. His sweaty shirt was oppressive to his back.

"We did not inherit my uncle's papers," said Don Luis. "—Enough, *Duglas!*" He threw the stick down the well. "My brother and I inherited his old house and other land but if there were papers they probably went to my cousin Pedro Alvarez-Polvo who lives in Segovia. He's a very interesting fellow. He works for the *Banco Español* but is a cultivated person. The countess had no family. She was fond of my uncle. My uncle was extremely fond of Alvarez-Polvo. They shared the same interests."

"Did your uncle ever speak of Gonzaga?"

"I don't recall. The countess had a large number of artistic admirers. This Gonzaga interests you very much, doesn't he?"

"Yes. Why shouldn't I be interested in him? You may some day be interested in an American poet."

"I? No!" Don Luis laughed, but he was startled.

What people! Damn these dirty laughers! Clarence waited until Don Luis's shocked and latterly somewhat guilty laughter ended, and his broad yap and spacious teeth, set wide like a hippo's, closed—shook with resistance to closing, and finally remained closed.

"Do you think your cousin Alvarez-Polvo would know. . ."

"He would know a lot," said Don Luis, composed. "My uncle confided in him. *He* can tell you something definite, you can count on him. I'll give you a letter of introduction to him."

"If it's not too much trouble."

"No, no, the pleasure is mine." Don Luis was all courtesy.

Returning to Madrid on the bus through the baking plain of Castile, Clarence phoned Miss Ungar. He wanted her sympathy and comforting. But she didn't invite him to come over. She said, "I can give you the *pesetas* tomorrow." That was her tactful way of informing him that the pilot had landed, and he thought she sounded regretful. Perhaps she was not really in love with her fiancé. Clarence now had the impression that the black-marketing was not her idea but the pilot's. It embarrassed her, but she was too loyal to admit it.

"I'll come by later in the week. There's no hurry," he said. "I'm busy anyway."

It would hurt him to do it, but he'd cash a check at the American Express tomorrow.

Disappointed, Clarence hung up. *He* should have a woman like that. It passed dimly over his mind that a live woman would make a better quest than a dead poet. But the poet was *there*; the woman not. He sent a letter to Alvarez-Polvo, washed all over, and lay reading Gonzaga by a buzzing light in the canopied bed.

He arrived in Segovia early one Sunday morning. It was filled with sunlight, the clouds were silk-white in the mountain air. Their shadows wandered over the slopes of the bare Sierra like creatures that crept and warmed themselves on the soil and rock. All over the old valley were convents, hermitages, churches, towers, the graves of San Juan and other mystical saints. At the highest point of Segovia was the Alcázar of Isabella the Catholic. And passing over the town with its many knobby granite curves that divided the sky was the aqueduct, this noble Roman remnant, as bushy as old men's ears. Clarence stood at the window of his hotel and looked at this conjured rise of stones that bridged the streets. It got him, all of it—the ancient mountain slopes worn as if by the struggles of Jacobs with angels, the spires, the dry glistening of the atmosphere, the hermit places in green hideaways, the sheep bells' clunk, the cistern water dropping, while beams came as straight as harpwires from the sun. All of this, like a mild weight, seemed to press on him; it opened him up. He felt his breath creep within him like a tiny pet animal kept for tenderness.

He went down through the courtyard. There the cistern of fat stone held green water, full of bottom-radiations from the golden brass of the faucets. Framed above it in an archway were ladies' hair styles of twenty years ago—a brilliantine advertisement. Ten or so beautiful señoritas with bangs, shingles and windswept bobs smiled like various confrontations of love. Therefore Clarence had the idea that this cistern was the Fountain of Youth. And also that it was something Arcadian. He said, *"Ye glorious nymphs!"* and burst out laughing. He felt happy—magnificent! The sun poured hotly over his head and embraced his back.

Smiling, he rambled up and down the streets. He went to the Alcázar. Soldiers in German helmets were on guard. He went to the cathedral. It was ancient but the stones looked brand-new. After lunch he sat at the café in front of the aqueduct waiting for Alvarez-Polvo. On the wide sloping sidewalk there were hundreds of folding chairs, empty, the paint blazed off them and the wood emerging as gray as silver-fish. The long low windows were open, so that inside and outside mingled their air, the yellow and the sombre, the bar brown and the clear blue. A gypsy woman came out and gave Clarence the eye. She was an entertainer, but whether a real gypsy or not was conjectural. In the phrase he had heard, some of these girls were *Gitanas de miedo,* or strictly from hunger. But he sat and studied the aqueduct, trying to imagine what sort of machinery they could have used to raise the stones.

A black hearse with mourners who trod after it slow, and with all the plumes, and carvings of angels and death-grimacers, went through the main arch to the cemetery. After ten minutes it came galloping back with furious lashing of the horses, the silk-hatted coachman standing, yacking at them. Only a little later the same hearse returned with another procession of mourners who supported one another, grief pushing on their backs, weeping aloud. Through the arch again. And once more the hearse came flying back. With a sudden tightness of the guts Clarence thought, Why all these burials at once? Was this a plague: He looked at the frothy edge of his glass with horror.

But Alvarez-Polvo set his mind at rest. He said, "The hearse was broken all week. It has just been repaired."

He was a strange looking man. His face seemed to have been worked by three or four diseases and then abandoned. His nose swelled out and shrunk his eyes. He had a huge mouth, like his cousin Don Luis. He had on a beret, and a yellow silk sash was wound around his belly. Clarence often had noticed that short men with big bellies often held their arms ready for defense as they walked, but at heart expected defeat. Alvarez-Polvo too, had that posture. However, his brown, mottled, creased, sunlit face with kinky gray hair escaping from the beret seemed to declare that he had a soul like a drum. If you struck, you wouldn't injure him. You'd hear a sound.

"You know what I've come for?" said Clarence.

"Yes, I do know. But let's not start talking business right away. You've never been in Segovia before, I assume, and you must let me be hospitable. I'm a proud Segoviano—proud of this ancient, beautiful city, and it would give me pleasure to show you the principal places."

At the words "talking business" Clarence's heart rose a notch. Was it only a matter of settling the price? Then he had the poems! Something in Clarence flapped with eager joy, like a flag in the wind.

"By all means. For a while. It is beautiful. Never in my life have I seen anything so gorgeous as Segovia."

Alvarez-Polvo took his arm.

"With me you will not only see, you will also understand. I have made a study of it. I'm a lover of such things. I seldom have an opportunity to express it. Whenever I take my wife, she is interested only in *novelas morbosas*. At Versailles, she sat and read Ellery Queen. In Paris, the same. In Rome, the same. If she lives to the end of time, she will never run out of *novelas morbosas.*"

From this remark, without notice, he took a deep plunge into the subject of women, and he carried Clarence with him. Women, women, women! All the types of Spanish beauty. The Granadinas, the Malaguenas, the Castellanas, the Catalunas. And then the Germans, the Greeks, the French, the Swedes! He tightened his hold on Clarence and pulled him close as he boasted and complained and catalogued and confessed. He was ruined! They had taken his money, his health, his time, his years, his life, women had—innocent, mindless, beautiful, ravaging, insidious malevolent, chestnut, blond, red, black . . . Clarence felt hemmed in by women's faces, and by women's bodies.

"I suppose you'd call this a Romanesque church, wouldn't you?" Clarence said, stopping.

"Of course it is," said Alvarez-Polvo. "Just notice how the Renaissance building next to it was designed to harmonize with it."

Clarence was looking at the pillars and their blunted faces of humorous, devil-beast humanities, the stone birds, demon lollers, apostles. Two men rolled a spring and mattress by in a pushcart. They looked like the kings of Shinar and Elam after Abraham had beaten some sense into them with his sword.

"Come, have a glass of wine," said Alvarez-Polvo. "I'm not allowed to drink since my operation, but you must have something."

When could they begin to talk about the poems? Clarence was impatient. Gonzaga's poems would mean little if anything to a man like this, but in spite of his endless gallant bunk and his swagger and laments about having broken his springs in the service of love and beauty, he was probably a very cunning old fuff. He wanted to stall Clarence and find out what the poems were worth to him. And so Clarence gazed, or blinked, straight ahead, and kept a tight grip on his feelings.

In the *bodega* were huge barrels, copper fittings, innumerable bottles duplicated in the purple mirror, platters of *mariscos,* crawfish bugging their eyes on stalks, their feelers cooked into various last shapes. From the middle of the floor rose a narrow spiral staircase. It mounted—who—knew—where? Clarence tried to see but couldn't. A little torn-frocked beggar child came selling lot-

tery tickets. The old chaser petted her; she wheedled; she took
his small hand and laid her cheek to it. Still talking, he felt her
hair. He stroked his fill and sent her away with a coin.

Clarence drank down the sweet, yellow Malaga.

"Now," said Alvarez-Polvo, "I will show you a church few
visitors ever see."

They descended to the lower part of town, down littered stair-
ways of stone, by cavelike homes and a lot where runty boys were
passing a football with their heads, and dribbling and hooking it
with their boots.

"Here," Alvarez-Polvo said. "This wall is of the tenth century
and this one of the seventeenth."

The air inside was dark, cool, thick as ointment. Concavities of
dark red and dark blue and heavy yellow slowly formed, and
Clarence began to see shapes—the altar, the columns.

Alvarez-Polvo was silent. The two men were standing before a
harsh-crowned crucifixion, a figure deeply gored in the side, rust-
blooded. The awful head-cover of thorns was too wide and heavy
to be borne. As he confronted it, Clarence felt that it threatened
to scratch the life out of him, to scratch to the heart.

"The matter that interests us both. . ." Alvarez-Polvo then said.

"Yes, yes, let's go somewhere and have a talk about it. You got
the poems among your uncle's papers. Do you have them here in
Segovia?"

"Poems?" said Alvarez-Polvo turning the dark mass of his face
from the aisle. "That's a strange word to use for them."

"Do you mean they're not in that form? What are they, then?
What are they written in?"

"Why, the usual legal language. According to law."

"I don't understand."

"Neither do I. But I can show you what I'm talking about.
Here. I have one with me. I brought it along." He drew a document from his pocket.

Clarence held it, trembling. It was heavy, glossy and heavy. He
felt an embossed surface. Yes, there was a seal on it. What had
the Countess done with the poems? This paper was emblazoned
with a gilt star. He sought light and read, within an elaborate
border of wavy green, *Compania de Minas, S.A.*

"Is this. . . ? It can't be. You've given me the wrong thing. My heart's racing. Look in your pocket again."

"The wrong thing?"

"It looks like a share of stock."

"Then it isn't the wrong thing. It's what it's supposed to be, mining stock. Isn't that what you're interested in?"

"Of course not! Certainly not! What kind of mine?"

"It's a pitchblende mine in Morocco, that's what it is."

"What in the name of anything do I want with pitchblende!" Clarence shouted.

"What any sensible man would want. To sell it. Pitchblende has uranium in it. Uranium is used in atom bombs."

Again! Oh, dear God!

"Claro. Para la bomba atómica."

"What have I to do with atom bombs. What do I care about atom bombs! To hell with atom bombs!" Clarence cried out, furious.

"I understood you were a financier."

"Me? Do I look like one?"

"Yes, of course you do. More English than American, I thought. But a financier. Aren't you?"

"I am not. I came about the poems of Gonzaga, the poems owned by the Countess del Camino. Love poems dedicated to her by the poet Manuel Gonzaga."

"Manuel? The soldier? The little fellow? The one that was her lover in 1928? The one who was killed in Morocco?"

"Yes, yes! What did your uncle do with the poems?"

"Oh, that's what you were talking about. Why, my uncle did nothing with them. The Countess did, herself. She had them buried with her. She took them to the grave."

"Buried! With her, you say! And no copies?"

"I doubt it. My uncle had instructions from her, and he was very loyal. He lived by loyalty. My uncle. . ."

"Oh, damn! Oh, damn it! And didn't he leave you anything in that collection of papers that has to do with Gonzaga? No journals, no letters that mention Gonzaga? Nothing?"

"He left me these shares in the mine. They're valuable. Not yet, but they will be if I can get capital. But you can't raise money in Spain. Spanish capital is cowardly, ignorant of science. It is still back in the Counter-Reformation. Let me show you the location of this mine." He opened a map and began to explain the geography of the Atlas Mountains.

Clarence walked out on him—ran, rather than walked. He had to get out of Segovia. Quickly. Immediately. Panting, enraged, choking, he clambered from the lower town.

As soon as he entered his room at the hotel, he knew that his valise had been searched. Storming, he slammed it shut and dragged it down the stairs, past the cistern, and into the lobby.

He called in a shout to the manager, "Why must the police come and turn my things upside down?"

White-faced and stern, the manager said, "You must be mistaken, señor."

"I am not mistaken. Why must the police bother foreign visitors?"

A man rose angrily from a chair in the lobby. He wore an old suit with a mourning band on the arm.

"These Englishmen!" he said with fury. "They don't know what hospitality is. They come here and enjoy themselves, and criticize our country, and complain. What hypocrisy! There are more police in England. The whole world knows you have a huge jail in Liverpool, filled with Masons. Five thousand Masons are *encarcelados* in Liverpool alone."

Clarence couldn't reply. He stared. Then he paid his bill and left. All the way to Madrid he sat numb and motionless in his second-class seat.

As the train left the mountains, the heavens seemed to split; the rain began to fall, heavy and sudden, boiling on the wide plain.

He knew what to expect from that red-headed Miss Walsh at dinner.

HORTENSE CALISHER was born in New York City and graduated from Barnard College. Her stories have appeared in such magazines as The New Yorker, Harper's Bazaar, Mademoiselle, *and* Harper's. *Her story, "A Christmas Carillon," appeared in the 1955 edition of the O. Henry Prize Stories. She has published a collection of stories with Little, Brown entitled* In the Absence of Angels *(1951), and the first portion of a novel (abridged) appeared in* Harper's Bazaar *in May, 1955. Miss Calisher received two Guggenheim Fellowships in 1952–1953, and 1955–1956. She is married, the mother of two children, and a resident of Nyack, New York.*

THE NIGHT CLUB IN THE WOODS

From DISCOVERY NO. 5

We first saw her, Mrs. Hawthorn, sitting alone, the first one down in the tender that waited to take us off the Bermuda boat. She was wearing a quilted taffeta suit, expensively flared at shoulder and hip, and a matching hat—one of those deep, real hats we were all wearing in the fall of 1935—and her arms were full, crammed full of tea roses. Under a city marquee, she would have had an enviable chic, but on the white deck of the tender, in the buttery Bermuda sun, she looked outlandishly urban for that travel-folder scene. As the rest of us climbed down into the tender, she made room for us, with an apologetic shifting of the roses, but one could see, as she nestled her long, rouge-assisted face into the buds, that she was pleased with them.

Later on, in the week that followed, we saw her at our hotel, and Luke and I, drifting in the ambience of our honeymooner's table, idly watched her dinner entrances. Each evening, appearing late but consciously unflurried, in a different gown—one always too dominantly colorful and sparkling for the off-season crowd— she crossed to the table reserved for her and her companion, a dark, pear-shaped man, shorter than she, who received her with an anxious, hesitant courtesy.

On the first evening, Luke, nudging me, had pointed to the single bird-of-paradise bud with which the hotel kept the tables adorned, each beaked bloom soaring from its coarse glass holder like an immoderately hued bird, and every evening thereafter, the analogy had kept us amused. One evening, however, as she passed us, her tall, haggard figure sheathed in green sequins that boom-eranged the light, a child at a nearby table cried out: "Look, Mommy! Christmas tree!" As she stopped, and bent toward the child, the sequins poorly concealing the middle-aged line from breast to hip, we heard her say, in a mellow voice, as if she were indulgently amused at both the child and herself—"Yes, darling! Christmas tree!"—and we felt ashamed, and liked her.

We met the two of them again, as we were all herded docilely into one of the glass-bottomed sight-seeing boats, and she told us her name. The little man, tentative and deferential in the back-ground, was one of those hovering people whose names one never catches, and we never did, although she told us it too. Again we saw her, alone on the beach in front of the hotel, in a maillot that was still somewhat scandalous for that time. We were a little embarrassed for her, not at the suit, but at its cruel, sagging revela-tion, and I remember that both of us, looking away with instinctive distaste of the young for the fading, glanced down with satisfac-tion at our own bodies. One of her arms was almost covered from wrist to elbow with diamond and sapphire bracelets, and she must have seen me staring at them, or trying not to. She laughed, on the same mellow note.

"I'd feel naked without them." She turned, and slid into the water. She swam well, better than either of us, her long, water-sallowed face, which once must have been very handsome, sinking deep into the fervid blue of the water, the one mailed arm flash-ing in the sun.

In those days, the thing to do was to go down on the Monarch and come back on the Queen. The little stenographers squander-

ing their vacation on off-season rates, an "interchangeable" ward-
robe, and one shattering evening dress, the honeymooners, intent
on seeming otherwise, all said it airily: "We came down on the
Monarch and will go back on the Queen." On the return voyage,
we met Mrs. Hawthorn and her vague companion again. The
ship had run into bad weather, the usual October storms of the
Caribbean, and at dinnertime, the little stenographers had been
unable to appear in their evening dresses after all.

Luke had been affected too, although I was not. After dinner
alone, I wandered into one of the ornate lounges that hollowed
the ship. Seated in one of the gold chairs, her lamé gown blending
so well that at first I did not see her, was Mrs. Hawthorn. She
beckoned to me.

"I see you are a good sailor, too," she said. "I never get sick.
Dave—the friend who is traveling with me—is down in his cabin."
There was the slightest emphasis on 'his'. "Women are the
stronger sex, I always says. You two are newlyweds, aren't you?"

"Yes."

"Look," she said. "Why don't you and your husband come up
to my stateroom and have champagne. It's the best thing in the
world for seasickness—and after all we really should celebrate for
you two. Yes, do! We really must!"

I went down to our cabin, and roused Luke. "You think you're
inveigling me," he said. "But it is really Mrs. Hawthorn who
intrigues me."

We climbed the ladders from D deck to A. Up there, with no
feel of more ship above us, the ocean, silhouetted against the
looming slant of the stacks, seemed to shift its dark obliques more
pervasively near us.

"The water seems more intimate up here with the rich, doesn't
it?" I said.

"Hmmm," said Luke, "but it's not an intimacy I care to develop
at the moment." I giggled, and lurching together, hip to hip, half
with love, half with the movement of the deck, we entered Mrs.
Hawthorn's stateroom.

The room was banked with flowers. Mrs. Hawthorn and her
companion were waiting for us, sitting stiffly in the center of
the blooms like unintroduced visitors in the anteroom of a funeral

chapel. Wedged behind a coffee table blocked with bottles, Mrs. Hawthorn did not rise, but we greeted each other with that air of confederate gaiety adopted by hostess and guest at parties of whose success neither is sure. Across from her, behind an imitation hearth, a gas log burned insolently, as if a fireplace burning in the middle of the sea might serve to keep the elements in their place.

"Life on the hypotenuse," said Luke. He retrieved a bunch of gladioli, and set them back on the erring horizontal of a table.

Mrs. Hawthorn shifted her bracelets. "Dave is the florist in our home town—Hawthornton, Connecticut. I needed a rest, so Dave came down with me. Senator Hawthorn couldn't get away. He's the senator from there, you know."

Luke and I nodded, anxious to let her see that we took her explanation at its face value, unwilling to appear abashed at the malpractices of the rich and worn. I imagined her life—the idle, probably childless woman, burdened with an exuberance no longer matched by her exterior, drawing toward her, with the sequins of wealth and difference, the self-conscious little man, who was doggedly trying to fill the gap between them with the only largesse at his command—his tumultuous abracadabra of flowers. Luke and I exchanged looks across the flowers, secure in our cocoon of beginnings, seeing before us an itinerary that repudiated compromise, and made no concessions to the temporal.

As we drank, the fraudulent solidity of the room was displaced now and again by a deep, visceral sway that drained the chair arms from beneath our digging fingers, and the wine seemed only to accentuate the irrationality of the four of us so transiently, so unsuitably met. At one point, Mrs. Hawthorn told the blond, mild-featured Luke that he had a "sulphurous" look, which roused us all to unsteady laughter, and again I remember her asking, with the gaucherie so denied by her appearance, "if he were a college man."

Then, suddenly, with an incredulous look on his face, Dave, the little man, stood up. Edging backwards, he felt for the door-knob, caught it, and disappeared around it. Ignoring his defection, the three of us sat on; then Luke, with a wild look at me, lurched through the flapping door and was gone.

Mrs. Hawthorn and I sat on for a moment, united in that smug matriarchy which joins women whose men have acted similarly and disgracefully. The heat from the burning log brought out the reek of the flowers, until it seemed to me that I had drunk perfume instead of champagne. Slowly the log up-ended and pointed toward the ceiling, but that too had slid far to the right, so that the room hung in a momentary armistice with the storm, the implacable hearth still glowing in its centre. I stood up, and moved toward the door. It sidled toward me, and I achieved the corridor, but not before I had caught a last glimpse of Mrs. Hawthorn. She was sitting there like one of those children one often sees at dusk in the playground or the corner lot, still concentrated in fierce, solitary energy on the spinning top or the chalked squares of the deserted game, unwilling to admit the default of the others who have wilted, conceded in the afternoon's end, and acquiescently gone home.

By the time Luke and I had made our separate ways to the cabin, the ship had ridden out of the storm area, and was running smoothly. We would dock next morning in New York harbor. We greeted each other, and slid limply into bed. Luke put his arms around me with a protectiveness tinged, I could not help thinking, with a relief that I had not proved so indomitable after all. For a second, I held him at arm's length. "Tell me first," I said. "Are you a college man?" Then we nestled together, in the excluding, sure laughter of the young.

At the docking the next day, we got through the lines early, without seeing anyone we knew. We had exchanged addresses with Mrs. Hawthorn, never really expecting to see her again, and in the busy weeks after, during which we returned to our jobs and our life together, we forgot her completely.

About a month later, sometime in November, we got a note from her, written in a large, wasteful hand on highly colored, expensive notepaper, and followed, when we did not immediately answer, by a phone call, during which her voice came over the wire as gaily insistent as before. "Would we come up for dinner and stay the night?" We accepted without particular considera-tion, partly out of a reawakened interest in her, and what she would be like at home with the Senator, and partly because it was a place to go with the Chevvie—and no sense of the stringency of time had led us as yet to a carping evaluation of the people with whom we spent it.

On the way up that Saturday, a run of about seventy miles, we drove steadily through a long, umber autumn afternoon. At our left the sun dropped slowly, a red disc without penumbra. Along the country roads, the escarpments of pines and firs were black-green, with the somber deadness of a tyro's painting of Italy. Lights popped up in the soiled gray backs of towns, and a presage of winter tingled in our minds, its remembered icicle sliding down our spines. I was twenty-two, free, still catching up with a childhood where hot dogs had been forbidden. I made Luke stop for them twice. After that we drove silently, my head on Luke's shoulder. Inside the chugging little car, the heater warmed us; we were each with the one necessary person; we had made love the night before.

At seven, when we were expected, we were still twenty miles away. Luke stopped to phone. He came back to the car. "She says dinner will wait for us, not to rush. We're to go on to a night club afterwards."

In a second my mind had raked over everything in my suitcase, had placed me at the dinner table—perhaps not quite at the Senator's right—had moved me on to the little round table on the dance floor.

"I just remembered," I said. "I didn't put in my evening shoes."

"I just remembered," said Luke. "I didn't bring a proper tie."

We burst into laughter. "We'll swing round by way of New London," said Luke. "We can get things there."

When we got to the main street of the town, it was crowded, but the clothing stores were closing. Luke rushed into a haberdashery shop and came out with a tie. At the dark end of the shopping district we found a shoe store whose proprietor, counting stock in his dim interior, opened his locked door. I bought a pair of silver, girl-graduate sandals, the first pair he showed me. "Gee, lady," he said, as we whisked out of his shop, "I wish every lady was as quick as you."

Smiling to ourselves, we reentered the car. There was a charm that hung about us then, and we were not insensible of it, even aware that it had more to do with our situation than ourselves. We were still guests in the adult world of "lady" and "gentleman"; lightly we rode anchor in their harbor, partook of its perquisites, and escaped again to our enviable truancy. The rest of the world —we saw it in their faces—would be like us if it could. On the way through Hawthornton, I looked for a florist shop, but we passed too quickly by.

Five miles through the woodland of the Hawthorns' private road brought us to the house. There had been no others along the way. But the house that loomed before us, in a cleared area rather bleak and shrubless after the woods behind us, had no baronial mystery about it. By the lights under its porte-cochere, it looked to be about forty years old—one of those rambling, tasteless houses, half timbered, with thick stone porches, that "comfortably off" people built around the turn of the century, more for summer use, but providently made habitable for all year 'round. As we came to a stop under the porte-cochere, and the coupe's engine died, I heard the rushing sound of water, and saw that we seemed to be on the tip of a promontory that ended several hundred feet beyond.

"We on a lake?"

"Only the Atlantic," said Luke. "Don't you ever know where you are? We've been driving toward it all afternoon."

"Hardly ever," I said. "But we seem to be fated to meet Mrs. H. on one ocean or another."

A capped maid opened the door. Mrs. Hawthorn stood at the foot of the stairs to greet us. It was the first time I had seen her in black, a very low-cut, smart black, enlivened only by the cuff of bracelets on her right arm. It made her seem less of a "character," placing her almost in my mother's generation, although she may not have been quite that, and a little unsettling me. In my world, the different generations did not much visit each other, at least did not seek each other's company as she had ours.

She made a breezy stir of our welcome, giving us each a hand, directing the houseman as to our bags, referring us to separate corners for a wash. "Drinks in the dining room. See you there."

When we entered, she was seated at the long dining table,

alone. Three places were set, not at the head, but down toward the middle, ours opposite hers. There was no evidence that anyone else was to dine, or had.

I remember nothing of the room, except my surprise. As we clicked glasses, were served, I tried to recall her voice as it had come over the wire to New York; certainly her airy chit-chat had given me the impression that we were to be members of a house party. Otherwise, considering the gap between us of situation, money, age—how odd it was of her to have singled us out! Her conversation seemed to be newly flecked with slang, a kind of slang she perhaps thought we used. "That way for the johns," she had said, directing us to the bathrooms, and now, speaking of Bermuda, she asked us if we had not thought it "simply terrif." She had found European travel "rather a frost."

"I get more of a boot out of cutting a dash at home," she said, grinning.

A second manservant and maid were serving us. "I keep the estate staffed the way it's always been," she said. "Even though a good bit of the time it's only just me. Of course we've had to draw in our horns in lots of ways, like everyone else. But I've washed enough dishes in Hawthornton, I always say." She smiled down at her bracelets.

"Have you always lived in Hawthornton?" said Luke.

She nodded. "The Senator's people have always had the mills here. The Hawthorn Knitting Mills. And my father was the town parson—also the town drunk. But I married the millowner's son." She chuckled, and we had to laugh with her, at the picture she drew for us. It was the same with all her allusions to her possessions—allusions which were frequent and childlike. As they ballooned into boasting, she pricked them, careful to show that she claimed no kind of eminence because of them. What she did claim was the puzzling thing, for I felt that "the estate" meant something to her beyond the ordinary, and that her choice of our company was somehow connected with that meaning. Certainly she was shrewd enough to see that our scale of living was not hers, although for a while I dallied with the idea that a real social ignorance—that of the daughter of the down-at-the-heel parson, suddenly transmuted into the millowner's wife—had kept her insensitive to all the economic gradations between, had made her assume that because we were "college people," had been on the Bermuda boat, and had an anonymous East Side address, our jobs and our battered Chevvie were only our way of drawing in our horns. But she did not seem to be really interested in who we were, or what our parents had been. Something about what we had, or were now, had drawn her to us; in her queer little overtures of slang she seemed to be wistfully ranging herself on our side. But I did not know what she imagined "our side" to be.

We took our coffee in what she referred to as "the big room" —at first it was hard to categorize as anything else. Large as a hotel lounge, it had something of the same imperviousness to personality. Sofas and club chairs, stodgy but solid, filled its middle spaces; there was a grand piano at either end, and all along the edges, beneath the irregularly nooked windows, there were many worn wicker and chintz settees. But, looking further, I saw the dark bookshelves filled with Elbert Hubbard editions, the burnt-leather cushions, of the kind that last a lifetime, scattering the wicker, the ponderous floor lamps, whose parchment umbrella shades were bound with fringe—and I began to recognize the room for what it was. This was a room from which the stag's heads, the Tiffany glass had been cleared, perhaps, but it was still that room which lurked in albums and memoirs, behind pictures labelled "The Family at ——. Summer of 1910. Bottom row my son Ned, later to fall in the Ardennes, daughters Julie and Christine, and their school friend, Mary X, now wife of my son George."

"I never did much to this room except put in the pianos," said Mrs. Hawthorn. "It's practically the same as when we got married, the year Harry's mother died, and he came back from France. We had some helluva parties here, though. Wonderful!" And now, as I followed her glance, I fancied that I detected in the room a faint, raffish overglaze of the early twenties, when I was too young to go to parties—here and there a hassock, still loudly black-and-white, a few of those ballerina book ends everyone used to have, and yes, there, hung in a corner, a couple of old batiks. Dozens of people could have sprawled here, the young men with their bell-bottomed trousers, the girls with their Tutankhamen eardrops, pointed pumps, and orange-ice-colored knees. The weathered wicker would have absorbed the spilled drinks without comment, and cigarette burns would have been hilariously added to the burnt-leather cushions. Yes, it could have been a hell of a room for a party.

Mrs. Hawthorn led us to the windows and pointed out into the dark, staring through it with the sure, commanding eye of the householder. "You can't see, of course, but we're on three bodies of water here—the river, the Sound, and the ocean. There's the end of the dock—the coast guard still ties up there once in a while, although we don't keep it up anymore. When I was a kid, it used to be fitted out like a summer hotel. I used to swim around the point and watch them." Then, I thought, she would not have been one of the three little girls in the bottom row of the picture —she would never have been in that picture at all.

She closed the curtain. "Let me show you your room, then we'll be off." She led us upstairs, into a comfortable, nondescript bedroom. "That's my door, across the hall. Knock when you're ready."

"Oh, it won't take us a minute to change," I said.

"Change? Dear, you don't have to change."

"Oh, but we've brought our evening things," I said. "It'll only take us a minute." There was a slight wail to my voice.

"Really it won't," said Luke. "We're awfully sorry if we've delayed you, but we'll rush."

We continued our protests for a minute, standing there in the hall. She leaned down and patted my shoulder, looking at me with that musing smile older women wore when they leaned over baby carriages. I had encountered that look often that year, among my mother's friends. "No, run along, and never mind," she said. "Nobody else is going to be there."

In front of the mirror in our room, I ran a comb through my curls. "Nobody who *is* anybody, I suppose she meant. I can't imagine why else she picked on us. And when I think of those awful shoes!"

"You can wear them at home," said Luke. "I like women to be flashy around the house. Come on, you look wonderful."

"I'm going to change to them anyway. They'll dance better."

"You'll only have to dance half the dances."

"Luke—." I slid my feet into the shoes and twisted to check my stocking seams. "Do you suppose that little man, Dave, will be there? Do you suppose we're being used as a sort of *cover?*"

He laughed. "I don't know. Come on."

"Don't you think it's funny she doesn't say where the senator is? At least make his excuses or something?"

"Away on business, probably."

"Well, why isn't she in Washington with him, then? I would be,—if it were you."

"Thank *you*," he said. "But how come you got through college? There's no Connecticut senator to Washington named Hawthorn."

"Luke! I knew there was something fishy! Maybe there isn't any senator. Or maybe he's divorced her, and nobody around here will know her. Or maybe she's a little off, from his being dead, and wants to go on pretending he's alive. With people like us— who wouldn't know."

He put back his head in laughter. "Now I know how you did get through college." He kissed the back of my neck, and pushed me through the door. "State senator, dope," he whispered, as we knocked at Mrs. Hawthorn's.

"Ready?" She opened the door and held it back in such a way that we knew we were to look in. "This is the only room I changed," she said. "I had it done again last year, the same way. I thought the man from Sloane would drop in his tracks when I insisted on the same thing. All that pink. Ninety yards of it in the curtains alone." She laughed, as she had done at the child in Bermuda. "Of course I had no idea back then . . . I thought it was lovely, so help me. And now I'm used to it."

We looked around. All that pink, as she had said. The room, from its shape, must be directly above the big room below; its great windows jutted out like a huge pink prow, overlooking the three bodies of water. Chairs with the sickly sheen of hard candy pursed their Louis Quatorze legs on a rose madder rug, under lamps the tinge of old powder puffs. There were a few glossy prints on the walls—nymphs couched like bonbons in ambiguous verdure. Marble putti held back the curtains, and each morning, between ninety yards of rosy lingerie, there would rise the craggy, seamed face of the sea.

Mrs. Hawthorn put her hand on one of the cherubs, and looked out. "We sailed from there on our honeymoon," she said. "On the old Hawthorns' yacht, right from the end of the dock. I remember thinking it would give, there were so many people on the end of it." She took a fur from a chair, slung it around her shoulders, and walked to the door. At the door, she turned back and surveyed the room. "Ain't it orful!" she said, in her normal voice. "Harry can't bear it."

She had two voices, I thought, as we followed her downstairs and got in the car she referred to as her runabout, that she'd made Harry give her in place of the chauffeur-driven Rolls. One voice for that tranced tale of first possession—when the house, the dock, the boudoir, Harry were new. And one for now—slangy, agnostic, amused.

She drove well, the way she swam, with a crisp, physical intensity. There had been bridle paths through these woods, she told us, but she hadn't really minded giving up the horses; swimming was the only thing she liked to do alone. She swam every day; it kept her weight down to the same as when she married. "You'll be having to pick yourself some exercise now too, honey," she said, sighing. "And stick to it the rest of your days."

We would turn on to the main road soon, I thought, probably to one of those roadhouses full of Saturday night daters such as Luke and I had been the year before, spinning out the evening on the cover charge and a couple of setups, and looking down our noses at the fat middle-agers who did not have to watch the tab, but were such a nuisance on the floor.

The car veered suddenly to the left, and reduced speed. Now we seemed to be riding on one of the overgrown paths. Twigs whipped through the open window and slurred out again as we passed. Beside me, Luke rolled up the window. We were all in the front seat together. No one spoke.

We stopped. We must be in the heart of the woods, I thought. There was nothing except the blind probe of the head lamps against leaves, the scraping of the November wind.

"Guess the switch from the house doesn't work any more," she said, half to herself. She took a flashlight from the compartment. "Wait here," she said, and got out of the car. After she had gone,

I opened the window and leaned across Luke, holding on to his hand. Above me, the stars were enlarged by the pure air. Off somewhere to the right, the flashlight made a weak, disappearing nimbus.

Then, suddenly, the woods were *en fête*. Festoons of lights spattered from tree to tree. Ahead of us, necromanced from the dark wood, the pattern of a house sprang on the air. After a moment our slow eyes saw that strings of lights garlanded its low log-cabin eaves, and twined up the two thick thrusts of chimney at either end. The flashlight wig-wagged to us. We got out of the car, and walked toward it. Mrs. Hawthorn was leaning against one of the illuminated trees, looking up at the house. The furs slung back from her shoulders in a conqueror's arc. As we approached, she shook her head, in a swimmer's shake. "Well, ladies and gents," she said, in the cool, the vinaigrette voice. "here it is."

"Is it—is this the night club?" I said.

"This is it, baby," she said, and the way she said it made me feel as if she had reached down and ruffled my curls. Instead, she reached up, and pressed a fuse box attached to the tree. For a minute, the red dazzle of the sign on the roof of the house made us blink. 'GINGER AND HARRY'S' it said. There were one or two gaps in GINGER, and the second R of HARRY'S was gone, but the AND was perfect.

"Woods are death on electric lines," she said. Leading the way up the flagged path to the door, she bent down, muttering, and twitched at the weeds that had pushed up between the flags.

She unlocked the door. "We no longer heat it, of course. The pipes are drained. But I had them build fires this afternoon."

It was cold in the vestibule, just as it often was in the boxlike entrances of the roadhouses we knew, and, with its bare wood and plaster, it was just like them too—as if the flash and jump were reserved for the sure customers inside. To our right was the hat-check stall, with its brass tags hung on hooks, and a white dish for quarters and dimes.

"I never had any servants around here," said Mrs. Hawthorn. "The girls used to take turns in the cloakroom, and the men used to tumble over themselves for a chance to tend bar, or be bouncer.

Lord, it was fun. We had a kid from Hollywood here one night, one of the Wampus stars, and we sneaked her in as ladies' matron, before anyone knew who she was. What a stampede there was, when the boys found out!"

I bent down to decipher a tiled placque in the plaster, with three initials and a date—1918. Mrs. Hawthorn saw me looking at it.

"As my mother used to say," she said. "Never have your picture taken in a hat."

Inside, she showed us the lounges for the men and the women —the men's in red leather, hunting prints, and green baize. In the powder room, done in magenta and blue, with girandoles and ball fringe, with poufs and mirrored dressing tables, someone had hit even more precisely the exact note of the smart public retiring room—every woman a Pompadour, for ten minutes between dances.

"I did this all myself," she said. "From top to bottom. Harry had a bad leg when he came back—he was in an army hospital before we got married. He gave me my wedding present ahead of time—enough to remodel the old place, or build a new one. I surprised him. I built this place instead."

"Is his leg all right now?" I said.

"What?" she said.

"His leg. Is it all right now?"

"Yes, of course. That was donkey's years ago." She was vague, as if about a different person. Behind her, Luke shook his head at me.

"And now . . ." she said. "Now . . . come in where it's warm." And this time my ear picked up that tone of hers as it might a motif—that deep, rubato tone of possession fired by memory. She opened the door for us, but for a scant moment before, with her hand on the knob, she approached it as a curator might pause before his Cellini, or a hostess before the lion of her afternoon.

And here it was. The two fires burned at either end; the sultry hooded sidelights reflected here and there on the pale, unscarred dance floor. The little round tables were neatly stacked at its edge, all but one table that was set for service, as if now that it was 3 A.M. or four, the fat proprietor and his headwaiter might just be sitting down for their morning bowl of soup. On the wall, behind the tables, flickered the eternal mural, elongated bal-masque figures and vaudeville backdrops, painted dim even when new, and never meant to be really seen. It could be the one of the harlequin-faced young men with top hats and canes, doing a soft-shoe routine against an after-dark sky. Or it might be the one of the tapering Venuses with the not-quite bodies, behind prussian-blue intimations of Versailles. It did not matter. Here was the "Inn," the "Club," the "Spot," the Glen Island, where one danced to Ozzie Nelson, the Log Cabin at Armonk, the one near Rumson, with the hot guitarist, the innumerable ones where, for an evening or a week of evenings, Vincent Lopez' teeth glinted like piano keys under his mustache. The names would have varied somewhat from these names of the thirties, but here it was, with the orchestra shell waiting—the podium a little toward one end, so that the leader might ride sidesaddle, his suave cheek for the tables, his talented wrist for the band. Only the air was different, pure and still, without the hot, confectionery smell of the crowd. And the twin fires, though they were burning true and red, had fallen in a little, fallen back before the chill advance of the woods.

So, for the second time, we sat down to champagne with Mrs. Hawthorn. There was a big phonograph hidden in a corner; after a while she set it going, and we danced, Luke first with her, then with me. And now, as the champagne went to our heads, it was not the logs, or the chair arms that moved, but we who moved, looping and twirling to the succulent long-phrased music, laughing and excited with the extraordinary freedom of the floor. I thought of Dave, the little man, but Mrs. Hawthorn never mentioned his name. She was warm, gay—"like a young girl"— as I had heard it said now and then of an older woman. I had thought that this could not be so without grotesquerie, but now, with the wisdom of the wine, I imagined that it could—if it came from inside. She had the sudden, firm bloom of those people who really expand only in their own homes. For the first time, we were seeing her there.

Toward the evening's height, she brought out some old jazz records, made specially for her, with the drum and cymbal parts left out, and from the wings back of the podium she drew out the traps, the cymbals, and the snare. In the old days, she told us, everybody who came did a turn. The turn with the drums had been hers. We made her play some of the songs for us, songs I remembered, or thought I remembered, from childhood, things like *Dardanella* and *Jadda Jadda Jing Jing Jing.* She had some almost new ones too—*Melancholy Baby,* and *Those Little White Lies.* We gave her a big hand. ,

Then, just as we began to speak of tiring, of going to bed because we had to drive back early the next day, she let the drumsticks fall, and put her fingers to her mouth. "Why I forgot it!" she said. "I almost forgot to show you the best thing of all!" She reached up with the other hand, and turned off the big spotlight over the orchestra shell.

Once more, only the sidelights glowed, behind their tinted shades. Then the center ceiling light began to move. I hadn't noticed it before; it was so much like what one expected of these places. That was the point—that it was. It was one of those fixtures made of several tiers of stained glass, with concealed slots of lights focussed in some way, so that as it revolved, and the dancers revolved under it, bubbles of color would slide over their faces, run in chromatic patches over the tables, and dot the far corners of the room.

"Dance under it," she said. "I'll play for you." Obediently, we put our arms around one another, and danced. She played *Good Night Ladies.* The drums hardly sounded at all. When it was over, she let the sticks rest in her lap. The chandelier turned, silently. Oval blobs of light passed over her face, greening it and flushing it like long, colored tears. Between the lights, I imagined that she was looking at us, as if she knew something about us that we ourselves did not know. "It was lovely," she said. "That first year." And this time I could not have said which of the two voices she had used.

We left early the next morning. By prearrangement, she was to sleep late and not bother about us, and in a sense we did not see her again. But, as we drove down the private road, we stopped for a moment at a gap in the trees, to see the sun shining, great, over the sea. There was a tall, gray matchstick figure on the end of the dock. As we watched it dove. She could not have seen us; probably she would not have wanted to. She was doing the exercise to keep her weight down, perhaps, or swimming around the dock, as she had done as a child. Or perhaps she was doing the only thing she cared to do alone. It was certainly she. For as the figure came up, we saw its arm—the one mailed arm, flashing in the sun.

During the next few years I often used to tell the story of our visit to Hawthornton. So many casual topics brought it up so naturally—Bermuda, the people one meets when one travels, the magnified eccentricities of the rich. When it became fashionable to see the twenties as the great arterial spurt of the century's youth, I even told it that way, making her seem a symbol, a denizen of that time. I no longer speculated on why she had invited us; I never made that the point of the story. But for some time now I have known why, and now that I do, I know how to tell her story at last. For now that I know why, it is no longer Mrs. Hawthorn's story. It is ours.

It is almost eighteen years since we were at Mrs. Hawthorn's, just as it was then almost eighteen years since Harry had come back from France. I was never to meet anyone who knew them, nor was I ever to see her again. But I know now that there was never any special mystery about her and Harry. Only the ordinary mystery of the distance that seeps between people, even while they live and lie together as close as knives.

Luke is in the garden now. His face passes the window, intent on raking the leaves. Yet he is as far from me now as ever Harry was from Hawthornton, wherever Harry was that day. He and I are not rich; we do not have the externalizations of the rich. Yet, silently, silently, we too have drawn in our horns.

So, sometimes when I walk in the woods near our house, it is to a night club that I walk. I sit down on a patch of moss, and I am sitting at the little round table on the unscarred floor. I fold my hands. Above me, the glass dome turns. I watch them—the two people, about whom I know something they themselves do not know. This is what I see:

It is a long, umber autumn afternoon. To the left the sun drops slowly, a red disc without penumbra. Along the country roads, the pines and firs are black-green, with the somber deadness of a tyro's painting of Italy. Lights pop up in the soiled gray backs of towns. Inside the chugging little car the heater warms them; they are each with the one necessary person; they have made love the night before. The rest of the world, if it could, would be like them.

ARCHIE CARR, *Professor of Biological Sciences at the University of Florida, was born in Mobile, Alabama, on June 16, 1909. He received his M.S. from the University of Florida in 1934 and his Ph.D. in 1937. Since 1937 he has taught biology at the University of Florida, except for the years 1944 to 1949 when he was on leave of absence, teaching biology at Escuela Agricola Panamericana in Honduras. Among the books he has published,* High Jungles and Low *is an account for the general reader of people, animals and terrain in Honduras and Nicaragua. "The Black Beach" is a section from his latest book,* The Windward Road, *to be published by Alfred A. Knopf. Mr. Carr lives with his wife and five children in Florida.*

THE BLACK BEACH

From MADEMOISELLE

It was on the black beach that I met Mrs. Ybarra. It was the long, lonesome, log-strewn stretch from Tortuguero to Parismina. You don't see many people on that beach. Perhaps the chances against our meeting reinforced the impression Mrs. Ybarra made on me and caused her to seem more noteworthy than she really was. That you must judge when you have learned the circumstances.

I was looking for nests of trunkback turtles. I had walked five miles and had found no sign—no fresh trail that was not clearly that of hawksbill or green turtle. Even the greens were scarce. There was just a sprinkling of early layers in the van of the big nesting migration—the "fleet," as the people on the beach call it—

which was already long overdue. It was nearing noon of a flaming, cloudless day and the land breeze had killed the trade wind.

Two miles back I had met the Siquirres dogs—the seasonally feral packs of curs that Paco had pointed out from the plane two days before. Each May the dogs gather on the beach from Siquirres and the other towns along the railroad far inland, called by some unknown cue to cross as much as thirty miles of jungle, marsh and mangrove swamp and meet the fleet and batten on turtle eggs for the season. There were eight dogs in the pack I met, and they were hungry and irritable. They ran yapping before me for a while, as if they thought I was somehow to blame for the lateness of the fleet, and then they dashed off over the low dunes and disappeared among the coco plums. Besides the dogs and a scurrying sand crab now and then I had seen no living thing on land.

Seaward there was little more—no boat to watch, no cruising fin; no whitecaps even, nor any bar or promontory to break the sweeping surf line. Once in a thousand steps there came the thin, lost cry of a tern hidden out among the heat waves.

Once, for a moment, a black patch showed on the burnished, blue-white swells just beyond the breakers where a shoal of anchovy had come up from wherever they had been to flip and play and circle at the surface. I stopped to see what hungry things would gather from the sea and the air, as they always gather about such schools. Almost at once the jacks came—big, flat, gleaming five-pounders that slashed and ripped at the edges of the anchovy cloud, knocking chunks of it into the air in showers of chrome splinters, and sometimes throwing themselves out too in short parabolas, head over tail, stiff and sheepish-looking. I thought what I could do among the jacks with a bass rod and a Johnson spoon.

I shuffled on through the fine, hot sand. It was light, powdery dust of pumice and black glass that let you sink ankle-deep. It was so hot it burned my shanks above my shoe tops. The beach was piled with stranded timber—immense silver trunks of cedar and laurel and *cedro macho* from the Costa Rican rivers and mahogany from Panama or Nicaragua, stolen from the loggers by decades of June floods and then thrown back again onto the black beach by the wild seas that batter this open coast. No tropical beach is fun to walk on at cloudless, windless midday. This one, with its end-less, monstrous jetsam to send you weaving from the deep, hot dunes down into the brawling surf and back again, made following the narrow strip above high-water mark, where turtle trails are laid, a trying job. My ardor for trunkback nests was failing under the sun and I was on the point of crawling beneath a propped log to sleep out the midday calm when I saw what I had come after.

It was a short, broad-limbed V deeply engraved in the beach above the tide zone. The limbs of the V—the trails to and from the disturbed patch—were nearly as wide as the wheel trail of a tractor, and indeed the whole system of marks seemed to show that a heavy, wheeled vehicle had come up from the sea, had sunk deep in the sand drift and, after a great deal of backing and filling and churning, had returned to the water.

It was the nest of a trunkback. It was the first I had ever seen but there was no mistaking it. It was the first ever recorded for Central America but its significance to me far transcended that statistic. To me it was the long-sought land sign of a sea creature I had looked for since childhood—a monster of the deep ocean guided ashore one time in each year by the primal reptile drive to dig a hole in earth and drop in it the seeds of trunkbacks for to-morrow, and cover the hole with toeless flat feet, and pound back down to the sea and never look behind—the last vestige of land-craft left to a bloodline seabound for a hundred million years, and left then but to one sex for one hour on one night in the year.

For a while I just stood and looked at the nest. After a bit the trance of lightheaded exultation ran out and I put down my camera bag and canteen and set about appraising the site where the turtle had worked. There was a great deal of it. A female trunkback often weighs a thousand pounds or more and is full of a fanatical kind of gland-given zeal that would almost pass for in-genuity. Everything she does is calculated to keep her eggs from being dug up again. She can't hide the fact that she was on the beach, so she confounds the egg-hunter with a plethora of clues. In this case the area of flung sand in which I had to prospect for the egg chamber was at least fifteen feet in diameter and roughly circular in outline. Since it offered no evidence, at least to my eye, by which the field for search might be narrowed down, I had to cover every square foot of it; and since the clutch of eggs might lie waist-deep beneath the sand the job ahead was imposing.

I took up my egg stick. After making a few random test holes here and there I began moving systematically back and forth across the site, punching as deeply as I could drive the stick. When I had completed a regular and closely spaced gridwork of holes and had found nothing I began to realize that the slim section of cane I had found effective enough in prospecting for the nests of hawksbill and green turtles was too feeble for the work at hand. To get down through the hard sand that lay below the surface drift I needed a pole with backbone—something I could plant and swing my weight on.

I began looking about the beach for something suitable. I tested one silvery stick after another but all were either crooked as a snake or punky and spineless from salt water and sun. I found a section of timber bamboo that was sound, but you don't split stuff like that with a pocketknife, which was the only tool I carried. Halfheartedly I trimmed and sharpened a leaf stem of coco palm, and this collapsed at the first thrust.

I wanted the nest badly, and with the mounting realization that I probably would not get it my frustration grew apace. I cursed my lack of foresight in not bringing a machete. I grabbed up a sphere of drifted pumice stone and tried to put an edge on my knife blade with it, but the rounded face of the stone collapsed like sugar candy and only polished the metal. In a peevish fit I threw the stone at the face of a laurel log and it went to pieces there.

Suddenly a slight blue feist dog burst from behind the log and started shrieking at me, lifting its feet in indignation and looking backward at intervals as if for support from a source hidden from me by the rise of the log.

Then, for an instant, I saw a face above the six-foot loom of the trunk, and then the face was gone. I ran around the end of the log and saw a woman on horseback retreating at a dead run in the direction from which she had come. I could hear the splatting of the horse's feet in the wave wash and I could see in the slant of the rider's back that she was not party to the flight but was trying to stop and turn the horse. It was the horse who was alarmed at the sudden, unprecedented sight and stink of gringo behind a log on the black beach—not Mrs. Ybarra.

Mrs. Ybarra no doubt took an unenthusiastic view of me too. But she was a woman inured to the shocks of life on this beach. She was not the sort to turn back because of a stranger there, no matter how unaccounted for. She gradually dominated the horse and brought it to a grudging halt a hundred yards down the beach and turned it. I could see that it was an ash-colored *criollo* stallion —one of the tough, runty and cruelly selected remnants of the old Spanish horse that somehow survived the odds against horse-flesh on this tropical shore and that now, salt-cured, *torsola*-proof and vampire-tolerant and economical with its tissue water as a camel, will single-foot all night in sand fetlock-deep.

The example under Mrs. Ybarra had the odd, ratlike face and ewe-necked silhouette they all have. He came back toward me under pressure, against his judgment, his eyes rolling. He came because the will of his rider was stronger than his will.

As she approached Mrs. Ybarra steered her mount down-beach to pass well seaward of me, gripping the reins firmly and drumming at the horse's tight belly with her heels. She gave me a quick look.

"*Adios,*" she said.

Adios said that way means you are going on by. In a matrix of circumstance such as this it becomes a bivalent greeting, a salutation with connotation that a parting will follow immediately. It is a hello-good-by and a word that, so far as I know, has no counterpart in English or North American. Spanish can be shaded delicately. It is nowhere near as simple as my textbooks and teachers made out.

There was, of course, no reason at all why Mrs. Ybarra should not go on by. But at the moment she spoke I saw the pearly gleam of new turtle eggs in two arroba baskets swinging from her saddle; and this made it unthinkable that she should ride on and leave me with my dilemma.

So I said *"Buenas tardes,"* and the shift in salutation changed our relationship at once and made it a point of courtesy for her to rein up, a bit warily, and see what my intentions were.

She was not the sort of woman you would expect to see on this beach, even supposing you were expecting women of any sort. She was a short, turnip-shaped woman with a thin-lipped Madonna's face and a mass of snuff-colored hair piled under a man's old felt hat tied on with a scarf. She had spindly Spanish legs and a big bosom bound in by a bodice of muslin. She wore a brown cotton smock, and a skirt of the same stuff was cleverly tucked under and around her legs because she rode astride and not sidesaddle like the women in Honduras. Her racial origin and place in life were not evident from her appearance. She looked like no Costa Rican I had ever seen. Except for her almost-black skin and reddish hair, and for the shameless way she straddled the high wooden pack saddle, she more closely approached the kind of women you see in the mountains of Matagalpa or of southern Honduras, where the century of hardship the old revolutions brought bred thin-faced women with more than their share of character. She had much in common with them and much in common with her horse. She was weather-beaten, but she had the quiet confidence that goes with a full stomach.

"Buenas tardes," she said, stopping her horse. "The widow of Ybarra from Panal, this side of Parismina."

"Do you know what kind of a turtle did that?" I asked.

"Why not? *Es de canal*—a trunkback."

"That's what I thought," I said. "How do you know?"

"Only a trunkback tears up the beach like that. All this beach is torn up by trunkbacks. It's hard to ride except near the water."

I looked up and down the beach and for the first time noticed that the sand in front of the dunes had an oddly uneven topography that was not part of the wind-piled dune system and not like any beach I had ever seen before.

"Some of that is where the animals dig for eggs when the fleet of green turtles comes, but mostly it's trunkbacks that pile the sand like that. Like this nest here. . . . But why don't you go on a way? I saw several *carey* nests in the light sand yonder, and some of green turtles—various. I dug two." She patted the side of one of the egg baskets.

"I don't want hawksbill eggs," I said, "or green turtle either. I'm looking for trunkback eggs."

"They're not as good as *carey* eggs. They have a little taste."

"I don't want to eat them," I said. "I want to measure them."

She looked at me deprecatingly.

"They're this big. *Asi de grande.*" She cupped her hand to show me how big.

"I mean exactly. And I want to take pictures of them."

"They are very deep. A yard—yard and a half. The animals can't find them. Even the tigers. Even the Siquirres dogs that dig out all the rest don't try to dig trunkback eggs."

"I don't care how long it takes," I said. "I would dig all afternoon if I knew there was a nest there. Maybe this one scratched and went back. Loggerheads do that."

She studied the tumbled sand for a moment. Then she wagged her finger from side to side in front of her face in the gesture of negation that all Latins use.

"*Puso—*" she said. "*Ahi puso.*"

"But how do you find the nest?" I asked. "I've punched all around here and couldn't find a soft place anywhere."

Again she wagged her finger at me.

"You didn't punch deep enough. There is no soft place in a *canal* nest. You just have to find it. Please, what time is it? Midday?"

I brushed the sweat-soaked sand from the face of my watch.

"A quarter after. Are you in a hurry?"

"Today the Spaniard pays the Mosquitos. I am going to collect a debt and I want to get there before they are all drunk. I saw the airplane Thursday, and they will all be drunk by dark."

"How much is the debt?" I said.

"There are two of them. They add up to eight *colones.*"

"All right, look. I'll pay you ten if you will help me find the turtle nest."

She looked at the sand in front of her horse again and then up at the sun. She sighed and swung a leg over the tall saddle frame and stepped to the ground.

"We will try it." She said it with no great enthusiasm.

She led the horse into the sprinkled shade of a ragged old *mangineal,* the only real tree anywhere on the foreshore, and tied the reins to a branch.

"That is a poison tree," I said.

"It doesn't molest horses."

"But how about your hands? You have to hold the reins."

"Don't worry. It doesn't molest me either. Only the juice, or the smoke when it burns."

"I wouldn't tie a horse to that tree for anything," I said.

"It's all right. You are a stranger here and haven't found yourself."

She drew a wasted sliver of a machete from a rawhide scabbard tied to the saddle. She walked back to the turtle nest and called to the feist and it came bouncing down from the beach grass, eager to serve her with all its talents. She leaned and scratched suggestively at the sand to interest the dog in the place.

"*Huevos,*" she said.

I winced, because this word said by itself like that usually means something quite different; but the dog understood and began to dig in a crab hole six feet from the turtle nest.

"Don't be an imbecile," Mrs. Ybarra said. "Here—dig here!"

The dog dropped his ears, hurt by the tone of the words; then he moved over and started digging in the turtle nest.

"With green turtles and *careyes* Filin never deceives himself. With trunkbacks he doesn't serve. Let him dig here awhile. I have to cut a stick. You come too! You can climb better."

We pushed through the sea grapes and sea oats and coco plums, and behind the dunes we came to a coppice of tightly spaced saplings. We stopped and Mrs. Ybarra peered about in the dense thicket until she found what she wanted.

"*Aquel.*" She pointed into the dim interior of the thicket. "If you climb that *palito* and trim it we can get it out."

I shinnied up the slim, smooth stem and trimmed off all the branches I could reach. Then I slid down and cut the trunk through at the ground and dragged it out into the clear. Mrs. Ybarra cut a five-foot section from the stem, skinned the bark from it and tapered one end to a point.

"Ya," she said. "Maybe with this."

When we got back the feist had lost interest in the turtle nest and was digging out another sand crab hole.

"He doesn't serve," Mrs. Ybarra said.

She planted the tip of the stick in the center of the nest and pushed. The point grated to a stop in the dense sand two feet down. She tried again a foot away with the same result. She punched a dozen holes and from each the stick emerged only dusted with fine sand. She stopped and studied the site again on hands and knees, plucking at each twig or bit of debris that protruded above the ploughed surface. After a while she found a newly broken end of beach morning glory stem, and when she pulled on this a good three feet of green vine came out of the sand.

"Maybe here," she said. "The *canal* buried the vine."

She took up the stick and probed carefully all around where the vine had been. Still the rod broke through no nest roof and came out smeared with no yolk. Finally she stopped and shook her head.

"It is *fregada,* this question of the *canal* nests," she said.

She wiped her eyes with the backs of her forearms. Her hair was falling out from under her hat and the sweat-stuck sand had frosted the dark shine of her face. I thought I could see misgiving in her expression.

"I don't believe there's anything here," I said.

"Don't deceive yourself. *Aquí puso*—she laid here. It is sure. Always it is like this The *canal* is—ooo—very big. Her leg is like this—" She measured against her own thigh. "She reaches to a great depth and she is heavy and she packs the sand back with her belly harder than it was before. And the worst is she ploughs so much ground it is hard to locate the nest. If you do find the eggs they are too big to eat with comfort. It is not worth the trouble. But maybe if we both push on the stick. . . . The place should be exactly there."

I have seen a water witch point out the spot for a well with the judicious precision with which Mrs. Ybarra aimed the tip of her stick. She sighted as if she were aiming a rifle at the head of a snake.

"Exactly there," she repeated.

She stuck the point in the sand and we both leaned on the shaft and it broke with a snap and split back in our hands.

"It broke," Mrs. Ybarra said. "The wood was tender. . . . Look, do you want to try any more? I think it will be easier if you go out at night and find the *canal* when she is laying and before she has covered. Any time when the moon is over the sea, not over the land. In the black sand pieces they come out every night—one, two, three—to lay."

I said I thought she was right. I dug in my pocket and from under the sand there brought out some Costa Rican bills. I counted ten colons and held them out to her, saying I was grateful for her help and was sorry she had got so hot and sandy.

"Ah, no," she said. "I can't accept that. I said I would find the eggs. You owe me nothing. I'll reach the village in plenty of time."

"No, look—I stopped you. I'm going to put the money in your saddlebag."

I turned and walked toward the *mangineal* tree behind the screen of tall sea oats. My first sight of Mrs. Ybarra's horse was his feet waving and kicking in the air, all four of them. I ran toward him in sudden panic and burst through the grass and saw him on his back writhing and jerking and bending his short, stiff backbone in impossible, convulsive arcs.

"Come, quick, look at your horse!" I yelled.

She came running.

"Oh, my sainted mother, is he scratching? Yes, my God, he is scratching! He always scratches when he is hot, and I forgot to watch—and look at my *carga!* A la—! Get up! You! Flojo! Stand up!"

She seized a piece of driftwood and began pounding the horse on his unprotected underside. He stopped rolling and in awkward haste floundered to his feet and stood with flaring nostrils, ears back and eyes rolling at his mistress, stung and puzzled.

He was a frightful thing to see. The bridle was bunched at his chin. The saddle and the empty egg baskets and some bundles that had not broken their moorings hung beneath him, and a disheveled game rooster dangled from a cinch ring between his forelegs. His back and sides were heavily smeared with a thick, uneven mixture of egg yolks and whites and black sand, in which, here and there about his surface, leaves and rotting *mangineal* apples and bits of turtle egg shell were stuck. He looked as if a two-year-old child had made a frosting for him. He shook himself violently but looked no better for it.

A feeling of despondency spread over me. This poor woman; what misery I had brought her. How utterly my stubbornness had wrecked her hopes and her day. I turned to her, in my shame ready to crawl or to force on her every last colon I could claw out of my pockets.

She was laughing.

"What a barbarity!" she shrieked. "What a brutal animal! Oh, my sainted mother, what animal more brutal!"

She was so clearly delighted that I looked back at the horse with new eyes, and this time he looked funny to me too and I started to laugh. We both laughed for a long time.

After a while I said: "I am sorry. The blame is all mine. What can we do?"

"No," she said, "it doesn't matter. I only have to bathe the horse."

She began to untangle the bridle, stopping at intervals to bend over and shake and screech with laughter. I helped her unfasten the cinches and disengage the confusion of saddle and *carga*. She took the machete and cut some clumps of grass, which she doubled and bunched and bound to make a brush. She shed her shoes and smock and skirt and strode off to the surf clad only in a sacklike nether garment, leading the horse by the bridle.

I hurriedly made a crude copy of her grass brush; then I rolled up my trousers and followed her into the water.

Within fifteen minutes the little horse was clean, or nearly so, his blue barb skin showing through matted wet hair and only a few patches of coagulated yolk clinging to him here and there. Mrs. Ybarra led him back to the tree and rubbed his back with handfuls of dry grass and spread on the burlap saddle blanket. She tidied up the saddle a bit and I heaved it on the horse and fastened the cinches while she rearranged the *carga*. The game-cock was dead but seemed remarkably intact for having been under a horse. Mrs. Ybarra chopped part way through his neck with the machete and hung the body low on the saddle to bleed on the ground. Then she slipped on her skirt and dropped her shoes into one of the baskets. She brushed at the sand on her arms and put on her smock, then swung herself into the saddle.

Once again I held out the thin sheaf of bills.

"*Vea*," I said cajolingly. "It was my fault that you lost the eggs and the cock died."

"*Qué va!* The cock was to kill and there will be eggs enough. There is no lack of *carey* eggs and the fleet will not be long coming. Will you be going back now?"

I told her I was going on. I must have seemed depressed at the prospect, because she said:

"All right—there's a *cocal* no more than there—just a little way. You can get a *pipa* there [a drinking coconut] and there is shade. Then if you go on six miles there is another *cocal*, and my house is there. If you go that far it is almost certain that I can show you a *canal* tonight, laying on the high tide."

I thanked her and said I couldn't go that far. Without her noticing I slipped the money into the basket where her shoes were.

"I'm going to dig another *canal* nest," I said. "I don't believe this one laid."

"Ay-eeee," she yelped. "You will kill yourself for nothing. She laid. This one laid. Right there. No *canal* nest will be easier to dig than this one."

"O.K.," I said. "But I'm not going to dig here any more. I'll be seeing you."

She gave me a look of what I think was pity, then set her mount in motion with her bare heels, guided him into the surf wash and squeezed him into the mincing single-foot he would hold all the way to Tortuguero. Then she turned and waved. "*Adios, pues*," she said.

The little feist saw her leaving and ran to take the lead. A first sudden breath of the afternoon breeze wiped the gleam from the water and turned it black. The horse's hoof splash faded in the distance and when it was gone the only sounds were the roll of the waves and the fitful piping of a tern as it slipped and tilted on the swelling trade wind.

ALFRED CHESTER was born in Brooklyn, New York. He did graduate work at New York University and Columbia. In 1951, he went to Europe and has lived in Paris since that time. He has had stories published in Botteghe Oscure *as well as the* Paris Review *and other magazines in Europe. His first novel,* Jamie Is My Heart's Desire *will be published in French before it appears in English, and a book of his short stories, in English, is soon to be brought out in France. At present, Mr. Chester is at work on a new novel entitled* I, *etcetera.*

THE HEAD OF A SAD ANGEL

From BOTTEGHE OSCURE

Once, in autumn, I sat all night beside the immense stone wall that stands round the ancient cemetery of Père La Chaise. It was an ugly night, for the sky was black and rain dripped intermittently, and the capes of black ivy on the cemetery wall were loosed by the rain and swung like threats in the wind; sometimes swaying out far enough to fold for an instant into the glow of green gaslight. Between eleven o'clock—when, exhausted and feeling very old but not altogether hopeless, I had sunk to my place beside the wall—and dawn, nine policemen had stopped to ask me why I sat there; to each I said I mourned my Uncle Frédéric, buried within; three, rustling their capes with suspicion, examined my passport on the wrong pages, and two others asked if I did not mind the rain or the *pissotières* whose stink dripped like mold on the wet wind.

Dawn flecked the sky, then night, enraged, returned blacker, rougher; the lamps went out, the increased wind was stung with silver lines of rain, the ivy flapped and shuddered and groaned with such a violence it seemed come to grief and might in a moment writhe itself over the wall and scream into the dead city, and then the nervous young watchman would hear and be alarmed and at last open the gates to permit the live lady to emerge. I knew exactly where she sat behind the wall, for in summer we had gone one afternoon to Père La Chaise, our arms loaded with dahlias. We had walked through the paths of the still stone city, and I had been aware, among the sepulchres, of life—in ourselves, in the sunlight that bumped against the yellow trees, in veins of moss bursting through marble. At Chopin's grave we arranged the dahlias carefully, the Countess pushing other people's offerings out of sight; then she stood up, straightened her beret, and looked into the expressionless stone face of the muse in mourning.

"It is good they took his heart to Poland, you know. Claudio says he will cut out my heart and bring it to Warsaw when I am dead."

"O you!" I laughed, for it was a long time now since I had ceased being incapable of contradicting her. "You'll never die."

"Yes," she nodded, but did not look at me. "You would like that if I do not die. All my students would like me to live forever, only because they are selfish. No, Chopin, we never had it easy, you know. You think I have had it easy, Jesse? Look how I look—and I am only forty-six years old. You think it is the face of an easy life? When I have lost everyone: my husband, my sister, my mother, my friend." She indicated each loss by springing up a finger of her left hand; only the thumb remained unraised, yet tentative. "Now I have no one but my students. And what do they care of me? All egoists, one after the other."

"That isn't so. You know I'd do anything for you."

"Yes? You are not an egoist?" Turning to me, she laughed, her hand jumping to the small toothless mouth as if the dry sound of the laughter burned her gums. "You think I do not know that sometimes you go to amuse yourself? Sometimes with women?"

"Does that make me an egoist?" I mumbled, more as a token of self-respect than with any intention of disproving her statement.

"Yes, that is an egoist. One must give up everything for music. Claudio—"

"Yes, yes, I know. But he didn't come with you today, did he?"

"That is because he works. Never mind. Please not to argue in this place."

And she sank to the step below the monument and rearranged

the dahlias and spoke to Chopin in Polish; while speaking, she wept a little and dried her pale eyes with the ends of the grey chiffon scarf that was wound about her neck. Now and then she hummed a passage from a study or a waltz and seemed to discuss it with him.

Afterward, we went to see where the Rothschilds lay; and then, from the grave of Héloïse and Abelard, the Countess stole a pot of striped tulips which she gave to Oscar Wilde who she said had once worshipped her; but I knew this was impossible. Then she was in a great rush lest we keep Claudio waiting, so we said a quick goodbye to Chopin, and the Countess pushed some newly placed daisies to the side of the muse. We took a taxi to the Champs-Elysées and sat half an hour on the terrace of the Select before Claudio appeared.

The purple sky drooped with heat and twilight, softening the avenue and the people upon it. But neither the hour nor the climate seemed to affect Claudio: he moved through time and temperature like a statue—being perhaps subject to them, but only over the centuries. His nose, his head, his mouth, his eyes seemed abnormally large, although actually they were not; it was only that he had a sculptured look, too steady and well realized to be life-sized, and too determined.

When he was seated we had two rounds of cognac which I paid for while the Countess made a joke about the GI Bill of Rights. "It is a pity, you know, they do not give it to artists also as to Americans." And then, in detail, I told Claudio of the long afternoon I had just spent with the Countess. He smiled and nodded; sometimes he said yes or *très bien* and rolled the Italian *r* unnecessarily; but I do not think he listened.

"A beautiful afternoon," said the Countess. "You should have come with me into the air. One day you shall have consumption like me if you do not breathe sometimes. Never mind: all great talents have consumption. You worked the concerto today? Yes? How does it go?"

I stared at Claudio, forcing a cold knowing smile to my face; but he appeared not to notice.

"Very well. Except the passage with the triple notes. I tried the new exercises. . ."

And the conversation suddenly moved away from me, turning,

as it invariably did, into German which they said was easier for
them than either French or English, but which I could not understand. After a quarter of an hour, I pushed my chair back, trying
not to look offended, and told them I was leaving.

"No, you don't leave. You must stay to dine with us."

"I'd better get back to my room. I can still get a couple of hours
of work in."

"Yes? Then go when you feel like it. Do the second page of the
étude: fa-si-fa-so with second and third finger." She illustrated the
movement. "Come to me Tuesday at ten-thirty."

I backed away from them, not turning to face the street until a
waiter ran past me, breaking my view of the table and of the
fingers that continued to fly over it like steel moths.

II

I had heard, then seen, these moths for the first time on a
spring Sunday less than four months before the afternoon we went
to Père La Chaise. I had heard them from far away sending a
polonaise across the spread canvases and the kiosks and the plywood shops, rolling imperiously through the flea market so that
the piles of gilt and antique junk trembled despite the weight of
their ages. Following the music I went round to the back alleys
where the market glooms with overhanging roofs and narrows
with goods spilling from the kiosks into the lanes. There, perhaps
thirty people were semicircled about a frontless piano shop, and
the music held them still and made their faces pink. Their breath
was gone; all sound was gone under this polonaise which could
deny all because, like the heart, it incorporated all. It was *piano*;
it was *forte*; it was a dozen shades of tone between and beyond,
and always tender as if the pianist never exerted pressure, not even
for the grandest passages, but yet brought maximum voice from
the instrument; the chords were sensitive and took pleasure in a
lover's touch, and for joy sang the polonaise.

When it ended I was not frozen to my place but, while the
others applauded, I pushed through them, shoving paint-and-sequin
ladies whose jewelry tinkled with rancor, my elbows thudding into

fat men, and I emerged at the little clearing before the shop just
as the pianist lifted herself from the bench. I saw nothing at first
but the wide black beret and the streak of grey chiffon which
moved in rapid nervous circles as if pushed by the applause.

"*Bis! Bis!*" I cried with the others, and then louder than they:
"*Encore: jouez encore. Je vous en prie.*"

Turning her head, she smiled to me and her tiny colorless lips
flapped inward against her gums. This recognition, tenuous as it
was, seemed so personal that I reddened and whispered—too confi-
dentially even for me to hear my words—*encore, encore!*

"You do not hear such music in America?" she asked me, speaking English without any accent, flat, uninflected, with the soft
halting rapidity of one who knows but seldom uses a language.
"No, and you do not hear it in Europe too—only when *I* play."

"Then play some more."

"No, no. I cannot, you know. I am not as I used to be. Once—"
Interrupting herself, she faced the crowd which still applauded,
still insisted.

"*Mais non, mes amis. J'suis fatiguée; j'suis malade. Je—*"

"*Bis . . . bis . . . bis . . .*"

"*O écoutez . . .*" she pleaded, raising her hand to stop them,
but they continued and, shrugging, she sank once more to the
bench and unloosed four mazurkas and two nocturnes. Her
fingers, rounded and firm, astonished me for they seemed never
to touch the keys but to fly over them drawing sound like a
magnet, each note imposing yet submissive to its phrase; melodies
and harmonies set free by quiet emphasis, by pauses that roared
like storm, by a technique that made each pulse in every part
of my body throb under her fingers. Arpeggios leaped, chromatics
were aflame, repetitions were like stars: clearly the same, but
clearly different.

Afterwards she would play no more, and most of the audience
shuffled out of the dark alleys, leaving me and a few spectacular
women, some of whom had purple hair and others platinum, and
one had orange hair rolled in small puffed balls like mimosa. All
their mouthless faces were identical, vanished beneath smooth
death-white masks of powder except for asterisks of color standing
round their eyes. In their black-gloved hands were silver sticks or

carved cigarette holders or purses which, like their clothes, sparkled with sequins and rhinestones. Because they all shrieked at once (and much too quickly for me to understand them) and because they spat as they talked and smelled of garlic, I wandered into the unlighted shop behind and tested a broken harpsichord whose harsh stutter surprised the ladies: they were silent a moment, looking in at me. Then I walked to a Blütner grand which bore a polished bronze plaque telling of a first prize to Katherine de Charski in 1937.

At last the ladies, still shrieking and spitting and sparkling, started down the cluttered path, tossing back last compliments: "*Incomparable, maître, vraiment . . .*"—"*Au revoir, au revoir, vous êtes l'ange de la musique.*"

When they were out of sight, the angel growled then looked into the darkness of the shop. "So, American, you do not go away?"

"Well, I—"

"*Well,* you—always they say well, or then they are afraid, or else they guess. The angel of the music, you know: they call me that. Every Sunday they come and they call me that. They should fall to their knees like before God. But they do not even buy a piano or give money. Would I take their money, do you think?"

Not moving from the Blütner, I tried to stir the dusk up around me. "Do you sell pianos?" I asked her. "Don't you give concerts?"

"Ah, such children, these Americans. What do you know of difficulty in life? Never mind, do not tell me, please. You play the piano?"

Yes, I played the piano, and I had always said so, but now I replied, "I'm studying" because the question chafed with relativity, just as if she had asked: "You have heard *me* play the piano. Consider, and tell me, do *you* play the piano?"

"I'm studying."

"And say where, with whom."

I told her.

"So? Indeed? Very good. You have traveled very far to remain in ignorance. In sixty years if you have chance you will play your *Rhapsody in Blue* like a master. You play scales all day? Do-re-mi-fa—"

"No, not all day."

"You work ten-twelve hours a day? How many? Altogether. I mean everything—scales backwards and forwards."

"Well, actually I only work four or five hours a day. I'm at school all morning and then—"

"Excuse me, if you have chance you will play *Rhapsody in Blue* in ninety years."

"I've already given a recital in America," I muttered, moving back from the Blütner, further into the dusk.

"Ah so, *maître*. You have then nothing more to learn. You must then teach me. Come, play something for me. Come here. Come, please, do not hide yourself there. I am almost blind and cannot see you in that darkness. *Asseyez-vous*."

I went forward reluctantly, placed myself upon the bench and complained at once that it was too low.

"Never mind. You will keep your bottom in the air."

Unexpectedly, chords began to drop under my fingers. I wondered who had pushed them, and wondering, my face went damp and hot, my hands stiff and cold, and I stopped. But before she could say anything, I began again, my ears shut against the sounds, and I resisted the impulse to grumble about the hard touch of the piano. I played recklessly, stupidly, moving from embarrassment to fear and finally to fury—hating her, hating myself, hating the music. But instead of jumping from the bench when the piece was done, I pushed my fingers straight into the first movement of the *Appassionata*, and I heard Beethoven roar at me. I roared back.

"You have much courage," she said, nodding and serious, when I had stopped.

"My God, my God, my God. Believe me, please believe me: I've never played so badly in my life. I don't know—"

"Yes, what does it matter? I will make you good pianist; you have heart and strength and courage. You are young, no like me: everything is for you when you are young. But where is your logic, your technique? You know nothing of interpretation. Your fingers are like the legs of a—how do you say—*poulet*, you know. O I do not blame you. Today, the professors can teach you nothing. They think when you spend all day in school and two hours at piano you are big artist. No, you must give up everything for the piano; it is a jealous art. When my Claudio came to me, he was despairing. Now in two years he is big artist. In one more year he will sit on the world. You shall hear him play, you know. He gives up everything for me; he works twelve-fourteen hours a day. No going out, no women, nothing—only his music. He knows that I"—she pounded her chest rapidly—"I am the only one left today. Why do you smile, you American? Tell me who plays better than me? Rubinstein? Horowitz? Gieseking? Who?"

"That's not why I smiled."

"If I am the greatest pianist, why should I not say so? Who listens to me anyway? These few hypocrites who come here to the market—"

"But why don't you perform?"

"Ah!" she cried, her mouth shooting open. "Have I one tooth in this mouth? You would like to see me on the stage with no tooth and in filthy clothes and let them make a mockery of me? Here on my head, under my beret, I have tumor as big as a box of matches, and all day and night I have headaches. I cannot work my piano. You hear me play now, and I have not worked since 1940. I shall let them laugh at me—when once they put me on their shoulders? You know where my tradition comes from? *Do you?*"

I hesitated, wondering what answer she expected.

"From *Chopin!* I am the last exponent of the tradition, I"—she thumped her chest once more—"I: Katherine Juliette Beatrice Maria la comtesse de Charski." Her tongue rolled and thundered with her names, and I looked down at the keys of the piano. I was not embarrassed; in fact, I was not anything, except perhaps slightly beside the point, for her grandeur was asserting itself round and beyond me, and if I caught pieces of it, it was almost accidental.

From down the path, a fat woman in a lather of foxes and a tall man under a homburg approached the shop.

"*Des américains,*" she whispered. "*Vous pouvez parler français?*"

"*Bien sûr, Madame.*"

"*Madame?* Why you call me *Madame?*" she said, speaking in English, and her hands slid down her flat body indignantly. "You must call me Countess, you know. I *am* a countess. You do not believe me? I will show you marked on my passport." She ran back of the shop to a small desk where stood her black leather sack.

"No, please! I'm sorry, Countess. Of course I believe you. Please don't—"

But she pulled wide the mouth of the sack, her arm sinking to the elbow. *"Merde, je ne—tiens, voilà!"* The passport was held together by a rubber band which had cut deep into the shredded edges. As she lifted it, the American couple walked past her to the Blütner.

"O darling!" said the woman. "What a beautiful piano!"

"Says here . . ." the man began, bending to see the bronze plaque. "Says here it was for—"

"The Blütner is not for sale," called the Countess, waving her passport at them. "But next to it is a very rare Pleyel. Chopin and Liszt played on it one night *chez la duchesse de Cornouailles.*" Head slightly bent, she led them to the Pleyel. "Touch yourself and hear the beauty of its tone: diamonds on one end, trumpets on the other." When she returned to me, she was muttering: "To sell my Blütner—not while I am here anyway." Then raising her voice and thrusting her passport forward: "Here you see. It says countess. Here in French; here in Polish. I am a true countess of the blood by birth and marriage, but I have lost everything. I had to run from war. Yes, it is not happy—but go away now. I must sell piano or I will lose my Blütner. Come to me to my home Tuesday at eleven before noon. Here is my card with the address. I will make you big pianist. Now go away, you know."

Her card bore a gilt-relief coronet above the many names and I thought I felt the weight of it as I pushed the card into my pocket and started down the alley. Her voice, rasping at the Americans, came after me. "You like the harpsichord? Bach himself performed on it when he played before Louis Quatorze . . ."

III

Round her head, like a crown pushed over a forehead, was an elastic bandage, and patches of grey hair poked out below and rose frumpishly, like tattered clouds, above. Her body was indistinguishable in a pink robe which must once have been purple and velvet and ravaged by moths, and now hung shapeless and without interest straight down to the two blazing golden pumps studding her feet.

"Come in, please. Come in. Forgive me that I greet you like this. I have not the strength to dress, and the bandage is for my headaches. It does me no good, you know, but sometimes it makes the pain to change place." She sighed and led me through the small empty corridor. "It is not good to be old. But I am not so old as you think! Please, never mind, do not tell me you do not think I am old. You think I am a hundred years? I am only fifty. In here, please."

The room was awash with stale sunlight, although there was no sun anywhere in it. Perhaps the air itself was amber as if once the sun had come piling into the room, been reluctant to leave, and so remained, growing pale, growing dry, hanging to the walls and to the enormous chandelier whose thousand tearlike crystals rang against one another at the breath of our entry. Even the three eighteenth-century portraits, despite their deep blues and black shadows, seemed lacquered with sunlight, but this was not so of the faces: two frowning gentlemen, and a lady with an iron smile, her eyebrows S-shaped, like an angry woman in a cartoon. But there was little in the large room for her to be angry at: another prize piano, a black bench with four legs of inlaid pearl, two embroidered hassocks, and a white-and-gold table loaded with flowers: with tulips and lilies and roses and carnations—some fresh, some nearly dead, some like rust or burnt paper.

"What a room!" I said.

"Yes? You like? But all my furniture is sold. I have ten more rooms—all empty except for my bed. But here, you see, one may see from the windows l'Arc de Triomphe and the long avenue of *marroniers*. Trees give me peace, you know, especially in spring; here, they are like *tempo rubato*—yum-terum-te. I hope you shall not mind when I smoke. I smoke very much during lessons. I was teaching once a girl named Olga and she said: O pardon me, Madame la comtesse, but I cannot stand it when there is so much smoke. I must have fresh air. I have asthma. Yes, I said to her,

I have worse asthma than you, and when you want fresh air you must go to the Bois de Boulogne not to me. You do not come here to breathe but to learn piano. She went away and two weeks later came back and brought me twenty thousand francs. O, she said, I would mot choke to death than live without you. You do not believe me? I will show you letter from her; I will show you letters from biggest people in the world. They would give millions to learn from me. They—what is the matter with you? Why do you become red?"

"I thought—that is, I wondered. I mean, if I'm going to study with you, don't you think we ought to settle terms?"

"What is terms?"

"You know, for the lessons. Frankly, I can't afford very much because I've got to stay on at the school. Otherwise I won't get money under the GI Bill."

"Ah, money!" She growled a moment and rubbed her head. "All you can think of is money, Americans. I am artist. I do not talk of money. Besides you have not enough money to pay me how I am worth it. I ask only that you give up everything, only to keep music. Is that agreed?"

"That's a pretty hard thing to do."

"Yes, but it is not so hard as to run with the girls and try to learn piano at the same time. Also you must not go more to school. They teach only wrong—"

"But if I don't go, I won't get the money from the government. And I've got no money of my own."

"So you will go each month and pay them registration and then you go no more until next month. You shall find that the professors are also very happy when you give them money and do not trouble them again. But now no more talk, you know. *Allons*, to the piano."

From the deep low pocket of her robe she withdrew a package of cigarettes and a pair of steel-rimmed spectacles which, when she had arranged the broken temples behind her ears, forced her to keep her head at a constant angle, for otherwise the glasses might slide along her nose and fall to the floor. As the lesson began, her face closed down upon its bone, cheeks and jaw tightening toward concentration, and she became a different person, or rather no person at all but an abstraction of human qualities no longer hampered by the individual past. The characteristics of her self and of her life were gone; illness, nobility, exile, despair, were of no further consequence. We had become two brains working with logic, analyzing the dispassionate and least resistant path to the heart, and from it, into the fingers. Sometimes she might pause suddenly, as if hesitating, calculating, and then we might go on or she might push me aside and illustrate a point by playing a piece, and in doing so she would change again, softening, her face becoming full and tender, her eyes pieces of swollen beauty behind the steel spectacles which, although her head was always stiff, threatened to budge, began to slide, did at last bounce onto the keyboard or her lap. At the piano she was never impatient, pushing us both with her logic and with her unquestioning self-confidence; each word she spoke was indubitable, was truth. "You must be now a child, an innocent. You must forget all wrong ideas of music you have learned. You start now again from beginning. *Recommençons . . .*"

We worked on until four o'clock, almost without a rest, and would have continued had the doorbell not rung and shaken us out of our concentration.

"Is Claudio. We stop now," she said.

Plucking her spectacles off, she broke round, crossed the room, swung the door open, and closed it behind her—all actions completed so quickly and abruptly it seemed five hours at the piano had put her into better condition than she had been when I entered the flat. Left alone, I began to stretch my exhaustion away and ease the tightness in my neck and back. So involved was I with my stretching that it was some time before I realized how long the Countess had been gone. I paused, listening, but heard only a chirring whisper, a shadow of rapid tittering conversation. Then there was a sound like *ch-ch-ch*, and the door swung open into the room.

"Come," she said, taking long strides toward me. "You shall meet my American who thinks always about money."

A short young man followed her in, his pace as slow and lazy as his smile, and despite the set, old-man look of his face, he moved like a shy boy. One hand was in his pocket and the other seemed unsteady, hung fidgeting at his side, went once quickly through his hair, then extended itself toward me when he was only halfway across the room.

"Here is terrible Claudio. He takes from me all my strength."

"Enchanted," he said, giving me his hand.

"Me too." His smile trembled, almost ready, I thought, to erupt into a laugh, but instead it disappeared.

"You will be taking lessons with the Countess?" he asked.

"Well, I hope so." I looked to her, but her eyes were fixed on Claudio, her mouth firm, her head nodding slightly.

"She is a most severe master."

"I think she's very kind."

"And most demanding."

"I don't—"

"But if she demanded less, perhaps her students would play less good. A year ago, for example, I could not take an octave; now I can take nine notes."

"That's amaz—"

"Naturally, of course, I have had to sacrifice." He was obviously in a hurry to get his piece said and over; he spoke without interest or expression, and stood perfectly still. "But after all it has been no sacrifice at all but a pleasure. For music satisfies every desire. You are prepared to make all else in your life secondary to your art?"

I did not answer, because it was not quite a question and because, even if it had been, the tone of Claudio's voice clearly indicated that nothing could interest him less than what he was at present discussing. But he continued speaking while the Countess nodded silently and while I became embarrassed at their little game. Claudio too became embarrassed but not until he had finished, and then he turned away from me and put his hands in his pockets.

"I'd love to hear you play," I said to him. "The Countess tells me you're a wonderful pianist."

"She exaggerates. There is only one great artist in the world today, *n'est-ce pas, ma comtesse?*"

"Dirty mouth. *Salaud!*" she shrieked, and a train of giggles rattled out of her like hiccups. "And you think it is yourself! I give him everything and now he thinks he is bigger than me. But one day I will show you, *sale* Claudio, that there is still no one like Katherine de Charski." She turned to me. "I have eight students, you know—no, now I have nine. And no one gives me money; they are all poor filths, my students. One says, O I must have a new frock or I give you everything. Another says, I must pay for my piano. And I have a new frock? And I pay for my piano? No, I sell everything—even my beautiful Blütner."

"I didn't know you'd sold it," I said. "On Sunday—"

"Yes, I sold it a long time ago. And for whom? What have I? Only headaches and pains, you know. Come, feel here, the tumor on my head. You are afraid to? Never mind, so do not. If you would feel here in my private parts you would feel a piece of iron; yes, I am all ruptures, broken to pieces." Her knuckles struck the belt, and there was a clanking sound which caused a light tinkle among the crystal of the chandelier. Claudio burst into laughter.

"You are wonderful, St. Countess. You have four hundred maladies and still you are stronger than myself."

"Stronger? *Tête de vache*, I am so weak that I must take a dozen tablets in the morning or I will not rise from bed. You hear how he talks to me? I put him the world to his fingers and he says I am stronger. I do everything for him, you know. Is that true? And I have nothing in revenge of it."

"One day you will. I will give you a piano made of gold with diamond keys."

"Give me nothing. I want nothing. You do not respect me because I am alone in the world, because I have lost everyone, you know. I have lost my husband, my sister, my mother, my friend." Four fingers on her left hand rose like monuments to the losses, and she shook them at Claudio. He bent to kiss her hand, but she slapped him weakly on the lips. "All my life I must run from the wars, and I leave always behind *un bien-aimé*, dead, dead. *Rien, rien, rien—je n'ai plus rien, rien que ces crottes d'étudiants.*" And suddenly she was speaking German, her voice rising, reaching a tower of curses upon Claudio's head. His head rose with her curses, and he smiled, shrugged and went to the piano. She followed, still cursing, but gradually lowering her voice to a mutter in French. *"Je t'emmerde,"* she whispered, and then was altogether silent, listening to him play. At first her body was still, stiff, but almost imperceptibly she began to sway, and her hands fluttered slowly, hardening into fists which ultimately pounded the rhythm on the side of the piano. *"Vite, vite! Schneller, schneller! Die Hünde sind hier und sie beissen sich!"*

I sank to the embroidered hassock beside the windows and looked out toward Etoile, my eyes moving across the avenue of chestnut trees, a sadness stretching out of my fatigue to the pastel afternoon, to the white chestnut blossoms standing like lamps upon the trees. Behind me Claudio played and the Countess pounded. His hands were of roses, and of teams of wild horses, and of things I had often felt and shivered with, guessing darkly that through them I would approach myself and consequently all the world.

My sadness was wound with jealousy, and I tried not to listen while pastel evening slid across the afternoon.

"Nein, nein, Claudio. Jetzt Melankolie. Es ist Nacht und das Herz weint."

IV

Sometimes a word, spoken by an individual sensitized by its meaning, swells outward, pushing everything aside but itself; sometimes it expands from a person's mouth until it is no longer symbol but thing symbolized. So it was with *war, la guerre, die Krieg*—when the Countess said it. Bombs sprang like teeth from her gums, her lips were tumid with flame and blood, seared skulls and swollen bellies, and along her tongue roared a pageant as deep as time splattered with man's inhumanities, his organized uniformed hatreds, man marching gold into the golden flames, emerging, if emerging at all, melted, leaden, in pieces, and as cheap as breath.

"Que je déteste la guerre," she would shriek, like a cry against history, a fingered voice reaching into the grave of the past. "My friend was a Jew. She had blue eyes and her hair was like in Poland, fair. Here, outside Paris, she was weeping by the roadside.

You will ruin your lovely eyes, *ma chère*. And I took her to my home, you know, and hid her for three years. But someone knew. Yes, so they came and they went through all the rooms, one after the other, and they took her away to put her in the fire. That night I sat with Chopin, long, long, through the whole night, when the gates were closed. He has known war, Chopin. You have known war, Jesse?"

"I was—no, not really."

"Claudio has known it."

Claudio nodded and took her hand.

The Countess had made burnt offerings at the altar of war, but she did not understand the god which ate of the sacrifice, and so her gestures toward him were empty, and the cloud of holy smoke rising, rising, fed and rising, smelled not of frankincense and souls but smelled of gizzard and hair. Yet the god sucked up her offerings, lapped out at her as she sacrificed between Warsaw and Paris. Where was she to go in search of peace? Perhaps only upon the altar itself, into the column of smoke, into the jaws of the munching god she could not understand. Once, and for a little while, she had found peace by giving her music to the world. But her peace was sought out, and she no longer performed, and although we did not speak of it I believed she would never perform again, not if she had teeth and a hundred dresses and no tumor on her head nor rupture in her private parts.

"I am alone, yes, and I am always complaining. But I want no one more. In this world it is dangerous to love. When one loves, one gives. I shall not any more give—not of anything."

That she did not give was only partly true, for she gave a great deal, but not all. Often, during our lessons, I would become aware of an instant of hesitation rather than thought, and I would know she was refusing me, denying me her mastery. I wondered if she refused her other students too, but except for Claudio I either did not know them at all or not well enough to question. Claudio seldom spoke to me directly, and although I talked to him it would somehow never develop into a conversation; but even if it had, I could not have asked him about the Countess, for she was always with us.

Still, what she did give me was enough to set the pattern of my life into another order: I left school (but I continued to pay fees); I moved into a new neighborhood, away from distracting friends; I spent twelve or sometimes fourteen hours a day at the piano; and I almost never went out, except with the Countess. So I gave to music most of what it wanted; and then one day I learned it wanted more.

"I have to pay my rent," said the Countess. "And I have no one franc, you know. Please," and she handed me the bill, "when you pass downstairs you shall pay the concierge."

"O my God, you should have warned me. I haven't got that much money."

"Yes? So you will borrow. You do not know other Americans?"

"Of course I do, but—"

"Good. To come now to the piano."

Ten days later, while we were dining with Claudio at the small crowded restaurant near the Countess' home, she slid a sheet of paper to me across the table. I looked down at the sum very hard, hoping it might disappear, but it didn't and the three of us were silent while I wondered how a two-month electricity bill could possibly be so high.

"It's awfully expensive, isn't it?" I said.

"You find it so? It gets cheaper now; the days become long."

Suddenly I turned to Claudio. "Look, could you help me out with this? I've just paid the Countess' rent."

"That was very kind of you. Unfortunately I have no money." And he continued eating.

"I am not worth it?" cried the Countess, and then dropped her fork with a clatter.

"I didn't say that. I just asked Cl—"

"Am I or am I not? That is all what I ask you."

"Certainly you are—"

"So, well, no more discussion."

The next time we were alone, I began a carefully prepared speech. "Paris is a very expensive city, and although I hardly ever go out any more there are—"

"Claudio never goes out except to come to me."

"All right, so maybe Claudio's not human." The word bumped like thunder between us.

"It is not human to come to me? Please, come no more."

"I'm sorry. I didn't mean it that way. I meant he wasn't human for not going out. Everybody wants to have a little fun sometimes."

"An artist has no right to be human."

I was silent a long time before I spoke. "Then why don't you perform?"

"Yes? Give me money to make teeth and tomorrow I throw you all away—all, and go to give concerts."

"You'll throw Claudio away too?"

"Yes, Claudio too. I give him too much already. I should throw him anyway. None of you deserve me." She seated herself at the piano and began to play a waltz, trying to distract me. But I was firm and returned to my speech.

"What I mean is, it would be so much easier for me if I could give you a certain amount each week rather than get stuck with a pile of bills all at once."

"*American!*" she sneered. "Tomorrow I go back to Warsaw. The Polish embassy says all will be forgiven if I go back. The Communists are good to artists. Not like you people—money, money, money. Always money."

"If you go back to Poland—" She was trying to drum my voice away under a Liszt rhapsody. "If you go back to Poland," I roared, "you won't be a Countess any more."

She lifted her hands from the keyboard. "Do I care? I care only for my art. Tomorrow I leave."

After that, I never mentioned money again, but put a sum aside each week, under Chopin's *Mazurkas,* and waited for the bills. Nor did she mention going back to Warsaw again, except one morning late in June when I came for my lesson and Claudio, pale and obviously upset, opened the door.

"Is the Countess ill?"

He was about to answer when I heard her voice moaning out of the salon: "Yes, iiiillll. I shall die."

She was sitting on the hassock beside the window, her eyes bulging and red with tears. "My Blütner is gone; the beautiful instrument I won in Vienna. It is sold—to American people."

"But I don't understand. I thought you *had* sold it."

"Yes, but now it is really sold. Now where can I ever find it? It goes to a place called San-san-nat, I think."

"Cincinnati."

"Yes," she sighed. "Cincinnati. O Claudio, *mon enfant*, you will come with me back to Poland. They do not steal pianos in Warsaw."

"I would go with you wherever you want," he said, then went to the piano and we were all silent while he hammered out his exercises.

Since this was supposed to be my lesson, I was annoyed with him, but I waited about a quarter of an hour before I complained. "I guess," I said to the Countess, "you're not much in the mood for working today."

"No. I have no head . . ."

"Maybe you'd better take it easy with those octaves, Claudio." I felt myself shake as I spoke.

"Yes?" he said and stopped; then he went to the Countess. "You want to go out? To have champagne, perhaps?"

"No. Go home to work. I was selfish to send you the telegram, but I was unhappy. Go home, come tomorrow for your lesson, both of you."

"Are you sure you're all right?" I asked.

"I am never all right, you know. Today worse than ever. But I will sleep. Please leave me now alone."

On the way down the faded stairs Claudio walked slightly behind me.

"I still don't understand," I said without looking at him, "what she means about the piano being sold and *really* sold."

"She sold it in the winter to a merchant, but now he has sold it to someone else."

"But she must have expected that." We were in the street now, under a forest of chestnut trees.

"Perhaps she did." He put out his hand to say goodbye, but I didn't take it.

"That shop in the flea market, it isn't hers?"

"Of course not. She tended sometimes the shop in return because the merchant promised not to sell the piano for two years. She was hoping to buy it back one day."

"And now he's gone back on his word and sold it."

"Yes." He smiled. "To Cincinnati."

"My God, how could all of you stand around and let her sell it?"

He shrugged. "She is a lovely woman. Unhappy. She too makes sacrifices. When it was necessary to sell her piano, she did not hesitate. In the end there is nothing to regret."

I had not the least idea what he was talking about, and so when his hand stretched out again, I was too confused to do anything but take it, and to watch him turn away toward the Etoile.

V

Summer swooped over Paris like a butterfly net. The city trembled and shook, and beat itself against the heat, then toward the end of July folded its wings inward, was silent, seemed to be dead. Shutters went up and corrugated shop-fronts went down; workmen took off their denims and put on their morning clothes (the ones they had been married in), shoved their wives into sleazy satinets and their children into Communion clothes, and they all went away in trucks and buses to sit beside crumbling chateaux and stagnant buzzing lakes, to argue, swat mosquitoes, drink wine and break wind. Tourists came though, yawning and very hot, complained, took photographs of Sainte-Chapelle, and caught the night train to Rome.

In deference to summer, and to the Countess, I rearranged one further thing: my room, so that while sitting at the piano, I could look out over the still, sunlit avenue de Clichy and dream of Venice and of making love in a gondola. Early in July I had told the Countess I wanted to go to Italy for a short holiday.

"Very good. It is good to change scenery. It makes the blood change too. Otherwise a person's heart shall become as mine. It aches all the time, you know. I have never any holiday. I cannot remember to have holiday in my long fifty-six years."

She stared at me expressionless, waiting.

"Well," I said. "There must be some way we could send you on vacation."

"No, no, Jesse. No one thinks for me. Please not to trouble to think for me. Go to your holiday. You shall take airplane, no doubt?"

"I can't afford to take an airplane, and you know that very well. I can't even afford to take a train if I expect to keep any money to spend in Italy. As a matter of fact, I've been planning to hitchhike."

"That is expensive? You must—"

"No, it's free. *Je m'en vais par auto-stop.*"

"*Ah, c'est bien!*"

And she said nothing more about it that afternoon, not even to Claudio—unless she did so during their invariably whispered conversation at her door when he arrived. But the next morning a telegram was delivered to my room.

> TOO TIRED TOO SICK NO MORE TEACH FIND OTHER PRO-
> FESSOR STUDENTS ALL EGOISTS I ALONE HAVE NO ONE
> WAR WITHOUT STRENGTH GOOD PROFESSORS IN ITALIE
> BUT NOT SO GOOD AS ME GOODBYE BON VOYAGE.
>   KATHERINE DE CHARSKI

I did not get angry until after lunch. At first the telegram only amused me and I propped it on the music rest while my fingers ran by themselves across the keyboard. That was part of the Countess' strength: so long as her actions were associated with her music, so long was she in a position of control, for genius, like passion, can demand without limits when demanding in its own name. And because I sat at the piano marveling at the way my fingers and wrists had learned to dance, the Countess could ask whatever she pleased.

But during lunch, I began to react at her intrusion. I had been studying music for fifteen years, privately and at schools; I had been applauded and encouraged; I had won a scholarship and two prizes and had given a recital. And throughout all that time, when I stepped away from the piano no one had dared to interfere with my life, nor to link into confusion my needs as a man and my needs as a musician. Now here was this crazy, selfish, egomaniac of a woman who seemed to think it was a sin against art to have friends, to amuse oneself in any way, to be an American—

"I'll have no more of it," I said aloud and went downstairs and round the corner to the post office where I sent a telegram.

ALL RIGHT I HAVE ANOTHER PROFESSOR A GENIUS FROM CINCINNATI.

JESSE

I did not touch my piano again that day nor at all the next. Instead I slid the pile of money from under Chopin's *Mazurkas* and went out and got a dark woman with hot sunken eyes and moist flesh and we rode round Paris in a taxi with the curtains down, stopping to eat greasy meals and to drink iced wine. Somewhere—where?—I lost this woman so I visited friends who said I'd neglected them, and I promised I would never do it again. I told them I had fallen in love with a toothless hag who loved a three-year-old Italian, and they were *simply wild* about playing with each other's ruptures while I watched. My friends were delighted and we celebrated into the next evening, pouring wine upon ourselves, floating from cabaret to cabaret, from Montparnasse to Montmartre, through streets thick and wet with summer night, painted with neon, rumpled with crowds, sticky with cognac and stars and the sap oozing out of trees. And then, and then, suddenly, over there, on the terrace of a cafe, back in a corner, like birds looped into night, was Claudio with a fair round-faced girl. He whispered in her ear and her laugh was silly, girlish, desiring; and he kissed her, their mouths gluing together with the force of summer. My friends had gone on without me, had come back, now tugged at me: the night was not yet over. *Jesse, Jesse, come on, come on.* But I did not move until their shouts roused Claudio and the girl. We stared at each other across the terrace, and then I broke away from the arms that pulled and ran to the corner into a taxi.

The Countess' windows were aflame with light. All was darkness along the street except that long strip which formed one single blaze of white. When I pushed her bell, she came quickly to the door, opened it slightly, then threw it wide, but there was nothing extraordinary in her face. She said she hoped I had had a good time in Italy and that I should come on Tuesday *comme d'habitude* and to have the whole second movement done.

"Why are all your lights on?"

She shrugged. "It is lonely, you know. So many rooms, all empty. It is terrible when they are dark."

She took me through the apartment, through all the ten rooms—each with a chandelier ashriek, and ourselves mirrored on the windows—which I had never seen. They were all alike, all square and empty, with perfect walls and cupids on the ceiling. When she led me back to the door my head was reeling from the light, and she told me please not to come drunk to her again nor at three in the morning when she is always sick and does not fall to sleep anyway and yes! please (crushing a sheet of paper into my hand) to pay the concierge the gas next time I came. Good night.

VI

If, in the weeks that followed, Claudio had shown some reaction, if he had condescended to suspicion or worry, I know I would have felt an abundance of warmth for him, siding with and nursing his hypocrisy. But he showed nothing: no concern, no fear I might expose him. Consequently I became unpleasant in very subtle ways—perhaps too subtle for he never seemed to notice my nasty smile, my innuendoes, my killing stare. So, where we had touched as human beings we were pushed farther apart; surely he had seen me that night, and his refusal afterwards to acknowledge this made me understand that I was not even a threat, that it was after all my word against his, and that if it ever evolved to a contest the Countess would never doubt whose word was truth.

But I was not interested in contests, nor did I have the time for them, or for anything else. Almost anything else. For there were nights when, overtired, lying under a feather bed of late summer heat, deep deep my bones iced by lonesome days, I would leave my room for a while to sit in silence opposite a friend or to walk along the boulevard de Rochechouart feeling pale, frozen, emasculate among the roar of Arabs and American soldiers and soldiers of the French Union—until a girl would pull me through a dark doorway up to a dim red room. "Nice boy *mais* pale face. Why you *portes* not unyform?" Because I'm a musician. *"Tiens!"* And later: "The love, it is gooder as music, *hein?"* Yes, gooder and cheaper and so much less troublesome. Then out the dim red room, out the dark doorway. "Nice boy. *Vrai* man. Come tomorrow *mais portes* unyform, yes?"

At the end of August I could play the *Appassionata* while Beethoven smiled at me, each of us pleased with the other. Chopin, too, took pleasure in me, but without mercy, as I mastered his first concerto and played four studies so quickly I could not tell when I missed notes. As a reward, or possibly because Claudio did not go with her—five times that month he declined her invitations; "He must work," she said, "if he shall give recital in winter"—the Countess took me once to Père La Chaise and once to Salle Pleyel, the hall from which, after a recital in 1938, she had been carried on the shoulders of a crowd wild with her music.

"It was so cold and I had only on my gown. This way we went." And full of excitement we followed that long-ago midnight crowd to Place des Ternes. "And then—come, Jesse—through Avenue Wagram." And at last to the Arc de Triomphe. "I was sneezing already, and we were by the Arch. All the cars had to stop there were so many people, and all were singing and screaming. I said, come, come to my home all of you. And they came, hundreds of them, and we drank champagne and the rooms were full, full of furniture and full of young people and old people, and I played until the morning. I played on my Blütner, and then for a change I played on my Steinway, and then on my Pleyel, and then on my Gaveau. All night it was Chopin and Liszt—and then in the morning it was Bach. And then all of a sudden I was not there, and no one was there—and I was in bed two months with pneumonia. But did I care? I had so many journals to read, you know. I was everywhere in the paper: Katherine de Charski makes big riots in the Etoile." She sighed. "It is a pity I did not die from the pneumonia—then, when life was lovely to live."

" You don't mean that."

"Yes? I do not mean that?" She spat suddenly on the walk. "What do you know what I mean? You think I should not to have

died then? Only to live so my students can take take take from me
and give me nothing and kill me?"

We turned away from the route of her triumph, going silently
up another avenue where Claudio was to meet us later on.

VII

Autumn trembled across September in a warm tattered veil,
shutting the sun away at first in early morning, then throughout
the morning, then for a string of days. When the mist lowered, the
cold came, an acid insidious cold that cut from the bone outward
so that one's innards felt like broken glass. The air was made of a
smoky rain that neither dropped nor lifted but hung, undulating
slightly, a wall between subject and object, but a wall which after
days became an object in itself, developed its own special and
bewildering personality. It became ultimately something to gaze
at and wonder about, and I was doing just that that morning in
October as I walked up the avenue. There was nothing else to see:
not my legs below me nor the tempo-rubato line of chestnut trees
above, not the houses, nor the Arch.

When I turned from the fog into the Countess' building, the
usually pale walls and pink carpeting dazzled me. I passed the
girl, almost without noticing, on the landing of the second floor,
for she was back against the wall, waiting for me to pass. I did
not recognize her immediately for her face had seemed fuller that
summer night; now it had gone thin, slightly blue, and small; the
eyes bulged dark and watery, their large heavy lids shucking up
and down rapidly. When I paused on the step above and stared at
her, she thumped her hands into the pockets of her coat and
walked to the edge of the landing, about to descend.

"*Je m'excuse, Mademoiselle,*" I began, my voice harsh as a
bark; and it was through this harshness that I realized how much
I hated the girl, how far I would go to avoid any contest with
Claudio and to protect the Countess from his deceit.

She hesitated, then turned, terrified. "*Monsieur?*"

"I remember you."

"I'm sorry, I don't—"

"What are you doing here?"

Instead of answering she gave a small shriek, a sound given from every part of her body, and she started to cry, flying wildly down the steps, her coat blowing out behind her. I ran up to the third floor and pushed the Countess' bell, but she did not come to the door. I continued to push the buzzer, my finger turning red with the pressure, and I heard the steady scream of the bell within. Then suddenly, her voice was behind the door, the words muffled and indistinguishable.

"It's me; Jesse."

"Leave, please."

"Let me in. What's the matter? Is anything wrong?"

"Leave."

"If you don't let me in I'll ring your bell all day."

"Do I care? Please to leave."

"No, I won't."

"I go now."

"No, no, listen to me." I hesitated. "I've seen the girl."

The locks clucked back and the door opened and although she was dressed in kimono and golden pumps, the elastic bandage was not on her head but twined round her arm. Her hair stood straight up on her head like frosted glass.

"I don't know what she told you," I said, pushing my way in and shoving the door closed behind us. "But whatever it was, it isn't true. I know her—"

"Yes?" In the gloom of the corridor, her face was yellow and parched, all flesh drawn like threads to the small puckered lips. "She has told me you saw her once."

"Listen to me, please listen to me. I don't care what she said to you. You mustn't care either. Nothing matters but music. Do you hear? Nothing else matters. You've taught me that. Do you understand? I know that nothing else matters. And you know it. And Claudio knows it. He doesn't care about anyone but you."

"Yes? Get out. Get out of here. I want nothing more from you or none of you. Get out."

"I won't."

"Yes, if not I call police. Go both of you, make babies not music."

"Babies?"

"Yes." She nodded, rounding her arms before her belly. "She is poor child, a student. She says he will not marry her because of me. Did I stop him making love to her?"

"Did he send her here?"

"He does not know. While he was sleeping she was looking in his papers. It was only one address he had. Now you know—get out, and do not never come back. I am alone and I want always to be alone. I have lost everyone: my husband, my sister, my mother, my friend." But now all five fingers went up. "I give him everything, you know. Why do I sell my Blutner? It was for him— all the money. I sell it to Americans and break my heart so he shall have money to live, so he shall not go back to Italy. Does he care? Yes, go all, make babies."

"So what if he makes babies? Bach made twenty-five babies."

"No, twenty-one."

"All right, twen—"

"After he was big artist. I told the girl, go, my child, tell him to marry you, make many babies, but I make no more musicians." Her face was set, and she snapped the elastic bandage on her arm. I went past her, throwing open the door to the salon, and seated myself at the piano, beginning the Chopin concerto. She strode in after me, paused, and said in a voice deep and severe as an angry man's: "Stop to play or I break your fingers." I stopped. "Now, go. I care nothing for you. I would make him great artist; now he is finished. I teach him everything; I tell him all the mysteries of piano. To you, nothing. I could make—"

"Shut up."

"You are an American; you have no culture. You shall never be anything."

"You're disgusting. You don't care about music. You only care about yourself, and your own—"

"Yes? So get out."

"All right. I'm getting out."

"Filthy American. Filthy stupid American," she screamed after me as I ran through the salon, through the corridor, out of the apartment and down the stairs.

In the street, in the fog, I continued running until I slammed into the wet bark of a chestnut tree. Then I paused, my cheek against the tree, my anger run out, and I wondered if I had ever heard the Countess mention Claudio's address. I would go to see him, but what could I possibly say? I knew she gave him several lessons a week, and I knew that one followed mine on Tuesdays, so I went down the avenue to do my waiting in a cinema. I sat through two showings of an Italian comedy and there was much screaming in which my spirit participated and rejoiced; it gave me a headache but I left the theater calm and reasonable. Why, this was only another aspect of the Countess' return to Warsaw or my trip to Venice; by this time the voyages were over, and she was preparing to give Claudio his lesson.

Part of my optimism was perhaps due to the weather, for the mist had begun to draw back, snapping into a light cold rain which sharpened and cleared the air. When I reached the building, Claudio was coming out the door, looking down at his feet, a music folder under his arm. He jumped when I spoke to him.

"Did she let you in?" I asked.

"Wh—no."

"Do you know why?"

"Yes." He looked round the street. "Such a foolish girl. I could kill her." Then he stopped looking round and with some effort brought his eyes to staring at me. "You had your lesson?"

"Yes."

"You are not speaking the truth." But I think at that moment he believed me.

"Would it have been so awful for you if I'd got my lesson and you hadn't got yours?"

"It would have been impossible. I know the Countess. It could not have happened."

"Why?"

"One day we shall talk about many things. But now it is better we shut up and work the piano. She will be better tomorrow."

"You think so?"

"Yes, I think so." His teeth clamped together, his lips fluttering rapidly across the words: "Nothing will stop me."

And then, his back bent slightly under the rain, he went up the street looking thin beneath the chestnut trees which had gone full green into the fog and had come out skeletal, knotted.

I went up to the Countess' flat and pushed her bell for a quarter of an hour and then I went to another film, but this one I neither saw nor heard. Instead I rewatched and relistened to each of the day's incidents, cheating myself into the center of it all, as if I were the core of every conversation. Now and then my mind would thrust me to the outside and I would feel like an enormous wound, intrusive and irrelevant, throbbing, ugly.

It was almost seven o'clock when I went back to the house, but this time, before I reached the stair, I heard the concierge rapping at her glass.

"*Elle est sortie,*" she said, looking troubled.

"*Sortie?* Where did she go?"

She shrugged her fat shoulders and writhed her mouth. "I don't know. She looked terrible. What's the matter?"

"Didn't you talk to her?"

"Only for a minute. She said she must hurry or it would be too late. Too late for what? I don't know. She talked otherwise as always—how she is alone in the world. Poor thing: but we're all alone, aren't we?" She smiled.

"No," I said coldly. "Are you sure she didn't say where she was going?"

"She said nothing. Perhaps some nonsense about Chopin—"

"She said she was going to Chopin?"

"Something like that."

On the dark street again, as I waved for a taxi, I looked back at the building now all lit but for the long black strip on the third floor. A cab pulled up for me and I told the driver to hurry to Père La Chaise, but he went slowly because the streets were filled with evening traffic, and later, when we rode upon the emptier boulevards, the tires whistled and skidded along the wet roads. When we stopped before the cemetery, the gates were bolted, the rain pouring on the walls and on the two swollen *pissotières* which stood, under their moon-shaped lights, before the gates, like pompous sentinels.

I paid, left the cab, and ran along the wall to the end of the street, then into the tunnel and up the stone stairs leading to the watchman's tower. He was an old man in a uniform, and he was reading a newspaper, his legs upon the windowledge, his trousers unbottoned to ease his belly. When I tapped at the glass above the door, he pushed the newspaper several inches to the side of his face and squinted at me. "What is it?"

"Open the door, please."

He shook his head. "Forbidden."

"Look, there's a woman hiding in the cemetery."

He shook his head. "No. The cemetery is closed and everyone is out."

"Let me talk to you a minute. Can't I come in? It's pouring out here."

"Forbidden," he said again. "Come back in the morning."

"Don't you understand? She's hiding in there at Chopin's grave and it's pouring. She'll die there."

"Why not? It's a cemetery." And he went back to his paper, but I pounded on the window until he looked at me again.

"Listen, if you let me in the cemetery I'll give you money."

"How much?"

I looked through my pockets. "Six hundred francs. That's all I've got." He shook his head. "But I'll bring you ten thousand later on. Just let me in now."

He laughed. "Forbidden. Go away or I'll telephone for the police."

The police. "Never mind. I'll go myself. Where's the station?"

His directions were vague and complicated and, in fact, altogether wrong, for the building was just around the corner. The station was one high wide room furnished with a long desk, an empty bicycle rack, and a chicken-wire cage emprisoning a half-dozen prostitutes who screamed about freedom and justice. The two men at the desk laughed all the time I spoke and shouted back at the prostitutes.

"So, for the love of God," I concluded, "get the watchman to let me in."

One of the men picked his nose, and the other said: "Let's see your papers."

"What have my papers got to do with it?"

"Give me your papers!" he roared.

I handed him my passport, and he flipped through it. "It seems to be in order," and he passed it to the other man who took his finger out of his nose and put it on my photograph. "In order," he agreed.

"Now will you come over with me so that I can—"

"Come back in the morning when the office is open upstairs."

"But she's there now. She's a sick woman. You can't—"

"Get out."

"Aren't you human?"

"If you open your mouth again, I'll rip it out of your face. Get out."

So I took a taxi home and had it wait while I slid all the fifteen thousand francs from under the *Mazurkas,* and on the way back to the cemetery I asked the driver to pass the Countess' house. He did, but her flat was still dark, and the concierge said no, she had not returned.

It was after ten o'clock when I climbed once more to the watchman's tower, and now someone else was there: a young nervous man with a sharp nose to whom I offered five, then ten, then all the fifteen thousand francs. He was not to be bribed and said he supposed I had come to steal flowers, and because I continued to plead he pulled a shade over the window and over the door. I pounded a while, then left, and walked round the cemetery and at last stepped into a cafe across the way where a sign hung in the window: *On est mieux ici qu'en face.* Within, the air steamed full of smoke and the smell of coffee, and the tiled floor was aslush with mud and sawdust. Two workers, in blue overalls, played chess in a corner and the bartender sang to himself while he turned glasses upside down for the night. I took a white wine at the bar and was soon talking to the other three men who recognized my accent and wondered how I came to be so far from home. Eventually I told them about the Countess and what had happened.

"Thou are certain she is in there?" asked the bartender.

"Yes."

"Well," said one of the workers, "I would let her stay there if she called *me* a filthy American, I can tell thee."

"She didn't mean it. She was just upset."

"All the same," said the second worker. "How can an American be filthy when they all have baths?"

So we laughed and I ordered wine for all of us, and then the bartender said: "I have a small ladder in back and perhaps thou canst climb over the wall." He hesitated. "Of course it would be trouble if they caught us."

"We can go around behind," one of the workers said, "where the factory is."

The bartender brought the ladder and we crossed the street and walked to the far side of the cemetery where there were no street lights and where the factory shadowed away the wall. The two workers started arguing about the best place to lean the ladder, and soon they were shouting.

"Close your skull," said the bartender. "And watch to see if anyone passes."

Then, where the wall seemed most concealed from the street, we put the ladder up against the flood of ivy. I climbed to the last rung and the three men took my legs and hoisted me

"Canst thou reach?" they whispered.

"No, lift me a bit more."

And they did, one of them going up the ladder behind me, pushing me while the ladder began to slide along the wall, my hands clutching the ivy until it tore. "Straighten the ladder," I begged. "Straighten it. A bit more and I'll reach."

They lifted me higher, but the ivy was thin toward the top and my fingers could not cling to the wall. Finally, shivering and exhausted, I had to come down, and we brought the ladder back to the cafe. I had more wine and talked with the bartender until I realized he would rather close up and go to bed. So I left and walked once more round the wall, past the heap of shredded ivy in the factory shadows, past the watchman's tower—his window now uncloaked, and since I could think of nowhere else to go, I went back to the gates and sank to the walk before them. Thus, I waited, while the rain fell, then stopped, then fell again, while the smell of the *pissotières* clogged the air, while the gaslight haunted the ivy and the street, while I almost forgot why I waited or for whom—remembering only that morning must come and that, even unbribed, the watchman would descend from his tower and swing open the gates

ROBERT MYRON COATES was born in New Haven, Conn., in 1897 and was graduated from Yale in 1919. He is the author of numerous books, among them The Outlaw Years, Yesterday's Burdens, The Bitter Season *and* Wisteria Cottage. *His latest book,* The Farther Shore, *was published in August, 1955, by Harcourt Brace & Co. Mr. Coates is a frequent contributor to* The New Yorker *magazine. He lives with his wife in Chatham, New York.*

IN A FOREIGN CITY

From THE NEW YORKER

It was the craziest, silliest thing in the world to do, and Chuck Cormoran never did quite know why he did it, except, of course, that he'd had about three drinks more than he needed at the time, and in that state he was likely to do anything. He had been at the Princeton Club that evening—not that he liked the damned place particularly, but it was one of the spots around town where he was still in good standing—and his drinking had been done mostly at the bar, with Willy Preston, an old classmate of his, God help them both, Frank Schumacher, and a few others. And then, instead of taking a taxi over to the station, as he should have done (it was that damned economy again), he'd decided to walk; and so he had gone zigzag, down a block or two and across one, more or less at random, angling over from Madison Avenue to the Long Island.

And it was dark, dark, dark, at that hour, in that region; he was on a short block between Sixth Avenue and Broadway, above Thirty-fourth Street—and feeling cheerful, too, because here he was on his way home, in good time for the twelve-thirty-two, which would get him out there, well, not much after one, so there wouldn't be too much trouble on that score; and not drunk, either, or not too drunk—when, then, suddenly, there was this plump little round-bellied fellow scurrying toward him, white-faced and worried-looking as a rabbit. And just as they met, Chuck got this impulse.

He didn't stop to think about the why or wherefore; the situation just seemed to demand it. Pulling both hands up from the hips with the thumbs cocked and the forefingers rigid, he aimed them at the poor bastard. "Stick 'em up, pal," he growled, in his growlingest voice. "It's a holdup."

Actually, the results went beyond his fondest expectations. The guy jumped, and his face jerked up, round and pale as an agitated little moon; he gave a strangled sort of high-pitched yelp, like *eep,* and then—just like a rabbit again—he was off, running madly back down the street toward the corner of Broadway. Chuck stamped his feet on the pavement a few times, making a clatter as if he, too, were running, but of course he didn't take out after him. For one thing, he was laughing too hard for that. He just stood there watching until the little guy reached the corner and rounded it, and then slowly, still laughing, he walked on his way after him.

That, he found out later, was his mistake. He had almost got up to the corner himself when the little guy appeared again, this time with a policeman; it was the sight of the thin little sliver of light on the barrel of the gun in the policeman's hand that gave Chuck his first intimation that he might be in for a major operation. Even then, though, he really wasn't much worried. God sakes, he had outtalked cops before, from his college days onward, and as the pair bore down on him—"There he is! That's him, Officer! There he is!" the little twerp kept yelping—it made the whole thing seem somehow sillier to see that the cop, too, looked nervous.

He was one of those long-faced young Irishmen, Chuck noticed, slow, dumb-witted, and all the more solemn and serious-looking because of it—but from then on, things got to happening a good deal faster than Chuck could handle them. "Hold on, there! Get your hands up!" the cop cried out sharply as Chuch approached. And he meant it, for as Chuck, still maintaining his leisurely attitude, took a step or two forward—"Hold on to what, Officer? What's the matter?" he was about to say—the cop backed up one step and then jerked up the pistol suddenly till it pointed directly at Chuck's belly.

"Get your hands up!" he cried again. "Do you want me to shoot?" And though his voice went up almost panically at the end, there was something in his face, and still more in that round little bullet-charged orifice, aimed relentlessly, that brought Chuck, almost stumbling, to a stop. And—it happened so easily, almost so naturally, that it sort of surprised him—he felt his arms rising over his head. It was a gesture that he'd never in his life had to make before, though in wartime especially he had thought about it, and wondered. Now, he found, the hands went up before his mind even knew they were doing it.

And in an odd sort of way he noticed, too—for whatever his body was doing, his mind remained clear—the fact that he'd put up his hands, on command, seemed to change the whole situation. "Turn around!" the cop barked. He'd gained confidence. "Keep your hands up!" He was on top of things now. He was really in charge, and as Chuck turned—and hated himself for it, even as he turned—he found himself swivelling his head around, trying awkwardly to keep the dumb bastard in focus. "What's up, Officer?" he said. It was sort of the same thing he'd meant to say earlier, but now when he brought it out it sounded different. Weaker, possibly. "What's the matter?"

They gave him no time—that was what was mainly the matter. And if it was bad enough there on the street, it was even worse when they got to the station house. They walked over there, down a few blocks and then over a couple; it was over on Thirtieth Street, and all the way, though by then he'd begun having his slight ups and downs—he was partly sobering—on the whole he couldn't help laughing about it. But the trouble was wisecracks fell flat. Even at the time of the holdup—*his* holdup, he'd started calling it, when he'd had to put up his hands for that dumb cop—there'd been a moment when the cop had been patting his back and his sides and under his armpits, and the twerp had kept yelping, "Get his gun, Officer. He's got a gun, I tell you. I saw it." And Chuck, half giggling—he couldn't help it—had said innocently, "Oh, you mean that gun back there? That was just my Buck Rogers space pistol."

To the cop, though, it wasn't funny. "Yeah? Well, where's it now?" he demanded, and when Chuck said, still blandly, "I disintegrated it," he could, even behind his back, feel the cop stop a moment and stare at him before going on with his eternal patting and prodding.

It made you wonder just how dumb people could get. A little later, but while they were still standing there, in the frosty isolation of the corner street lamp, a police car had come cruising slowly down Broadway, made a U turn, and stopped at the curb, and the two cops in it had piled out and stared at him; and the impact of so many gazes had made Chuck teeter a little, so that he probably looked drunker to them than he really was. It occurred to him then, for one tempting moment, that if he just folded up and collapsed on them it might even be the best way out of the situation. Instead, he pulled himself together and stared right back at them.

"The big, bold, bandit," he said, speaking slowly and ironically. He had reached the point, too, where he hoped they would see the effort it caused him. He was ready, really, to fall on anyone's shoulder. "Take a look at him."

They looked, but they didn't say anything—to Chuck, anyway. And, in fact, from then on the conversation seemed to get parenthetical, as if somehow he had no place in it. They talked among themselves ("Where'd you say . . . ?" "Down the block? And he walked right up to you . . . ?" "Cock-eyed, anyway") and occasionally to the twerp, who now claimed—for laughs, maybe, though nobody laughed—that he had over five hundred and fifty dollars in his pocket that he'd been carrying to his bank for a night deposit. But it was the gun again, mostly, Chuck gathered, that occupied them. Already, to the first cop, the dumb one, Chuck had tried to explain that there wasn't any gun, hadn't been one; it had all been a joke, a gag, a momentary impulse. And now he tried again—but again it got him nowhere.

"Do I look like a holdup man?" he demanded, and they looked at him. And it was discouraging. "I'm a business-man. I'm respectable. Can't you dumb clucks see that?"

"Don't get snotty, or it may be the worse for ya, chum," the older of the two new cops had said, incredibly. ("I only done my juty," Chuck expected him to say next.) "You look just like any other bum to me." Then he turned to the first cop. "Whyn't you take him in, Frank?" he said. "Get it over with. We'll clean up around here."

Chuck had been in police stations before—once or twice when he was in college, and it had only been a matter of calling up old Jack Fierce, the campus cop, to straighten things out; and once, soon after college, in Paris, where the fact that you were American, and presumably wealthy, insured a certain amount of partly ironic consideration—and the station house here had pretty much the same atmosphere as all the others. The same mixture of menace and melancholy, the same tired, heavy atmosphere. The green walls and the yellow lights, the too-solid brown furniture, and wainscoting. And the pinpointed officer in charge, lieutenant or sergeant, sitting solemnly, somnolently, under his lampshade, behind his high desk.

All the way over to the place, Chuck had been remembering the Paris adventure. It had been with Matt Schorrell, Rafe Benziner, and some other guy, and it had all grown out of something that had happened in that big all-night market; they had snitched too many carrots from the big piles of vegetables that were strewn around there, or Matt had fallen right into one of the piles and knocked it over. Or something. Anyway, there had been a row and the cops had been called. Chuck remembered them still, and how they looked—short and apple-cheeked, black-eyed, black-mustached, and all seemingly almost identical in their flat-visored caps and their flung-back capes, with their little short billies, standing grinning at him and the other fellows, and at the wailing vegetable woman, in the station.

Chuck remembered, too, how he, the only one in the crowd who spoke any French at all, had been forced to take charge of things, and how, eventually, he had ended by dominating them. He'd been scared there, for a few moments.

After all, there they were, in a foreign city, unknown, and all tight, to a greater or lesser degree, so that in addition to all the other things he had to think of—such as trying to listen to what the desk sergeant was saying, and outargue the wailing woman, and so on—he had had to keep Schorrell from tangling with a couple of the gendarmes, just for the hell of it. Matt had kept prowling back and forth in front of them, with his fists cocked and a funny grin on his face; and the cops—for all their small size they looked like pretty tough babies, and besides there'd been eight or ten of them, against four—had just stood there, tight and compact, in a group, waiting, grinning still, and watching Matt. "Hey, Chuck! These are just messenger boys, from the Western Union," Matt kept saying to him. "They can't do anything to us. Hey! You! *Savez-vous le* Western Union?" And he pointed at one of the cops and snapped his fingers. "*J'ai le* telegram—*Je—je*—Hey, Chuck! How do you say you want to send a telegram?"

Oh, yes, he'd been scared that time, for a while. But it had ended all right, just the same, and, as it seemed to him now, it had been because he had kept his dignity. He had listened to the cops, or had seemed to; he had listened to the wailing woman. But he had kept his air of injured dignity all the while, and when the moment came—and he had timed it just right, too, by luck or something—and he started talking himself, he had talked right through them all. "*Américain*," he had said. "*Justice, La France*," and anything else he could think of; and in the end he had cut the sergeant down to the point where he (the sergeant) was trying to talk American to *him*, haltingly, slowly, almost apologetically, while the woman, instead of wailing, listened.

It was simply a matter of a few francs' worth of vegetables, the sergeant had told him. They had been destroyed, they had been rendered inedible. The whole thing, understandably, had been simply a prank on the young gentlemen's part. But the woman herself was poor, and the loss to her, obviously, was considerable. And if the gentlemen—

Then Chuck, starting back dramatically . . . "Oh, but never!" he'd cried. A misunderstanding! "*Jamais souffrir, la pauvre femme*," he had said. And then he and Rafe spewing out franc notes (he had been in the chips, then; the old man was still alive), and the woman all smiles, and the cops, too, and everyone shaking hands (except Matt, who'd still wanted to take a poke at somebody), and the four of them exiting. It had all ended happily.

Matt, he thought; the last time he had heard of Matt was in the twenty-year yearbook, where it said he was general manager for some plywood factory out in Minnesota. And Rafe Benziner, he had vanished completely.

And, of course, one thing now was that Chuck didn't have the dough that he'd had in those days. Just the same, though, when they got to the police station he walked up to the desk sergeant stalwartly. "Listen, Sergeant, or Lieutenant, or whatever you are. I want to get this matter straightened out, and fast. This man here"—and Chuck pointed to the little twerp—"has been accusing me of the most fantastic things," and then so on and so on, being very much the righteously indignant, substantial citizen.

This time, though, it got him nowhere. The sergeant, in fact, hardly looked up. "Name?" he said, and then the address, the occupation. "Account executive, advertising," Chuck told him crisply, stretching the truth a little, or at least postdating it, for it was over eight months now since he had had a steady job. Sure enough, the bastards soon found that out, too, for when they asked him his employer's name and address all he could say was "At present, I'm free-lancing," and when he tried to reel off a list of firms he had worked for the words fell on stony ground, or whatever the phrase was. The sergeant merely transferred his attention to the young cop, and began asking the charge, and so on; and at that—and with the little twerp twittering away as usual—it seemed best for him to stand back and wait, smiling superciliously.

He was waiting, of course, for the proper, dramatic moment to break in and take over. But he waited too long; he was off on his timing, or something, because all of a sudden, apparently, and with no sense of transition, they were preparing to put him away. "Well, Mister, into the cooler," the cop said. He took Chuck by the arm, and at that the enormity of what was happening began to penetrate.

Chuck yanked back and braced himself. "No . . . but . . . look here!" he cried, and he found that for once he was having a hard time keeping the right ring of confidence in his voice. "Damn it all, man, you just can't *do* this!"

"No?"

"No!" And then, feeling the cop's pull still strong on his arm, Chuck found himself temporizing. "For one thing, how'll my wife know? How'll anyone know? I've got to notify people!"

This time, anyway, the sergeant paid some attention. He was taking down the little twerp's statement—if that was the word—by now, but he glanced up quickly at the disturbance.

"You can make one call," he said, and since they'd already confiscated Chuck's belongings, he pushed a dime at him over the desk top. "There's the phone over there."

And then (and maybe, he thought afterward, it had been the very rage and disillusionment of the phone calls that had caused it), incredibly he was out in the night-dark street, and running; and in that strange way that unknown capabilities—instincts, almost—will arise within a man to help him cope with unknown situations, he knew, after a dash around a corner, a skip through traffic to the opposite sidewalk, a breathless slowing, and then a quick turn down another street: he knew, without even looking back, that pursuit had ended.

He was in the clear, and as he slowed at last it occurred to him that maybe he always had been. Maybe he had impressed them, after all, with his manner, and more than he'd known; or it might have been the call to Frank, especially—when he'd made sure to bring out the club name loud and clear, so the cops could hear it— that had convinced them at last that they'd bitten off more than they could chew; and the business in the corridor afterward had been merely their roundabout way of just letting him go, if he wanted to take advantage of the opportunity.

It was all, still, confusing, and he was in no shape now, at the moment, to think about it clearly. He was walking down a dank, blank street, mostly warehouses—walking not too fast, not too slow, and he could feel his confidence rising; in a few minutes, he was sure, he'd be able to laugh about the whole matter. And yet, when a car turned in from the avenue, its lights, searchlight-like, swinging over and past him, he could feel himself almost physically shrinking, and he had to fight hard not to just cut loose and start running again. But the car went by.

No, he wasn't steady in his mind yet, by any means, and in a way the telephoning had been the most confusing thing of all. For he had made his call—two calls, really, though there had been a hassle about that—and the one to Alice, as he'd half known it would be, had been the worst. He'd called Schumacher first—after all, Frank was a lawyer—and when he got the club, and then got Frank, it was somehow comforting to hear, till Frank closed the booth door over there, the faint hint of the club sounds, the talking, the laughing, behind Frank's voice itself. Poor fool that he'd been! In two minutes, he'd learned the worst.

"Listen, Frank, can you help me?" he had started in. "Here's the damnedest thing. I'm in jail."

"In jail!" Frank exclaimed, and somehow the way he said it made Chuck think again of the humor of the situation. That was his mistake.

"That's right. Robbery," he said.

"Robbery!" Good old Frank; he was still trying to catch up.

"Armed robbery. A holdup. I'm supposed to have held up a guy."

"A holdup!" cried Frank, and it was then that the bottom fell out of things for Chuck. "My God, Chuck!" Frank was saying. "My God, man, why didn't you tell me?" And it was so obvious that he really believed it that it stopped Chuck dead for a second; for a second, all he could do was to stare at the telephone dial in front of him in simple astonishment. He went on with it, though; in the mood he was in now, explanations could wait.

"Tell you what?"

"Well, that—well, I mean, what can I do? Can I help you?"

"By God, I'll say you can. If you can get over here, get me out of this . . ." He broke off for a moment. They had made him leave the booth door open, and the cop had posted himself just outside it. "Where are we, anyway?" he said over his shoulder to the cop.

And then so on and so on. For it turned out that in the time it had taken Chuck to turn to the cop, get the station address, and give it to Frank, good old Frank had been thinking; from then on, caution flowed over the wire like a wave. No, he couldn't get over there now, he said, and even if he could it would do no good. If Chuck had been booked—and he had, hadn't he, someone had made a complaint?—then he'd have to be held for arraignment. And that, undoubtedly, would be next morning.

And he, Frank, Chuck's old pal, would be there then, certainly, to see what he could do. And then so on and so on, mealymouth, mealymouth; it was the lawyer speaking now, not the friend. "And I guess I need hardly say, boy . . . Well, I can't tell you, fellah; all I can say is I hope it's a big mistake . . ." Chuck sat fuming, listening, wondering if the cop could be listening too.

As he knew now he'd known it would be, the call to Alice was worse. The cops made trouble about that; seemed the law said you only had one call coming to you, or some such. ("Who's the law?" Chuck demanded, at his patience's end now, and the sergeant said wearily, "I am.") But in the end they got generous or something, and they gave him a quarter, *his* quarter, to put the call through to Great Neck.

It was tears from the start, and Chuck, already fuming from the call to Schumacher, was in no condition to stand it. "Oh, God, Chuck! Chuck! What have you done now?" was the way it started; and though to give her her due she tried to pull herself together later—"But what shall I do, Chuck? Shall I come in there now?" she asked once. "Only what'll I do about Chickie? Shall I try to get Mother to come over?"—there was something disheartening about the whole business. The truth was that he didn't know *what* he wanted her to do, except not what she *was* doing, and the trouble was that this time, with her wailing, Chuck was sure that the cop, standing there, heard her too. Anyway, when he hung up at last, the cop was grinning. "Seems to me like you're learning things the hard way, Brother," he said, as he reached out to lead Chuck away.

And maybe it was sympathy, maybe it was inexperience; maybe it was simply that they'd realized they just didn't have any ordinary sneak thief to contend with—anyway, in the corridor, his moment came. It was a little tile-floored, oak-walled passageway, with a barred gate at one end and a door open onto the street at the other, and with that choice before him Chuck didn't hesitate. The cop was careless. He wasn't holding Chuck now, he was simply herding him, and when Chuck swung it certainly staggered him. In five seconds, three maybe, Chuck was out the door, and away.

He was away still, now, and getting farther away, too, and fast.

He had gone a block after turning the corner, and then turned again—west, he thought—and gone another block and then—south?—a block more. When he came to the next corner, he turned again—west again, if it really was west—and kept walking. Slowly now, he wasn't hurrying, and this time when a car's lights swung in from the avenue he didn't bother at all. He was sure now, right now, that they had passed him up, really.

He'd had luck, of course, at the outset, with the two big trailer trucks for him to dodge behind, and, on the sidewalk beyond, no pedestrians, so he could run like hell, unseen, to the next corner turning. But then, he thought, cops had some sense, too, and even in New York they must have a little realization of the pranks and gags that college men were up to; maybe, even if Schumacher, the bastard, had failed him, the mere fact that he'd called him at the club might have helped a little. And, God knew, the address in Great Neck was a good one. Cops kept up on such matters—and fortunately they couldn't be expected to know about mortgages.

Oh, he was all right all right, and the only thing to do was to be more sensible in the future. Meantime, he couldn't help grinning at the thought of Frank turning up at some court next morning, ready with bail, maybe, and a lecture, and being told that no Chuck Cormoran was there—being told, maybe, if the cops were really smart, that he had never been arrested, and the telephone call was probably just some ill-timed joke on his part. Cops had a way of covering up for each other like that; they were famous for it.

He was on Tenth Avenue now, as he learned from a street sign, and walking toward a heavy, dark railway overpass that said, oddly enough, "New York Central." Freight cars lay in long parallel rows underneath and beside it, and beyond it tall, gaunt buildings rose sparsely, with here and there a whole floor lighted bluely, and probably racketing with machinery, while the rest was dark. Across the street, at the sidewalk level of a square, squat concrete building, obviously a warehouse, rows of trucks were loading at their ramps, and in the recesses within he could make out figures moving. It was a part of the city he had never been in before, and the whole look and feel of the region was strange to him; it was like being in a foreign city, but beyond the warehouse a corner gas station showed the Amoco sign over its pumps. Across from it was a bar, and when he saw that he headed for it. He could use a drink, at this moment, God knew he could use one, and he was almost at the entrance before he remembered that he had no money at all.

They had his money back there at the station house. They had his billfold, his commutation ticket, his name and address—and small wonder they hadn't bothered to chase him much; they knew everything they needed to know about him to begin with. More than that— But now, for the space of a minute or so, he held himself off from thinking.

Wire fencing bordered the sidewalk where it ran past the railroad siding, and when he came to that, he leaned against one of its posts and stood looking blankly back along the way he had come. It had come over him suddenly, fully, that nobody had believed him at all. Frank hadn't; he had realized that almost from the start, though he had taken it only as a sign of Frank's caution. And once, toward the end of their talk, Chuck had cried out to him, "You don't think I really did it, do you, damn it?" And Frank had said, in that pursy little way of his, "I don't know what to think, Chuck. But whatever the truth is, I'll do what I can to help you." But he couldn't ask Alice that, too—not before the damned grinning cop—and it occurred to him now that he hadn't had to. It had not been what she said so much as her manner, and it made him wonder: What in God's name did people think he had come to, anyway?

Now, it struck him suddenly, he didn't have to ask that, either. The answer was all too clear, and after a few moments, as if the post he was leaning against were somehow ill-omened, he shoved himself away from it and moved on to lean against another one. Off a little to his left, above the buildings, he could see the pink glow in the sky that meant Times Square and the center of the city. He knew where he was, in relation to it.

But where he was going was another matter. He could bull his way home on the train without a ticket, easily enough. He had done it before; all you did was sign a slip with your name and address, and promise to pay. But for all he knew the trainmen had been alerted, or cops had been posted at Long Island Station, and even if they hadn't they could pick him up at the house, as soon as he got there.

No, he couldn't go home, that was obvious. And he couldn't go to a hotel, for he had no money, not to mention the fact that he'd have to sign the register. He could give a false name, of course—if he had the money. It was always that question of money, and he realized now that he wasn't thinking very clearly, either. He was getting a little weavy and wavy, from the drinking and then the not drinking; he knew, too, that waiting somewhere deep in his mind was the realization that he'd acted like a dope from the start, and if he *had* collapsed on the sidewalk back there, at the time they'd arrested him, or if he'd just let them put him in jail and waited till morning . . . But he pushed that thought away, as he pushed himself away from the fence again. Something would occur to him, later. Something always had, and, God knew, whatever they thought of him, they couldn't *all* let him down. But, meantime, he had a long, hard night ahead of him, with nothing but trouble at the end of it. For the first time, as he started walking, he found himself wishing that he *had* had a gun, a real one. If he had, or if he had one now, there might be a real holdup, somewhere that night.

WILLIAM FAULKNER was born in New Albany, Mississippi, in 1897. He attended school only desultorily after the fifth grade and took some special courses at the University of Mississippi. He became a lieutenant in the R.A.F. during World War I, after which he returned and set himself to various jobs. The publication of Soldier's Pay *and* Mosquitoes *did not bring him either financial rewards or literary acclaim; these were to come later with the publication of* The Sound and the Fury *and* As I Lay Dying *and later,* Sanctuary. *His story, "Barn Burning," won first prize in the 1939 O. Henry Memorial Awards. He was awarded the Nobel Prize for Literature in 1949 and his latest novel,* A Fable, *won both the National Book Award and the Pulitzer Prize for 1955.*

RACE AT MORNING

From THE SATURDAY EVENING POST

I was in the boat when I seen him. It was jest dusk-dark; I had jest fed the horses and clumb back down the bank to the boat and shoved off to cross back to camp when I seen him, about half a quarter up the river, swimming; jest his head above the water, and it no more than a dot in that light. But I could see that rocking chair he toted on it and I knowed it was him, going right back to that canebrake in the fork of the bayou where he lived all year until the day before the season opened, like the game wardens had give him a calendar, when he would clear out and disappear, nobody knowed where, until the day after the season closed. But here he was, coming back a day ahead of time, like maybe he had got mixed up and was using last year's calendar by mistake. Which was jest too bad for him, because me and

Mister Ernest would be setting on the horse right over him when the sun rose tomorrow morning.

So I told Mister Ernest and we et supper and fed the dogs, and then I help Mister Ernest in the poker game, standing behind his chair until about ten o'clock, when Roth Edmonds said, "Why don't you go to bed, boy?"

"Or if you're going to set up," Willy Legate said, "why don't you take a spelling book to set up over? . . . He knows every cuss word in the dictionary, every poker hand in the deck and every whiskey label in the distillery, but he can't even write his name . . . Can you?" he says to me.

"I don't need to write my name down," I said. "I can remember in my mind who I am."

"You're twelve years old," Walter Ewell said. "Man to man, now, how many days in your life did you ever spend in school?"

"He ain't got time to go to school," Willy Legate said. "What's the use in going to school from September to middle of November, when he'll have to quit then to come in here and do Ernest's hearing for him? And what's the use in going back to school in January, when in jest eleven months it will be November fifteenth again and he'll have to start all over telling Ernest which way the dogs went?"

"Well, stop looking into my hand, anyway," Roth Edmonds said.

"What's that? What's that?" Mister Ernest said. He wore his listening button in his ear all the time, but he never brought the battery to camp with him because the cord would bound to get snagged ever time we run through a thicket.

"Willy says for me to go to bed!" I hollered.

"Don't you never call nobody 'mister'?" Willy said.

"I call Mister Ernest 'mister'," I said.

"All right," Mister Ernest said. "Go to bed then. I don't need you."

"That ain't no lie," Willy said. "Deaf or no deaf, he can hear a fifty-dollar raise if you don't even move your lips."

So I went to bed, and after a while Mister Ernest come in and I wanted to tell him again how big them horns looked even half a quarter away in the river. Only I would 'a' had to holler, and the only time Mister Ernest agreed he couldn't hear was when we would be setting on Dan, waiting for me to point which way the dogs was going. So we jest laid down, and it wasn't no time Simon was beating the bottom of the dishpan with the spoon, hollering, "Raise up and get your four-o'clock coffee!" and I crossed the river in the dark this time, with the lantern, and fed Dan and Roth Edmondziz horse. It was going to be a fine day, cold and bright; even in the dark I could see the white frost on the leaves and bushes—jest exactly the kind of day that big old son of a gun laying up there in that brake would like to run.

Then we et, and set the stand-holder across for Uncle Ike McCaslin to put them on the stands where he thought they ought to be, because he was the oldest one in camp. He had been hunting deer in these woods for about a hundred years, I reckon, and if anybody would know where a buck would pass, it would be him. Maybe with a big old buck like this one, that had been running the woods for what would amount to a hundred years in a deer's life, too, him and Uncle Ike would sholy manage to be at the same place at the same time this morning—provided, of course, he managed to git away from me and Mister Ernest on the jump. Because me and Mister Ernest was going to git him.

Then me and Mister Ernest and Roth Edmonds set the dogs over, with Simon holding Eagle and the other old dogs on leash because the young ones, the puppies, wasn't going nowhere until Eagle let them, nohow. Then me and Mister Ernest and Roth saddled up, and Mister Ernest got up and I handed him up his pump gun and let Dan's bridle go for him to git rid of the spell of bucking he had to git shut of ever morning until Mister Ernest hit him between the ears with the gun barrel. Then Mister Ernest loaded the gun and give me the stirrup, and I got up behind him and we taken the fire road up toward the bayou, the five big dogs dragging Simon along in front with his single-barrel britchloader slung on a piece of plow line across his back, and the puppies moiling along in ever'body's way. It was light now and it was going to be jest fine; the east already yellow for the sun and our breaths smoking in the cold still bright air until the sun would come up and warm it, and a little skim of ice in the ruts, and ever leaf and twig and switch and even the frozen clods frosted over, waiting to sparkle like a rainbow when the sun finally come up and hit them. Until all my insides felt light and strong as a balloon, full of that light cold strong air, so that it seemed to me like I couldn't even feel the horse's back I was straddle of—jest the hot strong muscles moving under the hot strong skin, setting up there without no weight atall, so that when old Eagle struck and jumped, me and Dan and Mister Ernest would go jest like a bird, not even touching the ground. It was jest fine. When that big old buck got killed today, I knowed that even if he had put it off another ten years, he couldn't 'a' picked a better one.

And sho enough, as soon as we come to the bayou we seen his foot in the mud where he had come up out of the river last night, spread in the soft mud like a cow's foot, big as a cow's, big as a mule's, with Eagle and the other dogs laying into the leash rope now until Mister Ernest told me to jump down and help Simon hold them. Because me and Mister Ernest knowed exactly where he would be—a little canebrake island in the middle of the bayou, where he could lay up until whatever doe or little deer the dogs had happened to jump could go up or down the bayou in either direction and take the dogs on away, so he could steal out and creep back down the bayou to the river and swim it, and leave the country like he always done the day the season opened.

Which is jest what we never aimed for him to do this time. So we left Roth on his horse to cut him off and turn him over Uncle Ike's standers if he tried to slip back down the bayou, and me and Simon, with the leashed dogs, walked on up the bayou until Mister Ernest on the horse said it was fur enough; then turned up into the woods about half a quarter above the brake because the wind was going to be south this morning when it riz, and turned down toward the brake, and Mister Ernest give the word to cast them, and we slipped the leash and Mister Ernest give me the stirrup again and I got up.

Old Eagle had done already took off because he knowed where that old son of a gun would be laying as good as we did, not making no racket atall yet, but jest boring on through the buck vines with the other dogs trailing along behind him, and even Dan seemed to know about that buck, too, beginning to souple up and jump a little through the vines, so that I taken my holt on Mister Ernest's belt already before the time had come for Mister Ernest to touch him. Because when we got strung out, going fast behind a deer, I wasn't on Dan's back much of the time nohow, but mostly jest strung out from my holt on Mister Ernest's belt, so that Willy Legate said that when we was going through the wood fast, it looked like Mister Ernest had a boy-size pair of empty overhalls blowing out of his hind pocket.

So it wasn't even a strike, it was a jump. Eagle must 'a' walked right up behind him or maybe even stepped on him while he was laying there still thinking it was day after tomorrow. Eagle jest throwed his head back and up and said, "There he goes," and we even heard the buck crashing through the first of the cane. Then all the other dogs was hollering behind him, and Dan give a squat to jump, but it was against the curb this time, not jest the snaffle, and Mister Ernest let him down into the bayou and swung him around the brake and up the other bank. Only he never had to say, "Which way?" because I was already pointing past his shoulder, freshening my holt on the belt jest as Mister Ernest touched Dan with that big old rusty spur on his nigh heel, because when Dan felt it he would go off jest like a stick of dynamite, straight through whatever he could bust and over or under what he couldn't.

The dogs was already almost out of hearing. Eagle must 'a' been looking right up that big son of a gun's tail until he finally decided he better git on out of there. And now they must 'a' been getting pretty close to Uncle Ike's standers, and Mister Ernest reined Dan back and held him, squatting and bouncing and trembling like a mule having his tail roached, while we listened for the shots. But never none come, and I hollered to Mister Ernest we better go on while I could still hear the dogs, and he let Dan off, but still there wasn't no shots, and now we knowed the race had done already passed the standers; and we busted out of a thicket, and sho enough there was Uncle Ike and Willy standing beside his foot in a soft patch.

"He got through us all," Uncle Ike said. "I don't know how he done it. I just had a glimpse of him. He looked big as a elephant, with a rack on his head you could cradle a yellin' calf in. He went right on down the ridge. You better get on, too; that Hog Bayou camp might not miss him."

So I freshened my holt and Mister Ernest touched Dan again. The ridge run due south; it was clear of vines and bushes so we could go fast, into the wind, too, because it had riz now, and now the sun was up too. So we would hear the dogs again any time now as the wind get up; we could make time now, but still holding Dan to a canter, because it was either going to be quick, when he got down to the standers from that Hog Bayou camp eight miles below ourn, or a long time, in case he got by them too. And sho enough, after a while we heard the dogs; we was walking Dan now to let him blow a while, and we heard them, the sound coming faint up the wind, not running now, but trailing because the big son of a gun had decided a good piece back, probably, to put an end to this foolishness, and picked hisself up and soupled out and put about a mile between hisself and the dogs— until he run up on them other standers from that camp below. I could almost see him stopped behind a bush, peeping out and saying, "What's this? What's this? Is this whole durn country full of folks this morning?" Then looking back over his shoulder at where old Eagle and the others was hollering along after him while he decided how much time he had to decide what to do next.

Except he almost shaved it too fine. We heard the shots; it sounded like a war. Old Eagle must 'a' been looking right up his tail again and he had to bust on through the best way he could. "Pow, pow, pow, pow" and then "Pow, pow, pow, pow," like it must 'a' been three or four ganged right up on him before he had time even to swerve, and me hollering, "No! No! No! No!" because he was ourn. It was our beans and oats he et and our brake he laid in; we had been watching him ever year, and it was like we had raised him, to be killed at last on our jump, in front of our dogs, by some strangers that would probably try to beat the dogs off and drag him away before we could even git a piece of the meat.

"Shut up and listen," Mister Ernest said. So I done it and we could hear the dogs; not just the others, but Eagle, too, not trailing no scent now and not baying no downed meat, neither, but running hot on sight long after the shooting was over. I jest had time to freshen my holt. Yes, sir, they was running on sight. Like Willy Legate would say, if Eagle jest had a drink of whisky he would ketch that deer; going on, done already gone when we broke out of the thicket and seen the fellers that had done the shooting, five or six of them, squatting and crawling around, looking at the ground and the bushes, like maybe if they looked hard enough, spots of blood would bloom out on the stalks and leaves like frogstools or hawberries.

"Have any luck, boys?" Mister Ernest said.

"I think I hit him," one of them said. "I know I did. We're hunting blood, now."

"Well, when you have found him, blow your horn and I'll come back and tote him in to camp for you," Mister Ernest said.

So we went on, going fast now because the race was almost out of hearing again, going fast, too, like not jest the buck, but the dogs, too, had took a new leash on life from all the excitement and shooting.

We was in strange country now because we never had to run this fur before, we had always killed before now; now we had come to Hog Bayou that runs into the river a good fifteen miles below our camp. It had water in it, not to mention a mess of down trees and logs and such, and Mister Ernest checked Dan again, saying, "Which way?" I could just barely hear them, off to the east a little, like the old son of a gun had give up the idea Vicksburg or New Orleans, like he first seemed to have, and had decided to have a look at Alabama; so I pointed and we turned up the bayou hunting for a crossing, and maybe we could 'a' found one, except that I reckon Mister Ernest decided we never had time to wait.

We come to a place where the bayou had narrowed down to about twelve or fifteen feet, and Mister Ernest said, "Look out, I'm going to touch him," and done it.

I didn't even have time to freshen my holt when we was already in the air, and then I seen the vine—it was a loop of grapevine nigh as big as my wrist, looping down right across the middle of the bayou—and I thought he seen it, too, and was jest waiting to grab it and fling it up over our heads to go under it, and I know

Dan seen it because he even ducked his head to jump under it. But Mister Ernest never seen it atall until it skun back along Dan's neck and hooked under the head of the saddle horn, us flying on through the air, the loop of the vine gitting tighter and tighter until something somewhere was going to have to give. It was the saddle girth. It broke, and Dan going on and scrabbling up the other bank bare nekkid except for the bridle, and me and Mister Ernest and the saddle, Mister Ernest still setting in the saddle holding the gun, and me still holding onto Mister Ernest's belt, hanging in the air over the bayou in the tightened loop of that vine like in the drawed-back loop of a big rubber-banded slingshot, until it snapped back and shot us back across the bayou and flang us clear, me still holding onto Mister Ernest's belt and on the bottom now, so that when we lit I would 'a' had Mister Ernest and the saddle both on top of me if I hadn't clumb fast around the saddle and up Mister Ernest's side, so that when we landed, it was the saddle first, then Mister Ernest, and me on top, until I jumped up, and Mister Ernest still laying there with jest the white rim of his eyes showing.

"Mister Ernest!" I hollered, and then clumb down to the bayou and scopped my cap full of water and clumb back and throwed it in his face, and he opened his eyes and laid there on the saddle cussing me.

"God dawg it," he said, "why didn't you stay behind where you started out?"

"You was the biggest!" I said. "You would 'a' mashed me flat!"

"What do you think you done to me?" Mister Ernest said. "Next time, if you can't stay where you start out, jump clear. Don't climb up on top of me no more. You hear?"

"Yes, sir," I said.

So he got up then, still cussing and holding his back, and clumb down to the water and dipped some in his hand onto his face and neck and dipped some more up and drunk it, and I drunk some, too, and clumb back and got the saddle and the gun, and we crossed the bayou on the down logs. If we could jest ketch Dan; not that he would have went them fifteen miles back to camp, because, if anything, he would have went on by hisself to try to help Eagle ketch that buck. But he was about fifty yards away, eating buck vines, so I brought him back, and we taken Mister Ernest's galluses and my belt and the whang leather loop off Mister Ernest's horn and tied the saddle back on Dan. It didn't look like much, but maybe it would hold.

"Provided you don't let me jump him through no more grapevines without hollering first," Mister Ernest said.

"Yes, sir," I said. "I'll holler first next time—provided you'll holler a little quicker when you touch him next time too." But it was all right; we jest had to be a little easy getting up. "Now which-a-way?" I said. Because we couldn't hear nothing now, after wasting all this time. And this was new country, sho enough. It had been cut over and growed up in thickets we couldn't 'a' seen over even standing up on Dan.

But Mister Ernest never even answered. He jest turned Dan along the bank of the bayou where it was a little more open, and we could move faster again, soon as Dan and us got used to that homemade cinch strop and got a little confidence in it. Which jest happened to be east, or so I thought then, because I never paid no particular attention to east then because the sun—I don't know where the morning had went, but it was gone, the morning and the frost, too—was up high now.

And then we heard him. No, that's wrong; what we heard was shots. And that was when we realized how fur we had come, because the only camp we knowed about in that direction was the Hollyknowe camp, and Hollyknowe was exactly twenty-eight miles from Van Dorn, where me and Mister Ernest lived—just the shots, no dogs nor nothing. If old Eagle was still behind him and the buck was still alive, he was too wore out now to even say, "Here he comes."

"Don't touch him!" I hollered. But Mister Ernest remembered that cinch strop, too, and he jest let Dan off the snaffle. And Dan heard them shots, too, picking his way through the thickets, hopping the vines and logs when he could and going under them when he couldn't. And sho enough, it was jest like before—two or three men squatting and creeping among the bushes, looking for blood that Eagle had done already told them wasn't there. But we never stopped this time, jest trotting on by. Then Mister Ernest swung Dan until we was going due north.

"Wait!" I hollered. "Not this way."

But Mister Ernest jest turned his face back over his shoulder. It looked tired, too, and there was a smear of mud on it where that 'ere grapevine had snatched him off the horse.

"Don't you know where he's heading?" he said. "He's done done his part, give everybody a fair open shot at him, and now he's going home, back to that brake in our bayou. He ought to make it exactly at dark."

And that's what he was doing. We went on. It didn't matter to hurry now. There wasn't no sound nowhere; it was that time in the early afternoon in November when don't nothing move or cry, not even birds, the peckerwoods and yellowhammers and jays, and it seemed to me like I could see all three of us—me and Mister Ernest and Dan—and Eagle, and the other dogs, and that big old buck, moving through the quiet woods in the same direction, headed for the same place, not running now but walking, that had all run the fine race the best we knowed how, and all three of us now turned like on a agreement to walk back home, not together in a bunch because we didn't want to worry or tempt one another, because what we had all three spent this morning doing was no play-acting jest for fun, but was serious, and all three of us was still what we was—that old buck that had to run, not because he was skeered, but because running was what he done the best and was proudest at; and Eagle and the dogs that chased him, not because they hated or feared him, but because that was the thing they done the best and was proudest at; and me and Mister Ernest and Dan, that run him not because we wanted his meat, which would be too tough to eat anyhow, or his head to hang on a wall, but because now we could go back and work hard for eleven months making a crop, so we would have the right to come back here next November—all three of us going back home now, peaceful and separate, until next year, next time.

Then we seen him for the first time. We was out of the cut-over now; we could even 'a' cantered, except that all three of us was long past that. So we was walking, too, when we come on the dogs—the puppies and one of the old ones—played out, laying in a little wet swag, panting, jest looking up at us when we passed. Then we come to a long open glade, and we seen the three other old dogs and about a hundred yards ahead of them Eagle, all walking, not making no sound; and then suddenly, at the fur end of the glade, the buck hisself getting up from where he had been resting for the dogs to come up, getting up without no hurry, big, big as a mule, tall as a mule, and turned, and the white underside of his tail for a second or two more before the thicket taken him.

It might 'a' been a signal, a good-by, a farewell. Still walking, we passed the other three old dogs in the middle of the glade, laying down, too; and still that hundred yards ahead of them, Eagle, too, not laying down, because he was still on his feet, but his legs was spraddled and his head was down; maybe jest waiting until we was out of sight of his shame, his eyes saying plain as talk when we passed, "I'm sorry, boys, but this here is all."

Mister Ernest stopped Dan. "Jump down and look at his feet," he said.

"Nothing wrong with his feet," I said. "It's his wind has done give out."

"Jump down and look at his feet," Mister Ernest said.

So I done it, and while I was stooping over Eagle I could hear the pump gun go, "Snick-cluck. Snick-cluck. Snick-cluck" three times, except that I never thought nothing then. Maybe he was jest running the shells through to be sho it would work when we seen him again or maybe to make sho they was all buckshot. Then I got up again, and we went on, still walking; a little west of north now, because when we seen his white flag that second or two before the thicket hid it, it was on a beeline for that notch in the bayou. And it was evening, too, now. The wind had done dropped and there was a edge to the air and the sun jest touched the tops of the trees. And he was taking the easiest way, too, now, going straight as he could. When we seen his foot in the soft places he was running for a while at first after his rest. But soon he was walking, too, like he knowed, too, where Eagle and the dogs was.

And then we seen him again. It was the last time—a thicket, with the sun coming through a hole onto it like a searchlight. He crashed jest once; then he was standing there broadside to us, not twenty yards away, big as a statue and red as gold in the sun, and the sun sparking on the tips of his horns—they was twelve of them—so that he looked like he had twelve lighted candles branched around his head, standing there looking at us while Mister Ernest raised the gun and aimed at his neck, and the gun went, "Click. Snick-cluck. Click. Snick-cluck. Click. Snick-cluck" three times, and Mister Ernest still holding the gun aimed while the buck turned and give one long bound, the white underside of his tail like a blaze of fire, too, until the thicket and the shadows put it out; and Mister Ernest laid the gun slow and gentle back across the saddle in front of him, saying quiet and peaceful, and not much louder than jest breathing, "God dawg. God dawg."

Then he jogged me with his elbow and we got down, easy and careful because of that ere cinch strop, and he reached into his vest and taken out one of the cigars. It was busted where I had fell on it, I reckon, when we hit the ground. He throwed it away and taken out the other one. It was busted, too, so he bit off a hunk of it to chew and throwed the rest away. And now the sun was gone even from the tops of the trees and there wasn't nothing left but a big red glare in the west.

"Don't worry," I said. "I ain't going to tell them you forgot to load your gun. For that matter, they don't need to know we ever seed him."

"Much oblige," Mister Ernest said. There wasn't going to be no moon tonight neither, so he taken the compass off the whang leather loop in his buttonhole and handed me the gun and set the compass on a stump and stepped back and looked at it. "Jest about the way we're headed now," he said, and taken the gun from me and opened it and put one shell in the britch and taken up the compass, and I taken Dan's reins and we started, with him in front with the compass in his hand.

And after a while it was full dark; Mister Ernest would have to strike a match ever now and then to read the compass, until the stars come out good and we could pick out one to follow, because I said, "How fur do you reckon it is?" and he said, "A little more than one box of matches." So we used a star when we could, only we couldn't see it all the time because the woods was too dense and we would git a little off until he would have to spend another match. And now it was good and late, and he stopped and said, "Get on the horse."

"I ain't tired," I said.

"Get on the horse," he said. "We don't want to spoil him."

Because he had been a good feller ever since I had knowed him, which was even before that day two years ago when maw went off with the Vicksburg roadhouse feller and the next day pap didn't come home neither, and on the third one Mister Ernest rid Dan up to the door of the cabin on the river he let us live in, so pap could work his piece of land and run his fish line, too, and said, "Put that gun down and come on here and climb up behind."

So I got in the saddle even if I couldn't reach the stirrups, and Mister Ernest taken the reins and I must 'a' went to sleep, because the next thing I knowed a buttonhole of my lumberjack was tied to the saddle horn with that ere whang cord off the compass, and it was good and late now and we wasn't fur, because Dan was already smelling water, the river. Or maybe it was the feed lot itself he smelled, because we struck the fire road not a quarter below it, and soon I could see the river, too, with the white mist laying on it soft and still as cotton. Then the lot, home; and up yonder in the dark, not no piece akchully, close enough to hear us unsaddling and shucking corn prob'ly, and sholy close enough to hear Mister Ernest blowing his horn at the dark camp for Simon to come in the boat and git us, that old buck in his brake in the bayou; home, too, resting, too, after the hard run, waking hisself now and then, dreaming of dogs behind him or maybe it was the racket we was making would wake him.

Then Mister Ernest stood on the bank blowing until Simon's lantern went bobbing down into the mist; then we clumb down to the landing and Mister Ernest blowed again now and then to guide Simon, until we seen the lantern in the mist, and then Simon and the boat; only it looked like ever time I set down and got still, I went back to sleep, because Mister Ernest was shaking me again to git out and climb the bank into the dark camp, until I felt a bed against my knees and tumbled into it.

Then it was morning, tomorrow; it was all over now until next November, next year, and we could come back. Uncle Ike and Willy and Walter and Roth and the rest of them had come in yestiddy, soon as Eagle taken the buck out of hearing, and they knowed that deer was gone, to pack up and be ready to leave this morning for Yoknapatawpha, where they lived, until it would be November again and they could come back again.

So, as soon as we et breakfast, Simon run them back up the river in the big boat to where they left their cars and pickups, and now it wasn't nobody but jest me and Mister Ernest setting on the bench against the kitchen wall in the sun; Mister Ernest smoking a cigar—a whole one this time that Dan hadn't had no chance to jump him through a grapevine and bust. He hadn't washed his face neither where that vine had throwed him into the mud. But that was all right, too; his face usually did have a smudge of mud or tractor grease or beard stubble on it, because he wasn't jest a planter; he was a farmer, he worked as hard as ara one of his hands and tenants—which is why I knowed from the very first that we would git along, that I wouldn't have no trouble with him and he wouldn't have no trouble with me, from that very first day when I woke up and maw had done gone off with that Vicksburg roadhouse feller without even waiting to cook breakfast, and the next morning pap was gone, too, and it was almost night the next day when I heard a horse coming up and I taken the gun that I had already throwed a shell into the britch when pap never come home last night, and stood in the door while Mister Ernest rid up and said, "Come on. Your paw ain't coming back neither."

"You mean he give me to you?" I said.

"Who cares?" he said. "Come on. I brought a lock for the door. We'll send the pickup back tomorrow for whatever you want."

So I come home with him and it was all right, it was jest fine— his wife had died about three years ago—without no women to worry us or take off in the middle of the night with a durn Vicksburg roadhouse jake without even waiting to cook breakfast. And we would go home this afternoon, too, but not jest yet; we always stayed one more day after the others left because Uncle Ike always left what grub they hadn't et, and the rest of the home-made corn whisky he drunk and that town whisky of Roth Edmondziz he called Scotch that smelled like it come out of a old bucket of roof paint; setting in the sun for one more day before we went back home to git ready to put in next year's crop of cotton and oats and beans and hay; and across the river yonder, behind the wall of trees where the big woods started, that old buck laying up today in the sun, too—resting today, too, without nobody to bother him until next November.

So at least one of us was glad it would be eleven months and two weeks before he would have to run that fur that fast again. So he was glad of the very same thing we was sorry of, and so all of a sudden I thought about how maybe planting and working and then harvesting oats and cotton and beans and hay wasn't jest something me and Mister Ernest done three hundred and fifty-one days to fill in the time until we could come back hunting again, but it was something we had to do, and do honest and good during the three hundred and fifty-one days, to have the right to come back into the big woods and hunt for the other fourteen; and the fourteen days that the old buck run in front of dogs wasn't jest something to fill his time until the three hundred and fifty-one when he didn't have to, but the running and the risking in front of guns and dogs was something he had to do for fourteen days to have the right not to be bothered for the other three hundred and fifty-one. And so the hunting and the farming wasn't two different things atall—they was jest the other side of each other.

"Yes," I said. "All we got to do now is put in that next year's crop. Then November won't be no time away."

"You ain't going to put in the crop next year," Mister Ernest said. "You're going to school."

So at first I didn't even believe I had heard him. "What?" I said. "Me? Go to school?"

"Yes," Mister Ernest said. "You must make something out of yourself."

"I am," I said. "I'm doing it now. I'm going to be a hunter and a farmer like you."

"No," Mister Ernest said. "That ain't enough any more. Time was when all a man had to do was just farm eleven and a half months, and hunt the other half. But not now. Now just to belong to the farming business and the hunting business ain't enough. You got to belong to the business of mankind."

"Mankind?" I said.

"Yes," Mister Ernest said. "So you're going to school. Because you got to know why. You can belong to the farming and hunting business and you can learn the difference between what's right and what's wrong, and do right. And that used to be enough—just to do right. But not now. You got to know why it's right and why it's wrong, and be able to tell the folks that never had no chance to learn it; teach them how to do what's right, not just because they know it's right, but because they know now why it's right because you just showed them, told them, taught them why. So you're going to school."

"It's because you been listening to that durn Will Legate and Walter Ewell!" I said.

"No," Mister Ernest said.

"Yes!" I said. "No wonder you missed that buck yestiddy, taking ideas from the very fellers that let him git away, after me and you had run Dan and the dogs durn nigh clean to death! Because you never even missed him! You never forgot to load that gun! You had done already unloaded it a purpose! I heard you!"

"All right, all right," Mister Ernest said. "Which would you rather have? His bloody head and hide on the kitchen floor yonder and half his meat in a pickup truck on the way to Yoknapatawpha County, or him with his head and hide and meat still together over yonder in that brake, waiting for next November for us to run him again?"

"And git him, too," I said. "We won't even fool with no Willy Legate and Walter Ewell next time."

"Maybe," Mister Ernest said.

"Yes," I said.

"Maybe," Mister Ernest said. "The best word in our language, the best of all. That's what mankind keeps going on: Maybe. The best days of his life ain't the ones when he said 'Yes' beforehand: they're the ones when all he knew to say was 'Maybe.' He can't say 'Yes' until afterward because he not only don't know it until then, he don't want to know. 'Yes' until then. . . Step in the kitchen and make me a toddy. Then we'll see about dinner."

"All right," I said. I got up. "You want some of Uncle Ike's corn or that town whisky of Roth Edmondziz?"

"Can't you say Mister Roth or Mister Edmonds?" Mister Ernest said.

"Yes, sir," I said. "Well, which do you want? Uncle Ike's corn or that ere stuff of Roth Edmondziz?"

HERBERT GOLD was born in Cleveland, Ohio, in 1924. When he was in grade school a teacher told him that he would be a writer, and this impressed him so much that "I had to spend years learning to undo my eleven-year-old notion of what good writing is." He received his M.A. from Columbia University in 1948 and continued his studies in philosophy at the Sorbonne on a Fulbright Fellowship. From 1951 to 1953 he lectured on philosophy and literature at Western Reserve University in Cleveland. Mr. Gold has published two novels, Birth of a Hero *and* The Prospect Before Us, *and his short stories have appeared in* The New Yorker, Mademoiselle, Harper's Bazaar *and many other magazines. At present he is teaching at Wayne University in Detroit, where he lives with his wife and two daughters.*

A CELEBRATION FOR JOE

From THE ANTIOCH REVIEW

Cousin Joe said: "Stay young? Live more? But can you stop the wind from blowing?"

I wanted to wear the black for him. For this departure I needed a band of black rage, tucked into my collar like a bib to catch the gravy of tears. "Don't be in a hurry, Joe," I said.

"The wind from blowing?"

It was agreed that he had to die. The doctors and the nurses whispered and clucked and hurried to present their bills and went on the other consultations. The house was full of death; it moved in the corridors as if the windows had been opened to this subtle breeze. His room was flower-soft with it. His great head lay embedded in the wide bull neck and the mouth grinned its gold teeth at us. His wife cried, Elsie and the other daughters cried, I cried. Joe wept for us all, told us to be brave, but did not interfere with our pleasure in tears.

"It's not so bad, they're finding a cure for me," he said.

"Wh-what?"

"Next time it won't happen again. I'll go to the doc, he'll give me an examination and a pill like in the magazines it says you should. They got a foundation working on how to cure it."

"Joe!" everyone sobbed during those last days.

"I'm an old man anyway. It would have been something else," he said.

When the telegram came, I rushed to him without closing the door to my room, perhaps dreaming of revenge against my father's flesh, death the one answer to love, health, and power. But he was Elsie's father, not mine, and I wanted to see him because it was Joe: Cousin Joe, the good cousin in our family. Once he had peddled fruit, then sold yardgoods, then opened and closed a shop without even a fire sale; then suddenly he talked his way into the bricklayer's union. A mason who could lay thirteen hundred bricks a day, although the union said to him, "Please, Joe, six hundred is enough. *Plenty.*"

"Okay, the vacation's over," he had answered. "Only six hundred." And he got married. And he had four daughters—two married, two working for pay.

A second cousin, a skinny adolescent with a new collegiate flannel sportcoat and a mouth freshly astounded by Contemporary Civilization (A and B), I came to visit him because I was lonely at school and because "you can always count on the family for thicker blood than water." (My mother's insight, of course.) Now, the blankets pulled up high, I was aware of fixing the memory of his huge bald head shiny and bulging like a honeydew, with phrenological bumps and glints as he turned on the pillow. The weight was more than a pillow can take. A tuft of feathers was working itself out. "What you looking, Danny?" he asked me. "Dropped a penny in the sheets?" His nonchalance at present was a sign more deadly than the lamb's blood. The other nonchalance —the one mated to him which he had put on his family and no human being but Elsie had overcome it—was a thing which, under the watching of his daughters and his wife, might make him ugly or comic to himself in the sight of his finish. The cheeks cracked for his grin, but this was no longer the grin that he enjoyed for the way it did justice to his teeth.

"Pa, be careful," said Elsie, the art school girl, her father's favorite—the ballet-slippered and flush-cheeked and hanging-on-her-father's-neck girl. She had never grown too tall or too heavy to take him about and jump to redden her cheeks against his. The dark hair, captured behind, of course, in a rubber band, leaped when she shook with laughter; it leaped now, although she was not laughing. "Do you want something, Pa?" Elsie held her hand on his forehead.

"How did you ever learn construction?" I asked, because he liked to talk about it.

Doris was saying, "He's not going to die." (He can't do this to me.) Sandra was saying, "He's not going to die." (He never did before.) Sulky Marilyn was saying, "He's not going to pass away." (Knock on wood.)

Elsie's lips were moving. She turned her tears toward me in a complicity of bereavement which, when Joe discovered it, included and eased him. Elsie moved her lips to say nothing but their silence. Her father wanted to talk for her.

Sarah said, thwarted as always, first by her husband's health, then by his sickness, now by both: "Don't! Don't! O don't, Yussel!"

"That's all right, Saraleh."

"So don't wiggle around so much, you heard what the doctor said."

He had never kept the promise which America was for them: *You will be comfortable, my children.* They could not believe that he would leave them alone now after having bothered them so long. (But Elsie believed it.) They could not accept that he would depart without ever once calling out in need of them, furious in their sense of his flaw—he needed nothing except himself and his work. Stubborn? the nervous shake of Sarah's head asked. That man is stubborn, the shake replied. (But he needed Elsie.)

"He's going to be all right," I said, patting the nearest soft back without looking to see who it was. He had been to the hospital twice already. Both times he had threatened to walk out unless they carried him home. Once they found him standing in the hall with his pants half pulled on.

The back jumped and said, "Don't!"—it was Marilyn.

"So how did you ever learn construction?" I repeated.

"Brick-laying," he said, grinning.

"The mason trade was all right, you have a good union," I argued, "but you could have opened a fruit store, be your own boss again, or a little ready-to-wear place. There's money in dry goods. The war proves it."

The blankets rippled; he was laughing, which hurt him but was still worth the crackling in his chest. "Whoever!" he choked. "Whoever! Whoever! Whoever heard of a man was his own boss? The Jews were in Egypt, they built the pyramids, you think they'd take a chance like that crossing the Red Sea if they were thinking about semi-annual inventories? At least bricks you do it and you're done, ready for the next job, you get a habit to stand off with the Irishers and look at it."

I looked.

"Yes, yessir, just like that, Danny. A pile of bricks is nice." He thumped himself, wheezed, unbuttoned the pajama shirt and showed the gray-black hairs curling off his chest.

Because the wheezing embarrassed me, I repeated a childish joke—"A man's best friend is his mortar"—and blushed.

Such generosity! He laughed in his biblical fatness, a fatness of oil, sleek and glossy. He laughed in his fatness and his sleekness while death chipped at his heart in this house which he had built, brick by brick, himself. He could afford laughter and patience even for a pimply boy in sports clothes and abashed by illness. "You stand off from the lot and say, Hum, with bricks. You say Hum to them. Listen to me, Danny. With bricks you carried that wall on your back, and that one. You carried that house, you set it down, you stuck it together."

"Okay, it's time to be quiet," Doris said.

"You go from job to job, and what you carry with you is how-to-do-it. Plus the union card, I didn't forget. You can build your own like that."

When it came to his own house, someone helped him with the

plumbing and wiring. He had taken his wife to the country and given her a shack like a skeleton. A man of sixty with four grown girls left behind in the Bronx, he had fleshed out this skeleton. "They cry, they don't have to bother with us no more," he said. "Let them cry, it makes them feel good."

"*Sh!*"

"I was only saying what is true."

"Pa, you promised you'd be good if we let you come home."

There was a sad slanting fall of eyelid, and a hilarious fleshing at his mouth. "*Let* me," he said to Elsie. "*Let—*"

"I meant it another way, Pa."

"Be careful, girl," he said. "Don't stop it from blowing."

Upon the idea of a house which was this shack, he had begun to lay bricks. He learned support and insulation and joining; he had friends to give him a Sunday. And he learned carpentry, his voice ringing over the hoarse ravening of an electric saw. Mostly he lay bricks—that's how I remember him. Rising from a shack on a weedy lot came a house, while his bald dome glistened and he leaned against the hod and shook his head *yes*.

"What for?" three of the daughters had demanded.

"What do you mean all by yourself to build a house?" I asked, falling by respect into the parody of his speech. "With your bare hands?"

Elsie said softly to me: "You know how he likes it."

"Sometimes my friends help me weekends and the fourth of July. Sometimes I wear gloves. No bare hands—you want to try?"

"Don't bother," the girls had counselled me.

I even learned to mix cement, that grainy spitting soup with bubbles like saliva.

When it was closed in for the first winter, there occurred a moment of pensiveness in the family. "Well, a nice little bunga-low," murmured his wife, Sarah.

"I don't know," said Marilyn, "No modrun conveniences yet."

"A house!" he yelled. "A place to live, getting bigger every year. Look! Taste it! Workrooms, storerooms for our junk, places to sleep."

Elsie admonished the others. "Pa gets a kick out of it. That's nice. Be quiet already."

"It's almost a ranch-style," Doris mused. "Stanley," (her husband) "he says you could sell it and get a nice little apartment in the Bronicks." She pronounced the second syllable of *Bronx* with the negligent culture of a girl to whom museums come natural.

"What could you get for a home-made house like that?" And the answer was easy: "Beans."

He didn't blame his children for being American; it was a waste of exasperation. Besides, Elsie was American *plus*—plus something which felt like the pleasure of work, which he could not say in any of his languages. But he announced: "I don't want no nice apartment. . . . Want to see how I mark off the ground?" he had asked me. "Every man his own surveyor,"—and he paced exactly one yard with each straining thick-thighed step.

On that Ocotber day his daughter Marilyn had gone to the kitchen, which still smelled of wet cement. He watched her wipe the dirt from her shoes with a newspaper. "Clean children I raised," he said, "they lived in the city with smoke and garbage, no real dirt, no work dirt. Well, everybody enjoys like he can."

"It's not their fault," I said.

"Who said anything was wrong?" he said. He had learned in middle age to wield tools, to lift, to carry, and to swing down with his legs apart and the fixed grin of labour running with sweat. He was barrel-staved with hair and tight high-colored skin, a housebuilder with ambition for red bricks mixed with straw. "I ain't building me no pyramid, it's a house," he said. But it was a memorial all the same.

A sphynx—that monument of brick stolidly facing out over the deserts of Connecticut. Foundation and insulation by the builder, windows by the same. It had been brought on the back of a hard squat round old man from the Bronx. This, and not the bitter unleavened bread, was to be carried across the desert. And Elsie loved him! Is there anything more? He would sit in his kitchenette and eat buttered saltines and radishes and figure how to keep the fireplace from smoking.

The fireplace was smoking and he was dying.

I found him among the paraphernalia of death. Back from the hospital to finish himself out at home, he panted and gasped like a played-out child, still wide awake and challenging his family with the suspicion that they wanted to put him away. Except only Elsie. The room was filled with a melon-fragrance, the sweet ripeness of decay. Under the sheet—it was now summer again—illness had tightened his skin. His body had swollen, containing death, holding it, embracing; he had swollen like a mother's breast groped by famished death, the blind baby.

"Aie!" wailed his wife.

"Oh! Oh!" said his polite daughters. More than their love for him, they felt and feared what remained of him in his dying. Elsie said nothing.

"I know," he said, "I didn't make no wills. Split it up someways, but don't sell the house."

"What should we do with it, Pa?" Marilyn demanded. "You can't expect us to live out in the sticks."

"Hello to Danny," he said to me, "come to see an old man off. The terrible thing, let me tell you, is all those doctors and relatives in the hospital. At least now the docs went away. Glad to see you, boy, but don't bawl me out. I had enough from them already."

I couldn't cry. He seemed pleased. A happy death?—that is, sad with the sense of waste which increases the gladness that such waste is still possible. Another way of saying it: Bricks were piled in the yard, mortar was drying in a bin, windows still wore the glazier's stickers, but the house was finished enough. You could live in it already, which means that you could die in it. He said to me at one time during those hours while we waited, astounded by his wakefulness: "It's tough on the women." And then: "Well, take this house for a for-instance. It might be hard on her, but it's something to remember with."

The doctor had anticipated a paralysis, but there was none. "Stop talking so much. Don't be a dumb-bell," Marilyn said.

"Eat your dinner, it's getting late," he said. "Make them something good to eat, Sarah. It's getting dark already."

It was as if we were waiting. He waited, too, but did not insist. "I build a house, I make my own mortar. Bricks dried in the sun with red clay and straw—the straw sticks the clay together, the mortar sticks the bricks together." Naked under a sheet and pajamas, the chest rolled like a barrel and the tight high-colored skin shimmered like a ripe pear. Obscure disabilities and failures were occurring one after the next within his body, but Joe's eyes still recreated Joe at each instant, blazing from the great fat expanse of his head. The bald lids of his eyes fell in a moment's respite. If there was pain, we knew only by his withdrawal from it. Elsie, all youth and agelessness, waited by his side in complicity with this old man.

Someone's tears awakened him. In the air of his daughters' discontent his mouth gulped like that of a fish. "What's the matter?" he asked. "Should I hurry?"

We pulled closer as his face darkened with blood, smooth and strange with effort. His wife whispered, "What's the matter?"

"This time it's for me."

"What?"

He pulled himself half out of the sheets. "I got to go—"

"What?"—and she pushed his chest with her hands. "Lie down. Don't move."

"To the bathroom!" Part of his face went awry with laughter. "I got to go to the toilet."

"Stay in bed, Pa!"

"Yussel!" his wife cried. "We'll get you the pan."

"Get away from me," he said.

"I'll tell the doctor on you," Sarah said.

He pushed her away with a slow sweeping motion, unhesitating in will although, to his face, there came a look of surprise at his own slowness. Still smiling, uncaring about our watching, he grunted and ponderously rolled off the bed onto his feet. He stood swaying naked before his daughters, his wife, and me, his pendant belly dark and rolls of fat over the cord of his pajamas, his huge swollen old man's backside bulging. "I can do it myself," he said.

No one moved.

His daughters stared as if they had never seen him before, Elsie turned away, but the others went on looking. There was a bluish bed-sore like a beetle on his back, and discolored marks where the pajama cord had cut him.

"Some baby, eh?" he said.

"Joe!" his wife cried again. She was too afraid of him to touch him.

"All right, all right."

"Joe!"—I heard my own voice. He could not get to the bathroom alone; he would take no help.

"I told you he'd try something like that," Marilyn hissed. "In the hospital they got facilities—"

"Listen, everybody," his voice came. "Listen, don't cry, anybody."

My tear-ducts and the apple of grief in my throat turned with regret that his shoulders and chest and belly could give none of their strength to the sapped limbs. His glare was fixed on the door. He stretched, propped with his thick legs straddling. He stretched again and scratched the hairy flanks under cotton, but his face was pulled tight with effort. "Don't say nothing," he muttered stiffly, and he stumbled, and his arms beat at his side, and he scampered against the bed which creaked and rolled, and he fell half-naked to the floor while we all jumped to him. *Oh no,* Elsie turned her head away into her arms. I think all of us yelled at once, but he was silent now. There was even a slight bleeding where he scratched his flank against the bed. The heart was unequipped for his desire. It heaved, it turned over, it busted.

Afterwards, long past suppertime, I remembered that he would want me to eat, and with this thought in my throat the warm tears came loosened to wash me. At midnight I took the bus, then the subway back to my dormitory. I sat in a Bickford's and ate.

The bin of mortar in the yard hardened, whitened, flaked until his wife threw it out like spoiled soup. But even ten years later, the three times of Joe and all of us are joined in a single moment which still hovers over his bed in that house where his legs were a-straddle on their way—the past time of the idea of a house, the present time when he does work with bricks, and the time to come when, nothing yet finished, Elsie would sacrifice her bereavement in order to marry. Their presence in a moment supposes a law about the happy and unwilling death of the man who finds a work that he likes.

ROBIE MACAULEY *is a native of Grand Rapids, Michigan, where he was born in 1919. He wrote his first novel at the age of twelve,* The Boy Crusader. *He studied under Ford Madox Ford at Olivet College and under John Crowe Ransom at Kenyon. He says these two men taught him most of what he knows about writing. Mr. Macauley spent four years in the Army, doing counterintelligence work in France, Germany, and Czechoslovakia, winding up finally in Japan. Afterward he taught at Bard College and at the University of Iowa. He began writing seriously several years ago and won the* Furioso *prize for fiction in 1949 with a story called* "A Nest of Gentlefolk." *Since then his stories have appeared in several magazines, and he has published a novel,* The Disguises of Love. *He now lives in Alexandria, Virginia, and is at work on a book of short stories. A story of his,* "The Invaders," *appeared in the 1951 O. Henry collection.*

THE CHEVIGNY MAN

From KENYON REVIEW

"The last of the Renaissance men," said Paul Teeling, tipping the bottle uncertainly at the jigger as if trying to salt the tail of an elusive bird. "Poet, art-critic, novelist, playwright, traveller, officer —he was in the British Navy during the first war, you know— editor and a dozen other things. Veritably an *uomo universale.*" This sounded a little pedantic. "A man of parts, really. He's had a dozen distinguished careers." That made it better. He now noticed that in his excitement he had given Marian, his wife, a double shot of the good Bourbon and the Dean a single one of the imitation Scotch.

"But will he *live?*" asked Watters from the sofa.

Poor Watters. Paul looked at him and almost smiled. Still sniping from the bushes even after he'd been completely out-maneuvered. Watters' man was Samuel Daniel, who died in 1619 —no chance of *his* ever coming to the campus to lecture.

"Not a doubt," said Paul pointedly. "His *Collected Poems* alone makes him one of the outstanding figures of the 20th Century." Watters blinked behind his spectacles and nervously dipped up a handful of cheese crackers. For the past year or so his greatest apprehension had been that Daniel was fading. He had almost disappeared from PMLA altogether, the Oxford Press man had shown only the mildest interest in Watters' manuscript of the *Life,* and a library talk on "Several Themes in the *Civil Wars*" had been saved at the last minute only by the compulsory attendance of Sophomore English classes.

"Do you know Mr. Chevigny?" asked the Dean. "Personally, I mean?"

The crucial question, Paul thought. The question that had galled him so often in the past. He deftly switched the little straw glass-holders with their identifying colors between Marian's glass and the Dean's before he answered. "No," he said with just a tinge of smugness. "Not *yet.*"

How often he'd seen the look of interest fade. The old lady who approached him after his lecture in Dayton two years ago. The bright students in his modern literature course. The young writer from Chicago who'd called on him. "Do you know . . . personally, I mean?" they'd all asked at various times and, trying to choke back that sense of insufficiency, he'd had to answer, "I must admit . . . !" And they had all stared at his apology in the same way: He got it all out of books. The talk ebbing, the questions dying off, people turning away. "Well, nevertheless, it was a very informative discussion." He'd never felt the magic touch, seen the face that appeared so often in the *Times* Sunday book section, couldn't quote a single anecdote that began, "I remember Geoffrey saying to me once, 'Now Paul, I'm astonished at your perception when you say . . .'" Letters to Chevigny had drawn only a brief reply from a secretary.

"Not *yet,*" he said again.

"Now aren't we fortunate," Martha Baker, the Dean's wife, said, "to have the greatest authority on Geoffrey Chevigny right here just at the time he decided to make an American lecture tour. I think it's a wonderful coincidence." Martha always babbled on.

"Thank you, Martha," he said with a smile a little broader than genuine and handed her the glass of sherry he had just refilled. "The man and his work have always fascinated me—ever since I discovered one of his plays when I was a junior in college. *The Exiled*—it's about the old age of Prince Charles Stuart. A wealth of material about the Stuart character in it."

"I heard he'll be passed over for the laureateship—that is, when Masefield dies," said Watters rudely.

Didn't the man know when he was demolished? There were so many answers to this that he hardly knew which weapon to choose —or whether it wouldn't be more damning just to keep silent. He wondered if the thought weren't passing through the Dean's mind that a man who had never heard of *The Exiled* and who still thought of the poet laureateship as a great distinction ought not to be teaching English on the college level. Then he suddenly realized that he was mistaken to attribute these fine distinctions of his own to Baker. As a matter of fact, the Dean *did* love Masefield. He remembered hearing him say so.

Confused by the wide range of possibilities, he suddenly realized that they were all coming out in one sentence. "Surely after its history—after Shadwell, Cibber and Austin—you can't take that thing seriously and so Chevigny stands with Milton, Pope, Byron, Yeats . . . he has nothing to do with such faded official honors, or can you imagine the author of *The British Consul* ever *wanting* it and anyway he's quite old, you know, rarely ever stirs from his house in Rome—can you imagine what satire there'd be in Chevigny's *Ode to the Youngest Princess on the Occasion of Her Ninth Birthday?*" Seeing that he was going wrong, he stopped. They were looking at him in a slightly puzzled way, he thought. He'd meant to be a load of bricks on Watters, but he'd only succeeded in burying himself.

From his seat in the corner Dr. Dunmeade chuckled at him. For years the head of the English Department had practised and cultivated that sound until now it was rich, rattly and, more than any other sound in the world, fitted the word "chuckle." It sounded like a pair of oversized dice being rattled around in his throat.

"Teeling, my boy," he said. Whenever Dr. Dunmeade called him that, Paul felt confusedly that it had some reference to his disappearing hairline. Dr. Dunmeade still had an ugly black shock on his head. "Teeling, we understand your natural warmth of interest in Chevigny. Admirable. But I don't think Watters meant anything by his remark. After all, it's an academic question, isn't it, with Masefield still hale and hearty?" Dunmeade was a Wordsworth man—therefore unassailable. Paul was often irritated with his absolute neutrality; as a matter of fact, when the Donne man in the department has been nominated for the headship in opposition to the Shelley man, Dunmeade had finally come out as the compromise choice; Wordsworth was felt to be safe and middle-of-the-road.

"No offense meant," Watters said offensively. "How old *is* this Chevigny? He must be up in his eighties, isn't he?"

He didn't die at the beginning of the 17th Century—but Paul thought better of saying this.

"He's sixty-nine," said the Dean, "born in 1871." The Dean must have been looking him up in *Who's Who,* or perhaps he had been reading one of Paul's own articles in *The Northeast Review* or *The Journal of Modern Literary Scholarship.*

"I think he owes a debt of gratitude to Paul," Marian said loyally. "In spite of his reputation, he's never had the serious consideration he deserves—outside of Europe, at least. Why, do you know, Paul's book will be the first biography to appear in English?" She *had* been listening to him these past ten years, in spite of her distracted looks and frequent interruptions to ask if he'd paid the grocery bill. Good girl.

"I'm dying to meet him," said Mrs. Dunmeade, "I enjoyed his *Brief Encounter* so much." Here was support. Let Watters notice that even Mrs. Dunmeade, who read almost nothing but Lloyd Douglas—even *she* knew something of Chevigny.

"*The Curt Reply,*" he said.

"Why, I didn't mean to be," said Mrs. Dunmeade.

"No—that's the name of the play. *The Curt Reply.*"

"Of *course*. I *knew* the other was by Bernard Shaw the moment I said it."

He thought Watters was looking sly. Wasn't there some way of reminding him how the conscripted Sophomores had hawked and shuffled during his interminable droning about the *Civil Wars?* Teeling had refreshed the last of the drinks and now he sat down again.

"Well, now, tell us something more about Chevigny," said the Dean, who always threw a good deal of heartiness as a kind of makeweight into his most banal remarks. "I know him by his popular reputation, of course (*Who's Who,* Teeling thought again) but I'm not too well acquainted with the details."

Leaning back in his chair, Paul Teeling said, "Geoffrey Chevigny was born of an old family of Norman descent in York, England, in 1871."

"The Dean already gave us that," said Watters.

"I'm sorry, George," Teeling said mildly. Watters looked sheepish.

"No, I'*m* sorry," said Watters. "Shouldn't have interrupted you. It was a very good beginning."

"His father, Sir Manfred Chevigny—named for Byron's hero, by the way—was high in the councils of the Tory party during his lifetime . . ." This oft-told story had now become a part of his life and it was with a sense of satisfaction that he realized while shaving in the morning that he had been thinking of Geoffrey Chevigny ever since he had arisen—that period between 1885 and '87. Weren't there any letters still in existence to account for Chevigny's whereabouts and, more importantly, his thoughts at that period? In the department store a pretty girl waited on him and he had some trouble in describing the curtains that Marian wanted. He wondered what Chevigny would have thought of the girl. Wasn't she rather like "the sinuous girl with the ivory face" in *Ucalegon?* Perhaps the same one mentioned in the journal as "the jade-and-ivory Jeanette." He read the war headlines in the paper and thought, "Chevigny said that historians have misunderstood the Battle of Jutland. It was actually more than decisive." He had read and mastered every maneuver of that conflict, finding, to his disappointment however, no mention of Chevigny in the official report and very little mention of his ship, *The Indispensable,* which had, it appeared, arrived a little late and had returned to drydock before the battle was completely over.

What epigram would Chevigny have coined to dispose of Watters at lunch? What was the reason for Chevigny's great attraction to ballet dancers in that 1895 period? Was it that the movement of the classical ballet was very much akin to the kind of movement on his plays and poetry? Teeling had waited anxiously for the appearance of the Ballet Russe in town and then, to his mortification, had fallen asleep in the middle of the second ballet.

As he walked to the bus stop, he wondered what Geoffrey Chevigny had been doing on this sunlit morning thirty years ago. Let's see—he had been living in Venice at the time, working over *The Three Roisterers.* Had he, at this exact time, been walking along the Grand Canal (he had lived two houses away from the one in which Browning had died and Teeling had a map of the neighborhood) signalling for a gondola, just as Teeling, on this fine May morning thirty years later, was signalling for the King Power Co. Trolley Car? What had Chevigny been thinking? Undoubtedly the theme of self-destruction that runs so brilliantly and gloomily through *The Three Roisterers* was more connected with the suicide of his friend Caldwell than himself. Chevigny had always been in favor of life.

And so Chevigny had become almost a part of him. Paul knew considerably more about the man, he reflected, than most of Chevigny's closest friends. It was really amazing how much could be learned—to the minutest detail—about the life of a man who had never come within a thousand miles of you. In fact it was probably true that Paul knew many things that Chevigny had forgotten or had never realized about himself. It would be amazing when they met. He imagined the two of them in his study late at night. "Do you realize," Paul was saying, "that at the same time you were working on *Dead Mansions* a very good friend of yours was writing a poetic drama with the identical idea?—stemming from the anecdote about General Burgoyne and the children that you told one evening—June first, 1905, I believe—at a dinner party at the Byerley's house in Paris?" "No!" Chevigny would say, starting from his seat. "I never suspected. Not . . . ?" Paul would nod gravely. "I'm afraid so. A brilliant man, but he outlived his genius, don't you agree?"

That recalled a delicate problem, a problem that was actually more one of introduction than accomplishment. How was he going to get Chevigny aside for a long session of tactful questioning that would serve to fill in those baffling gaps in the biography? The truth had to be known, for instance, about that two months in 1907 that Chevigny had spent on an island in the Cyclades. Teeling was absolutely convinced that it had been neither Lady Judith Perrigeau nor the "Turkish girl with odd tastes" that malicious gossips had hinted at—but a long poem on a classical subject that had apparently never been printed. He had a clue to that. And the six months in the Swiss hospital that ensued? And the mysterious Dane with whom Geoffrey had taken that walking trip in North Africa? His opinion of Winston Churchill? The famous quarrel with Yeats? Had he actually called Pound a "damned, dirty, stinking —" as Widdicomb had reported or had he actually been referring to Widdicomb?

But all this had to be approached with the greatest smoothness —it all had to be in context. For the last two months, ever since he had heard from the agent that Chevigny would accept the lecture engagement, he had been wondering about a setting that would induce the reminiscent mood. Nothing seemed to help very much here. At Cambridge, he knew, Chevigny had been known as a "four bottle man." The encyclopedia was unfortunately blank on this term. Dunmeade, who had been at Oxford, wasn't much help. He had said, "Might be Vichy water. That's all I drank when *I* was there. Couldn't stand English beer." Then, Chevigny liked long walking trips and mountain-climbing—almost out of the question here in Indiana. Brilliant women were supposed to stimulate his conversation—then Paul thought of the faculty wives, a great many of whom, unhappily, seemed to be pregnant just at this moment, and the college girls, most of whom were trying to look like Lana Turner just now and—what was worse—succeeding. There was one pretty girl in the English Department but, Paul reflected, she was a Swinburne man—in the middle of her thesis about Swinburne. Nothing would enrage Chevigny more than to hear all about *that*.

". . . and so," Paul began to wind up, "at the outbreak of the war he was forced to remove from his house in Rome whence he travelled to Majorca, where he now lives. It's a delightful place, I understand. He has a study overlooking the 'wine-dark waters' of the Mediterranean where he sits every morning from nine to twelve and writes on his work-in-progress, which is to be a grand critical study of all his literary contemporaries."

There was a brief silence. "It's snowing outside," Watters remarked.

But he had lost the patience of the group. "Illuminating. Most illuminating," said the Dean. "I shall look forward to your biography with the greatest pleasure."

"*Very* interesting. I'm dying to meet him," said Mrs. Dunmeade.

"I hope he won't be too—well, you know how some of those writers are," said Mrs. Baker.

"Please try to be here at six-thirty for a drink or two before dinner. You remember that the lecture is at eight-thirty," said Marian.

They went out into the hall, putting on coats and rubbers. Watters lingered a little behind the others and Paul saw a forlorn look on his face. With a sudden warmth of forgiveness, he helped him on with his coat.

With his hand at the knob, Watters turned and leaned towards him, the wretched look magnified behind the show-windows of his large spectacles. In a low voice he said, "I envy you, Paul. I wish *my* man were alive."

To Paul the next two days were intense but hazy. They spent a lot of their time doing what Marian called "stocking up." At the liquor store Paul took an annoying half-hour trying to get several wines he had never tasted, wines famous to literature but nearly unknown in the Dandy-Corner Liquor Store. Claret, Port, Bristol Cream Sherry and sack—no, sack was Falstaff—it must be hock.

"Have you any good hock?" he asked.

"This ain't a pawn shop, Mister," said the fat man, laughing heavily.

He laid in an extravagant stock of Benson and Hedges cigarettes and pipe tobacco and Marian made two heavy hauls at the delicatessen. The house was cleaned and their part-time maid was engaged full time for the next three days. After some debate, Marian even bought her a uniform.

Coming into his study the evening before the arrival, Paul saw how thoroughly it had been cleaned—and even rearranged, a bit ostentatiously, he thought. All of the Chevigny books, for instance, (his collection was complete) were now on the top shelf of the bookcase along with the magazines containing Paul's articles. *The Manchester Guardians* for the last six months had been brought out of the closet and laid in a neat overlapping file on the lamp-table. His big book of newspaper clippings relating to Chevigny, his friends and the places where he had lived for the past twenty years, had been placed on top of the desk. Over the desk, Paul noticed something missing. On one side always hung the greatly-enlarged photograph of Chevigny that Paul had had made from a publisher's publicity picture and on the other side hung a reproduction of a portrait of Landor—an old love from Ph.D. days, now forsaken. Landor had been stored away. A small feeling of guilt prickled in his mind and he wondered if Chevigny hadn't taken somewhat of an advantage with him over Landor—a rather unfair advantage simply by being alive.

Watters had made that point, but Paul still wasn't sure of all the ins and outs of it. Until recently he had hardly ever thought of Chevigny as actually being alive; he was still breathing somewhere, of course, and still furnishing material for the last chapter but, in a sense, not really living. He moved the Chevigny picture over to the Landor hook, judging that there it could be seen a little better on first entrance into the room.

He slept badly that night and Marian accused him of mumbling. The next morning in his ten o'clock class he felt a little tired and on edge. He talked about Chevigny's life and read a selection of his poems. There were ten minutes left then and he called for comments or questions. A discouraging silence followed. Finally a boy in the last row raised his hand. "Yes?"

"Did Robert Frost know him?" he asked.

"I doubt if Chevigny would have noticed Frost," Paul snapped, being unfair and knowing it. "Any other questions?"

"You said *Ucalegon* is one of the greatest modern poems," one of the girls said. "It isn't in our textbook and . . ."

"Simply ignorance on the part of the editors," Paul said grimly. "These questions are all pretty frivolous, it seems to me."

Perry Reynolds, a great smoother-over, trying to nurse his athletic scholarship along for another year, said, "Sir, I understand that some critics place it above *The Wasteland* in importance. Isn't that true?"

So the class ended on a sweeter note and after a good lunch, Teeling felt somewhat better. It was just nerves, he told himself as he sat in his office going over the typescript of his little introductory speech. "A modern Odysseus on a voyage of intellectual discovery through . . ." Didn't that phrase sound a little too rhetorical? And the reference to his own work on Chevigny? However modest it might seem here in the quiet of his office, wasn't it possible that it might have another ring when spoken into the microphone in the auditorium? Finally he drew a light pencil line through several sentences, leaving them optional, to be decided on later. From time to time he had glanced out of the window and at last with a feeling of displeasure he went and stood at it, looking out on the snowy campus. It was only three o'clock and already it was becoming alarmingly dark. A sweeping wind coming out of the west kept the deserted walks bare but cast up odd drifts around the bases of the tree boles and at the edges of buildings. One moment, when the wind died, the air seemed salted with granular snow and the next moment was cleared with a vicious new blast. Standing there, Paul had an odd, almost portentous feeling, a half-wish that Chevigny wouldn't come or that he had already gone.

But he had to leave; it was already only a half-hour before train time. He muffled up and went out to the lot for his car. The streets seemed tortuous with slowly-moving traffic, cars looking like monstrous buns with a layer of frosting. As he drove down the long street of gloomy warehouses and wholesale establishments that led to the railway station, he thought how dreary this must be and how strange to a man accustomed to the bright air and colors of the Mediterranean. But he censored that thought quickly; it had no bearing whatsoever, he told himself.

At the station he found that he still had fifteen minutes to wait and so he walked around aimlessly, peering at the magazines on the stand, stopping for a moment to call Marian to let her know everything was all right, getting caught in the middle of two embracing families who were about to be parted.

Five minutes early he got out on the platform in the vicious wind. The light down the tracks was green but the train seemed to take a long time coming into the yards even after its whistle. But finally it was slowing up alongside. The porters were jumping down and beginning to haul bags off. Passengers stood waiting on the steps with money showing between the fingers of their gloves. A great crowd had appeared from somewhere and he was shoved in the legs with suitcases and sideswiped by children, caught in a sudden steam bath from beneath the train. How in the world was he going to find Chevigny in this mess? He started down the platform.

Then he suddenly discovered that he had been gazing at the face of an old man without understanding who he was. It was partly the overpowering familiarity of his looks that made him unrecognizable. It was partly that Paul, almost unconsciously, had been hearing the long physical description with which he had begun chapter five: "those eagle eyes beneath the sharp-cut brows . . . the military moustache . . . the clean angle of the cheekbone . . . the clear, reddish tone of the skin." Chevigny was taller than he had imagined, broader in the shoulders. With a gulp, Paul rushed up and spoke to him.

"Eh?" he answered. "No—CHIVingee. CHIVingee. Yes. You're the boy sent down from the school?"

It was a terrible blast for Paul. For years he had been calling him SheVEENye and everybody in college knew it. No time to worry about that now.

"I'm *Paul Teeling*," he said, waiting for the fierce face to soften into a recognitory smile.

It didn't. "Howjado."

"Paul Teeling," he said again with despair, but Chevigny was already getting his bags away from the redcap. "Now, sir, here is my luggage," he said brusquely.

On the ramp, Paul couldn't help staggering under the weight of the three fat bags. Chevigny strode ahead of him like a brigadier leading a charge into the thick-packed but demoralized natives.

Paul finally caught up with him in the middle of the station and panted directions to the car. Once they got there, Paul nearly dropped the luggage. His muscles felt like broken threads. He leaned against the fender and caught his breath. Then he raised the cover of the trunk and slowly and carefully stowed the bags away.

When he turned he saw that Chevigny was still waiting for him to open the car door, though it wasn't locked.

"Inevitable awkwardness at first," Paul thought as they went down the street. "There's a kind of genuine hauteur that surrounds a truly great man." He'd decided that by no means would he ask Chevigny what he thought of America or Indiana—he'd have only scorn for such a hackneyed opening. Better let him speak first.

"Damned depressing place," Chevigny said. "Reminds me of Manchester and the Naples slums scrambled together at the North Pole."

"Yes, it does, rather," said Paul, weakly, trying to accommodate himself.

"I'm used to the bright colors of the Mediterranean, y'know," Chevigny remarked again.

CHIVingee. CHIVingee. CHIVingee. He must drill himself and remember to say it that way. "Mr. CHIVingee, your talk has been much anticipated. I think you'll find that your work is well-known and appreciated here."

Wait until he saw the study—he'd tumble then. In the excitement at the station he probably hadn't connected the name with Paul's writing.

"Mph?"

"The weather *is* nasty but I think we can offer you a little bit of compensation at least with a warm fire and a good glass of Scotch."

"Bawph."

Paul tried once or twice more, but got nothing. When they came to a stoplight he took a quick sideglance at the author. "You look a little pale, Mr. Chevigny. Are you tired?"

"Oh. Quite. That is, not really." He put a fine carved hand to his forehead. "I was a bit dizzy in the train, you know. I had a fall. Nothing, really. I'll soon be right as rain." He seemed to slump even as he said this.

"Some sleep and all's well," he said. Paul thought of the people coming for cocktails, the dinner, the lecture, the Dean's reception after the lecture, and began to pass cars recklessly on the slippery pavement. It would have to be a quick nap. Marian would be firm about that.

At last he turned into the driveway and stopped at the walk. Chevigny seemed to waken from a slight doze. He looked out of the window. "Where are we?" he asked.

"Right here at our house," Paul said heartily, "and only a minute away from a good drink."

"But, my good fellow," Chevigny said abruptly, "those people at the school are expecting me. You'd better take me there at once. I do appreciate your offer, but . . ."

"I should have explained," Paul said in a rush. "You're staying with us. We have the honor . . ."

Chevigny got out of the car somewhat doubtfully, opening the door by himself this time. He followed Paul, who carried the bags. Marian had been waiting. She threw the front door open before he could touch the knob. "Mr. SheVEENye!" she exclaimed. But it was only Paul and the luggage. Chevigny was standing several yards back, looking uncertainly down the street as if wondering whether any rescue was in sight.

They bundled him inside and got his hat and coat away from him. Marian was brisk and forceful and full of bright conversational bits. Chevigny was marched upstairs with the maid to be shown his room. He was given five minutes to wash and then marched down again—this time to the study where Paul had a fantastic battalion of bottles arranged on a silver tray in preparation for "a little drink before they all get here." Chevigny, to

Paul's alarm, looked paler than ever and he saw him sink into the easy chair with a feeling of relief—even though his eye had passed blankly over the photograph and the books.

"A Scotch and soda, sir?" Paul asked.

"No. Just a little Martini. Very dry."

Horrors! Englishmen *never* drank cocktails if they could help it, never Martinis.

"Just a moment. I thought my wife called," said Paul, turning whiter than Chevigny.

Ten minutes later it turned out that the Claphams next door had just half a pint of gin left and a nearly full bottle of American vermouth they had intended to throw away because of its unexpected sweetness.

"He wants to take a nap before dinner," Paul whispered to Marian.

"Out of the question!" she hissed, dropping an olive into the glass.

Back in the study, Paul wondered how to begin the friendship, how to get Chevigny around to literary matters. "I suppose you realize, Mr. Chevigny, that American critics have been increasingly absorbed in your work? A great deal has been written about you over here during the past few years."

Chevigny tested his Martini and set it down. "Oh? 'tso? Somebody sent me a copy of a piece by some damned fool. Didn't read it. On a frightful juvenile thing of mine called *Ucalegon*. I daresay there're better, though."

The insufferable old —! This was getting impossible. It was not only insulting to Paul but it was insulting to Chevigny as well! Then he remembered that this *was* Chevigny. He almost said, "Sir, I happen to be the damned fool . . ." but he thought better of it and after he had taken a long draught from his glass, another thought crept in. It might be just as well that Chevigny *hadn't* connected him. But, oh, the moment when he did.

The situation had to be straightened out somehow, sooner or later. Paul tried again. "I think you're being too modest, Mr. Chevigny," he said in a slightly-strained voice. "It seems to me that *Ucalegon* is one of the few modern poems that successfully exploits the thematic and ideational conflicts of our times—in the very cacophony of the language and the dichotomy of the structure. In a time when poetry is growing increasingly hieratic . . ."

"Heard of it, eh?" Chevigny asked and relapsed into silence.

The clock on the wall ticked and Marian and the maid knocked and rattled things in a subdued way in the kitchen. At last Paul began. "Mr. Chevigny, I wanted to ask . . ."

"Better go up if I'm to have that sleep," said Chevigny, rising.

Paul went along with him and followed up the stairs, not knowing quite how he was to put it. At the door of the bedroom, just as Chevigny was going in, he finally managed to get something out. "Mr. Chevigny, I'm afraid it's a little late for a nap right now. We have guests coming in for cocktails—all of whom want especially to meet you—and then we're having dinner. The lecture is at eight-thirty you know and after that"—it began to sound worse —"the Dean, Dean Baker, is giving a reception at his house." Chevigny had turned around in the doorway and his pale face seemed to darken. Paul stumbled on, "Of course, you'll have a chance to get a nice long sleep in the morning—er—your train doesn't leave until ten-thirty . . ."

Chevigny's sharp eyebrows, pulled down, seemed to stab at him. "Well!" he barked. "Such awful damned bloody nonsense!" He shut the door.

Paul went slowly down the stairs again and sat in a chair in his study. He tried to think of every rationalization. The man was very old and used to a different kind of living. Besides that, he was evidently tired and out of sorts. Perhaps after a few drinks he would begin to be a little more convivial and the rudeness would wear off. Paul had often smiled at the anecdotes about Chevigny's sharp replies and Johnsonian squelches, but this—this was just plain— He looked over at Chevigny's chair and saw the full Martini on the table beside it.

Paul tried not to think of what Watters would say or how the Dean would look at him and all he could hope for was a miracle that would change Chevigny. He sat there with his head in his hands for nearly half an hour, hearing Marian's voice occasionally and dreading to look at the clock.

He couldn't avoid it finally and he saw that people would be arriving any minute now. Then he heard a car stop in the street outside. He pulled himself to his feet and he realized that all his muscles felt strained and sore from the heavy bags. He went slowly to the stairs and began to climb them.

He hesitated outside Chevigny's door, not knowing what to say again. Then he heard the knocker at the front door and so he rapped twice. "Mr. Chevigny? I don't want to hurry you, but I wonder if there's anything you need before you come down?" No answer.

"Mr. Chevigny?" He knocked again. No answer. "Mr. Chevigny!"

He *had* gone to sleep, the old fool. Paul tried the door quietly and found that it wasn't locked. He began to push it open slowly.

Just as he had expected, Chevigny was lying stretched out on the bed with his eyes closed. He had, however, started to change and he wore evening trousers and a dress shirt. Paul stopped a moment when he saw that he was barefooted. The surprisingly narrow long feet were very white with dark blue veins, like queer outcrops of water-eroded rock. Teeling halted, then heard the Dean's voice downstairs in the hall, which urged him on.

He touched Chevigny gently on the shoulder. "I'm sorry, sir, but I'm afraid you'll have to wake up." There was no response. "The guests are coming and we're about ready to begin. If I can help you in any way . . .? *Wake up,* Mr. Chevigny."

But Mr. Chevigny would never begin again or wake up again and he no longer needed any help. It took Paul quite a long time to realize this and to believe it. With increasing hurry and confusion, he discovered first that the hands were cold, that there was no heartbeat at all, that no breath came from the thin nostrils. He knelt down and put his ear to Chevigny's stiff shirt front. There was nothing.

He stood up slowly, feeling sick. He felt as if he were in a whirlpool and about to go down the drain. He steadied himself against the wall and looked down at Chevigny. Already the man seemed to be looking better. Paul began to think of his face as "benign," perhaps "noble." The hard sarcastic lines had all been eased out of it and the lips seemed to be smiling gently at him. "A certain calmness and greatness of spirit shone through . . ."

Paul wrote in his mind. "The white hair still neat, the classic brow unruffled, the magnificent eyes now closed in . . ."

He turned away and walked slowly out of the room, closing the door behind him gently. The noise of arrival had increased and he stepped softly along the hall to his own bedroom. When he was there, he walked up and down from window to dresser several times with no particular object but with the thought that he must gather all his ideas, must synthesize all the aspects.

He had been walking for several minutes when he stopped before the mirror. He saw a smile on the face of the man there and realized that he was rubbing his hands together. Only then did he know that the miracle had happened. He began to walk again, hardly able to contain himself.

He would not have to face everybody with Chevigny—but that was only an added blessing. The important thing was like a kind of grand legacy. Already the last chapter of the book had begun to take form in his mind and, magnificently, he himself was a part of it. He had shaken the hand, he had looked into the face, he had shared the last moments of the great man! For all practical purposes, he had been at the bedside in the last extremity *and* without a doubt he had heard his last words. "Paul Teeling, his biographer and close friend, describes in his book the fortitude and resignation with which Chevigny . . ."

"Did you . . . I mean, personally?" What an answer he could give to that question now! He was almost too full of it to think what the answer would be—perhaps simply a bowed head and a mournful "Yes."

He began to wonder about this evening. Perhaps a little elegy-like speech, dignified, touching, simple—in the tradition of the French *oraison funèbre?* And that too would go in the last chapter, would be quoted in future studies.

One idea glowed in his mind after another and he paced up and down the bedroom for a long time, the titles for articles occurring to him, the name "Paul Teeling" in various kinds of type on various bindings coming before his eyes, a vision of the photographs and the long reviews in the Sunday book sections.

At last he was aware that there had been a tapping at the door for two or three minutes. It opened and Marian stood there.

"*Paul!* You're not dressed! Everybody's been waiting for just hours. For God's sake, hurry up."

"Oh! Yes, yes. Sorry," he said and began to go to the closet for his tuxedo.

"And listen," she said, "What's happend to your man? He hasn't come downstairs either."

Reminded, he turned around exultantly, "Oh, Marian. He's dead! He's dead! At last he's dead!"

HOWARD NEMEROV *was born in New York City in 1920 and educated at the Fieldston School and Harvard. During the war he served as a pilot for both the Royal Canadian Air Force and the U.S. Army Air Force. Since 1948 he has been teaching at Bennington College in Vermont, where he lives with his wife and son. He was an editor of* Furioso *from 1946 to 1950 and was the 1955 winner of the Kenyon Review Fellowship in Fiction. Mr. Nemerov has published three volumes of poems and two novels, the latest of which,* Frederigo, or The Power of Love *appeared in 1954.*

TRADITION

From KENYON REVIEW

Below the village of Ravensburg, at the edge of the woods and facing the swampy bottom lands that spread to the river, old Mr. Birch had his cabin where he lived alone and did nothing, or almost nothing. People driving the highway on the other side of the river could look across and have a glimpse of him—a faded denim shirt, flowering white hair—sitting peaceably in a rocker on his porch, one end of which had sagged; and those people, if they were just passing through on their way from one city to another, would sometimes be reminded of the firm rural virtues, frugality and toil, upon which our civilization is reared. In a flash —before even slowing down for the stop-signal which marks Ravensburg's one cross-roads—they would have a vision, touched by nostalgia, of the fine thing it was to live close to the soil, to be born, spend your days, and die old in a cabin beside a river. Ravensburg itself, an unenterprising and largely decaying little place, would perhaps change their minds, as they passed the abandoned stove factory with its heap of rusting iron bellies and limbs like the carnage of some robot battlefield; but by that time they would have had the vision, and for the fact that it rested entirely on illusion, on nothing, nobody—certainly not Mr. Adam Birch—could be held responsible. But that is often how it is with our edifications. People are driven to noble and desperate actions by, it may be, a lie in a schoolbook; perhaps Alexander the Great imitated in his conquests some perfectly fantastic notion of ancient virtues which his tutor had heard fables of.

Old Mr. Birch had not been born in Ravensburg but in Brooklyn. To his present habitation he had come many years ago, during Prohibition, and the rumor was that he had been a small beer baron, a rum-runner, a hijacker, a dynamiter of safes—some such thing, anyhow—who had not only evaded the law but piled up, also, a sufficiency of funds to enable his quite modest retirement to the country. We see Mr. Birch from outside, and do not know if these things said about him are true, but certainly he seems to have had some experience with dynamite.

If Mr. Birch presented no living illumination of the truth that Crime Does Not Pay, he could at least be used to illustrate the proposition that Crime Does Not Pay Very Well. If a beer baron at all, he must have been an extremely small one, for he drank nothing but beer except if someone stood him the odd glass of whisky now and then at the Blue Light Tavern where he usually went in the evenings to read the paper. This treat happened seldom, though, for while he was a nice, friendly old man, he didn't talk much, he seemed to have little to talk about. When he had first come—and not many people clearly remembered that time, jealous as for some reason they all were about the high privilege of having been born in Ravensburg—Mr. Birch used to talk some about Brooklyn, and how good it was to have been born there, to know that you had, so to say, all that life and infinite rumbling variety behind you. But then Brooklyn dropped out of his talk, and he began to tell people that as a matter of fact he had been born right in Ravensburg, but moved to Brooklyn at an early age—that he had really, in moving to the country, come back home. People did not exactly believe this, but they did not exactly out loud refuse to believe it; partly because Mr. Adam Birch was an extremely powerful (though gentle) old person, and partly because this story of his seemed to them less an outright lie than an honest and praiseworthy ambition to have been born in Ravensburg. Also they thought him a bit queer, though not seriously so.

The Lord alone knows what he did with his days, old Adam Birch. In the good weather he sat before that shack of his and watched, presumably, the world go by; which at that place it did very leisurely, at about the pace of the Manadoc River flowing slowly from right to left in front of him. Perhaps he counted the cars going by across the river and thought it a good day when more cars went from left to right than from right to left, or vice versa. Perhaps he thought about his boyhood, about being born in Brooklyn or Ravensburg. Perhaps he watched, with slow, perceptive care, the seasons change in hundreds of slight allusions and indications which over twenty years he had come to know quite well, though probably without calling them by their names. Behind his white head lay the poky, prospectively dirty and unneat mystery of his shack, which no one but himself entered, and behind the shack lay the forest rising up over the hills and the wild country of deer and bear and badger and fox and skunk and maybe bobcat; and over his white head sailed the immense sky like a sea with turreted galleons of cloud and distant lines of surf of cloud.

One thing he must have done was watch the crows, the crows and ravens which had given his village of adoption its name long ago. Ravensburg had a huge population of these birds, not so noticeable by day when they were dispersed over the countryside as at evening, when they returned to roost, which they did all around Adam Birch's house, in the massed trees at the forest's edge, and in the lonely single elms, oaks and hickory that stood out in the swamp land between there and the river. At sundown in this place the sky would thicken with wheels of crow, their voices in deafening volume would rebound from the hills behind and fill the damp bottoms with continuous sound; then, as though by a single command, they would settle for the night into their ridiculously unkempt, huge and rickety nests. Henry Ward Beecher is supposed to have summed up the crow's reputation for wisdom, or at least intelligence, by saying that not many men, if they had wings and feathers, would have the sense to be crows; but probably any man, even without wings and feathers, could make a better-looking nest. Anyhow, there were thousands upon thousands of these crows, it was like an airport for them out where Adam Birch had his residence; so there can be hardly any doubt he must have watched the crows, though what he thought about them it is impossible to know except by inference from the things that happened, and such inference is always at best a dubious business.

Ravensburg had its name, as I said, from this circumstance of birds. No one knew any more whether the first settlers had called it so because there were in fact more ravens than crows, or whether it was from the simple consideration that the raven, even before Poe's celebrated poem, had a more attractive and high-sounding reputation. It is true that a place called Crowville (or even Crowburg) could scarcely be expected to get very far in the world; but then, neither had Ravensburg got very far in the world. At any rate, there were now many more crows than ravens, perhaps for the same reason that "more geese than swans now live, more fools than wise," and perhaps for no reason at all. But they are very different birds, the raven and the crow, the former being much larger, and flying more like a hawk, with passages of planing on perfectly flat wings alternated with passages of wing-beating, while the latter beats his wings more continuously, and in his slight soarings is observed to have a dihedral tilt to the wings. They also make different noises, the crow saying "caw" and the raven something altogether less humanly imitable, such as "krauuuk," described by authorities as "hoarse, uncouth, dismal and prolonged," though whether they mean something entirely different is open to question. And it is doubtful if these distinctions much occupied old Mr. Birch's mind; probably to him they were all crows, or all ravens.

As to his physical appearance, Mr. Birch was tall and fat, though as a matter of fact he was one of those persons who look fat and are not, whose sagging paunches seem resting cruelly on the edges of their belts but turn out, if anyone dares to touch them, to be hard as a tire; so all the beer which old Mr. Birch had drunk in his life seemed to have transmuted itself magically, and without any particular help from himself, into muscle. His face was broad, browned and weathered, with a large, twisted nose that fattened like a root prospering in mid-air, with jagged teeth brown as kernels of indian corn, with eyes of a pale blue like fringed gentians. His hair was soft and fine and white as the silk which in autumn spills from milkweed when it bursts, and carries the seed away on the wind.

He might have been a poacher, a great huntsman outside the law, except that upon his first arriving in Ravensburg he seemed to have attempted some such thing and got lost on the hills, in the deep forest, to be found two days later by accident (for no one knew he had gone) when a couple of real poachers came across him sitting on a fallen tree with his rifle on his lap. Since then old Adam Birch had stayed away from the deep forest, and though it was thought he might not be above taking a deer out of season, or in season at night by jack-lantern, that would be very likely because the deer was wandering past his front door, where it could really be regarded as a nuisance on his property and killed quite legally. But as a true poacher he exemplified something that must happen more frequently than we know, a career of crime prevented by simple incompetence. It remained true to say, when asked what Adam Birch did, that he did nothing.

Now one of the newspapers that Adam Birch used to read in the Blue Light Tavern evenings was the Hartland Press, and as Hartland was the county seat that paper used to publish a page or so of doings around the county generally; one of the things they would run from time to time, just to make up the end of a column, was a little stick of a sentence or two saying how Ravensburg had got its name, and once they added another sentence to the effect that in one year the birds had been so numerous, and such a pest to farmers, that a bounty had been put on their heads of twenty-five cents per bird. And that was all it said, but it seems to have been enough. People find their destiny by the most trivial indications.

That little stick of filler could doubtless lie around a printer's shop for fifty years or more, and even be printed three or four times or more, without becoming an occasion of anxiety to any large number of crows or ravens or both, without inciting any person to the kind of large-scale activity implicit in its premises. The sensible person, the person with a business and a life of his own, skimming over the article in the first place as of no real interest and clearly inserted just to fill space, would think—if he fleetingly thought of it at all—that this bounty must have been withdrawn long, long ago. A less sensible person might pause to think: why, there's money in crows—why not go out and . . . . ? But by this time even he would have concluded dismally that probably the bounty had been withdrawn long, long ago, and even if it hadn't been he would look seven kinds of damn fool out blasting away at crows, which were very wily birds; and he would think of the cost of shotgun shells (or rifle bullets if he had so high an opinion of his skill) and what his friends would say (not to mention his wife), and he would by that time anyhow be half-way through the next column of type, dozing off a little maybe, and that would be that.

Adam Birch was not a sensible person, in this sense, and not even a less sensible person; it seems likely he thought quite a lot about that stick of type (it is at least a plausible inference that he did) and that somewhere in his hypothetical background (beer baron, rum-runner, etc.) there lay the possible application of modern industrial methods to the problem of crows; there may have been also in that background the vague suggestion that ordinances and laws do not get repealed but get forgotten instead. The conclusion had to be that a bounty offered on the premise that farm boys would here and there loose off at a crow with a flintlock (or whatever they had back then) was perfectly liable to survive in oblivion, and, like so many ancient customs, traditions and what-not, provide modern opportunities and modern embarrassments. Such at any rate may have been the mechanics of the matter; as to what were the deeper motives which caused Adam Birch to leave his seat on the shaky porch and come to be the scourge of crows, little or nothing can be said. Maybe he had come in all that time to hate crows, and needed only the slight financial incentive to get him off his behind and into action; maybe he loved the crows and sacrificed them regretfully to his well-being; or maybe the crows had never really existed for him, and he had thought nothing about them until given an abstract equivalent—that a crow was, a crow meant, twenty-five cents—which had the possibility of being thought about.

But whatever he thought—to take things in their apparent order—the village of Ravensburg did not know for some time, though there had been the following indications of increased activity on Birch's part: that he took his old Ford (which he had got when he planned on doing some farming which he did not do) over to Hartland several times; that he was often to be seen snooping around the stove factory picking up old bits and pieces (there may have been a law against that, but who would enforce such a thing?); that he got the Village Records from the clerk and spent hours going through them, his lips moving silently while he ran his forefinger down page after page looking for what ought not to be there; that finally, one day, he came into the clerk's office holding a dead crow and said he had come for the bounty on that crow. The clerk looked at him vaguely, but old Birch showed him the Records with the announcement of the bounty, and prepared to take him right through to show that the bounty was still on the book. "All right, I believe you," the clerk said after a few minutes of this, and threw him a quarter across the counter, taking in exchange the dead crow and tossing it thoughtlessly in the waste basket behind him. He remembered thinking, the clerk did, that maybe he ought to mention that bounty to the Mayor or the Judge, but he put it off from laziness, thinking, "If he comes in again, I'll let someone know."

The foregoing suggests—it is easy to be wise after the event—the care with which Adam Birch, having discovered doubtless from the Records the difficulty of negative proof, sought to put the burden of it altogether on the other side; and established him a precedent with the clerk; for it followed, once the principle was admitted that a quarter would be paid for a crow, that n crows would bring n quarters.

What else followed was that toward dusk a few days later Ravensburg was startled out of its suppertime wits by numerous and rapid explosions. Everyone rushed out of doors, but it was too dark to see much, no glare of fire lit the horizon, silence had already settled back down (though a number of crows, startled by

the blast no doubt, were flying about overhead and screaming),
so everyone went back inside to supper and speculation—the latter
quite useless, for there were no industries in Ravensburg which
would go off with anything like that effect; so people finally began
to declare it must have been over to Hartland, and sounded so
loud on account of echoing from the hills. Anyone out walking
the highway, however, would have seen, probably without tying
it to the explosions, a lantern bobbing ceaselessly and jerkily up
and down as it moved this way and that around the swamp-lands
by the river; this lantern was attached to Adam Birch's belt. The
milkman saw this light next day at dawn, it was still bobbing up
and down, but he did not give it much thought because of the
gloom and mist of morning which made all else impossible to see.

Full sunlight disclosed a horrible mess, there on the marshes
before old Mr. Birch's house. Trees, split and fallen, lay every
which way, and between the trees the ground was covered with
crows. Among these crows still strode Adam Birch, the lantern at
his belt still jerking up and down (it was still lit, as a matter of
fact) as he methodically and according to some definite pattern
he had laid out in his head moved about bashing at the black
bodies with a baseball bat in his right hand and a length of lead
pipe in his left. Here and there a crow still feebly fluttered or
cawed, but mostly those crows were through. Mr. Birch must
presently have thought so, or had enough anyhow, for just as he
was he got into his Ford and drove off to the office of the clerk.

It was still quite early, the clerk had only just got there and was
occupied rubbing the sleep from his eyes, when in came Adam
Birch covered in mud, sweat, blood and feathers, with pieces of
bone and crow's eyes sticking to his clothing, his hair all bloody
and black with mud where he must have pushed it back out of his
eyes with a gory hand—in came Adam Birch and said that so far
as he had reckoned he was entitled to the bounty on about two
thousand crows and a hard night's work it'd been.

The clerk, as soon as he recovered from the terrible fright the
sight of old Mr. Birch had given him by coming in covered with
blood and so forth, realized that the matter was beyond his com-
petence, and so he told Mr. Birch that nothing could be done
until the Mayor came in, which would be in about half an hour.

"I'll wait," Mr. Birch replied. And so he would have, had that clerk not been greatly taken with his own cleverness and after a moment said, with a slight, civil sneer, "We don't pay no bounty but for crows in hand, crows in the field is not enough." That, he thought, would discourage the old man.

But Mr. Birch was not discouraged, he acknowledged the logic of what the clerk had said, so he simply turned back and loaded his Ford up to the roof with dead crows and came up to the office again while the clerk was out at the barber shop telling everyone what had happened; with the result that when the Mayor arrived at the Town Hall the floor of the outer office, where his clerk worked, had on it a substantial first load of dead crows; Adam Birch having meanwhile gone back for more. "Clerk!" shouted the Mayor, in a voice that could be and was heard clear down to the barber shop; and the clerk came running back to be denounced by the Mayor. Before this clerk could get in a word edgewise, back came Mr. Adam Birch with another load of dead crows, which he began dumping slowly, two by two, on the floor in the office.

When the Mayor finally understood what had happened, he used his wits. First he told the clerk to tell Mr. Birch to get those crows out of there. They would count the crows on the field, he said, and (with an edge in his voice) Mr. Birch would get everything that was coming to him. Mr. Birch obediently began removing the crows, which he put back on the field in front of his house to be counted. Meanwhile the Mayor, after instructing his clerk to wash the floor, summoned to a conference the Chief of Police, the Judge and the Game Warden. This conference lasted into the mid-morning, and when it was over all these officials drove out to see just what had taken place; by that time the whole town, more or less, was standing around with hands in pockets, smoking and making remarks. It was a public holiday.

It was clear by now that what Mr. Birch had done, with great effort and at some cost, was to manufacture a number of bombs from sticks of dynamite placed in stovepipes and packed from end to end with fragments of iron stove. These bombs, wired to storage batteries, had been placed quite high in the trees where the crows most numerously nested; there on the ground lay the ladder which Mr. Birch had evidently constructed himself, a very crude ladder; and from the group of batteries on the porch wires still led away everywhere. And there on the ground were all those crows. It was a sickening spectacle. Among the crows, when they came to be counted, lay a number of innocent victims—presuming the crows to have been in some way guilty: squirrels, rabbits, a brace of pheasant, three woodchuck, a few dozen sparrows, starlings, robins, three or four jays, and there was even one doe lying dead at the edge of the wood, a piece of stove-door in her head. What was more, several fragments of a bomb incautiously planted too close by had gone through the side window of Mr. Birch's cabin, breaking the glass, a hanging bulb and the mirror on the far wall. It looked probable, as this window was but a few feet from the porch, that Mr. Birch himself might easily have destroyed himself with the crows; and some people were of the opinion that this would have been a good thing.

But this kind of indignation came from a very small minority, inspired perhaps most of all by the clerk, whose motives for indignation could not have been purely in favor of the crows. Most people were a little dazed by the whole affair, did not know what to make of it—for it seemed unlikely that the appearance of so much blood could be unconnected with some sort of crime—and were waiting for someone to take an official view. Mr. Birch by this time, whether to avoid questions or simply because he was tired, had gone into his cabin and shut the door. It is noteworthy that practically everyone among the confused majority had gone over to look at the dead doe and remarked on the pity of that, as though a certain size and distinction of gender were necessary to make innocence visible. Apart from this, though, many people were inclined to laugh at the whole business—if they had had nothing against crows they did not know so much in their favor either—and to make the outstanding thing the "unholy mess" that Mr. Birch had caused. Some said he was mad, and most likely all would have agreed that his action had been at least queer; yet there was also, to such as imagined it in any detail, something ludicrously yet frighteningly homeric and titanic in the idea of the brute old man with the white hair slaughtering wounded crows the whole night long by lantern light. It was not the Vale of Roncesvalles, nor the Valley of Ajalah where Joshua made the sun stand still, but remotely it parodied such scenes, and Mr. Birch implicitly had the sort of reputation from his deed that the tailor had in the fairy tale, who slaughtered six at one blow. As for the old man's being in fact and in law mad, there had to be set over against that the irreproachable cold sanity of his having done all this for money; and in some people's minds the question of his madness resolved itself into two more basic questions: was it enough money? and would he get the money? It should be added that a few people, looking at the ground, became sick to their stomachs.

The remainder of the morning was taken up with an official tally of the crows. The clerk, carrying a writing board, moved through the field marking off each crow which Adam Birch, summoned from his house, placed in a pile until there were twenty-five; then they would both, followed by the Mayor and the Judge and the Chief of Police and the Game Warden, move a few feet over and begin again. The crowd spread raggedly around them.

It turned out that the number of crows came to 2,102, or, translated, a bounty of $525.50. Allowing the odd dollars over for expenses (the dynamite, the batteries) Adam Birch could be said roughly to clear five hundred dollars. The Mayor was almost in a stupor from the sun and indignation.

The Village of Ravensburg did not have five hundred dollars to spend on this old man, and was not certain (in the person of the Mayor) if it would be morally right to spend it so granting the money to be available. Legally, legalistically, it appeared to be old Adam Birch's just reward for ridding the village of such a number of crows which for all practical purposes it had not even known it had. There was not such a deal of farming around Ravensburg any more, the land being mostly poor and worked out, and besides, as the Game Warden had assured him that morning, the modern view of crows, rather different from what had been believed when the bounty was established, held them to be as useful as they were destructive, inasmuch as the contents of their stomachs proved they ate not merely corn but so much else besides that the corn scarcely mattered: all sorts of offal, refuse, carrion, garbage; young birds, adult ones now and then, eggs, mice and snakes. A neutral sort of bird, in the modern view.

To a reporter who had come from Hartland the Mayor said
(again) that Mr. Birch would get everything that was coming to
him.

At his conference that morning, he had found the other dig-
nitaries of the village entirely agreed that something must be done,
though no one was altogether sure what it would be. But the
Chief of Police (and Fire Chief) had been reassuring when he
said: "You can't make that much noise and not commit a crime,"
while the Game Warden, echoing him, had said: "You can't kill
that many anythings and not commit a crime," and the Judge had
said: "We'll see to it that the man eats crow," at which all four
of them dourly smiled.

So when old Adam Birch showed, by instruction, to collect his
reward—it was now mid-afternoon, and he had cleaned himself up
and changed his clothes—he found waiting for him not only the
clerk but the Mayor, and not only the clerk and the Mayor but
also the Chief of Police and the Game Warden and the Judge,
all of whose offices gave off the clerk's room, and all of them were
standing in the doors of their offices, smiling.

The Mayor congratulated Mr. Birch upon ridding the village of
all those crows, and asked him to step over to the clerk, who
would make him out a check for five hundred and twenty-five
dollars and fifty cents. When this was done the Chief of Police
tapped him on the shoulder and said: "Adam Birch, I arrest you in
the name of the law," and brought him over to where the Judge
was standing.

"This man is charged with disturbing the peace," said the Chief,
"also with the unlicensed possession and use of explosives."

"Guilty or not guilty?" asked the Judge, and old Adam, who
saw very well where things were tending, replied that he was
guilty.

"Fifty dollars on each count," said the Judge. "Case dismissed.
Pay the clerk as you leave."

But, before he could even pay, the Game Warden had arrested
Adam, too, on four charges. First, killing a deer out of season.
Second, killing a deer by illegal means. Third, killing a doe.
Fourth, as some of those crows had fallen in the river, polluting a
stream. To all these charges Adam Birch had to plead guilty, and

was sentenced to pay a total of three hundred dollars in fines. He also lost his hunting license on this account, and it was a lucky thing he had one, as the officials were planning to get another fine with the charge of killing a deer without a license.

Because they could not get this other fine they were puzzled for a moment; Adam was handing the clerk his check and would have received $125.50 in change. But the Judge spoke up in time and said there was the matter of destruction of public property; the trees were public property: fifty dollars. And this inspired him to add that the crows also, inasmuch as the village was named after them, or after the ravens anyhow, no difference—the crows also were public property. That would be fifty dollars.

There was a great chance, now, of Adam's escaping with $25.50 in pocket, to pay him for the dynamite. But the Mayor, at this moment, became very clever.

"Of course, you could plead innocent to all these charges," he said, and Adam turned toward him looking bewildered.

"I mean, nobody *saw* you do all those things," insisted the Mayor. "Maybe you didn't do them?"

"In that case," said Adam Birch, "I plead innocent."

"In that case," said the Mayor, "you didn't kill those crows, so there will be no bounty."

"Sonofagun," said Adam, "there's no justice. I plead guilty."

"Profanity," said the Judge cheerfully, "which is in contempt of court. Twenty-five dollars."

"And fifty cents, Judge," the Mayor reminded him.

"And fifty cents."

After Adam had gone, leaving the check on the clerk's counter, the Mayor sighed.

"Thank God for that doe," he said, or perhaps it was "dough."

But the history does not end on this sordid consideration. No one knew what Mr. Adam Birch thought about all that had happened, for he answered to no laughter and kept his own ideas to himself, sitting on the porch before his place, surveying the field of killed crows. When the Chief of Police came by next day to tell him to clean up and get rid of all those birds and so forth, or there would be another fine, Adam nodded and set about it. By that night, in a true bonfire, a great pyre of crows soaked in kerosene began to burn, and burned for three days. The smell at first was quite good, and led some to say he might have sold the birds for eating, but after a while it became oppressive, and on the third day a downright stink. There might have been another fine imposed for this, but the Mayor did not want (he said) to go beyond justice into tyranny, he pitied the poor old man (in a way) and the fire would soon be over. Besides, there were some who thought that Mr. Birch had got a raw deal, and sympathized with him. It seemed better to let the whole episode die away. Perhaps the only person who did not fully agree with this judgment was, again, Mr. Birch.

Though at the heart of the fire his crows were burnt to indistinctive ash, all round the edges and a certain way in their skulls and their bones remained, intact and beautifully white. These Mr. Birch collected all of the third day, and also thousands of feathers which lay scattered about the field; he even rescued from the periphery of the fire a fairly large number of crow's feet.

Of all this material he patiently began to make souvenirs: quill pens at first, and feathers for hats, and feather Indian headdresses; then, more ambitiously, little lattice houses of bone, a tray of patterned crow-feathers under glass, reflecting brilliantly blue-black lights shot with green; the skulls of the crows were left as they were for macabre stamp-boxes, or the little hole in the top of the skull allowed it to be filled with dirt and a violet or other small flower planted there; the lacquered legs and claws, mounted on rocks (later on polished hardwood), made attractive paperweights. In all this Mr. Birch displayed considerable ingenuity and manual skill; and by midsummer he had made a stand by the highway over the river and was selling these objects, with a certain small success.

Or was it the objects, exactly, which he sold? Each person who stopped at his roadside stand, whether he bought or no, was given a throwaway which old Mr. Birch had had printed in Hartland. This consisted of a single sheet of paper, narrow but about a foot long, on which was printed (in the horrible green type such things often use) an account of the entire incident; or not of the entire incident, for there was no mention of fines or injustices; or more than the entire incident, considered in another way, for what the account omitted at the end it made up for in the beginning; Mr. Birch had placed the massacre of the crows back in the last years of the 19th Century and assigned it to his grandfather (also named Adam Birch), who was described as one of the earliest settlers of Ravensburg Village. The head of the sheet bore a green picture of this grandfather, a majestic and bearded old man who resembled (and happened to be) John Greenleaf Whittier. The account itself described the crows (and ravens) of Ravensburg as, in those days, a menace to farming, a plague comparable to those in the Bible, which the relatively primitive methods of the times had no way of stopping until Grandfather Adam single-handedly, by the ingenious use of dynamite bombs, made the great massacre of crows and became thereby the benefactor of his native place, in witness whereof hardly a crow (and it is true there were now very few) could be seen today in Ravensburg. A final paragraph described the souvenirs offered for sale as family treasures, made by the grandfather and sold now out of absolute necessity.

So that it may have been not the sale of crow-relics at all which Mr. Birch had in mind; the crows were possibly but a means to the sale of a certain idea which he had entertained for some time, an idea of himself as born in Ravensburg and native there; born, moreover, of an old established stock. For how long might he have entertained this idea? That is easily answered, for it was many years since he had begun to speak of himself as born in Ravensburg. But it leads to another question not so easily answered, and rather dreadful to ask—with what intensity had he held this idea? The crows, of course, were killed for the five hundred odd dollars he did not get—or were they? On the night he waded about in the squawking flesh of crows, beating at them, was the further motive already in view? But the mind boggles worse at that than at the bounty of five hundred dollars.

At any rate the scheme more or less succeeded, if that was indeed the scheme. Not that the crow relic business ever really flourished—though it went on—but that a notion of old Adam Birch, grandfather or grandson, got put about and more or less accepted, as people will negatively or implicitly accept something that they do not believe worth disputing; so that when Mr. Adam

Birch died, without remaining kin to claim the bits of nothing that were left, those green-print circulars got just so much in the way of the reality that the Hartland Press referred to him as "the last surviving member of one of Ravensburg's oldest families," and had a line or two about his grandfather ("a colorful figure of earlier times") and the crows ("who were then so numerous and so destructive") and so on.

It may rightfully be objected that Mr. Adam Birch could not have seen this obituary. But a man who can, even in so small a way, change the past so that as it were he grows back into it, and now has a publicly attested being where he had not it before—such a man might have stumbled on some trivial secret of time, at least enough to know his own obituary, and perhaps so much that, becoming a legend, he does not die but after his human death is made the king of the crows, who will one day lead them back to Ravensburg, where indeed a few are beginning to return even now.

*JEAN STAFFORD rose to immediate literary
prominence with the publication of her first novel,*
Boston Adventure, *in 1944. Two others,* The Mountain Lion *and* The Catherine Wheel, *followed in
1947 and 1950. Her stories have appeared regularly
in* The New Yorker *and similar magazines, and a
collection,* Children Are Bored on Sundays, *was
published in 1953. Born in 1915 in Covina, California, she was educated at the University of Colorado
and the University of Heidelberg. She has received
two Guggenheim Fellowships, in 1945 and 1948,
and a grant from the National Institute of Arts and
Letters. Her story, "In the Zoo," won the First Prize
in the 1955 O. Henry Awards.*

BEATRICE TRUEBLOOD'S STORY

From THE NEW YORKER

When Beatrice Trueblood was in her middle thirties and on the
very eve of her second marriage, to a rich and reliable man—when,
that is, she was in the prime of life and on the threshold of a
rosier phase of it than she had ever known before—she overnight
was stricken with total deafness.

"The vile unkindness of fate!" cried Mrs. Onslager, the hostess
on whose royal Newport lawn, on a summer day at lunchtime,
poor Beatrice had made her awful discovery. Mrs. Onslager was
addressing a group of house guests a few weeks after the catas-
trophe and after the departure of its victim—or, more properly, of
its victims, since Marten ten Brink, Mrs. Trueblood's fiance, had
been there, too. The guests were sitting on the same lawn on the
same sort of dapper afternoon, and if the attitudes of some of Mrs.
Onslager's audience seemed to be somnolent, they were so because
the sun was so taming and the sound of the waves was a glamorous

lullaby as the Atlantic kneaded the rocks toward which the lawn sloped down. They were by no means indifferent to this sad story; a few of them knew Marten ten Brink, and all of them knew Beatrice Trueblood, who had been Mrs. Onslager's best friend since their girlhood in St. Louis.

"I'm obliged to call it fate," continued Mrs. Onslager. "Because there's nothing wrong with her. All the doctors have reported the same thing to us, and she's been to a battalion of them. At first she refused to go to anyone on the ground that it would be a waste of money, of which she has next to none, but Jack and I finally persuaded her that if she didn't see the best men in the country and let us foot the bills, we'd look on it as unfriendliness. So, from Johns Hopkins, New York Hospital, the Presbyterian, the Leahy Clinic, and God knows where, the same account comes back: there's nothing physical to explain it, no disease, no lesion, there's been no shock, there were no hints of any kind before- hand. And *I'll* not allow the word 'psychosomatic' to be uttered in my presence—not in this connection, at any rate—because I know Bea as well as I know myself and she is not hysterical. Therefore, it has to be fate. And there's a particularly spiteful irony in it if you take a backward glance at her life. If ever a woman deserved a holiday from tribulation, it's Bea. There was first of all a posi- tively hideous childhood. The classic roles were reversed in the family, and it was the mother who drank and the father who nagged. Her brother took to low life like a duck to water and was a juvenile delinquent before he was out of knickers—I'm sure he must have ended up in Alcatraz. They were unspeakably poor, and Bea's aunts dressed her in their hand-me-downs. It was a house of the most humiliating squalor, all terribly genteel. You know what I mean—the mother prettying up her drunkenness by those transparent dodges like 'Two's my limit,' and keeping the gin in a Waterford decanter, and the father looking as if butter wouldn't melt in his mouth when they were out together publicly, although everyone knew that he was a perfectly ferocious tartar. Perhaps it isn't true that he threw things at his wife and children and whipped them with a razorstrop—he didn't have to, because he could use his tongue like a bludgeon. And then after all that horror, Bea married Tom Trueblood—really to escape her family,

I think, because she couldn't possibly have loved him. I mean it isn't possible to love a man who is both a beast and a fool. *He* was drunker than her mother ever thought of being; he was obscene, he was raucous, his infidelities to that good, beautiful girl were of a vulgarity that caused the mind to boggle. I'll never know how she managed to live with him for seven mortal years. And then at last, after all those tempests, came Marten ten Brink, like redemption itself. There's nothing sensational in Marten, I'll admit. He's rather a stick, he was born rather old, he's rather jokeless and bossy. But, oh, Lord, he's so *safe,* he was so protective of her, and he is so scrumptiously rich! And two months before the wedding *this* thunderbolt comes out of nowhere. It's indecent! It makes me so angry!" And this faithful friend shook her pretty red head rapidly in indignation, as if she were about to hunt down fate with a posse and hale it into court.

"Are you saying that the engagement has been broken?" asked Jennie Fowler, who had just got back from Europe and to whom all this was news.

Mrs. Onslager nodded, closing her eyes as if the pain she suffered were unbearable. "They'd been here for a week, Marten and Bea, and we were making the wedding plans, since they were to be married from my house. And the very day after this gruesome thing happened, she broke the engagement. She wrote him a note and sent it in to his room by one of the maids. I don't know what she said in it, though I suppose she told him she didn't want to be a burden, something like that—much more gracefully, of course, since Bea *is* the soul of courtesy. But whatever it was, it must have been absolutely unconditional, because he went back to town before dinner the same night. The letter I got from him afterward scarcely mentioned it—he only said he was sorry his visit here had ended on 'an unsettling note.' I daresay he was still too shocked to say more."

"Hard times on ten Brink," said Harry McEvoy, who had never married.

"What do you mean, 'hard lines on *ten Brink?'*" cried Mrs. Fowler, who had married often, and equally often had gone, livid with rage, to Nevada.

"Well, if he was in love with her, if he counted on this . . .

Not much fun to have everything blow up in your face. Lucky in a way, I suppose, that it happened before, and not afterward."

The whole party glowered at McEvoy, but he was entirely innocent of their disapproval and of his stupidity that had provoked it, since he was looking through a pair of binoculars at a catboat that seemed to be in trouble.

"If he was in love with her," preached Mrs. Fowler rabidly, "he would have stuck by her. He would have refused to let her break the engagement. He would have been the one to insist on the specialists, he would have moved Heaven and *earth,* instead of which he fled like a scared rabbit at the first sign of bad luck. I thought he was only a bore—I didn't know he was such a venomous pill."

"No, dear, he isn't that," said Priscilla Onslager. "Not the most sensitive man alive, but I'd never call him a venomous pill. After all, remember it was *she* who dismissed *him.*"

"Yes, but if he'd had an ounce of manliness in him, he would have put up a fight. No decent man, no manly man, would abandon ship at a time like that." Mrs. Fowler hated men so passionately that no one could dream why she married so many of them.

"Has it occurred to any of you that she sent him packing because she didn't want to marry him?" The question came from Douglas Clyde, a former clergyman, whose worldliness, though it was very wise, had cost him his parish and his cloth.

"Certainly no," said Priscilla. "I tell you, Doug, I know Bea. But at the moment the important thing isn't the engagement, because I'm sure it could be salvaged if she could be cured. And how's she to be cured if nothing's wrong? I'd gladly have the Eumenides chase me for a while if they'd only give her a rest."

Jack Onslager gazed through half-closed eyes at his wholesome, gabbling wife—he loved her very much, but her public dicta were always overwrought and nearly always wrong—and then he closed his eyes tight against the cluster of his guests, and he thought how blessed it would be if with the same kind of simple physical gesture one could also temporarily close one's ears. One could decline to touch, to taste, to see, but it required a skill he had not mastered to govern the ears. Those stopples made of wax and cotton

would be insulting at a party; besides, they made him claustropho-
bic, and when he used them, he could hear the interior workings
of his skull, the boiling of his brains in his brain-pan, a rustling
behind his jaws. He would not like to go so far as Beatrice had
gone, but he would give ten years of his life (he had been about
to say he would give his eyes and changed it) to be able, when he
wanted, to seal himself into an impenetrable silence.

To a certain extent, however, one could insulate the mind
against the invasion of voices by an act of will, by causing them
to blur together into a general hubbub. And this is what he did
now; in order to consider Mrs. Trueblood's deafness, he deafened
himself to the people who were talking about it. He thought of
the day in the early summer when the extraordinary thing had
taken place.

It had been Sunday. The night before, the Onslagers and their
house-party—the young Allinghams, Mary and Leon Herbert,
Beatrice and ten Brink—had gone to a ball. It was the kind of
party to which Onslager had never got used, although he had been
a multimillionaire for twenty years and not only had danced
through many such evenings but had been the host at many more,
in his own houses or in blazoned halls that he had hired. He was
used to opulence in other ways, and took for granted his boats and
horses and foreign cars. He also took for granted, and was bored
by, most of the rites of the rich: the formal dinner parties at which
the protocol was flawlessly maneuvered and conversation moved
on stilts and the food was platitudinous; evenings of music to bene-
fit a worthy cause (How papery the turkey always was at the
buffet supper after the Grieg!); the tea parties to which one went
obediently to placate old belles who had lost their looks and their
husbands and the roles that, at their first assembly, they had
assumed they would play forever. Well-mannered and patient,
Onslager did his duty suavely, and he was seldom thrilled.

But these lavish, enormous midsummer dancing parties in the
fabulous, foolish villas on Bellevue Avenue and along the Ocean
Drive did make his backbone tingle, did make him glow. Even
when he was dancing, or proposing a toast, or fetching a wrap for
a woman who had found the garden air too cool, he always felt

on these occasions that he was static, looking at a colossal *tableau vivant* that would vanish at the wave of a magic golden wand. He was bewitched by the women, by all those *soignee* or demure or jubilant or saucy or dreaming creatures in their caressing, airy dresses and their jewels whose priceless hearts flashed in the light from superb chandeliers. They seemed, these dancing, laughing, incandescent goddesses, to move in inaccessible spheres; indeed, his wife, Priscilla, was transfigured, and, dancing with her, he was moon-struck. No matter how much he drank (the champagne of those evenings was invested with a special property—one tasted the grapes, and the grapes had come from celestial vineyards), he remained sober and amazed and, in spite of his amazement, so alert that he missed nothing and recorded everything. He did not fail to see, in the looks and shrugs and the clicking of glasses, the genesis of certain adulteries, and the demise of others in a glance of contempt or an arrogant withdrawal. With the accuracy of the uninvolved bystander, he heard and saw amongst these incredible women moving in the aura of their heady perfume their majestic passions—tragic heartbreak, sublime fulfillment, dangerous jealousy, the desire to murder. When, on the next day, he had come back to earth, he would reason that his senses had devised a fiction to amuse his mind, and that in fact he had witnessed nothing grander than flirtations and impromptu pangs as ephemeral as the flowers in the supper room.

So, at the Paines' vast marble house that night, Onslager, aloof and beguiled as always, had found himself watching Beatrice Trueblood and Marten ten Brink with so much interest that whenever he could he guided his dancing partner near them, and if they left the ballroom for a breath of air on a bench beside a playing fountain, or for a glass of champagne, he managed, if he could do so without being uncivil to his interlocutor and without being observed by them, to excuse himself and follow. If he had stopped to think, this merciful and moral man would have been ashamed of his spying and eavesdropping, but morality was irrelevant to the spell that enveloped him. Besides, he felt invisible.

Consequently, he knew something about that evening that Priscilla did not know and that he had no intention of telling her, partly because she would not believe him, partly because she would be displeased at the schoolboyish (and parvenu) way he put in his time at balls. The fact was that the betrothed were having a quarrel. He heard not a word of it—not at the dance, that is—and he saw not a gesture or a grimace of anger, but he nevertheless knew surely, as he watched them dance together, that ten Brink was using every ounce of his strength not to shout, and to keep in check a whole menagerie of passions—fire-breathing dragons and bone-crushing serpents and sabretoothed tigers—and he knew also that Beatrice was running for dear life against the moment when they would be unleashed, ready to gobble her up. Her broad, wide-eyed, gentle face was so still it could have been a painting of a face that had been left behind when the woman who owned it had faded from view, and Bea's golden hand lay on ten Brink's white sleeve as tentatively as a butterfly. Her lover's face, on the other hand, was—Onslager wanted to say "writhing," and the long fingers of the hand that pressed against her back were splayed out and rigid, looking grafted onto the sunny flesh beneath the diaphanous blue stuff of her dress. He supposed that another observer might with justification have said that the man was animated and that his fiancee was becomingly engrossed in all he said, that ten Brink was in a state of euphoria as his wedding approached, while Beatrice moved in a wordless haze of happiness. He heard people admiringly remark on the compatibility of their good looks; they were said to look as if they were "dancing on air"; women thanked goodness that Mrs. Trueblood had come at last into a safe harbor, and men said that ten Brink was in luck.

As soon as the Onslagers and their guests had driven away from the ball and the last echo of the music had perished and the smell of roses had been drowned by the smell of the sea and the magic had started to wane from Onslager's blood, he began to doubt his observations. He was prepared to elide and then forget his heightened insights, as he had always done in the past. The group had come in two cars, and the Allinghams were with him and Priscilla on the short ride home. Lucy Allingham, whose own honeymoon was of late and blushing memory, said, with mock petulance, "I thought *young* love was supposed to be what caught the eye.

But I never saw anything half so grand and wonderful as the looks of those two." And Priscilla said, "How true! How magnificently right you are, Lucy! They were radiant, both of them."

Late as it was, Priscilla proposed a last drink and a recapitulation of the party—everyone had found it a joy—but ten Brink said, "Beatrice and I want to go down and have a look at the waves, if you don't mind," and when no one minded but, on the contrary, fondly sped them on their pastoral way, the two walked down across the lawn and presently were gone from sight in the romantic mist. Their friends watched them and sighed, charmed, and went inside to drink a substitute for nectar.

Hours later (he looked at his watch and saw that it was close on five o'clock), Jack woke, made restless by something he had sensed or dreamed, and, going to the east windows of his bedroom to look at the water and see what the sailing would be like that day, he was arrested by the sight of Beatrice and Marten standing on the broad front step below. They were still in their evening clothes. Beatrice's stance was tired; she looked bedraggled. They stood confronting each other beside the balustrade; ten Brink held her shoulders tightly, his sharp, handsome (but, thought Onslager suddenly, Mephistophelean) face bent down to hers.

"You mustn't think you can shut your mind to these things," he said. "You can't shut your ears to them." Their voices were clear in the hush of the last of the night.

"I am exhausted with talk, Marten," said Beatrice softly. "I will not hear another word."

An hour afterward, the fairest of days dawned on Newport, and Jack Onslager took out his sloop by himself in a perfect breeze, so that he saw none of his guests until just before lunch, when he joined them for cocktails on the lawn. Everyone was there except Beatrice Trueblood, who had slept straight through the morning but a moment before had called down from her windows that she was nearly ready. It was a flawless day to spend beside the sea; the chiaroscuro of the elm trees and the sun on the broad buoyant lawn shifted as the sea winds disarrayed the leaves, and yonder, on the hyacinthine water, the whitecaps shuddered and the white sails swelled; to the left of the archipelago of chairs

and tables where they sat, Mrs. Onslager's famous rosary was heavily in bloom with every shade of red there was and the subtlest hues
of yellow, and her equally famous blue hydrangeas were at their
zenith against the house, exactly the color of this holiday sky, so
large they nodded on their stems like drowsing heads.

The Allinghams, newly out of their families' comfortable houses
in St. Louis and now living impecuniously in a railroad flat in
New York that they found both adventurous and odious, took in
the lawn and seascape with a look of real greed, and even of
guile, on their faces, as if they planned to steal something or eat
forbidden fruit.

In its pleasurable fatigue from the evening before and too much
sleep this morning, the gathering was momentarily disinclined
to conversation, and they all sat with faces uplifted and eyes closed
against the sun. They listened to the gulls and terns shrieking
with their evergreen gluttony; they heard the buzz-saw rasp of
outboard motors and the quick, cleaving roar of an invisible jet;
they heard automobiles on the Ocean Drive, a power mower
nasally shearing the grass at the house next door, and from that
house they heard, as well, the wail of an infant and the panicky
barking of an infant dog.

"I wish this day would never end," said Lucy Allingham. "This
is the kind of day when you want to kiss the earth. You want to
have an affair with the sky."

"Don't be maudlin, Lucy," said her husband. "And above all,
don't be inaccurate." He was a finicking young cub who had been
saying things like this all weekend.

Onslager's own wife, just as foolishly euphoric but with a
good deal more style, simply through being older, said, "Look,
here comes Beatrice. She looks as if her eyes were fixed in the
Garden of Eden before the Fall and as if she were being sere-
naded by angels."

Marten ten Brink, an empiricist not given to flights of fancy,
said, "Is that a depth bomb I hear?"

No one answered him, for everyone was watching Beatrice as
she came slowly, smiling, down the stone steps from the terrace
and across the lawn, dulcifying the very ground she walked upon.
She was accompanied by Mrs. Onslager's two Siamese cats, who

cantered ahead of her, then stopped, forgetful of their intention, and closely observed the life among the blades of grass, then frolicked on, from time to time emitting that ugly parody of a human cry that is one of the many facets of the Siamese cat's scornful nature. But the insouciant woman paid no attention to them, even when they stopped to fight each other, briefly, with noises straight from Hell.

"You look as fresh as dew, dear," said Priscilla. "Did you simply sleep and sleep?"

"Where on earth did you get that fabric?" asked Mrs. Herbert. "Surely not here. It must have come from Paris. Bea, I do declare your clothes are always the ones I want for myself."

"Sit here, Beatrice," said ten Brink, who had stood up and was indicating the chair next to himself. But Beatrice, ignoring him, chose another chair. The cats, still flirting with her, romped at her feet; one of them pretended to find a sporting prey between her instep and her heel, and he pounced and buck-jumped silently, his tail a fast, fierce whip. Beatrice, who delighted in these animals, bent down to stroke the lean flanks of the other one, momentarily quiescent in a glade of sunshine.

"What do you think of the pathetic fallacy, Mrs. Trueblood?" said Peter Allingham, addressing her averted head. "Don't you think it's pathetic?" By now, Onslager was wishing to do him bodily harm for his schoolmasterish teasing of Lucy.

"Monkeys," murmured Beatrice to the cats. "Darlings."

"Beatrice!" said Marten ten Brink sharply, and strode across to whisper something in her ear. She brushed him away as if he were a fly, and she straightened up and said to Priscilla Onslager, "Why is everyone so solemn? Are you doing a charade of a Quaker meeting?"

"Solemn?" said Priscilla, with a laugh. "If we seem solemn, it's because we're all smitten with this day. Isn't it supreme? Heaven can't possibly be nicer."

"Is this a new game?" asked Beatrice, puzzled, her kind eyes on her hostess's face.

"Is what a new game, dear?"

"What *is* going on?" She had begun to be ever so slightly annoyed. "Is it some sort of silence test? We're to see if we can keep still till teatime? Is it that? I'll be delighted—only, for pity's sake, tell me the rules and the object."

"Silence test! Sweetheart, you're still asleep. Give her a Martini, Jack," said Priscilla nervously, and to divert the attention of the company from her friend's quixotic mood she turned to ten Brink. "I believe you're right," she said, "I believe they're detonating depth bombs. Why on Sunday? I thought sailors got a day of rest like everybody else."

A deep, rumbling subterranean thunder rolled, it seemed, beneath the chairs they sat on.

"It sounds like ninepins in the Catskills," said Priscilla.

"I never could abide that story," said Mary Herbert. "Or the Ichabod Crane one, either."

Jack Onslager, his back toward the others as he poured a drink for Beatrice, observed to himself that the trying thing about these weekends was not the late hours, not the overeating and the over-drinking and the excessive batting of tennis balls and shuttlecocks; it was, instead, this kind of aimless prattle that never ceased. There seemed to exist, on weekends in the country, a universal terror of pauses in conversation, so that it was imperative for Mary Herbert to drag in Washington Irving by the hair of his irrelevant head. Beatrice Trueblood, however, was not addicted to prattle, and he silently congratulated her on the way, in the last few minutes, she had risen above their fatuous questions and compliments. That woman was as peaceful as a pool in the heart of a forest. He turned to her, handing her the drink and looking directly into her eyes (blue and green, like an elegant tropic sea) and he said, "I have never seen you looking prettier."

For just a second, a look of alarm usurped her native and per-petual calm, but then she said, "So you're playing it, too. I don't think it's fair not to tell me—unless this is a joke on me. Am I 'it'?"

At last, Jack was unsettled; Priscilla was really scared; ten Brink was angry, and, getting up again to stand over her like a prose-cuting attorney interrogating a witness of bad character, he said, "You're not being droll, Beatrice, you're being tiresome."

Mrs. Onslager said, "Did you go swimming this morning, lamb? Perhaps you got water in your ears. Lean over—see, like this," and she bent her head low to the left and then to the right while

Beatrice, to whom these calisthenics were inexplicable, watched her, baffled.

Beatrice put her drink on the coffee table, and she ran her forefingers around the shells of her ears. What was the look that came into her face, spreading over it as tangibly as a blush? Onslager afterward could not be sure. At the time he had thought it was terror; he had thought this because, in the confusion that ensued, he had followed, sheeplike with the others, in his wife's lead. But later, when he recaptured it for long reflection, he thought that it had not been terror, but rather that Priscilla in naming it that later was acually speaking of the high color of her own state of mind, and that the look in Beatrice's eyes and on her mouth had been one of revelation, as if she had opened a door and had found behind it a new world so strange, so foreign to all her knowledge and her experience and the history of her senses, that she had spoken only approximately when, in a far, soft, modest voice, she said, "I am deaf. That explains it."

When Onslager had come to the end of his review of those hours of that other weekend and had returned to the present one, he discovered that he had so effectively obliterated the voices around him that he now could not recall a single word of any of the talk, although he had been conscious of it, just as some part of his mind was always conscious of the tension and solution of the tides.

"But you haven't told us yet how she's taking it now," Mrs. Fowler was saying.

"I can't really tell," replied Priscilla. "I haven't been able to go to town to see her, and she refuses to come up here—the place probably has bad associations for her now. And I'm no good at reading between the lines of her letters. She has adjusted to it, I'll say that." Priscilla was thoughtful, and her silence commanded her guests to be silent. After a time, she went on, "I'll say more than that. I'll say she has adjusted too well for my liking. There is a note of gaiety in her letters—she is almost jocose. For example, in the last one she said that although she had lost Handel and music boxes and the purring of my Siamese, she had gained a valuable immunity to the voices of professional Irishmen."

"Does she mention ten Brink?" asked someone.

"Never," said Priscilla. "It's as if he had never existed. There's more in her letters than the joking tone. I wish I could put my finger on it. The closest I can come is to say she sounds *bemused*."

"Do you think she's given up?" asked Jennie Fowler. "Or has she done everything there is to be done?"

"The doctors recommend psychiatry, of course," said Priscilla, with distaste. "It's a dreary, ghastly, humiliating thought, but I suppose—"

"I should think you *would* suppose!" cried Mrs. Fowler. "You shouldn't leave a stone unturned. Plainly someone's got to *make* her go to an analyst. They're not that dire, Priscilla. I've heard some very decent things about several of them."

"It won't be I who'll make her go," said Priscilla, sighing. "I disapprove too much."

"But you don't disapprove of the medical people," persisted Jennie. "Why fly in the face of their prescription?"

"Because . . . I *couldn't* do it. Propose to Beatrice that she is mental? I can't support the thought of it."

"Then Jack must do it," said the managerial divorcee. "Jack must go straight down to town and get her to a good man and then patch things up with Marten ten Brink. I still detest the sound of him, but *de gustibus*, and I think she ought to have a husband."

The whole gathering—even the cynical ex-pastor—agreed that this proposal made sense, and Onslager, while he doubted his right to invade Bea's soft and secret and eccentric world, found himself so curious to see her again to learn whether some of his conjectures were right that he fell in with the plan and agreed to go to New York in the course of the week. As, after lunch, they dispersed, some going off for *boccie* and others to improve their shining skin with sun, Douglas Clyde said sotto-voce to Onslager, "Why doesn't it occur to anyone but you and me that perhaps she doesn't *want* to hear?"

Startled, the host turned to his guest. "How did you know I thought that?"

"I watched you imitating deafness just now," said the other. "You looked beatific. But if I were you, I wouldn't go too far."

"Then you believe . . . contrary to Priscilla and her Eumenides . . . ?"

"I believe what you believe—that the will is free and very strong," Clyde answered, and he added, "I believe further that it can cease to be an agent and become a despot. I suspect hers *has*."

Mrs. Trueblood lived in the East Seventies, in the kind of apartment building that Jack Onslager found infinitely more melancholy than the slum tenements that flanked and faced it in the sultry city murk of August. It was large and new and commonplace and jerry-built, although it strove to look as solid as Gibraltar. Its brick facade was an odious mustardy brown. The doorman was fat and choleric, and when Onslager descended from his cab, he was engaged in scolding a band of vile-looking little boys, who stood on the curb doubled up with giggles, now and again screaming out an unbelievable obscenity when the pain of their wicked glee abated for a moment. A bum was lying spread-eagled on the sidewalk a few doors down; his face was bloody but he was not dead, for he was snoring fearsomely. Across the street, a brindle boxer leaned out a window, his forepaws sedately crossed on the sill in a parody of the folded arms of the many women who were situated in other windows, irascibly agreeing with one another at the tops of their voices that the heat was Hell.

But the builders of the house where Mrs. Trueblood lived had pretended that none of this was so; they had pretended that the neighborhood was bourgeois and there was no seamy side, and they had commemorated their swindle in a big facsimile of rectitude. Its square foyer was papered with a design of sanitary ferns upon a field of hygienic beige; two untruthful mirrors mirrored each other upon either lateral wall, and beneath them stood love seats with aseptic green plastic cushions and straight blond legs. The slow self-service elevator was an asphyxiating chamber with a fan that blew a withering sirocco; its tinny walls were embossed with a meaningless pattern of fleurs-de-lis; light, dim and reluctant, came though a fixture with a shade of some ersatz material made esoterically in the form of a starfish. As Onslager ascended to the sixth floor at a hot snail's pace, hearing alarming *rales* and exhalations in the machinery, he was fretful with his discomfort and fretful with snobbishness. He deplored the circumstances that required Beatrice, who was so openhearted a woman, to live in surroundings so mean-minded; he could not help thinking sorrowfully that the ideal place for her was Marten ten Brink's house on Fifty-fifth Street, with all its depths of richness and its sophisticated planes. The bastard, he thought, taking Jennie Fowler's line—why did he let her down? And then he shook his head, because, of course, he knew it hadn't been like that.

This was not his first visit to Beatrice. He and Priscilla had been here often to cocktail parties since she had lived in New York, but the place had made no impression on him; he liked cocktail parties so little that he went to them with blinders on and looked at nothing except, furtively, his watch. But today, in the middle of a hostile heat wave and straight from the felicities of Newport, he was heavyhearted thinking how her apartment was going to look; he dreaded it; he wished he had not come. He was struck suddenly with the importunity of his mission. How had they *dared* be so possessive and dictatorial? And why had *he* been delegated to urge her to go to a psychiatrist? To be sure, his letter to her had said only that since he was going to be in the city, he would like to call on her, but she was wise and sensitive and she was bound to know that he had come to snoop and recommend. He was so embarrassed that he considered going right down again and sending her some flowers and a note of apology for failing to show up. She could not know he was on his way, for it had not been possible to announce himself over the house telephone—and how, indeed, he wondered, would she know when her doorbell rang?

But when the doors of the elevator slid open, he found her standing in the entrance of her apartment. She looked at her watch and said, "You're punctual." Her smiling, welcoming face was cool and tranquil; unsmirched by the heat and the dreariness of the corridor and, so far as he could judge, by the upheaval of her life, she was as proud and secret-living as a flower. He admired her and he dearly loved her. He cherished her as one of life's most beautiful appointments.

"That you should have to come to town on such a day!" she exclaimed. "I'm terribly touched that you fitted me in."

He started to speak; he was on the point of showering on her a cornucopia of praise and love, and then he remembered that she would not hear. So, instead, he kissed her on either cheek and hoped the gesture, mild and partial, obscured his turmoil. She smelled of roses; she seemed the embodiment of everything most pricelessly feminine, and he felt as diffident as he did at those lovely summer balls.

Her darkened, pretty sitting room—he should not have been so fearful, he should have had more faith in her—smelled of roses, too, for everywhere there were bowls of them from Priscilla's garden, brought down by the last weekend's guests.

"I'm terribly glad you fitted me in," repeated Beatrice when she had given him a drink, and a pad of paper and a pencil, by means of which he was to communicate with her (she did this serenely and without explanation, as if it were the most natural thing in the world), "because yesterday my bravura began to peter out. In fact, I'm scared to death."

He wrote, "You shouldn't be alone. Why not come back to us? You know nothing would please us more." How asinine, he thought. What a worthless sop.

She laughed. "Priscilla couldn't bear it. Disaster makes her cry, good soul that she is. No, company wouldn't make me less scared."

"Tell me about it," he wrote, and again he felt like a fool.

It was not the deafness itself that scared her, she said—not the fear of being run down by an automobile she had not heard or violated by an intruder whose footfall had escaped her. These anxieties, which beset Priscilla, did not touch Beatrice. Nor had she yet begun so very much to miss voices or other sounds she liked; it was a little unnerving, she said, never to know if the telephone was ringing, and it was strange to go into the streets and see the fast commotion and hear not a sound, but it had its comic side and it had its compensations—it amused her to see the peevish snapping of a dog whose bark her deafness had forever silenced, she was happy to be spared her neighbors' vociferous television sets. But she was scared all the same. What had begun to harry her was that her wish to be deaf had been granted. This was exactly how she put it, and Onslager received her secret uneasily. She had not bargained for banishment, she said; she had only wanted a holiday. Now, though, she felt that the Devil lived with her, eternally wearing a self-congratulatory smile.

"You are being fanciful," Onslager wrote, although he did not think she was at all fanciful. "You can't wish yourself deaf."

But Beatrice insisted that she *had* done just that.

She emphasized that she had *elected* to hear no more, would not permit of accident, and ridiculed the doting Priscilla's sentimental fate. She had done it suddenly and out of despair, and she was sorry now. "I am ashamed. It was an act of cowardice," she said.

"How cowardice?" wrote Onslager.

"I could have broken with Marten in a franker way. I could simply have told him I had changed my mind. I didn't have to make him mute by making myself deaf."

"Was there a quarrel?" he wrote, knowing already the question was superfluous.

"Not *a* quarrel. An incessant wrangle. Marten is jealous and he is indefatigably vocal. I wanted terribly to marry him—I don't suppose I loved him very much but he seemed good, seemed safe. But all of a sudden I thought, I cannot and I will not listen to another word. And now I'm sorry because I'm so lonely here, inside my skull. Not hearing makes one helplessly egocentric."

She hated any kind of quarrel, she said—she shuddered at raised voices and quailed before looks of hate—but she could better endure a howling brawl amongst vicious hoodlums, a shrill squabble of shrews, a degrading jangle between servant and mistress, than she could the least altercation between a man and a woman whose conjunction has had as its origin tenderness and a concord of desire. A relationship that was predicated upon love was far too delicate of composition to be threatened by cross-purposes. There were houses where she would never visit again because she had seen a husband and wife in ugly battle dress; there were restaurants she went to unwillingly because in them she had seen lovers in harsh dispute. How could things ever be the same between them again? How could two people possibly continue to associate with each other after such humiliating, disrobing displays?

As Beatrice talked in discreet and general terms and candidly met Jack Onslager's eyes, in another part of her mind she was looking down the shadowy avenue of all the years of her life. As a girl and, before that, as a child, in the rambling, shambling house in St. Louis, Beatrice in her bedroom doing her lessons would hear a rocking chair on a squeaking board two flights down; this was the chair in which her tipsy mother seesawed, dressed for the street and wearing a hat, drinking gin and humming a Venetian barcarole to which she had forgotten the words. Her mother drank from noon, when, with lamentations, she got up, till midnight, when, the bottle dry, she fell into a groaning, nightmare-ridden unconsciousness that resembled the condition immediately preceding death. This mortal sickness was terrifying; her removal from reality was an ordeal for everyone, but not even the frequent and flamboyant threats of suicide, the sobbed proclamations that she was the chief of sinners, not all the excruciating embarrassments that were created by that interminable and joyless spree, were a fraction as painful as the daily quarrels that commenced as soon as her father came home, just before six, and continued, unmitigated, until he—a methodical man—went to bed, at ten. Dinner, nightly, was a hideous experience for a child, since the parents were not inhibited by their children or the maid and went on heaping atrocious abuse upon each other, using sarcasms, threats, lies—every imaginable expression of loathing and contempt. They swam in their own blood, but it was an ocean that seemed to foster and nourish them; their awful wounds were their necessities. Freshly appalled each evening, unforgiving, disgraced, Beatrice miserably pushed her food about on her plate, never hungry, and often she imagined herself alone on a desert, far away from any human voice. The moment the meal was finished, she fled to her schoolbooks, but even when she put her fingers in her ears, she could hear her parents raving, whining, bullying, laughing horrible, malign laughs. Sometimes, in counterpoint to this vendetta, another would start in the kitchen, where the impudent and slatternly maid and one of her lovers would ask *their* cross questions and give crooked answers.

In spite of all this hatefulness, Beatrice did not mistrust marriage, and, moreover, she had faith in her own even temper. She was certain that sweetness could put an end to strife; she believed that her tolerance was limitless, and she vowed that when she married there would be no quarrels.

But there were. The dew in her eyes as a bride gave way nearly at once to a glaze when she was a wife. She left home at twenty, and at twenty-one married Tom Trueblood, who scolded her for seven years. Since she maintained that it took two to make a quarrel, she tried in the beginning, with all the cleverness and fortitude she had, to refuse to be a party to the storms that rocked her house and left it a squalid shambles, but her silence only made her husband more passionately angry, and at last, ripped and raw, she had to defend herself. Her dignity tramped to death, her honor mutilated, she fought back, and felt estranged from the very principles of her being. Like her parents, Tom Trueblood was sustained by rancor and contentiousness; he really seemed to love these malevolent collisions which made her faint and hot and ill, and he seemed, moreover, to regard them as essential to the married state, and so, needing them, he would not let Beatrice go but tricked and snared her and strewed her path with obstacles, until finally she had been obliged to run away and melodramatically leave behind a note.

Beatrice was a reticent woman and had too much taste to bare all these grubby secret details, but she limned a general picture for him and, when she had finished, she said, "Was it any wonder, then, that when the first blush wore off and Marten showed himself to be cantankerous my heart sank?"

Onslager had listened to her with dismay. He and Priscilla were not blameless of the sin she so deplored—no married people were—but their differences were minor and rare and guarded, their sulks were short-lived. Poor, poor Beatrice, he thought. Poor lamb led to the slaughter.

He wrote, "Have you heard from Marten?"

She nodded, and closed her eyes in a dragging weariness. "He has written me volumes," she said. "In the first place, he doesn't believe that I am deaf but thinks it's an act. He says I am indulging myself, but he is willing to forgive me if I will only come to my senses. Coming to my senses involves, among other things, obliterating the seven years I lived with Tom—I told you he was madly jealous? But how do you amputate experience? How do you eliminate what intransigently *was?*"

"If that's Marten's line," wrote Onslager, revolted by such

childishness, "obviously you can't give him a second thought. The question is what's to be done about *you?*"

"Oh, I don't know, I *do* not know!" There were tears in her voice, and she clasped her hands to hide their trembling. "I am afraid that I am too afraid ever to hear again. And you see how I speak as if I had a choice?"

Now she was frankly wringing her hands, and the terror in her face was sheer. "My God, the mind is diabolical!" she cried. "Even in someone as simple as I."

The stifling day was advancing into the stifling evening, and Jack Onslager, wilted by heat and unmanned by his futile pity, wanted, though he admired and loved her, to leave her. There was nothing he could do.

She saw this, and said, "You must go. Tomorrow I am starting with an analyst. Reassure Priscilla. Tell her I know that everything is going to be all right. I know it not because I am naive but because I *still* have faith in the kindness of life." He could not help thinking that it was will instead of faith that put these words in her mouth.

And, exteriorly, everything was all right for Beatrice. Almost at once, when she began treatment with a celebrated man, her friends began to worry less, and to marvel more at her strength and the wholeness of her worthy soul and the diligence with which she and the remarkable doctor hunted down her troublesome quarry. During this time, she went about socially, lent herself to conversation by reading lips, grew even prettier. Her analysis was a dramatic success, and after a little more than a year she regained her hearing. Some months later, she married a man, Arthur Talbot, who was far gayer than Marten ten Brink and far less rich; indeed, a research chemist, he was poor. Priscilla deplored this aspect of him, but she was carried away by the romance (he looked like a poet, he adored Beatrice) and at last found it in her heart to forgive him for being penniless.

When the Talbots came to Newport for a long weekend not long after they had married, Jack Onslager watched them both with care. No mention had ever been made by either Jack or Beatrice of their conversation on that summer afternoon, and when his wife, who had now become a fervent supporter of psychiatry, exclaimed after the second evening that she had never seen Beatrice so radiant, Onslager agreed with her. Why not? There would be no sense in quarreling with his happy wife. He himself had never seen a face so drained of joy, or even of the memory of joy; he had not been able to meet Bea's eyes.

That Sunday—it was again a summer day beside the sea—Jack Onslager came to join his two guests, who were sitting alone on the lawn. Their backs were to him and they did not hear his approach, so Talbot did not lower his voice when he said to his wife, "I have told you a thousand times that my life has to be exactly as I want it. So stop these hints. *Any* dedicated scientist worth his salt is bad-tempered."

Beatrice saw that her host had heard him; she and Onslager travailed in the brief look they exchanged. It was again an enrapturing day. The weather overhead was fair and bland, but the water was a mass of little wrathful whitecaps.

JOHN STEINBECK was born in 1902 in Salinas, California. After graduating from the Salinas High School, he spent four years at Stanford University as a special student, where his primary interest was in science. He has held many jobs before turning seriously to writing, among them a reporter on a New York paper, an apprentice painter, a chemist and a fruit-picker. His The Grapes of Wrath *was made into a prize winning motion picture as well as winning for him the Pulitzer award. He has achieved literary eminence with such books as* Tortilla Flat, In Dubious Battle, Of Mice and Men, The Moon Is Down, Cannery Row, East of Eden, *and many short stories*

THE AFFAIR AT 7, RUE DE M——

From HARPER'S BAZAAR

I had hoped to withhold from public scrutiny those rather curious events which have given me some concern for the past month. I knew of course that there was talk in the neighborhood. I have even heard some of the distortions current in my district, stories, I hasten to add, in which there is no particle of truth. However, my desire for privacy was shattered yesterday by a visit of two members of the fourth estate who assured me that the story, or rather *a* story, had escaped the boundaries of my *arrondissement*.

In the light of impending publicity I think it only fair to issue the true details of those happenings which have come to be known as The Affair at 7, rue de M——, in order that nonsense may not be added to a set of circumstances which are not without their bizarrerie. I shall set down the events as they happened without comment, thereby allowing the public to judge of the situation.

At the beginning of the summer I carried my family to Paris

and took up residence in a pretty little house at 7, rue de M———,
a building which in another period had been the mews of the
great house beside it. The whole property is now owned and part
of it inhabited by a noble French family of such age and purity
that its members still consider the Bourbons unacceptable as
claimants to the throne of France.

To this pretty little converted stable with three floors of rooms
above a well-paved courtyard, I brought my immediate family,
consisting of my wife, my three children, two small boys and a
grown daughter, and of course myself. Our domestic arrangement
in addition to the concierge who, as you might say, came with the
house, consists of a French cook of great ability, a Spanish maid
and my own secretary, a girl of Swiss nationality whose high at-
tainments and ambitions are only equaled by her moral altitude.
This then was our little family group when the events I am about
to chronicle were ushered in.

If one must have an agency in this matter, I can find no alter-
native to placing not the blame but rather the authorship, albeit
innocent, on my younger son John who has only recently attained
his eighth year, a lively child of singular beauty and buck teeth.

This young man has, during the last several years in America,
become not so much an addict as an aficionado of that curious
American practice, the chewing of bubble gum, and one of the
pleasanter aspects of the early summer in Paris lay in the fact that
the Cadet John had neglected to bring any of the atrocious substance with him from America. The child's speech became clear
and unobstructed and the hypnotized look went out of his eyes.

Alas, this delightful situation was not long to continue. An old
family friend traveling in Europe brought as a present to the
children a more than adequate supply of this beastly gum, thinking to do them a kindness. Thereupon the old familiar situation
reasserted itself. Speech fought its damp way past a huge wad of
the gum and emerged with the sound of a faulty water trap. The
jaws were in constant motion, giving the face at best a look of
agony while the eyes took on a glaze like those of a pig with a
recently severed jugular. Since I do not believe in inhibiting my
children I resigned myself to a summer not quite so pleasant as I
had at first hoped.

On occasion I do not follow my ordinary practice of laissez-faire. When I am composing the material for a book or play or essay, in a word, when the utmost of concentration is required, I am prone to establish tyrannical rules for my own comfort and effectiveness. One of these rules is that there shall be neither chewing nor bubbling while I am trying to concentrate. This rule is so thoroughly understood by the Cadet John that he accepts it as one of the laws of nature and does not either complain or attempt to evade the ruling. It is his pleasure and my solace for my son to come sometimes into my workroom, there to sit quietly beside me for a time. He knows he must be silent and when he has remained so for as long a time as his character permits, he goes out quietly, leaving us both enriched by the wordless association.

Two weeks ago in the late afternoon, I sat at my desk composing a short essay for *Figaro Litteraire,* an essay which later aroused some controversy when it was printed under the title "Sartre Resartus." I had come to that passage concerning the proper clothing for the soul when to my astonishment and chagrin I heard the unmistakable soft plopping sound of a bursting balloon of bubble gum. I looked sternly at my offspring and saw him chewing away. His cheeks were colored with embarrassment and the muscles of his jaws stood rigidly out.

"You know the rule," I said coldly.

To my amazement tears came into his eyes and while his jaws continued to masticate hugely, his blubbery voice forced its way past the huge lump of bubble gum in his mouth.

"I didn't do it," he cried.

"What do you mean, you didn't do it?" I demanded in a rage. "I distinctly heard and now I distinctly see."

"Oh sir!" he moaned, "I really didn't. I'm not chewing it, sir. It's chewing me."

For a moment I inspected him closely. He is an honest child, only under the greatest pressure of gain permitting himself an untruth. I had the horrible thought that the bubble gum had finally had its way and that my son's reason was tottering. If this were so, it were better to tread softly. Quietly I put out my hand. "Lay it here," I said kindly.

My child manfully tried to disengage the gum from his jaws. "It won't let me go," he sputtered.

"Open up," I said and then inserting my fingers in his mouth I seized hold of the large lump of gum and after a struggle in which my fingers slipped again and again, managed to drag it forth and to deposit the ugly blob on my desk on top of a pile of white manuscript paper.

For a moment it seemed to shudder there on the paper and then with an easy slowness it began to undulate, to swell and recede with the exact motion of being chewed while my son and I regarded it with popping eyes.

For a long time we watched it while I drove through my mind for some kind of explanation. Either I was dreaming or some principle as yet unknown had taken its seat in the pulsing bubble gum on the desk. I am not unintelligent. While I considered the indecent thing, a hundred little thoughts and glimmerings of understanding raced through my brain. At last I asked, "How long has it been chewing you?"

"Since last night," he replied.

"And when did you first notice this, this propensity on its part?"

He spoke with perfect candor. "I will ask you to believe me, sir," he said. "Last night before I went to sleep I put it under my pillow as is my invariable custom. In the night I was awakened to find that it was in my mouth. I again placed it under my pillow and this morning it was again in my mouth, lying quietly. When, however, I became thoroughly awakened, I was conscious of a slight motion and shortly afterward the situation dawned on me that I was no longer master of the gum. It had taken its head. I tried to remove it, sir, and could not. You yourself with all of your strength have seen how difficult it was to extract. I came to your workroom to await your first disengagement, wishing to acquaint you with my difficulty. Oh, Daddy, what do you think has happened?"

The cancerous thing held my complete attention.

"I must think," I said. "This is something a little out of the ordinary, and I do not believe it should be passed over without some investigation."

As I spoke a change came over the gum. It ceased to chew itself and seemed to rest for a while, and then with a flowing movement like those monocellular animals of the order Paramecium, the gum slid across the desk straight in the direction of my son. For a moment I was stricken with astonishment and for an even longer time I failed to discern its intent. It dropped to his knee, climbed horribly up his shirt front. Only then did I understand. It was trying to get back into his mouth. He looked down on it paralyzed with fright.

"Stop," I cried, for I realized that my third-born was in danger and at such times I am capable of a violence which verges on the murderous. I seized the monster from his chin and striding from my workroom, entered the salon, opened the window and hurled the thing into the busy traffic on the rue de M———.

I believe it is the duty of a parent to ward off those shocks which may cause dreams or trauma whenever possible. I went back to my study to find young John sitting where I had left him. He was staring into space. There was a troubled line between his brows.

"Son," I said, "you and I have seen something which, while we know it to have happened, we might find difficult to describe with any degree of success to others. I ask you to imagine the scene if we should tell this story to the other members of the family. I greatly fear we should be laughed out of the house."

"Yes, sir," he said passively.

"Therefore I am going to propose to you, my son, that we lock the episode deep in our memories and never mention it to a soul as long as we live." I waited for his assent and when it did not come, glanced up at his face to see it a ravaged field of terror. His eyes were starting out of his head. I turned in the direction of his gaze. Under the door there crept a paper-thin sheet which, once it had entered the room, grew to a gray blob and rested on the rug pulsing and chewing. After a moment it moved again by pseudopodian progression toward my son.

I fought down panic as I rushed at it. I grabbed it up and flung it on my desk, then seizing an African war club from among the trophies on the wall, a dreadful instrument studded with brass, I beat the gum until I was breathless and it a torn piece of plastic fabric. The moment I rested, it drew itself together and for a few moments chewed very rapidly as though it chuckled at my impotence, and then inexorably it moved toward my son, who by this time was crouched in a corner moaning with terror.

Now a coldness came over me. I picked up the filthy thing and wrapped it in my handkerchief, strode out of the house, walked three blocks to the Seine and flung the handkerchief into the slowly moving current.

I spent a good part of the afternoon soothing my son and trying to reassure him that his fears were over. But such was his nervousness that I had to give him half a barbiturate tablet to get him to sleep that night, while my wife insisted that I call a doctor. I did not at that time dare to tell her why I could not obey her wish.

I was awakened, indeed the whole house was awakened, in the night by a terrified muffled scream from the children's room. I took the stairs two at a time and burst in the room, flicking the light switch as I went. John sat up in bed squalling, while with his fingers he dug at his half-open mouth, a mouth which horrifyingly went right on chewing. As I looked a bubble emerged between his fingers and burst with a wet plopping sound.

What chance of keeping our secret now! All had to be explained, but with the plopping gum pinned to a breadboard with an ice pick the explanation was easier than it might have been. And I am proud of the help and comfort given me. There is no strength like that of the family. Our French cook solved the problem by refusing to believe it even when she saw it. It was not reasonable, she explained, and she was a reasonable member of a reasonable people. The Spanish maid ordered and paid for an exorcism by the parish priest who, poor man, after two hours of strenuous effort went away muttering that this was more a matter of the stomach than the soul.

For two weeks we were besieged by the monster. We burned it in the fireplace, causing it to splutter in blue flames and melt in a nasty mess among the ashes. Before morning it had crawled through the keyhole of the children's room, leaving a trail of wood ash on the door, and again we were awakened by screams from the Cadet.

In despair I drove far into the country and threw it from my automobile. It was back before morning. Apparently it had crept to the highway and placed itself in the Paris traffic until picked up by a truck tire. When we tore it from John's mouth it had still the nonskid marks of Michelin imprinted on its side.

Fatigue and frustration will take their toll. In exhaustion, with my will to fight back sapped, and after we had tried every possible method to lose or destroy the bubble gum, I placed it at last under a bell jar which I ordinarily use to cover my microscope. I collapsed in a chair to gaze at it with weary defeated eyes. John slept in his little bed under the influence of sedatives backed by my assurance that I would not let the Thing out of my sight.

I lighted a pipe and settled back to watch it. Inside the bell jar the gray tumorous lump moved restlessly about searching for some means of exit from its prison. Now and then it paused as though in thought and emitted a bubble in my direction. I could feel the hatred it had for me. In my weariness I found my mind slipping into an analysis which had so far escaped me.

The background I had been over hurriedly. It must be that from constant association with the lambent life which is my son, the magic of life had been created in the bubble gum. And with life had come intelligence, not the manly open intelligence of the boy, but an evil calculating wiliness.

How could it be otherwise? Intelligence without the soul to balance it must of necessity be evil. The gum had not absorbed any part of John's soul.

Very well, said my mind, now we have a hypothesis of its origin, let us consider its nature. What does it think? What does it want? What does it need? My mind leaped like a terrier. It needs and wants to get back to its host, my son. It wants to be chewed. It must be chewed to survive.

Inside the bell jar the gum inserted a thin wedge of itself under the heavy glass foot and constricted so that the whole jar lifted a fraction of an inch. I laughed as I drove it back. I laughed with almost insane triumph. I had the answer.

In the dining room I procured a clear plastic plate, one of a dozen my wife had bought for picnics in the country. Then turning the bell jar over and securing the monster in its bottom, I smeared the mouth of it with a heavy plastic cement guaranteed to be water-, alcohol- and acidproof. I forced the plate over the opening and pressed it down until the glue took hold and bound the plate to the glass, making an airtight container. And last I turned the jar upright again and adjusted the reading light so that I could observe every movement of my prisoner.

Again it searched the circle for escape. Then it faced me and emitted a great number of bubbles very rapidly. I could hear the little bursting plops through the glass.

"I have you, my beauty," I cried. "I have you at last."

That was a week ago. I have not left the side of the bell jar since, and have only turned my head to accept a cup of coffee. When I go to the bathroom, my wife takes my place. I can now report the following hopeful news.

During the first day and night, the bubble gum tried every means to escape. Then for a day and a night it seemed to be agitated and nervous as though it had for the first time realized its predicament. The third day it went to work with its chewing motion, only the action was speeded up greatly, like the chewing of a baseball fan. On the fourth day it began to weaken and I observed with joy a kind of dryness on its once slick and shiny exterior.

I am now in the seventh day and I believe it is almost over. The gum is lying in the center of the plate. At intervals it heaves and subsides. Its color has turned to a nasty yellow. Once today when my son entered the room, it leaped up excitedly, then seemed to realize its hopelessness and collapsed on the plate. It will die tonight I think and only then will I dig a deep hole in the garden, and I will deposit the sealed bell jar and cover it up and plant geraniums over it.

It is my hope that this account will set straight some of the silly tales that are being hawked in the neighborhood.

JOSEPH WHITEHILL, *twenty-eight, is an ex-machinist and electronics design engineer. He has served in the Navy as a Seaman First Class. Having been dissatisfied with his former occupations, Mr. Whitehill turned to writing. Since writing "Able Baker" he has contributed "The Academicians" to the* Atlantic Monthly *and "Stay Away from My Mother" to* Ellery Queen's Mystery Magazine, *where his first published story also appeared, in 1954.*

ABLE BAKER

From ATLANTIC MONTHLY

Chief Engineer Baker, who had been called Able Baker for so long now that he resignedly believed it to be his real name, was sympathetically examining the monkey's scalp ringworm when the fan belt in the blower housing broke. Baker closed his stubby hands over the bony bundle of fur in his lap and raised his heavy head to listen. When a unique noise overrides the complex, intricate roars of the main engine and the auxiliary, it is generally impossible to use the practiced human sense to discover its source. A new sound must repeat itself many times in a hinting rhythm before one can zero in on it and find out what went wrong; like the children's game in which all but one are blindfolded, and he who is It must go "peep, peep" at regular intervals to lead the others to him. Able Baker released the monkey and rose from his stool to hear better, should the sound come again. He stood still on the soapy-feeling deck plates, steadying himself with a grip on the main engine guard-rail, and he looked about the cream-painted engine room with his head thrust up and out in a wall-eyed, bovine fashion, as a man will do when his ears have a mystery.

Orion, the monkey, climbed happily up to the sloping top of the gray-painted, stand-up log desk and nestled in the basketful of fuel reports to scratch. Orion hated these daily examinations of his ringworm because after the attentive petting always came a burning applicaion of salicylic acid which sent him slinging around the engine room in a stung rage until the pain stopped.

At first, as Able Baker stood there beside the magnificent old twelve-cylinder diesel, gimbaling slowly with the roll of the ship, he wondered whether the sound he had heard might not have been the scraping of flotsam along the ship's side; but because the Captain was on Conn, this seemed unlikely. The Captain had an old maid's eye for floating things. Able Baker, sixty-four years old, never considered that he might have heard something that was not. There was a new, unusual air about the engine room which told him something was markedly amiss. The air now seemed hotter—closer.

Then his wandering eyes surprised him by discovering the fault. Years ago, when he had first joined this ship, he had tied a pennant strand of white blonde manila to the grill of the ventilator inlet over his head, and for all these years it had fluttered gaily, losing weight and growing dirty, telling him that the exhaust blower on the other side of the compartment was doing well. But now this telltale was hanging limp and dead.

Engineer Baker found a blackened electrical-burned screwdriver on the tool board and, after poking affectionately at the monkey with it, started around the main engine. Baker, a man of efficiency, moved in his thwartships progress with the roll of the ship, shuffling forward when the catwalk slanted downward and stopping to wait on the rise. There was a heavy roll on today, after yesterday's half-gale.

At the blower housing, which looked like a washtub-sized snail, Able Baker peered into the screened intake and saw the big squirrel-cage rotor standing still in the darkness. He went around to the other side of the housing, skinning under a sweating fire main, and used the screwdriver to loosen the painted-over Dzeus fasteners holding the side cover on. The cream-colored paint around the edges of the cover popped and scaled as he pried the cover loose, and some of the flakes snowed down into the bilge.

Engineer Baker leaned the freed cover against the fire main carefully, with a good cant to it so that it would not fall with the ship's roll, and turned with medical professionalism to look into the cavity of the blower housing.

There the fuzzy black belt, like a long snake in the agony of exuviation, lay helplessly twisted over the shaft of the rotor, irreparably parted. The dusty black electric motor was running fast and quietly in relief. Baker untwisted the broken Vee belt and, climbing *over* the fire main this time, carried it back to the cluttered little tool bench by the power panel. Counting in his head from left to right along the row of disconnect switches, he stopped at the seventh and flipped it off to shut down the blower motor. Then, with his intractable steel tape, he fumblingly measured the length of the broken belt and its width across its back.

He went to the communicator handset hanging on the bulkhead by the log desk and pushed the button marked "Conn." While he waited for them to answer, he scratched the monkey's ringworm between the shoulders where it was difficult for Orion to reach.

"Conn."

"This is the Engine Room," Baker said, squinting. These telephones were highly irritating, being of the sort called "dead microphone transmission," which do not permit the speaker to hear his voice in his own ear. With telephones like these, one tends to speak louder and more distinctly than otherwise, but there is a frustrating deadness about them which gives a man the feeling he is trying to talk to God and is not getting through. Baker stopped scratching Orion and put his scratching finger in his uncovered ear. "Hello, Conn? That you, Mate?"

"This is the Captain," came the linear answer.

"Oh, hello, Captain. Is the Mate up there?"

There was a long pause, during which Engineer Baker wrote on the open page of the Engine Room Log, "0940—Cast and Broke Belt of Engine Room Ventilator Blower." Then the Mate came on: "Yeah, Able?"

"Belt on the ventilator blower just broke. I wondered if you would drop me a spare down the hatch so I won't have to leave watch?"

"What size?"

"It's eighty-two inches around and it's three quarters of an inch across the flat. I expect that's a C or D section belt."

"Just a minute," the Mate said. "I gotta write that down. It's rolling like hell up here."

Able Baker smiled at his own wit and said, "It's rolling down here, too. That must mean we're on the same ship."

"Oh, you're a funny one, you are. What was that again, now?"

"Eighty-two inches around and three quarters of an inch across the flat."

"Eighter-two around and tharee quarter across. I'll look around. I think your spares are in the aft lazaret. I'll call you back."

Able Baker licked the corner of his mouth where a little tobacco juice had escaped: "Kind of hurry, will you? It's getting hotter down here."

But the Mate had hung up without hearing. Baker collared the monkey and held him up where he could see the air temperature thermometer. Orion reached out with his delicate fist and rapped the round glass of the thermometer to make the needle bounce properly. The slim black needle quivered, then settled finally on a hundred and eleven degrees Fahrenheit. Baker poured each of them a drink from the iced scuttle butt and punched out into his palm two salt tablets from the phallic dispenser. He spit his used charge of plug into the bilge by the main engine and swallowed one of the pills. He gave the other to the monkey, who retired to the log desk to suck it meditatively

2

To kill time until the return call from the Mate, Baker went to his gage panel and shopped over it with his eyes, not really intending to buy anything, but interested just the same. . . . That main engine was a fine old thing. Its rpm's had hung right at five-seventy for more than two hours without a touch to the fuel-oil feeds. The auxiliary, the little eight-cylinder affair which generated electrical power of several kinds, was only a year old and was still youthfully erratic. Its speed wandered between nine hundred and

fifty and nine hundred and seventy-five revolutions with no
evident purpose. When he saw the tachometer needle again
begin its upward hunting, Baker shook his head in irritation. At
the shake of his head, drops of sweat from his eyebrows scurried
down inside the lenses of his steel-rimmed bifocals, making everything look wavy. He took them off and cleaned them, then wiped
his forehead and the folds of fat at the nape of his neck with a
blue bandana.

Able Baker, like all white men who work sensibly in hot places,
always wore full clothing—long khaki pants and a long-sleeved
khaki shirt. Let the youngsters in the deck gang cultivate their
tans—he intended to stay cool. Once, when some seamen were
twitting him about dressing so formally, he had tried to explain
how it was that wearing thoroughly sweat-soaked rough cotton
increased one's evaporation efficiency, but he had run aground
in their laughter and had been silenced.

"Pooh!" he said at the recollection. "Here, Orion." Able snapped
his fingers and the monkey swung onto his knees. Holding him
firmly about the chest with one hand so that the animal could not
escape, Baker uncorked the bottle of salicylic acid and fished a
Kleenex out of the box in his drawer. When Orion saw what was
imminent, he shook his little ball-like head as though his neck
were a free swivel, then ducked his head and bit the hand which
held him. Able was not startled. He had been expecting the bite
and knew it would not hurt excessively, so he held firm and began
swabbing the monkey's ringworm. After squirming twice in panic,
the monkey grudgingly submitted and lay trembling quietly in
Able's hand. When he was done, Able released the monkey to
career wildly about the compartment to run out its pain, and he
used the other end of the Kleenex to daub some of Orion's medi-
cine on the bitten place on his hand.

The gong of the communicator hammered out shrilly over the
din of the engines. As Baker answered it, he positioned himself
so that he could look reassuringly up at the limp manila telltale
dangling from the grill of the air intake overhead. He wanted to
tell it that everything would be all right in a little bit, just as soon
as he had installed the new belt. "Engine Room," he said into the
handset as he corked his ear with his forefinger."

"Engine Room? Conn. La'ona'ika noka dice."

Able Baker shoved his finger farther into his ear canal: "What?"

"What d'ya mean, *what?*" came the thin sound of the Mate's insolent voice.

"Excuse me," Baker said humbly. "*Repeat,* then."

"That's better. You got big tough tit, Dad. No belt."

"Are you sure? It must be on board somewhere."

"Nope. None."

Able Baker's mouth worked as he groped for words. He pushed his finger harder into his ear in the despairing hope that something constructive would come out of his mouth. At length, he said, "There *should* be a belt on board. I put in for one at Honolulu. Are you sure there isn't?"

"You don't believe me, then go look for yourself."

"I think I'll go on up there."

"Come ahead. Out."

"Out." Able Baker hung up the handset and again mopped the sweat from his shining red face. Sometime before a man's hair turns gray, sometimes early, sometimes late, he learns one thing well. He learns that even with a willing cooperator on the other end of the line, if he wishes to achieve the exact end he dreams of he must do the errand himself. Of course there was a belt aboard. Had he not put in for one? And did he not, because of his trusted conservatism in the matter of spares, always receive what he put in for?

Standing before the log desk on hot, tired feet, in high black shoes that squished with the sweat inside, Baker marveled at how hot the engine room had grown because of the failure of the blower. The air temperature thermometer now stood at an incredible hundred and twenty-one degrees; virtually too hot to open one's eyes.

Baker found in the drawer his stiff-grease-caked gauntlets and dropped them over his hands. He beckoned to Orion to accompany him topside, but the monkey, over its pain now and basking sleepily in the increasing heat, clung to the wires of the basket with all four hands to indicate that it was quite satisfied to remain behind. At the foot of the ladder, before he began the arduous climb, Baker looked down over his clothing with minute care and found with wonder that, for the first time he could remember, there was not a dry spot on him. His faded khakis had turned back to the color they were when new.

3

As he climbed the welded ladder to the main deck the temperature dropped some, but Able Baker was unprepared for the shocking blast of cold air which struck him as he turned back the hatch in the sunlight and blinked at the far blue sea. He swung his thick legs clumsily over the hatch coaming and stood up dizzily, clinging for support to the lifeline at the rail. In the cold Force Five wind, bits of his wetly matted gray hair raised and ruffled stiffly. Shivering in his wet clothes, Able Baker lumbered aft and climbed to the flying bridge.

The Mate and the Captain were there, leaning against the forward rail, silently watching the coming horizon. At the top of the ladder, Baker stopped to catch his breath. From the engine room up to the flying bridge was a climb of seventy feet, as Baker had once measured when he wondered if he were growing old. "It's cold up here!" Baker said loudly, his ears still full of the roar of the engines. Both the Mate and the Captain started and turned. "Good morning, Captain," he added.

"Good morning, Mister Baker," the Captain answered, standing at attention. The Mate, though not addressed, nodded.

"Uh—Captain, when we were in Honolulu a couple of months ago, I put in for a new belt for that blower fan, so it must be aboard somewhere." Baker fluffed his hair before the wind with his hand, that it might dry.

"Mate says it isn't," said the Captain, looking at Able Baker's stomach where it bulged over the top of his pants.

Baker drew in a breath to raise his chest to a protrusion approximating that of his stomach. "Well, sir," he persisted, "we could look at the stores records for Honolulu and see what happened."

The Captain, seemingly now aware that Baker was not to be

distracted by verbal finalities, said to the Mate, "The bridge is yours, Mister," and led the way below to the ship's office. Baker followed, full of breathless satisfaction at having incepted progressive action in his commander.

From the file cabinet in the office the Captain withdrew a sheaf of material requisitions and leafed through them until he found the Engineering Department sheet which had been sent ashore at Honolulu. Baker, impolitely reading over his captain's shoulder, was the first to find the item about the belt, and pointed at it with a dirty finger. The Captain pulled the paper away, out of the reach of soil, and put it on the desk, where it might be safely examined without being touched.

"There it is, sir," Baker said, peering gratefully at the typed line which proved him not a fool.

The Captain was tapping his foot to illustrate his impatience. "Yes," he said, "but the shore office sent it back marked T.X. Just a minute. I'll read you what that means." The Captain found a thin black book with the Company's seal embossed in varnished gold on the cover. "Here. See right here? It says, 'T.X. indicates that the requisition has been set aside on the ground that the item or items requested fall in the group of supplies which have a service expectancy greater than the time between scheduled wharfside overhauls. Items in this group must be replaced at the time of overhaul, by Company shore personnel.' There, Baker, you see? The belt didn't come aboard at all."

Baker blinked at such arrant injustice, and moved between the Captain and the door, so the Captain could not escape. "But *sir!* Nobody told me. It's a mistake. It's all wrong. You know it is, sir." Knowing he was beginning to whine, he took a rale-sounding breath before he went on more calmly. "The kind of stuff they mean there is stuff like cylinder liners and shaft log packing glands and things that are expensive. Not fan belts!"

"There it is," the Captain said shortly, and there it was indeed. Baker had in his lifetime heard the ending of enough things to know with certainty when the end had arrived—the point beyond which further pursuit was futile. Baker put his hands under his damp stomach and lifted it a little, and turned to go. The Captain said as Baker stepped up over the sill, "You could rig a canvas wind scoop at the intake on deck. As long as we're in the Trades, you'd get some circulation down there. It'll only be eight more days and we'll get you a belt at Balboa." Able Baker paused to hear his captain out, then nodded and left.

He found the Third Mate working with a rust-brushing detail of deck hands on the starboard quarter of the main deck, and said to him, "You got the key to the rope locker? I need some supplies."

The Third Mate stood up and shut off his electric rotary brush. His hair and face were covered with a Ben Day of rust flakes. "Whadda you need?"

Able Baker thought a moment, calculating in his head, then said, "Twenty-five feet of three-quarter manila and four rolls of Okonite tape."

"*Four* rolls! My God, what're you settin' out on?"

Baker loathed going to this red-haired young pup for supplies. Somehow the Third Mate, with his slack-jawed expression of chronic shock, made Baker feel that he was the most prodigal user of stores aboard and that his ends were frivolous. "I have my uses, sonny, don't you worry," he said.

"You know how much that tape *costs?* It costs a dollar a roll, that's how much. You're not getting it for inventory, are you?"

"I am not," Baker said firmly, as if the idea were unthinkable. "I have to jury up something, is all, and I'd appreciate a little speed. There's nobody down in the engine room but Orion."

Baker stood a moment at the main-deck hatch leading below to the engine room, arranging his new supplies for the climb down. He hung the coil of bright, clean manila rope around his neck, and stuffed the four rolls of self-vulcanizing rubber tape inside his shirt front. Then he stood stiffly by the rail, breathing deeply of the cool sea wind. Unconsciously, he tried to pre-chill himself for the coming plunge into the inferno of the engine room. It was not in Baker's nature to rail uselessly against the Company, or against the human obtuseness of its agents, but now, standing in the bright Pacific sun, he felt he was about to be swallowed up in a rising wrath of delicious indignation. Hurriedly, before he said something to himself he might regret, he laid back the hatch and started down the ladder.

4

Down in the engine room, Baker quickly regretted even having gone topside; it seemed so much hotter now, partly by contrast with the coolness he had just quitted. Because it was important to Baker to know precisely to what measurable extent he was suffering, he went to look at the thermometer. The pointer read a hundred and twenty-nine degrees, one degree short of its maximum. "My Lord!" Baker said to himself, but his voice fell dead under the tappeting roar of the engines and he could not hear it. This was not air he was breathing, he felt, but a denser, hot fluid with a pronouncedly sweet taste. A mortal man, and proud of his mortality, he wondered how long he could survive down here in this hell.

Baker, gasping this furnace air which seemed to have no extractable good in it, looked about him to see how Orion was taking it, but the monkey was nowhere in sight. Then, avoiding the burning touch of the steel everywhere near him, Able Baker shambled around the main engine feeling its glow upon the left side of his face, and took his new rope around behind the broken blower. With a cool crescent wrench from his hip pocket, he loosened the mounting bolts of the electric motor and heaved it along its slots toward the axle of the squirrel cage rotor. Having thus minimized the belt span, he looped one end of his rope around the big pulley of the fan shaft, around the small pulley on the motor, and back to the big pulley again. Pinching the rope with one hand to mark the place, he dabbed up with his fingertip a bit of dirty grease which had exuded from one of the shaft bearings, and marked the rope.

On his way back to the small workbench, a seizure of heat-risen ague racked his shoulders, and he was obliged to catch at the blistering guardrail to halt his teetering. When the fit had passed, he rubbed his smarting palm over the wet front of his shirt, then spread the rope out loosely on the open area of steel deck before the workbench. With fingers circling nimbly, he began to unlay one strand of the three composing the rope. He worked by blind touch, for his spectacles were so smeared and wet that they were useless. A great, heaving groan of misery escaped him and he did not hear it; nor did his freckled, mottled hands pause in their spiraling race. It was as though he had only thought the groan.

When he had unlaid the entire twenty-five foot rope, he began re-laying one strand upon itself at the grease mark, making a closed loop, or grommet. Suddenly, as though birthed by a ghost, the wet, homuncular shape of the monkey dropped to Able's shoulder and scrabbled weakly for a hold. Able started, then helped the monkey down to the bench and took off his glasses to see. The monkey's fur was wet with dirty, oily water. Able was horrified. "You've been in the bilge!" He held up the monkey to look into its eyes, and what he saw there made him close his own in pain. Orion's eyes, always black and bright, now had a glazed and vapid look, as though it did not care any more. "You silly!" Baker shouted, wanting to shake the little beast. "Why didn't you run topside to cool off? No, not you, you Goddam engineer, you! You poor little fool. I'll bet you swallowed a lot of that muck down there under the engine, didn't you? And to think that's where I *spit!* Oh, Mister, I'm sorry!" Sadly, he laid the ill monkey on a clean rag on the bench and turned again to his work.

His sweaty, trembling fingers slipped often on the rope. Once around the loop made two strands laid up, and once more made three. Engineer Baker now held a seemingly endless loop of three-quarter-inch rope. He tucked the two strand ends together in a half-overhand and commenced wrapping the rope with the gummy rubber tape. The heat was now so intense that the rubber worked ideally under his hands, sticking hungrily to itself and smoothing neatly into the roughness of the rope.

When Able had used two full rolls of tape, he saw out of the corner of his eye that the monkey was in distress. It lay tangled in the rag, squirming and nibbling at the hem. Baker put down his work and tried to dry the monkey, but the little thing would not help him. It stayed curled up, with tense and quivering limbs, so the grieving old man had to put the monkey down again.

Impulsively, Baker stumbled to the gage board. The needle of the air thermometer was resting on the pin, having gone off scale. The water temperature of the main engine was already a hundred and ninety, far too hot for the health of the lubricating films.

While Able paused, watching the gage, he was suddenly blood-hammered at the sides of his head, and knew positively he was about to faint. He clung to the valve handles and bent his head down to his knees until he was all right again, then straightened with blood-blinded eyes and tottered back to the bench.

With his hands grown clumsy, he somehow managed to finish taping the new fan belt he had made, and broke the tape to end it. He bent over the monkey and peered shortsightedly at it, but Orion's eyes were closed. Several drops of sweat-mixed tears fell from his face onto the monkey's messy gray fur, and the monkey twitched.

Thus reassured that Orion still lived, and might not die, Able Baker took his newly fashioned fan belt and staggered with it toward the blower. Twice on the way the unruly belt caught on obstructions and jerked itself from Able's hands, and each time he patiently recovered it and went on. At the blower he looped it over both pulleys, then shoved the motor back until the belt was tight. He cried out softly in pain when the perfidious vertebra low in his back jumped with his effort. He had to use his arms to help him straighten up. Now carefully keeping his back straight, he tightened the motor mounting bolts and replaced the side cover of the blower housing.

As he climbed over the fire main to return to the switchboard, he sat for a moment astride the cool, wet pipe, loving the coolness in his groin and loving the sitting still. He did not so pamper himself long, however, for he was not yet done. He dragged his back leg over the fire main and hobbled stiffly to the electric panel. Counting over, it was number seven, and he threw the switch. Instantly, the limp shred of manila on the grill of the intake duct fluttered, then stood out wagging happily. The blessed change of moving, cooler air at once enwrapped him in its kindness, and Able wiped his face in gratitude.

He went back to the workbench to tell Orion what he had done, and that everything was all right now, but when he picked it up gently, the monkey's head lolled out over his hand, and it was smiling a crooked little dead smile.

Knowing now the pass that things had come to, knowing he had been truly robbed by someone else's heedless stupidity, Able

Baker nestled the monkey's body in the crook of his arm and carried it in cold intentness over to the main engine control station. Here, he held Orion up so that the dead eyes might watch too, and he pulled down the great brass handle of the throttle. The huge main engine shuddered loosely in surprise, then slowed and stopped.

With the strength of rage, Able Baker wrenched back the long lever of the transmission, unclutching the drive. Near silence was his prize. All Able Baker now could hear was the muttering of the auxiliary, and the slow rushing sound of the great drive shaft as it rolled over slowly, free-wheeling, driven by the propeller under the stern as the ship ghosted quietly through the water.

As soon as Baker had dragged his stool over into the cool wind from the duct, and had sat down, the clangor of the communicator began. It rang once shortly, then once again in a steady, shrill tremor of alarm. The fat, tired old man hugged the monkey's body until the ringing stopped. Then the chain-driven pointer on the dial of the engine-room telegraph oscillated peevishly, making fussy loud clangs at each oscillation. Engineer Able Baker leaned his stool back against the hard steel bulkhead and stroked the monkey. He smiled through his tears while he waited for what came next.

RICHARD YATES was born in Hastings-on-Hudson, N.Y., in 1926, and raised in various parts of New York City and its suburbs. He spent two years in the Army, mostly in Europe, and following his discharge in 1946 he held a succession of newspaper and publicity jobs in New York until 1951. He then returned to Europe for two years, with his wife and small daughter, and has been a free-lance writer ever since. One of his short stories won the Atlantic Monthly's *annual Atlantic "First" Award for 1953, and a number of others have appeared in other national magazines.*

THE BEST OF EVERYTHING

From CHARM

Nobody expected Grace to do any work the Friday before her wedding. In fact, nobody would let her, whether she wanted to or not.

A gardenia corsage lay in a cellophane box beside her typewriter —from Mr. Atwood, her boss—and tucked inside the envelope that came with it was a ten-dollar gift certificate from Bloomingdale's. Mr. Atwood had treated her with a special shy courtliness ever since the time she necked with him at the office Christmas party, and now when she went in to thank him he was all hunched over, rattling desk drawers, blushing and grinning and barely meeting her eyes.

"Aw, now, don't mention it, Grace," he said. "Pleasure's all mine. Here, you need a pin to put that gadget on with?"

"There's a pin that came with it," she said, holding up the corsage. "See? A nice white one."

Beaming, he watched her pin the flowers high on the lapel of her suit. Then he cleared his throat importantly and pulled out the writing panel of his desk, ready to give the morning's dictation. But it turned out there were only two short letters, and it wasn't until an hour later, when she caught him handing over a pile of Dictaphone cylinders to Central Typing, that she realized he had done her a favor.

"That's very sweet of you, Mr. Atwood," she said, "but I do think you ought to give me all your work today, just like any oth—"

"Aw, now, Grace," he said, "you only get married once."

The girls all made a fuss over her too, crowding around her desk and giggling, asking again and again to see Ralph's photograph ("Oh, he's *cute!*"), while the office manager looked on nervously, reluctant to be a spoilsport, but anxious to point out that it was, after all, a working day.

Then at lunch there was the traditional little party at Schrafft's— nine women and girls, giddy on their unfamiliar cocktails, letting their chicken à la king grow cold while they pummeled her with old times and good wishes. There were more flowers and another gift—a silver candy dish for which all the girls had whisperingly chipped in.

Grace said "Thank you" and "I certainly do appreciate it" and "I don't know what to say" until her head rang with the words and the corners of her mouth ached from smiling, and she thought the afternoon would never end.

Ralph called up about four o'clock, exuberant. "How ya doin', honey?" he asked, and before she could answer he said, "Listen. Guess what I got?"

"I don't know. A present or something? What?" She tried to sound excited but it wasn't easy.

"A bonus. Fifty dollars." She could almost see the flattening of his lips as he said "fifty dollars" with the particular earnestness he reserved for pronouncing sums of money.

"Why, that's lovely, Ralph," she said, and if there was any tiredness in her voice he didn't notice it.

"Lovely, huh?" he said with a laugh, mocking the girlishness of the word. "Ya *like* that, huh Gracie? No, but I mean I was really surprised, ya know it? The boss siz, 'Here, Ralph,' and he hands me this envelope. He don't even crack a smile or nothin', and I'm wonderin', what's the deal here? I'm getting fired here, or what? He siz, 'G'ahead, Ralph, open it.' So I open it, and then I look at the boss and he's grinning a mile wide." He chuckled and sighed. "Well, so listen honey. What time ya want me to come over tonight?"

"Oh, I don't know. Soon as you can, I guess."

"Well listen. I gotta go over to Eddie's house and pick up that bag he's gonna loan me, so I might as well do that, go on home and eat, and then come over to your place around eight-thirty, nine o'clock. Okay?"

"All right," she said. "I'll see you then, darling." She had been calling him "darling" for only a short time—since it had become irrevocably clear that she was, after all, going to marry him—and the word still had an alien sound. As she straightened the stacks of stationery in her desk (because there was nothing else to do) a familiar little panic gripped her: She couldn't marry him—she hardly even *knew* him. Sometimes it occurred to her differently, that she couldn't marry him because she knew him too well, and either way it left her badly shaken, vulnerable to all the things that Martha, her roommate, had said from the very beginning.

"Isn't he funny?" Martha had said after their first date. "He says 'terlet.' I didn't know people really said 'terlet.'" And Grace had giggled, ready enough to agree that it *was* funny. That was a time when she had been ready to agree with Martha on practically anything—when it often seemed, in fact, that finding a girl like Martha from an ad in the *Times* was just about the luckiest thing that ever happened to her.

But Ralph had persisted all through the summer, and by fall she had begun standing up for him. "But what don't you *like* about him, Martha? He's perfectly nice."

"Oh, everybody's perfectly nice, Grace," Martha would say in her college voice, making perfectly nice a faintly absurd thing to be, and then she'd look up crossly from the careful painting of her fingernails. "It's just that he's such a little—a little *white worm.* Can't you see that?"

"Well, I certainly don't see what his *complexion* has to do with—"

"Oh, God, *you* know what I mean. Can't you see what I *mean?*

Oh, and all those friends of his, his Eddie and his Marty and his George with their mean, ratty little clerks' lives and their mean, ratty little . . . It's just that they're all *alike*, those people. All they ever say is 'Hey, wha' happen t'ya Giants?' and 'Hey, wha' happen t'ya Yankees?,' and they all live way out in some crowded little community, and their mothers have those damn little china elephants on the mantelpiece." And Martha would frown over her nail polish again, making it clear that the subject was closed.

All that fall and winter she was confused. For a while she tried going out only with Martha's kind of men—the kind that used words like "amusing" all the time and wore small-shouldered flannel suits like a uniform; and for a while she tried going out with no men at all. She even tried that crazy business with Mr. Atwood at the office Christmas party. And all the time Ralph kept calling up, hanging around, waiting for her to make up her mind. Once she took him home to meet her parents in Pennsylvania (where she never would have dreamed of taking Martha), but it wasn't until Easter time that she finally gave in.

They had gone to a dance somewhere in Queens, one of those big American Legion dances that Ralph's crowd was always going to, and when the band played "Easter Parade" he held her very close, hardly moving, and sang to her in a faint, whispering tenor. It was the kind of thing she'd never have expected Ralph to do— a sweet, gentle thing—and although it probably wasn't just then that she decided to marry him, it always seemed so afterwards.

That night she had told Martha, and she could still see the look on Martha's face. "Oh, Grace, you're not—surely you're not *serious*. I mean, I mean, I thought he was more or less of a *joke*—you can't really mean you want to—"

"Shut up! You just shut up, Martha!" And she'd cried all night. Even now she hated Martha for it; even as she stared blindly at a row of filing cabinets along the office wall, half sick with fear that Martha was right.

The noise of giggles swept over her, and she saw with a start that two of the girls—Irene and Rose—were grinning over their typewriters and pointing at her. "*We* saw ya!" Irene sang. "*We* saw ya! Mooning again, huh Grace?" Then Rose did a burlesque of mooning, heaving her meager breasts and batting her eyes, and they both collapsed in laughter.

With an effort of will Grace resumed the guileless, open smile of a bride. The thing to do was concentrate on plans.

Tomorrow morning, "bright and early" as her mother would say, she would meet Ralph at Penn Station for the trip home. They'd arrive about one, and her parents would meet the train. "Good t'see ya, Ralph!" her father would say, and her mother would probably kiss him. A warm, homely love filled her; *they* wouldn't call him a white worm; *they* didn't have any ideas about Princeton men and "interesting" men and all the other kinds of men Martha was so stuck-up about. Then her father would probably take Ralph out for a beer and show him the paper mill where he worked (and at least Ralph wouldn't be snobby about a person working in a paper mill, either), and then Ralph's family and friends would come down from New York in the evening.

She'd have time for a long talk with her mother that night, and the next morning, "bright and early" (her eyes stung at the thought of her mother's plain, happy face), they would start getting dressed for the wedding. Then the church and the ceremony, and then the reception (Would her father get drunk? Would Muriel Ketchel sulk about not being a bridesmaid?), and finally the train to Atlantic City, and the hotel. But from the hotel on she couldn't plan any more. A door would lock behind her and there would be a wild, fantastic silence, and nobody else in all the world but Ralph to lead the way.

"Well, Grace," Mr. Atwood was saying, "I want to wish you every happiness." He was standing at her desk with his hat and coat on, and all around her was the chattering and scraping-back of chairs that meant it was five o'clock.

"Thank you, Mr. Atwood." She got to her feet, suddenly surrounded by all the girls in a bedlam of farewell.

"All the luck in the world, Grace."

"Drop us a card, huh, Grace? From Atlantic City?"

"So long, Grace."

"G'night, Grace, and listen: the best of everything."

Finally she was free of them all, out at the elevator, out of the building, hurrying through the crowds to the subway.

When she got home Martha was standing in the door of the kitchenette, looking very svelte in a crisp, new dress.

"Hi, Grace, I bet they ate you alive today, didn't they?"

"Oh no," Grace said. "Everybody was—real nice." She sat down, exhausted, and dropped the flowers and the wrapped candy dish on a table. Then she noticed that the whole apartment was swept and dusted, and the dinner was cooking in the kitchenette. "Gee, everything looks wonderful," she said. "What'd you do all this for?"

"Oh, well, I got home early anyway," Martha said. Then she smiled, and it was one of the few times Grace had ever seen her look shy. "I just thought it might be nice to have the place looking decent for a change, when Ralph comes over."

"Well," Grace said, "it certainly was nice of you."

The way Martha looked now was even more surprising: she looked awkward. She was turning a greasy spatula in her fingers, holding it delicately away from her dress and examining it, as if she had something difficult to say. "Look, Grace," she began. "You do understand why I can't come to the wedding, don't you?"

"Oh sure," Grace said, although in fact she didn't, exactly. It was something about having to go up to Harvard to see her brother before he went into the Army, but it had sounded like a lie from the beginning.

"It's just that I'd hate you to think I—well, anyway, I'm glad if you do understand. And the other thing I wanted to say is more important."

"What?"

"Well, just that I'm sorry for all the awful things that I used to say about Ralph. I never had a right to talk to you that way. He's a very sweet boy and I—well, I'm sorry, that's all."

It wasn't easy for Grace to hide a rush of gratitude and relief when she said, "Why, that's all right, Martha. I—"

"The chops are on fire!" Martha bolted for the kitchenette. "It's all right," she called back. "They're edible." And when she came out to serve dinner all her old composure was restored. "I'll have to eat and run," she said as they sat down. "My train leaves in forty minutes."

"But I thought you didn't have to go until *tomorrow!*"

"Well, I don't, actually," Martha said, "but I decided to go tonight. Because you see, Grace, another thing—if you can stand one more apology—another thing I'm sorry for is that I've hardly ever given you and Ralph a chance to be alone here. So tonight I'm going to clear out." She hesitated. "It'll be a sort of wedding gift from me, okay?" And then she smiled, not shyly this time but in a way that was more in character—the eyes subtly averted after a flicker of special meaning. It was a smile that Grace—through stages of suspicion, bewilderment, awe, and practiced imitation— had long ago come to associate with the word "sophisticated."

"Well, that's very sweet of you," Grace said, but she really didn't get the point just then. It wasn't until long after the meal was over and the dishes washed, until Martha had left for her train in a whirl of cosmetics and luggage and quick good-bys, that she began to understand.

She took a deep, voluptuous bath and spent a long time drying herself, posing in the mirror, filled with a strange, slow excitement. In her bedroom, from the rustling tissues of an expensive white box, she drew the prizes of her trousseau—a sheer nightgown of white nylon and a matching negligee—put them on, and went to the mirror again. She had never worn anything like this before, or felt like this, and the thought of letting Ralph see her like this sent her into the kitchenette for a glass of the special dry sherry Martha kept for cocktail parties. Then she turned out all the lights but one and, carrying her glass, went to the sofa and arranged herself there to wait for him. After a while she got up and brought the sherry bottle over to the coffee table, where she set it on a tray with another glass.

When Ralph left the office he felt vaguely let down. Somehow, he'd expected more of the Friday before his wedding. The bonus check had been all right (though secretly he'd been counting on twice that amount), and the boys had bought him a drink at lunch and kidded around in the appropriate way ("Ah, don't feel too bad, Ralph—worse things could happen"), but still, there ought to have been a real party. Not just the boys in the office, but Eddie, and *all* his friends. Instead there would only be meeting Eddie at the White Rose like every other night of the year, and riding home to borrow Eddie's suitcase and to eat, and then having to ride all the way back to Manhattan just to see Grace for an hour or two. Eddie wasn't in the bar when he arrived, which sharpened the edge of his loneliness. Morosely he drank a beer, waiting.

Eddie was his best friend and an ideal Best Man because he'd been in on the courtship of Grace from the start. It was in this very bar, in fact, that Ralph had told him about their first date last summer: "Ooh, Eddie—what a figger!"

And Eddie had grinned. "Yeah? So what's the roommate like?"

"Ah, you don't want the roommate, Eddie. The roommate's a dog. A snob, too, I think. No, but this *other* one, this little *Gracie*—boy, I mean, she is *stacked*."

Half the fun of every date—even more than half—had been telling Eddie about it afterwards, exaggerating a little here and there, asking Eddie's advice on tactics. But after today, like so many other pleasures, it would all be left behind. Gracie had promised him at least one night off a week to spend with the boys, after they were married, but even so it would never be the same. Girls never understood a thing like friendship.

There was a ball game on the bar's television screen and he watched it idly, his throat swelling in a sentimental pain of loss. Nearly all his life had been devoted to the friendship of boys and men, to trying to be a good guy, and now the best of it was over.

Finally Eddie's stiff finger jabbed the seat of his pants in greeting. "Whaddya say, sport?"

Ralph narrowed his eyes to indolent contempt, and slowly turned around. "Wha' happen ta you, wise guy? Get lost?"

"Whaddya—in a hurry a somethin'?" Eddie barely moved his lips when he spoke. "Can't wait two minutes?" He slouched on a stool and slid a quarter at the bartender. "Draw one, there, Jack."

They drank in silence for a while, staring at the television. "Got a little bonus today," Ralph said. "Fifty dollars."

"Yeah?" Eddie said. "Good."

A batter struck out; the inning was over and the commercial came on. "So?" Eddie said, rocking the beer around in his glass. "Still gonna get married?"

"Why not?" Ralph said with a shrug. "Listen, finish that, willya? I wanna get a move on."

"Wait awhile, wait awhile. What's ya hurry?"

"C'mon, willya? Ralph stepped impatiently away from the bar. "I wanna go pick up ya bag."

"Ah, bag schmagg."

Ralph moved up close again and glowered at him. "Look, wise guy. Nobody's gonna *make* ya loan me the goddam bag, ya know. I don't wanna break ya *heart* or nothin'—"

"Arright, arright, arright. You'll getcha bag. Don't worry so much." He finished the beer and wiped his mouth. "Let's go."

Having to borrow a bag for his wedding trip was a sore point with Ralph; he'd much rather have bought one of his own. There was a fine one displayed in the window of a luggage shop they passed every night on their way to the subway—a big, tawny Gladstone with a zippered compartment on the side, at thirty-nine ninety-five—and Ralph had had his eye on it ever since Easter time. "Think I'll buy that," he'd told Eddie, in the same offhand way that a day or so before he had announced his engagement ("Think I'll marry the girl"). Eddie's response to both remarks had been the same: "Whaddya—crazy?" Both times Ralph had said, "Why not?" and in defense of the bag he had added, "Gonna get married, I'll *need* somethin' like that." From then on it was as if the bag, almost as much as Gracie herself, had become the symbol of the new and richer life he sought. But after the ring and the new clothes and all the other expenses, he'd found at last that he couldn't afford it; he had settled for the loan of Eddie's which was similar but cheaper and worn, and without the zippered compartment.

Now as they passed the luggage shop he stopped, caught in the grip of a reckless idea. "Hey wait awhile, Eddie. Know what I think I'll do with that fifty-dollar bonus? I think I'll buy that bag right now." He felt breathless.

"Whaddya—*crazy*? Forty bucks for a bag you'll use maybe one time a year? Ya crazy, Ralph. C'mon."

"Ah—I dunno. Ya think so?"

"Listen, you better *keep* ya money, boy. You're gonna *need* it."

"Ah—yeah," Ralph said at last. "I guess ya right." And he fell in step with Eddie again, heading for the subway. This was the way things usually turned out in his life; he could never own a bag like that until he made a better salary, and he accepted it—just as he'd accepted without question, after the first thin sigh, the knowledge that he'd never possess his bride until after the wedding.

The subway swallowed them, rattled and banged them along in a rocking, mindless trance for half an hour, and disgorged them at last into the cool early evening of Queens.

Removing their coats and loosening their ties, they let the breeze dry their sweated shirts as they walked. "So what's the deal?" Eddie asked. "What time we supposed to show up in this Pennsylvania burg tomorra?"

"Ah, suit yourself," Ralph said. "Any time in the evening's okay."

"So whadda we do then? What the hell can ya *do* in a hillbilly town like that, anyway?"

"Ah, I dunno," Ralph said defensively. "Sit around and talk, I guess; drink beer with Gracie's old man or somethin'."

"Some week end," Eddie said. "Big, big deal."

Ralph stopped on the sidewalk, suddenly enraged, his damp coat wadded in his fist. "Look, you bastid. Nobody's gonna *make* ya come, ya know—you or Marty or George or any a the rest of 'em. Get that straight. You're not doin' *me* no favors, unnastand?"

"Whatsa matta?" Eddie inquired. "Whatsa matta? Can'tcha take a joke?"

"Joke," Ralph said. "You're fulla jokes." And plodding sullenly in Eddie's wake he felt close to tears.

They turned off into the block where they both lived, a double row of neat, identical houses, bordering the street where they'd fought and loafed and played stickball all their lives. Eddie pushed open the front door of his house and ushered Ralph into the vestibule, with its homely smell of cauliflower and overshoes. "G'wan in," he said, jerking a thumb at the closed living-room door, and he hung back to let Ralph go first.

Ralph opened the door and took three steps inside it before it hit him like a sock on the jaw. The room, dead silent, was packed deep with grinning, red-faced men—Marty, George, the boys from the block, the boys from the office—everybody, all his friends, all on their feet and poised motionless in a solid mass. Skinny

Maguire was crouched at the upright piano, his spread fingers high over the keys, and when he struck the first rollicking chords they all roared into song, beating time with their fists, their enormous grins distorting the words:

> "Fa he's a jally guh fella
> Fa he's a jally guh fella
> Fa he's a jally guh fell-ah
> That nobody can deny!"

Weakly Ralph retreated a step on the carpet and stood there wide-eyed, swallowing, holding his coat. "That nobody can deny!" they sang, "That nobody can deny!" And as they swung into the second chorus Eddie's father appeared through the dining-room curtains, bald and beaming, in full song, with a great glass pitcher of beer in either hand. At last Skinny hammered out the final line:

> "That—no—bod—dee—can—dee—nye!"

And they all surged forward cheering, grabbing Ralph's hand, pounding his arms and his back while he stood trembling, his own voice lost under the noise. "Gee, fellas—thanks. I—I don't know what to—thanks, fellas. . . ."

Then the crowd cleaved in half, and Eddie made his way slowly down the middle. His eyes gleamed in a smile of love, and from his bashful hand hung the suitcase—not his own, but a new one: the big, tawny Gladstone with the zippered compartment on the side.

"*Speech!*" they were yelling. "*Speech! Speech!*"

But Ralph couldn't speak and couldn't smile. He could hardly even see.

At ten o'clock Grace began walking around the apartment and biting her lip. What if he wasn't coming? But of course he was coming. She sat down again and carefully smoothed the billows of nylon around her thighs, forcing herself to be calm. The whole thing would be ruined if she was nervous.

The noise of the doorbell was like an electric shock. She was halfway to the door before she stopped, breathing hard, and composed herself again. Then she pressed the buzzer and opened the door a crack to watch for him on the stairs.

When she saw he was carrying a suitcase, and saw the pale seriousness of his face as he mounted the stairs, she thought at first that he knew; he had come prepared to lock the door and take her in his arms. "Hello, darling," she said softly, and opened the door wider.

"Hi, baby." He brushed past her and walked inside. "Guess I'm late, huh? You in bed?"

"No." She closed the door and leaned against it with both hands holding the doorknob at the small of her back, the way heroines close doors in the movies. "I was just—waiting for you."

He wasn't looking at her. He went to the sofa and sat down, holding the suitcase on his lap and running his fingers over its surface. "Gracie," he said, barely above a whisper. "Look at this."

She looked at it, and then into his tragic eyes.

"Remember," he said, "I told you about that bag I wanted to buy? Forty dollars?" He stopped and looked around. "Hey, where's Martha? She in bed?"

"She's gone, darling," Grace said, moving slowly toward the sofa. "She's gone for the whole week end." She sat down beside him, leaned close and gave him Martha's special smile.

"Oh yeah?" he said. "Well anyway, listen. I said I was gonna borrow Eddie's bag instead, remember?"

"Yes."

"Well, so tonight at the White Rose I siz, 'C'mon, Eddie, let's go home pick up ya bag.' He siz, 'Ah, bag schmagg.' I siz, 'Whatsa matta?' but he don't say nothin', see? So we go home to his place and the living room door's shut, see?"

She squirmed closer and put her head on his chest. Automatically he raised an arm and dropped it around her shoulders, still talking. "He siz, 'G'head, Ralph, open the door.' I siz, 'Whatsa deal?' He siz, 'Never mind, Ralph, open the door.' So I open the door, and oh Jesus." His fingers gripped her shoulder with such intensity that she looked up at him in alarm.

"They was all there, Gracie," he said. "All the fellas. Playin' the piana, singin', cheerin'—" His voice wavered and his eyelids fluttered shut, their lashes wet. "A big surprise party," he said, trying to smile. "Fa me. Can ya beat that, Gracie? And then—and then Eddie comes out and—Eddie comes out and hands me this. The very same bag I been looking at all this time. He bought it with his own money and he didn't say nothin', just to give me a surprise. 'Here, Ralph,' he siz. 'Just to let ya know you're the greatest guy in the world.'" His fingers tightened again, trembling. "I cried, Gracie," he whispered. "I couldn't help it. I don't think the fellas saw it or anything, but I was cryin'." He turned his face away and worked his lips in a tremendous effort to hold back the tears.

"Would you like a drink, darling?" she asked tenderly.

"Nah, that's all right, Gracie. I'm all right." Gently he set the suitcase on the carpet. "Only, gimme a cigarette, huh?"

She got one from the coffee table, put it in his lips and lit it. "Let me get you a drink," she urged.

He frowned through the smoke. "Whaddya got, that sherry wine? Nah, I don't like that stuff. Anyway, I'm fulla beer." He leaned back and closed his eyes. "And then Eddie's mother feeds us this terrific meal," he went on, and his voice was almost normal now. "We had *steaks;* we had French-fried *potatas,"* his head rolled on the sofa-back with each item, "lettuce-and-tomata *salad, pickles, bread, butter—*everything. The works."

"Well," she said. "Wasn't that nice."

"And afterwards we had icecream and coffee," he said, "and all the beer we could drink. It was a real spread."

Grace ran her hands over her lap, partly to smooth the nylon and partly to dry the moisture on her palms. "Well, that was certainly nice of them," she said. They sat there silent for what seemed a long time.

"I can only stay a minute, Gracie," Ralph said at last. "I promised 'em I'd be back."

Her heart thumped under the nylon. "Ralph, do you—do you like this?"

"What, honey?"

"My negligee. You weren't supposed to see it until—after the wedding, but I thought I'd—"

"Nice," he said, feeling the flimsy material between thumb and index finger, like a merchant. "Very nice. Wudga pay fa this, honey?"

"Oh—I don't know. But do you like it?"

He kissed her and began, at last, to stroke her with his hands. "Nice," he kept saying. "Nice. Hey, I like this." His hand hesitated at the low neckline, then slipped inside.

"I do love you, Ralph," she whispered. "You know that, don't you?"

His fingers pinched her breast, once, and slid quickly out again. The policy of restraint, the habit of months was too strong to break. "Sure," he said. "And I love you, baby. Now, you be a good girl and get ya beauty sleep, and I'll see ya in the morning. Okay?"

"Oh, Ralph. Don't go. Stay."

"Ah, I promised the fellas, Gracie." He stood up and straightened his clothes. "They're waitin' fa me, out to Eddie's."

She blazed to her feet, but the cry that was meant for a woman's appeal came out, through her tightening lips, as the whine of a wife. "Can't they wait?"

"Whaddya—*crazy?*" He backed away, eyes round with righteousness. She would *have* to understand. If this was the way she acted *before* the wedding, how the hell was it going to be *afterwards?* "Have a *heart,* willya? Keep the fellas waitin' *tonight?* After all they done fa *me?*"

After a second or two, during which her face became less pretty than he had ever seen it before, she was able to smile. "Of course not, darling. You're right."

He came forward again and gently brushed the tip of her chin with his fist, a husband reassured. "'At's more like it," he said. "So I'll see ya, Penn Station, nine o'clock tomorra. Right, Gracie? Only, before I go—" He winked and slapped his belly. "I'm fulla beer. Mind if I use ya terlet?"

When he came out of the bathroom she was waiting to say goodnight, standing with her arms folded across her chest, as if for warmth. Lovingly he hefted the new suitcase and joined her at the door. "Okay, then, baby," he said, and kissed her. "Nine o'clock. Don't forget, now."

She smiled tiredly and opened the door for him. "Don't worry, Ralph," she said. "I'll be there."

MAGAZINES CONSULTED

ACCENT, Box 102, University Station, Urbana, Ill. ADVENTURE, 205 East 42nd Street, N.Y.C. AMERICAN MAGAZINE, 640 Fifth Avenue, N.Y.C. ANTIOCH REVIEW, 212 Xenia Avenue, Yellow Springs, O. ARGOSY, 205 East 42nd Street, N.Y.C. ARIZONA QUARTERLY, University of Arizona, Tucson, Ariz. ASTOUNDING SCIENCE FICTION, 575 Madison Avenue, N.Y.C. ATLANTIC MONTHLY, 8 Arlington Street, Boston, Mass. BETTER LIVING, 230 Park Avenue, N.Y.C. BEYOND, 421 Hudson Street, N.Y.C. BLUE BOOK, 230 Park Avenue, N.Y.C. BOTTEGHE OSCURE, via Botteghe Oscure 32, Rome, Italy. CALIFORNIA QUARTERLY, 7070 Hollywood Blvd., Los Angeles, Cal. CAROLINA QUARTERLY, Box 1117, Chapel Hill, N.C. CATHOLIC WORLD, 411 West 59th Street, N.Y.C. CHARM, 575 Madison Avenue, N.Y.C. COLLIER'S, 640 Fifth Avenue, N.Y.C. COMMENTARY, 34 West 33rd Street, N.Y.C. COSMOPOLITAN, 57th Street & Eighth Avenue, N.Y.C. COUNTRY GENTLEMAN, Independence Square, Philadelphia, Pa. DISCOVERY, 360 Fifth Avenue, N.Y.C. ELLERY QUEEN'S MYSTERY MAGAZINE, 570 Lexington Avenue, N.Y.C. EPOCH, 252 Goldwin Smith Hall, Cornell University, Ithaca, N.Y. ESQUIRE, 488 Madison Avenue, N.Y.C. EVERYWOMAN'S, 16 East 40th Street, N.Y.C. FAMILY CIRCLE, 25 West 45th Street, N.Y.C. FANTASY AND SCIENCE FICTION, 2643 Dana Street, Berkeley, Cal. FOLIO, Indiana University, Bloomington, Indiana. GALAXY SCIENCE FICTION, 421 Hudson Street, N.Y.C. GEORGIA REVIEW, University of Georgia, Athens, Ga. GOOD HOUSEKEEPING, 57th Street & Eighth Avenue, N.Y.C. HARPER'S BAZAAR, 572 Madison Avenue, N.Y.C. HARPER'S MAGAZINE, 49 East 33rd Street, N.Y.C. HARVARD ADVOCATE, 40 Bow

Street, Cambridge, Mass. HUDSON REVIEW, 439 West Street, N.Y.C. HUSK, Cornell College, Mount Vernon, Ia. JEWISH HORIZON, 154 Nassau Street, N.Y.C. KENYON REVIEW, Kenyon College, Gambier, O. LADIES' HOME JOURNAL, Independence Square, Philadelphia, Pa. MADEMOISELLE, 575 Madison Avenue, N.Y.C. MASSES & MAINSTREAM, 832 Broadway, N.Y.C. MCCALL'S, 230 Park Avenue, N.Y.C. NEW MEXICO QUARTERLY, Box 85, University of New Mexico, Albuquerque, N.M. NEW WORLD WRITING, 501 Madison Avenue, N.Y.C. NEW YORKER, 25 West 43rd Street, N.Y.C. PACIFIC SPECTATOR, Box 1948, Stanford, Cal. PARIS REVIEW, 8 Rue Garancière, Paris, France. PARTISAN REVIEW, 30 West 12th Street, N.Y.C. PERSPECTIVE, Washington University Post Office, St. Louis, Mo. PRAIRIE SCHOONER, 12th and R Streets, Lincoln, Neb. QUARTERLY REVIEW OF LITERATURE, Box 287, Bard College, Annandale-on-Hudson, N.Y. QUARTO, 801 Business, Columbia University, N.Y.C. REDBOOK, 230 Park Avenue, N.Y.C. THE REPORTER, 220 East 42nd Street, N.Y.C. SATURDAY EVENING POST, Independence Square, Philadelphia, Pa. SEWANEE REVIEW, University of the South, Sewanee, Tenn. SOUTHWEST REVIEW, Southern Methodist University, Dallas, Tex. THIS WEEK, 420 Lexington Avenue, N.Y.C. TODAY, 638 Deming Pl., Chicago, Ill. TOWN & COUNTRY, 572 Madison Avenue, N.Y.C. UNIVERSITY OF KANSAS CITY REVIEW, University of Kansas City, Kansas City, Mo. VIRGINIA QUARTERLY REVIEW, One West Range, Charlottesville, Va. WESTERN REVIEW, State University of Iowa, Iowa City, Ia. WOMAN'S DAY, 19 West 44th Street, N.Y.C. WOMAN'S HOME COMPANION, 640 Fifth Avenue, N.Y.C. YALE REVIEW, Box 1729, New Haven, Conn.

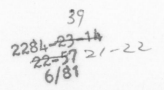